WHEN
the
WORLD
GOES
QUIET

ALSO BY GIAN SARDAR

Take What You Can Carry

You Were Here

Psychic Junkie

WHEN

the

WORLD
GOES
QUIET

A NOVEL

GIAN SARDAR

LAKE UNION
PUBLISHING

Published by Lake Union Publishing, Seattle

www.apub.com

Amazon, the Amazon logo, and Lake Union Publishing are trademarks of Amazon.com, Inc., or its affiliates.

ISBN-13: 9781662518669 (paperback)
ISBN-13: 9781662518676 (digital)

Cover design by James Iacobelli
Cover image: © Gonzalo Azumendi / Getty; © Brais Seara / Getty;
© vvvita / Shutterstock

Printed in the United States of America

For my mother, whose father was born into a house occupied by soldiers during the Great War, and whose Belgian family passed along strength, resilience, and a serious sweet tooth.

Sleep on, pale Bruges, beneath the waning moon,

For I must desecrate your silence soon,

And with my bombs' fierce roar, and fiercer fire,

Grim terror in your tired heart inspire:

For I must wake your children in their beds

And send the sparrows fluttering on the leads!

—*"The Bombing of Bruges"* by English pilot Paul Bewsher

PROLOGUE

There was nothing the wind couldn't do. It was alive and angry and eager. It was a world of hands, prying and cruel. It sprang from a sky that churned an odd mix of light and dark, good and bad, a twisting force that suddenly came into being and tugged at the door of the root cellar, rumbled the old wood, and made a sound like an open-mouthed growl. Inside the cellar, it was pitch-black, and Evelien crouched on the dirt floor, nails digging into the packed earth while just beyond the door, her mother went silent.

There is nothing worse than silence, in a moment *after*. Ask a woman who's just given birth. Ask a father who saw a wagon tip and is running, calling out names. Ask a daughter whose mother didn't make it into the shelter, because of her.

Silence screams loudest of all.

CHAPTER 1

October 10, 1918

More than a decade has passed since the storm, but the bombs and the noise seem to conjure that day. Bombs that land far away but not far enough. Bombs that rattle houses and doors and break panes of glass and send papers flying in the street, just like the wind once had. The first time Evelien took shelter in a cellar during a bombardment, right at the start of the war, the sounds and the shaking and the suffocating underground space grabbed her and yanked her through the years till she was back on her parents' small farm in their small corner of Belgium, till she was once again inside their root cellar, held in dark and blame because she was the reason her mother was outside, in the storm. Sometimes fault is also like a wind. It slips into cracks and fills spaces.

The first time she hid in the cellar during a bombardment was also the last. The memories of that day don't just exist in her mind, they pulse fast in her blood, increase the speed of her heart, and make her legs shake.

"I saw you the other night," Coletta, her mother-in-law, says.

Coletta, tall with curly red hair that's thinned during the war, handfuls often caught in the comb of her fingers. The opposite of Evelien's mother, in all ways that matter, though the two women grew up together and were once close. She comes into Evelien's room, then opens the shutters. A scarlet morning light pours in.

"In the alley," she continues, "during the shelling."

Bright shots of vermilion, blooms of blue, ribbons of green. The sky had been a beautiful horror, lit up with the Allied effort to hit the seaplane bases responsible for the bombings of London and southeast England. Evelien's futile attempt: to try to detach meaning and see the colors as only colors. Not just as a way to spare herself pain, but to provide a bit of refuge. To help live in an unlivable world. "It was far enough away."

"If something happened to you, and we're in the cellar and don't know—Evelien, what could we do?"

Secretly, Evelien loves the woman's concern. But she also understands that someone who survives four years of war might start feeling invincible, rather than lucky, and that she's begun taking too many chances. "I was right at the door. Almost inside."

"*Almost* inside means outside. And after curfew?"

Is it wrong that I tell myself what I'm hearing is thunder? One of the questions Evelien first asked when the war began. *I believe we're allowed a bit of self-preservation,* August, Coletta's husband, a short man with wide nostrils and flyaway graying hair, explained. Eventually they saw it this way: in the midst of a war that wasn't ending, entrenched with unspeakable horror and loss, the only correct way to live was whatever way they could. And though Evelien could never forget what the streaks of light mean, after so long, sometimes she chooses to try to only see the color. This, however, is not something she will admit to. There's already enough that's wrong with her.

Coletta continues. "Imagine Emiel coming home after all these years and *you're* dead, right at the end. A bullet kills at the end of the war the same way it does at the start."

Imagine Emiel coming home.

She wishes she could. It's been two years since they've heard from him, but a year ago she *felt* Emiel's death. A constriction of air, a sudden swelling of sadness. It was a day no different than any other, except in her inexplicable and overwhelming knowledge. She knew then he wouldn't come home, because she felt it—loss where before there'd been only an absence. And though the war is almost over and people are grasping at the tattered ends of hope, the dead can only stay dead.

~

Evelien is a twenty-one-year-old who has always wanted to be taller, a woman with eyes the blue-gray of an angry ocean and hair that is neither blonde nor brown. She is stubborn, someone who's knocked down webs while balancing on the top step of a ladder, despite a touch of vertigo, who once scrubbed the floor with a hand brush so vigorously that her fingers bled, and who refused to leave with the other refugees when the threat of war grew, because she wouldn't leave Coletta and August, parents she wasn't born with but knew she would die for.

She is also a woman who can't look away from the singed curl of a rose petal on a hot day, the valley of skin in the fold of a hand, or the shine on the curve of a dog's back. What people find mundane or ordinary or even unappealing—she's fascinated by all of it. It's problematic, this appreciation. It renders her the only one in a group of women more drawn to the shocked and tired set of a mother's face than the baby, the one who even now, after four years of war and occupation, stops walking when she should move, and looks at what she shouldn't see, always collecting textures and hues and expressions. One day she will find paints and brushes and canvases and let loose this storage of terrible beauty.

For now, though, for now she holds it in and indulges in art by looking at what's on the walls around her—or what's hidden *inside* the walls.

The paintings her employer asked her to hide when the war began: two are tucked into the voids where the pocket doors in the parlor once slid, before the Germans requisitioned wood, and one is strapped to the underside of a bottom shelf in a cabinet. Now and then she checks on them—not just to be sure they're still there and are undamaged, but to satisfy a craving, a longing to fall headlong into an alternate world.

Leaning on the floor in the parlor, she uses a billiard stick to reach into the space where the left pocket door once slid, to hook a string with a looped end. She pulls, just enough to feel the resistance and verify the canvas is still there and not stuck. Georges Braque's *Landscape Near Antwerp*. Antwerp, Belgium: a port city, urban and gray. And yet the painting—which captures a stretch of dunes on the bank of the Scheldt River, with a building in the background and a mass of schooners to the right—hardly resembles the landscape where Braque stood. It hardly resembles anything real at all, in fact. Instead, the dunes are lyrical and dreamy, with expressive though perhaps illogical color. Grass and sand and vegetation all emerge in threads of emerald green, swaths of pink, and buoyant curves of orange and red. The water is orchid and yellow and at times simply unpainted, bare stretches of canvas. There is a mint-taffy-colored sky. A horizon of violet rooftops.

It makes no sense, Evelien's mother, Leona, said when they saw the work. *There's no Antwerp in this.* It was 1906, and they were in Paris only so Leona could sign documents after an aunt passed. The trip was *not* supposed to involve art, art being something other people had time for, not Leona. But it was raining, and the door to a gallery on Rue Victor Massé was open, and so in they went. There it was. Laughing from its wall. Vibrant and alive as outside the rain came down and the world was flat and gray. *That's not Antwerp,* her mother said again, this time with finality, as if a matter had been settled. Standing off to the side, a woman leaned into Evelien. *Isn't it wonderful, when what someone perceives is even better than what's there?*

The painting was a promise: *Your world doesn't need to be the one others see.* Like a match that ignited a love for art, from that moment on, all Evelien thought of was painting and drawing and colors. The fact that one day, years later, she would be the housemaid for the man who bought the piece from the gallery still feels like fate, and right off the bat, a kinship existed between herself and Mr. Vanheule, her employer, all from a shared love of the painting. *It was like two strangers met,* he once said, *only to realize they shared a friend.*

Inside the void from the other pocket door is the second painting, a Renoir. The third, a little Matisse, is secured to a low shelf in a cabinet.

In the kitchen, Coletta has the last of their flour in a bowl. Somehow, she's kept meat and vegetables on the table—not an easy feat. "The painting fairies didn't make off with them in the night?"

"Not yet. The slackers."

"The problem, then, is this: our flour is half sawdust. That's the last time I go to S&P Market. And we could use the carrots from the garden. You told Father Louwagie you'd bring him a quilt?"

"He gets cold, but he won't admit it."

Coletta nods to a folded blanket on the kitchen chair. Lined in a delicate royal blue, the priest's favorite color. "Take that. But he leaves soon, so go to the garden first, but *no drawing.*"

Her garden, her *ruined garden,* as she calls it, is in an abandoned house that was damaged when Allies dropped a bomb on the building alongside it, all because windows were left uncovered and lights blazed inside, turning it into a target. Covertly grown carrots, lettuce, tomatoes—anything they can find seeds for she grows within the ruined building. But the real lure is what's up a set of broken stairs: a room where Evelien draws, the once-blank walls now covered in her work.

Coletta continues. "You'll need to watch him put it in his room, though, or he'll leave it somewhere. Like he did his glasses. And his ration card."

"And his replacement ration card."

7

"Which is why you can't let the man out of your sight till the quilt's locked away, or some German will sleep well and I won't have *that* on my shoulders. *And* he needs to keep quiet on where he got it from. Germans breathing down my neck about extra fabric is the last thing I need. What I do for that man."

Coletta, a Spiritualist in a country of Catholics. When she speaks of Father Louwagie, she likes to paint theirs as a friendship beyond her better judgment, even though in many ways it was the only reason that the most pious Catholics—which, in their country, is almost everyone—even spoke to her.

"Don't forget the carrots," Coletta adds as Evelien grabs the quilt.

Then the woman's back to measuring out the last of their flour, and Evelien steps into the alley behind their house. The air has a beige tinge and a note of destruction, as if from a sifted, settled catastrophe. Unending blue skies are a memory, a cerulean nostalgia.

Cobblestones and brick. Moss and violets. Bruges used to be a dreamer's city, with daffodils and tulips in window boxes and weeping willows whose boughs skimmed the water of the canals that vein the city. A fairy-tale land of medieval buildings and winding narrow roads, as well as shimmering water and bridges where couples stood to cast wishes into the air, the reflection below them a glossy, inverted world of red-tile rooftops and trees and white clouds scattered in cornflower-blue skies.

Now, people are forbidden from lingering on bridges, or anywhere for that matter. Now, too many trees are broken, and the sky is no longer blue.

She takes a street that was damaged, dodging puddles and stepping over a barrier, all so she can arrive at the house with the ruined garden with enough time to draw before meeting Father Louwagie. The facade is largely intact, though much of the glass in the windows was blown out long ago. The difference is in the roof, as it's barely there, yet not noticeable from the street. One more glance up and down the block, then a quick jiggle of the doorknob, four times while pushing to the right, and the broken lock unlatches.

Plants are everywhere. In trunks, sinks, the bathtub, open drawers. Vines hang and creep, and yellow oxalis flowers bloom alongside a green chaise she's worked to keep clean. Behind the house there was an actual garden, but people could see that. Since the Germans demand everything anyone grows be handed over to them for distribution—a distribution that lessens like a wave on a hot, dry shore by the time it reaches the Belgians—this garden is in violation of that. But she takes the risk, not just because the herbs help what little they have taste better, and the fresh vegetables are worth it, but because, other than this, nothing truly belongs to her. It never has. From her parents' house to her employer's house to her husband's family's house.

This place that is not hers is like coming home. She can lie on her back and face the sun through broken beams. She can get dirt under her nails and go barefoot and chew on parsley stems. And best of all, she can draw. Just to her left are the damaged stairs that lead to what's left of a partial second floor. Her *canvas room*, as she calls it. Once-white walls now covered in her charcoal drawings, courtesy of charred chunks of wood from the destroyed house next door.

But upstairs, a leak in what remains of the ceiling has dripped water onto one of the walls, forming what looks like a black rivulet in the charcoal. She stands before it, trying to shake an ominous feeling.

Though she's known this room can't last forever, this feels like the beginning of the end.

Then an idea, and she goes to work, incorporating the spill into a drawing: a coffeepot at the top of the wall, its spout pouring black liquid.

It doesn't take long, and she's done, back on the street and trying to walk in shadow. Germans still occupy most of Belgium, but change is in the air like static, a low-grade warning. Recently, troops who occupy Bruges have begun to leave. Every day, more are gone, while the ones who remain are fidgety with nerves. A reckoning is coming, it's clear, and while from the start Evelien's kept her heart safe by shielding it from hope, and her body safe by staying out of sight, now this is even more important. Head down. Feet forward.

She crosses a bridge, red clouds like carnations in the water's reflection. Across the road, soldiers drag mattresses from a home for deaf-mute and blind children, and men carry away lead pipes on their shoulders. From the corner, an older woman watches them openly, gaze heavy with admonition.

Behind the church is a brick building that seems to sit in a holy shadow. Father Louwagie is perched on the top step. Frail, like parchment. Sun shines through his thinned hair.

Slowly, he stands. "I thought you'd forgotten."

"I'm not the one who's forgetful." As she says this, she realizes she forgot the carrots. "So you've lost your replacement ration card."

He brushes the palms of his hands on his black pants. "Lies. All of it."

She glances in the direction of the children's school. "The Germans are taking mattresses from the blind children."

"Mattresses and lead pipes for heating. *Dismantle or destroy* seems to be their parting orders. Don't test them, though. We'll get through this." He smiles at the quilt. "Now, that is exquisite. But I didn't need it. If there's someone else—"

"There's no one else, anywhere, in all of Belgium, who needs it. So I'll leave it here."

He smiles. "The whole country, toasty in their beds."

"And full. Everyone, so full they can't move." Just the other day, Evelien saw two people faint in the street from hunger.

Help me with the gate? The first thing Father Louwagie said to her. She was thirteen when her parents sent her to Bruges to work, when they saw that her value on the farm was eclipsed by her value as a housemaid, and only a year later her mother passed away from pneumonia.

Not yet an adult, but far from a child, Evelien refused to cry for the woman who'd never once cried for her, who'd sent her away when she proved not useful enough and who blamed her for just about everything, including a leg that never worked right after that storm. *If you weren't off drawing, I would've found you and made it into the cellar.* Then, in Bruges one day, there was Father Louwagie with a stack of books, asking for help opening a gate. The day after that, he met Evelien on her walk home and offered her one of the books. Another day, a butterfly wing he'd found. And when finally she brought up her mother, he listened, and never broached her Sunday absences.

"Do you need help finding your ration card?" she asks.

He shrugs. "Whoever found it needs it more than I do."

She glances at his pants legs, which brush the ground. "I doubt that's true."

"Regardless, someone always shows up to feed me. God provides."

Just look for the way God provides, Emiel used to say. Emiel. Her husband for a night but her oldest friend. The long shadow to her every step. The calm hand on her shoulder and the logic to her wild mind. A Catholic despite his parents, Coletta and August, a man who attended and believed with a faith that only became stronger from swimming against the tide of his upbringing.

Evelien says, "God provides in the form of someone who didn't lose their ration card."

Father Louwagie smiles. "You and Coletta. Both of you, ruthless." On the street, a group of people hurries toward the church. Watching them, he takes a handkerchief from his pocket; inside, a crushed walnut. "The pews are full lately. Bombers flying overhead daily have made God very popular." He holds the walnut toward Evelien.

"No, *you* eat that."

He shrugs, picking a bit of walnut and popping it in his mouth. "Speaking of what's been lost, you know Mrs. Maarten's forgotten where they kept the deed to the house."

"I heard." Moniek Maarten asked for Coletta's help in locating the document. Help, by way of asking Coletta to ask Moniek's dead husband where he kept it. *I trance easily,* Coletta told her, *but I don't control* which *spirits come to me, so whatever you do, don't stop looking.*

Father Louwagie tilts his head to one side, as if he's heard someone calling. "Mrs. Maarten too? I wouldn't have thought she'd buy into—well. It's a different time we're in. There's comfort in believing our loved ones are still around us. With everyone losing someone, I imagine Coletta's busy. Though I didn't think Moniek Maarten—"

"You think it's wrong, that people go to Coletta?" Evelien's instigating, she knows.

"I think you're mad at God for the war," he says, reading her as he always does. "And you're not alone."

Explain to a Haitian why they're at war, August said when Haiti joined in. *It will make as much sense as wishing for winter.* Though Belgium was neutral and forced into the war when Germany invaded, the war's catalyst has reduced over the years and become simple in her mind, like something simmered on the stove too long: a little to do with an Austrian archduke who was shot point-blank when his motorcar took a wrong turn, landing him in the path of a young Serbian conspirator, and a lot to do with allegiances that sparked one to another to another like a long chain of dynamite, the entire world becoming bright with pain. *Can you imagine, our collective fate rested on that one choice,* Coletta has said. *Right or left.* From there, fighting not just in Europe, but Africa and the Middle East. Belgium, once forests and fields and blankets of bluebells, has since been blasted and cratered and veined with trenches, while the men who are lucky enough to survive are too often trapped in the cages of their minds, living an endless nightmare. If everything is in God's hands, Evelien reasons, there *is* much to be angry about.

For a moment, Father Louwagie is silent, eyes on the smoky, sun-held air. "More and more, I'm realizing we're shortsighted."

"We?"

He nods. "Humans. Maybe what we think of as *wrong* really isn't."

Evelien smiles. "You might want to keep quiet on that. I'm pretty sure the basis of your business is right and wrong."

"Right and wrong—those ideas not only depend on *who* tells the story, but on *when* the story stops. Or when it starts. Wouldn't you agree? Not everyone gets the full picture. When you're in the midst of something, it's hard to see that. Though we're at the end of this war, we're still very much in the midst. Now you go; I'm late."

She glances at the quilt. "I'm not going anywhere until I see you put that in your room. I'm under orders."

"My dear, if you'd gotten here even two minutes earlier, I'd indulge Coletta and go back to my room, but trams wait for no one, and so this quilt will go in the church closet, which I *promise* to lock. Now please, tell her thank you from me."

He waves her off, and she relents. When she's at the corner, she spots a torn flyer, swept against the side of a stoop—one of the announcements that's normally posted to the walls of the city. A quick nudge with her toe, just to see what it's about: a threatening notice about fines for not shuttering windows at night, a time when both sides use darkness to their advantage.

When she glances back, Father Louwagie is tossing a bit of walnut toward a squirrel.

Another handful of blocks and there's Emma Lemahieu, nine years old and always with her worn and dirtied cloth doll. She's standing in the middle of a bridge that spans the canal, the water below burnished gold and violet. Lately the girl has been limping, and now she stands mostly on one foot, something to do with being malnourished, Evelien thinks. It's common, children often too weak to even walk to school and then too cold to stay, since the Germans seizing coal means unheated classrooms.

Then there is the sound of a plane.

13

Emma looks up first. Then Evelien. Smoky, inflamed clouds obscure the aircraft. But no one's firing at it, which must mean it's German, coming home. Then she realizes that if she can't see it, neither can the Germans. No one's firing at it because it's hidden. For now.

A glance back down. The streets are empty of soldiers.

How one knows an attack is impending: the soldiers are gone. In place and ready.

With this, other sounds seem to stop and slide over and disappear, allowing only for the solitary noise of this plane in the sky. This war is the first fought with aircraft, and though at first the people in Bruges looked at the friendlies, the Allied planes, with sympathy and hope, now, after so many bombings, that's changed. If the plane above her isn't German, it's a threat—a twisted side effect of living in occupied territory, that they fear their own side.

Then, a break in the clouds. She backs against the nearest wall, heels against the brick. Time begins to creep. The noise goes long and wide, taking over everything.

The plane's nose. Then two sets of wings, stacked one above the other: a biplane. She squints, searching for the German black cross.

Suddenly it turns. Sound cuts into the air as it dips, and she sees that there is no black cross, which means it's not German. And she's not the only one who's seen this, because all at once the air bursts with a hail of upside-down rain from antiaircraft artillery.

Emma, in the middle of the bridge, is shocked still. Terrified. Her doll hangs at her side as she looks up.

"Off the bridge!" Evelien yells at her. "Off the bridge!"

But Emma stays where she is. Evelien races to her and gets her arm under the girl's shoulder—there's no way she can carry her—but still Emma won't move.

Something hits in the canal. Gold water jumps into the air, a burst of shining light, before the drops smash back into the water. Then something else, on the road to the right. Impact threads through the streets.

"Emma. You are strong and you are fast, and you are going to run with me."

Emma looks up at her, a child who's trying to be brave. Who wants to be good. She nods.

Evelien runs with her, half carrying her, to a building where they crouch and shelter as best they can. And then something else falls from the plane. Fast at first, it catches in the air. With a jerk, it lifts back up, and a tendril of white flows up. A parachute. Now a graceful drift in the orange sky.

The pilotless plane sails on, steady in its determined downward trajectory. Evelien tries to gauge where it will crash and only knows it will not be here, in these immediate blocks, and so watches the dark shape at the end of the parachute. A British man, she assumes. Someone's son. Here to rescue them, to help them, now hanging and exposed in enemy sky. More noise and that poor, helpless man bounces as he's hit, and Evelien tucks the girl into her, holding her head against her shoulder so she doesn't see. The drift continues. The shape's gone still. Parachute silk shifts in the wind and catches the colors of the morning, flaring crimson.

The plane disappears in the distance, lost behind rooftops, but is present again in a booming and a slight tremble in the ground. Just then, a door across the canal opens, and Emma's mother, Martine, runs out, frantic till she sees the girl and the two meet on the bridge. Evelien takes a deep, steadying breath and turns back in the direction of the house where she works.

Do not dwell. Head down, feet forward, don't think. *And so we pull the blanket of numbness tight around our shoulders,* August says. August, a writer prone to useless musings.

On the corner is a house where soldiers billet. In the window, a young German nods to a beat she cannot hear and most likely does not exist. Men have returned but are still gone. Checked out, eyes vacant, but technically present. *Shell shock,* they call it. Wild nerves and a thousand-yard stare.

Now the man is tapping his forehead on the pane of glass over and over. And she's about to look away, to give this poor man his privacy, when she sees something in the reflection of the window. Or rather, *doesn't* see something in the reflection.

The church tower, in the direction of where the plane went down, is gone.

One doesn't run in an occupied city—it's too suspect—but Evelien does. Her feet slap the cobblestones painfully, and at one point she hits one wrong and twists her ankle and someone barks German at her but she ignores him and continues, now hobbling and praying and making a deal with God, whom she believes in, she really does, just not as she was taught to, and when she turns the corner, she's before the church and for a second it looks as it should, the front still upright and sturdy despite the smoke that spills upward from where the roof once was. A buzzing grows in her ears. She hears herself breathe as if she's trapped inside a box, and keeps walking. Through the tall open doors, the light is brighter, hallowed and radiant. Stunning and terrible. A fire, she now sees, burns from the plane's wreckage.

A few Belgian men pass buckets of water in an assembly line, while others toss back bricks from a pile as fast as they can, disordered and frantic. Wordlessly, Evelien tucks herself against a wall, knowing they are digging toward something, that they are working with the speed of men motivated by knowledge. She doesn't need to ask whom they saw there, who they know was inside, because when a man lifts another brick, she sees it—small and dusty, the blue corner of the quilt. The men begin to shout and point and move faster and faster and then there's a foot, and a leg, and under that beautiful, inflamed gold light is Father Louwagie, his eyes open and kind and empty.

She sinks against the wall. War has taken male pride and provided men with the same amount of tears as women, and in this moment there seems to be a chorus of male voices, crying, imploring.

"That a priest would be killed," a man beside her says. "In this house. How could He let it happen."

It sits flat—not a question.

And then a deep voice.

"Aussteigen! Aussteigen!" A barrel-chested German in uniform. He sweeps his hand to the door over and over, angrily ushering people out, until another soldier, a German with sharp cheekbones, approaches. This man has a cane and a limp and a slightly sideways walk, a life no doubt held in skewed pain, and says something firmly to the barrel-chested man, who falls silent and starts to leave—but on his way, the barrel-chested man places his foot on the edge of a bucket of water. In one motion, the bucket is on its side, and while embers still burn and flames snake orange in the wreckage, water fills into the cracks of the floor, wasted.

All the anger she's held back, everything she's kept hidden in a corner of her heart, explodes. Her nails dig into her palms, and a scream works its way from her throat as she starts after the man, but then there's the soldier with the cane, stepped in front of her. For a second he studies her, surprised, as if unused to seeing rage in a woman. He shakes his head, and she takes a step back. When he turns, there is a tear in the back of his gray uniform coat, and his leaning shadow lengthens against the rubble.

CHAPTER 2

Everything is a daze. She needs to tell Coletta. She needs to be at work. She needs to be gone, to a place this doesn't happen, where a person who's good and decent and kind doesn't suffer through the entirety of the war only to be killed at the very end.

A bullet kills at the end of the war the same way it does at the start.

If she hadn't gone upstairs to draw, he would've left sooner. He wouldn't have been anywhere near the church when the plane hit. Heart racing, palms damp, she feels as though she's spiraling and leans against a building, eyeing steps to a front door, fighting the urge to sit in a corner to try to only breathe.

Because she did this.

At home, she stands in front of Coletta, who looks for the carrots she'd asked for and then sees tears Evelien had not even known were on her face. As Evelien tells her, the woman nods, flour wet on her own cheek when she wipes her eyes.

"I drew," Evelien says.

Coletta studies her, confused.

"You told me not to, but I did. I got there early, so I thought I had time. But if I hadn't done it—"

"You're saying this happened because you spent minutes drawing?"

"If I hadn't, he would've left."

"Evelien. Did you crash the plane? Was that you who did that?"

When Evelien says nothing, Coletta continues.

"Did you invade this country? Did you make it so an old man was cold when he slept at night? So he needed a quilt in the first place? The Germans took my son. Your husband. *They* took years of our lives we will never get back, the children you never had. We shouldn't be *thankful* we've survived; we should be *angry* we've not lived. And now this happens and you blame yourself?"

"If I didn't go upstairs to draw, I would've been there earlier and he'd have left earlier."

"How do you know what he would've done? He might have spent even *more* time in the church. Or feeding those damn squirrels. *The Germans* were why he was cold. Why he'd lost weight. Why he needed help." Tears now stream down Coletta's cheeks, and she sits heavily in a chair. "You can't control what falls from the sky. And you, you missed it by minutes."

"It would've been better if it was me."

"Not for me or August, or Emiel when he comes back. They've taken too much already—don't give them more by blaming yourself. Be *angry*, not guilty."

Anger is something she's only started to embrace. To be angry, you must feel. You must grasp the magnitude of loss or injustice—and she's not ready for that. Not completely. Not yet. Only lately have people begun to do this, to show their fury, anger settling into the cracks left by the war. As if now, with the end in sight, they tentatively believe it's safe to feel.

"Did you hear that?" Coletta suddenly asks. She looks toward the milk cubby, a rectangular box just above the ground and by the far kitchen window, where milkmen used to leave bottles, back when deliveries still happened and milk was something you just ordered.

Quietly, Evelien goes to the cubby. "I don't hear anything."

On the inside, there used to be an interior door—until the war, when August removed it when the Germans demanded wood. On the outside, in the alley, the milk door is still there, painted red. They hadn't realized, though, that with the interior door missing, sound at that one spot would carry. Standing outside the milk door, almost everything can be heard from within the kitchen, just as standing at that precise spot inside is like holding a stethoscope to the alley.

What did they just say? They've gotten too careless. No one is usually in their alley.

"Never mind," Coletta finally says, her voice catching. A deep, quivering breath. "We can't have you losing your job now. Not while they're still here, rounding the unemployed off to Germany. I won't lose you, too, so out you go."

"Are you—"

"I'm just fine. Out, please."

The woman wants privacy, Evelien knows, just as she knows Coletta is not just fine. No one is.

"It's all right to be angry," Coletta says quietly as Evelien leaves. "You should be. We all should be."

~

Evelien's almost to the end of the alley when there's a voice.

"*Guten Tag.*"

Most of the houses here were abandoned; that someone's on this street catches her off guard. But at the corner, a man leans against the wall. His hair appears pushed down, as if he'd just taken off a hat, though he holds none in his hand, and his brown tweed coat is too long on his arms, as if taken from a taller man. He steps forward.

Just barely, she nods in acknowledgment. This German, already in a location he has no business being in, is not someone she should engage with. *It's all right to be angry. You should be.* She stops walking and turns to face him. "Do you need something?" she asks in Flemish, which, in this part of Belgium, is what's spoken.

Surprisingly, he responds in Flemish. *"Jij bent Evelien?"*

You are Evelien? But he doesn't pronounce her name the way the Flemish do—*Ā-vuh-leen*—he says it as the French tend to, or the way someone might if they'd never heard it. *Ehv-uh-lee-yawn.* Nothing is adding up, and nothing about him knowing her name can be good. Quickly, she starts to turn, but he lifts his arm just slightly, just enough to reveal the end of an envelope he's hidden up his sleeve. She looks up at him, to eyes that are blue but threaded with red—a man who has not slept. Which, with the letter he's hiding, makes sense, because mail is supposed to be delivered, unsealed and open, to the *Kommandantur*—the local seat of the military authority—for inspection. A letter like this could land him in prison.

Fear threads through her. "Do I know you?"

"You know him," the man says, and now she hears what she thinks is an Irish accent, but then he's extending his arm in such a way that the back of the envelope with return information is visible, and there, in handwriting she knows too well, is Emiel's name.

What this man has is a letter, written by Emiel.

A flash of her last night with her husband, the night before he left to report, their wedding night: He'd sat on the edge of the bed in a towel, staring at the burgundy velvet drape that covered the window. Light brown hair damp from the bath. A drop of water on his neck. *What if this is it?* he'd asked, dramatic, but, it turned out, correct.

Or maybe not.

Coletta might be right. *He's my blood. If he were dead, I would feel it. I am telling you, he's alive and can't send us word.* Evelien's heard stories of letters that have made it over the *dodendraad*, or death wire: a fifteen-foot electrified fence that separates Belgium from neutral Holland. Family members toss letters over, desperate to reach those they love. But it rarely works, and those stuck within German territory remain isolated, cut off and controlled.

Evelien reaches for the envelope. But the man hides it in his sleeve.

"No," he says. "Not yet." He smiles. "He wrote this letter, but it's not addressed to you."

"His parents, then." She motions toward their kitchen door. Then turns back to the man. "How did you know my name? If it's not addressed to me?"

Again, a smile. "Because I was sent to find you. And I'll talk to you only. And this is what I'll tell you: he wrote the letter about a year ago, and no, it's not addressed to you." Again, he raises his arm, just slightly, so she can see the return address, and again there is that *E*, that beautiful, sad, swooping *E*.

"Written a year ago? And it's just now you're giving it to me?"

"A letter from an enemy soldier into occupied territory—you're lucky it made it at all. Or me, for that matter. The trains are only for the military, so if you think I've had a bad time getting here, you'd be right. Some thanks could be in order."

He says the last part quietly, and his gaze is steady.

She eyes the mouth of the alley, watching for the German who keeps sentry a block over. "I don't need the letter, then. If that's the way you're thinking."

The man laughs. "I'd bet I have the right person—I was told you didn't know how to hold your tongue. But I'll need more proof."

"Proof for what?"

"You have an arrangement."

She shifts her feet. "I don't know who you are."

"I can tell you I'm working with those who are furthering the Belgian cause."

"One of the resistance groups? With the Allies?"

He glances behind him, at the alley. "You might not say that so loud, please."

In her mind, she sees Emiel, working for the resistance. *Alive.* "My husband, he works with you?"

Ignoring her question, he says, "There's a number I'm supposed to give you. This sounds familiar?"

Memorize the auction number on the back of the Braque painting, Mr. Vanheule wrote in a letter he posted from the Paris apartment they'd just bought, sent off before the Germans arrived in Bruges. He told her that use of Bruges as a German naval base was all but assured, since the Ostend-Zeebrugge-Bruges triangle was deemed strategic, with canals linking Bruges—slightly inland—to both coastal port cities. Canals that were deep enough for torpedo boats. Mr. Vanheule was half-German and half-Belgian, but luckily his cousin was high up in the German military and through considerable trouble had agreed to see to it that should the Germans arrive, it would be he who would billet at their house, and Evelien could stay on and continue work as a housemaid. *He will be good to you,* Mr. Vanheule said of his cousin, Vizeadmiral Braun, *which is more than I can say of the others. And he trusts me, implicitly.* What seemed almost secondary was this: *Memorize the auction number on the back of the Braque painting. At some point, someone may ask you for a task. This person will recite the first part, and you are to recite the last. If the numbers are correct, you will know the request has come from me.*

She never knew what the nature of the request would be. To smuggle out silverware, she'd thought, or to find his marriage certificate and keep it safe. But that a resistance group is involved means the request would certainly be something *against* the Germans, against Mr. Vanheule's cousin. Was this the plan all along? Mr. and Mrs. Vanheule, whom she would do anything for, who made her attend school and frequent museums and go to bed at "reasonable" times, and who in return expected only a minimum of work. *Protect that job,* Coletta always said, as if it might be stolen in the night. Which, in essence, it was.

She looks to the mouth of the alley. For almost four years, there's been no request. "But it's ending." Distantly, the front thunders. Even she knows that *ending* does not mean *over.*

The Irishman looks back to her. "Is there ever an end? I think only new starts, and new needs."

"We've got weeks left, maybe. The Germans are leaving."

Now he's irritated, as if this is taking longer than he'd planned. "They said you'd receive something in exchange. That this would be a risk you'd *want* to take. That you'd *want* to help."

The painting, the Braque. Once Evelien informed the Vanheules she was planning on staying to watch over Coletta and August, they promised her the painting if she cared for their house, the three paintings that meant the most to them, as well as a few pieces of their jewelry—the main item being a family heirloom diamond ring, with a stone said to have formed from the earth's tears. Everything is at Evelien's house. The only thing she didn't keep with her was a tiny diamond-and-ruby ring that Coletta insisted be at her dress shop in case of an emergency. Possessions, they quickly learned, had value only if they could be used for food, warmth, or bribes.

"From the impression I got," the Irishman continues, "you had a deal. But most importantly, I see these." He motions to his own cheeks, mimicking the tracks of her dried tears. "Whatever you were crying over, *that's* why you do it."

She looks to the skyline, the empty place where the church tower once stood. *We shouldn't be thankful we've survived; we should be angry we've not lived.* Now is Evelien's chance to do something. To not just learn about her husband, but to make a difference and live instead of merely exist. But also, to do something that might bring Father Louwagie a shred of justice. To redeem herself. "Give me the numbers."

"Good girl," he says. "487."

"738-5."

He nods. "All right, then. There is a list in the office, in a drawer, where you work. This makes sense? You're to make a copy. The title of the list is *166.*"

"What does that mean?"

"It's numbers. A code. There are numbers at the top of the list, and the list is in a drawer—that's all I know. If you haven't figured this out by now, I'm a messenger. I don't even know where you work, and I don't want to know."

My cousin will emerge from this better off than before, Vizeadmiral Braun said to her on the first day she worked for him. Fuller cheeks back then, life with both feet planted in this world. *Petrus is invested, you might say, and I trust him. I always have. So I believe him when he vouches for you and tells me that you are good and honest. Which is lovely, and I'm happy to do him a favor—but only because I do not bring my work home. So, know this: nothing of interest to anyone will ever be in this house, and if it were, you would not be.*

"The German I work for," she says of the vizeadmiral, "is barely there. And he locks his office at home. Every time. But it doesn't matter because he doesn't work there. He's at the *MarineKorps Flandern* headquarters. *That's* where anything useful would be. There's nothing at the house."

"Nothing that *you* know of."

"No, he's smart. He wouldn't keep something of interest to the Allies in a house where a Belgian works." *My cousin believes me supportive of Germany,* Mr. Vanheule wrote. *That Anna and I will benefit if they prevail, and hence their victory will be ours. Please say nothing to dissuade him of this.*

The Irishman nods. "A smart man might lead you to think that."

She laughs. "I wish you'd told me this earlier; it would've saved us time. I'm telling you, he only uses that room for letter writing to his wife. Or reading newspapers he won't let me see. That's it. For years, nothing else."

Now the Irishman laughs. "You've worked for him for years, have you? Time is what takes your guard down. Whatever this list is, maybe it wouldn't have been there at the start, but now? When he's forgotten to suspect you? Forget what I said about him being smart—the man most likely *trusts* you." Trust, said like something laughable.

A faint booming. He turns in the direction of the sound. The inner port and coast get the brunt of the battering, with the city itself spared, for the most part, but bombs can be dropped in error. Last Evelien heard, at least five thousand have fallen on Bruges soil, and though they hit mostly on the outskirts, more than five hundred houses have been damaged and a hundred completely destroyed. Though, for a major naval base and target, the damage over the years has been minimal. *You don't think it was strategic?* August once asked. *That the Germans picked Bruges as a base? A much-loved place the British would think twice about decimating?* Lately, however, things have been changing, the rules rewritten daily. Every day, it seems, the skies grow heavier with smoke.

She glances toward the letter. This will focus her. Might be the distraction she needs, perhaps even a slight release from blame. "But I don't do this," she says. "I'm not—"

"In war, none of us is what we do." The Irishman leans toward her, his breath sharp with peppermint. "But this," he says, tapping the letter, "and whatever you were promised, only comes to you if you get the list." Then he softens. "I'm a teacher. So I'm not what you think either. But I believe in the Belgian cause, which happens to coincide with my own. Others, they believe in food for their family. Do your part or don't. It makes no difference to me. I've done what was asked. Like I said, in war, actions do not define the man." A pause. "Or the woman."

CHAPTER 3

The chance of Emiel surviving the entirety of the war is slim. But it doesn't matter. The second Coletta hears that there's a letter from him—even one written a year ago—she's crying, relieved.

"He's alive. I told you." She swipes at her eyes. "A letter that *he* wrote. Oh. Thank God."

Evelien looks to the empty chair in the corner, where he used to study. For hours, leaned in so close to his books, it was as if he was inhaling the information, letting facts sift and settle. When someone walked in the room, he'd look up, confused. And then he'd smile. *Forgive me. Did you say something?* One of his cheeks had a dimple, while the other did not. A slight undoing to his serious nature.

She turns from the empty chair to his mother. And then tells her the rest.

Coletta's mouth hangs open, her cheekbones chiseled by war's deprivation. "Mr. Vanheule wants to spy on his cousin? Mr. Vanheule's a spy?"

Mr. Vanheule is many things, most notably wealthy and an art collector. *Not* a spy. Wiry and tall, he has a neat beard and round glasses that he takes off when people are around, reducing the world to the soft haze he claims to sometimes prefer—a haze that meant he was exempt from military duty. "I don't think his eyes are good enough to be a spy."

"Evelien. As if that's to do with anything."

"Maybe the list is something from their past?"

"Oh, my girl. Don't be naive. It's for the war effort, of course it is. Mr. Vanheule might be half-German, but he's got a whole Flemish heart." The news is sinking in, color returning to Coletta's face. "Evelien. *A letter from Emiel.*"

"So I steal the list?"

Now Coletta presses on the side of her forehead, as if fending off a headache. "No. The vizeadmiral will see it's missing. Copy it into your sketchbook. You still take it everywhere?"

Evelien feels the outline of the pad in her pocket. The small sketch pad is always with her, along with a nub of a pencil—nubs being all that's left after four years of war. Art, after all, in a war, is the lowest of priorities, and supplies are hard to come by. Even stationery—she's managed to hold on to three envelopes, which have become symbols of hope, hope that one day she'll be able to reach Emiel.

"I have it, but he keeps his office locked."

"The man who found you—he's working as part of the resistance?"

Evelien nods, excitement building.

"Then they must need this list," Coletta continues.

"They must."

"And Emiel was safe and healthy when he sent this letter?"

"I only saw the back. But it was from him. His writing."

"Le Mot du Soldat," Coletta says. The soldier's word—a secret network that sends messengers between the occupied area and the front. In most cases, it's the only way soldiers are heard from. A friend of Coletta's received a letter through them years ago, letting her know that her son was injured and recuperating in the south of France. Though nothing's arrived since, the woman still believes he's there, reclined in a chair at the edge of a field of lavender.

Now Coletta lowers her head. Someone who didn't know her would suspect she was praying, but Evelien knows Coletta, and knows the woman's only trying to stay standing.

When she looks up, there's shine in her eyes. "I dreamed of him last night, did I tell you? I saw him with a friend, an infantryman. His best friend, I knew. And they were yelling at one of their superiors because the man only speaks to them in French, even though most of the regiment speaks Flemish." She laughs, crying now. "Imagine him yelling at a superior. But I saw him do it. The dream was a message—he's alive. I know it; I've always known it." Arms out, she hugs Evelien, full-bodied and swaying, the kind of hug that would have made Evelien's own mother stiffen. "He's coming back," Coletta whispers into her ear, still holding on. "I've told you. Do what you have to do, but get us that letter."

~

Though it's a risk, right at the end, it feels right. To do *something*. To bring Father Louwagie a shred of justice, to learn about her husband, and even just to feel alive after all these years—everything tells her to do this. The problem is the actual task: to do it, she has to get into a room that's kept locked, and the key is on a chain the vizeadmiral wears on his belt.

If there's a chance of getting him to leave his office without locking the door, it's first thing in the morning, when he likes to try to write letters to his wife. And though he's home only sporadically, this morning he has a haircut, and could be there now.

"You need honey," Coletta says. "To lure him out and make him forget to lock the door. You said he loves honey."

"So does Weber." Weber—the vizeadmiral's German cook, a man whose breath fumes with alcohol and whose face seems scrunched, like a drawing viewed from below. Weber, who sits at the kitchen table in the morning and eats any leftovers from the night before, chewing loudly as Evelien's stomach twists with knots of hunger. "But no one has honey." Honey, in demand for its ability to energize troops on the front.

Coletta riffles through her dresser drawer. "S&P Market does."

S&P Market. Owned by a German family, the Schmidts, who'd refused to move at the start of the war. Even after people broke their windows and scattered the white feathers bestowed to cowards inside, S&P Market stayed open, claiming Belgian loyalty, claiming that legitimate exemptions were the only reasons their men weren't fighting. Still, when the Germans arrived and took over the city, S&P's shelves were filled with products no one else had. And now the latest: flour mixed with sawdust. Next it would be sugar mixed with sand, or milk with water, and despite the German warnings about tampering with food, they never punish the Schmidts.

Coletta lifts a powder-blue dress from the drawer, wrinkled but pristine. "I planned on wearing it for our anniversary. Alixa's size, wouldn't you say?"

Alixa Schmidt, one of Evelien's closest friends. Until the war began, that is.

The dress is soon rolled up in Evelien's bag. Hurrying to the market, she tries to not think about her friend, who never bothered to hide her surprise when Evelien—almost overnight, Alixa claimed—developed feelings for Emiel. Letting Alixa think that this was the cause of their falling out has been easier than explaining that it's because of the war; each of them has been caught on waves of their own, differing nationalities. Every time Alixa neglected to ask about Emiel, the rift between them grew. Every day that Lukas, Alixa's brother, is there, in the flesh, while the men the Belgians love are gone, the gulf widens.

Still, despite the worry over seeing Alixa, Evelien is excited. If you'd told her four years ago to expect this day, a day when she—a housemaid, a no one—would be happy to put her life at risk, she would've laughed. But war has mixed roles and rules, has turned dogs into frontline messengers and elk hunters to snipers and mothers to ambulance drivers, and now, suddenly, Evelien is being asked to spy. Evelien, who loves art and sweets and is anything but a spy.

"Something's funny?"

Alixa. Sitting on a chair in the alley behind her shop, peeling potatoes. She's waiting for a response. Milky water froths in a bowl beneath her hands, and peels are scattered on the ground.

You don't know who she's reporting to, so don't give her anything worth reporting. Coletta's last words of advice.

"Why are you outside?" Evelien asks.

"It stinks in there. Lukas's got five men unloading boxes. What do you need?"

It hurts, to cut straight in like this, but Alixa's right. "Coletta made a dress for her anniversary, but they didn't celebrate." She doesn't need to say *why*. For years, people have skipped birthdays and anniversaries. "But we have the dress and it's beautiful and I heard you have honey." She holds up the dress, and Alixa eyes it, biting her lip.

At last, she nods. "Maybe. But it also might be promised to someone."

"A German."

Alixa starts peeling again. A long strip from one end to another. "Are they all bad? You work for a German too. Are you mean to him?"

Vizeadmiral Braun is a part of the MarineKorps Flandern, which is active on land, sea, and air and, unlike other branches, tends to remain in the same location for years. Keeping her job has been a sort of investment over the course of time, sparing her from much, much worse options. "It's different. If I wasn't nice to him, I would've had many employers and many problems. And no one can be mean to the vizeadmiral. He'd punish them."

"That's my point. There might be a reason, but you're nice to him. The enemy. And yet you sleep well at night?"

"I told you, I have no choice."

"Tell yourself that if you need to. But why is my situation different? Because we have a store?"

"Because you're German."

The words are out before she can stop them. Both women fall silent. The only sound is the ever-present drumming of the distant front.

"You sympathize with them," Evelien adds quietly. "It's different because it is."

Finally, Alixa nods. "Did you know my grandmother is starving, in Germany, because of the British blockade? What did she do? How does this war have anything to do with her?"

Alixa's grandmother, a tiny woman who always traveled with two identical tins in her purse—one with powdered cookies and the other with money. Once, when offering to pay for a snack for the girls, she'd pulled out the wrong tin and unleashed a puff of white. Evelien can still see her gnarled fingers prying loose the lid.

She's about to ask Alixa more when the back door opens. First there's the waft of tangy sauerkraut—currently at a surplus and thus a required purchase, as is anything that's at a surplus—and then the sound of boots, and when Evelien turns, she sees four soldiers, all smiling and laughing, their cigarettes flaring orange as they squint into the morning. All the men but the tallest one start down the alley, voices trailing. The one left behind stands with his back to Alixa as he breathes in smoke, and on the exhale cranes his head to the side to see her. His lashes catch the red light as he looks at her and smiles. Though it's subtle, Evelien notices the tug of a return grin on Alixa's face. Then the man is following the others down the alley, the smoke from his cigarette a drift behind him.

"You like him," Evelien says quietly when they're gone. Because she saw it, the look her friend gets when she tries to contain something. And for a moment it's the two of them, whispering behind the counter, and Evelien feels the push of words, a confessional torrent—*how did it get like this, I miss you, tell me I've been wrong about you.*

But Alixa must only hear accusation. She stands, annoyed, and wipes her hands on her apron. "I'll get the honey."

"But it's promised to someone."

"Do you want it or not?"

"I don't want you to get in trouble." The truth.

Alixa shakes her head as she glances down the alley. "Oh, Evelien, it's too late for that, isn't it?"

CHAPTER 4

It's too late for that, isn't it? An admission of a sort. People have kept to themselves since the war began—trust is a wager no one wants to make—but sometimes Evelien can feel it, the lack of friendship that seems to flatten their already flat country, deflating spirits further. Bombs and guns and starvation are obvious killers, but what loneliness does simply takes longer. What she would do for conversation, for jokes, for a reason to smile and not feel guilty for the smile. And though Evelien wants to be wrong about Alixa, in the same moment she also does *not* want to be wrong. Because if she is, if Alixa and her family were never collaborators, it would mean this whole time there was a rift when there didn't need to be. It's one thing to make it out of this war barely intact; it's another to know you inflicted some of the harm yourself.

Above, a lone green streak flares in the sky, and a whistling cores into the morning. Lately, the bombardments have increased, last-ditch efforts to maintain ground. In her bag, she feels the weight of the jar of honey. It's a ridiculous effort, really, and part of a plan that's destined to fail, but it's the first time she's felt proactive in years.

Now, there's a burning in the air, acrid yet faint with vanilla. War is a mesh of dark scents—the rotting eggs of gunpowder, the sweet burn of an oak wagon on fire, that heart-stopping iron bite of blood. But this smell she doesn't know. Her steps slow. Another turn and she sees it—a bonfire in the square, soldiers tossing books onto the flames. The books splay, pages fluttering, before they hit the flames.

Entire worlds extinguished, one by one. A slender book lands on the edge of the pile, half-burned, a bright seam of orange spreading. If August were here, he'd grab it. August—not only a writer but a professor of literature and a man who prefers books to people, for the most part. In their cellar is a pile of novels with burned edges and soot-stained pages. *Rescues,* he calls them. The way he runs his finger down their charred spines is like tracing the pain on someone he loves.

She doesn't realize she's stopped walking until a soldier yells at her. No one is allowed to stand around in the city, and especially not in the market square. Smoke burns in her throat as she goes, but then she stops again when a wagon loaded with freshly hewn boards bounces past. Another woman spots the boards and makes the sign of the cross, and that's all it takes. Grief, that insidious interloper, lives at the surface, and in a flash Evelien's crying, because no one will ever hear Father Louwagie's voice again.

The woman standing nearby clears her throat. "I'm praying it's not your loved one about to be stretched out on one of those. Your husband, maybe?"

Curious, she peers at Evelien's hand, then looks at a nearby stoop, as if wanting to sit. Even in the little space of exposed skin at her collar, Evelien can see the woman's bones.

"Not him. Or, if it is, I don't know. I don't know if he's alive. I don't think he is." Strangely, it feels good to say this truth, even to a stranger.

"That's the best way to think. Tell yourself he's gone. Then if by God's grace he returns, you'll be pleasantly surprised. Always better than being disappointed. But careful not to watch," the woman adds, motioning toward the burning.

"Books?"

"Books and newspapers. Started with the newspapers. Someone— and I heard this, but you didn't hear it from me—someone found newspapers that said over fifteen thousand men in the Sixth Army had caught that illness going around."

"What about the Fourth?" Evelien asks about the division stationed here.

"Doesn't matter, does it?" The woman leans in, her voice a whisper, her breath an acidic waft of hunger. "They're losing men. Scores of them. From fighting and this flu. Can't win a war with a ghost army. The krauts got mad when they found the paper and started burning anything they could. Head down as you go—they're in a mood."

Head down. Feet forward. Then she's taking the back entrance to the Vanheules' house, crossing the Boniface Bridge. Built in 1450, the brick mansion backs against the canal with walls that rise from the water, darkened with moss and time. Inside are wood ceilings and massive stone fireplaces taller than she is, as well as electricity—something only the wealthy had before the war, though the Germans have since installed a lighting network along the length of the harbor. But her favorite part of the house is the garden, sometimes dark in the shadow of the Church of Our Lady across the canal, as if under a protective arm. Clover between the stones. Boxwood hedges now wild and uneven.

Once there was a time when Evelien would stand in the third-floor window and repaint the world, mentally streaking reds and greens and purples over waterways and trees, thinking of the paintings she loved by some of her favorite artists, Derain, Matisse, Vlaminck—*the Fauves*, or *the wild beasts* as a stunned critic had called them, horrified by their undisguised brushstrokes and their unapologetic refusal to be realistic. Braque, as well, was a part of this when he painted *Landscape Near Antwerp*, though his own Fauvist period was even shorter than the movement itself, which burned bright and fast before it was gone. Viennese green and Prussian blue and scarlet lake and cadmium yellow. The Fauves let color break free, their canvases alive with scorching hues, with paint often applied directly from the tubes and in ways sometimes deemed illogical.

When I paint green, it doesn't mean grass, Matisse said. *When I paint blue, it doesn't mean sky.*

Now she's not allowed on the third floor. Something about the high view and the ability to see what she perhaps should not.

Her duties are anything household-related but also encompass spillover from any army departments that need assistance with things such as laundry or mending and once even polishing brass buttons on uniforms when Admiral von Schröder, the head of the MarineKorps Flandern, decided his half-starved soldiers could use a sprucing up. She's thinking about what she was supposed to do today when she sees a shape in a lower window—the office window. The vizeadmiral is home.

I'll come to you in two nights, the Irishman told her. Two nights.

Inside, she hears Weber in the kitchen, but instead of going there—where she deposits her purse, where it, as is she, is subject to spontaneous searches—she heads straight to Vizeadmiral Braun's office.

She's just knocked when the door swings open, as if he were standing right on the other side. Eyes like shaded wheat—a little gold in certain lights and darker in shadow—study her. Only in his late forties, gray threads his hair like tinsel, and his skin is tan. When he laughs, he coughs, unaccustomed to or perhaps bothered by his own happiness. For a bit longer, he stares at her, almost unseeing, still lost in schematics or numbers or positions in the war he won't admit is ending.

"I'm late," she says in French. French, the one thing her mother did to prepare her for life beyond their circumstance. *French in the parlor, Flemish in the kitchen,* the saying goes. While many low-ranked soldiers only speak German, the higher-ranking officers almost all speak French as well, so this ability has served her well.

Vizeadmiral Braun looks confused, his mind elsewhere. "My reason," she continues, taking the honey from her bag.

It takes him a moment, and his eyes widen. "For me?"

She nods, relieved. "I don't like honey. I never have. But I thought of you."

"And Weber just made *Kriegsbrot*."

War bread, which uses margarine from vegetable oil and not butter, a recipe that German soldiers passed along when they needed bread to be fast and to last on a battlefield. Weber uses carraway seeds, and even picturing the bread with the honey makes her stomach tighten and her mind latch on to the days of *koekebrood*, the sweet Sunday bread Coletta used to make.

She motions to the kitchen and starts to hurry down the hall, as if time is of the essence, praying he'll follow without bothering with his key. When she glances behind her, she sees him closing the door but not locking it. Could it be this easy?

"A week on the field and this bread is as good as new," he says. "It's the only thing I'd eat out there. *Drahtverhau*. That's the name for the dried vegetables they eat. I'm trying to think of the French equivalent for that word." A laugh. "Barbed wire. And *Stroh und Lehm*—straw and mud—for the yellow peas with sauerkraut. And *Schrapnellsuppe*—shrapnel soup for barely cooked pea-and-bean soup. They're creative, the men on the front, I'll give them that. I almost left, too, ten minutes ago."

His good mood is both a relief and a worry. Like a smile from someone holding a gun or a laugh from a lion tamer. Untrustworthy at best, sinister at worst. In the face of everything, he jokes about food.

"I was late because a church was hit," she tells him.

He replies without breaking stride. "I heard. The British will stop at nothing."

"A plane went down. It wasn't a bomb."

"One plane, in German territory. A suicide mission. Next, we'll be blamed. They'll print photographs and say we did it."

She steps aside to let him enter the kitchen first. In her mind, she sees the Belgian men as they lifted Father Louwagie, the way they could barely look down, knowing that in their hands was the result of a betrayal greater than anything they'd known. "I would hope the man didn't *aim* for a church."

"No?" the vizeadmiral asks. "A steeple is not visible from the sky? The British will stop at nothing. *Weber.*"

The cook appears from the pantry, where he keeps a bottle of booze. His cheeks are red, and already he's glaring at Evelien, clearly blaming her for the vizeadmiral's presence.

"Show him," the vizeadmiral says.

She puts the honey on the counter. But Weber just looks up at her, suspicious. He points to her and then the honey.

"I don't like honey," she says, even though Weber doesn't speak French.

Already he's dunked in a spoon and is holding it out to her. Evelien eyes the bread longingly as the vizeadmiral takes a knife and eases down on the crust.

The taste of honey. The rush of sugar, the bolt of flavor. Weber puts his hand up, demanding she stay put. She knows he's observing her, making sure she doesn't rinse out her mouth.

The vizeadmiral nods. "I don't see how anyone doesn't like honey. My grandmother had arthritis. Beestings to her knuckles helped. And they use it on the front for burns and other infections, did you know? The boys say the machine-gun bullets sound like bees, like swarms coming at them. Maybe I should look into getting a hive for the garden."

There is no reason to point out that there won't be time. No reason to point to the sky, to the observation balloons that have moved along with the front, an indication of the shrinking German territory, because Vizeadmiral Braun himself has overseen the movement of heavy equipment out of Bruges, and yet in his mind, this is all temporary. In his mind, none of this means defeat.

"We work well together, do we not?" he says suddenly.

"We do," she says, because it's the only answer.

Always look for the knife behind the back of kindness, Coletta likes to say. And though at first it felt wrong, to play nice with the enemy, Evelien quickly learned she had to, and ultimately it would help the people she loves. Since 1915, there's been full-country conscription to Germany, and anyone without work can be deported. Keeping her job means not being shipped off to work German farms or being forced to suffer bleeding fingers from peeling potatoes all day at the Potato Supply Center. It also means surprising benefits, such as the German doctor who tended to a deep cough Father Louwagie once had, all because the vizeadmiral saw the worry on her face and inquired as to what was on her mind. Walk to work, shut off her heart, and remember that the Vanheules asked for this—the Vanheules whom she did not realize she loved until they were gone.

"May I?" she asks, motioning to the hall. "I have work—"

"Yes, go," the vizeadmiral says, already slathering honey on a slice of bread. She knows he'll eat it standing where he is, because he's of the belief that food is never to leave the kitchen or dining room. *Ruffian,* he called a man once, who ate a piece of bread while walking.

Quickly she passes the front door, then the linen closet, where she grabs a feather duster for an excuse, then passes the parlor, where the Renoir—a dreamlike painting of woods and a glimpse of ocean, one of the paintings hidden in Evelien's walls—used to live, and then she's flying through the hall, where more art lines the wall, pieces that are also valuable but are mostly sacrificial, selling the lie that nothing was taken. *It's not that we don't trust my cousin,* Mr. Vanheule had written of Vizeadmiral Braun, *it's that we have no guarantee it will be him who billets there for the duration. We'd rather them not start looking for what they think is hidden and could help fund their war effort.* Then she's passing Mrs. Vanheule's sewing room, long emptied of its fabric and anything useful, and is at his office.

From the kitchen, she hears German. They must be eating and talking.

It's now or never. Feather duster under her arm, she opens the door.

A blast of light. The curtain's open, and German soldiers are right outside the window.

She drops to the floor, heart pounding. She'd thought the curtains were closed. Men were in front of the glass. Did they spot her?

A peek: a German vehicle on the street must have blocked her, but now she can't stand without them seeing her. Fingers pressed into the rug, she stays still, listening. The desk is all the way across the room, by the window. There's no way she can make it there without being seen.

Still on her hands and knees, she backs out of the room, then stands slowly, trying not to gather attention with a fast movement. Gradually, she brings the door shut.

Only when she's got the door completely closed does she turn around. And that's when she sees Weber, emerging at the far end of the hall. He looks at her just as she drops her hand from the doorknob.

There's a chance he doesn't know she was inside. A small, fragile chance, but she's clinging to it, hoping and praying—until she realizes the feather duster is no longer under her arm.

CHAPTER 5

There is no time. She needs to tell the vizeadmiral she was in his office before Weber does, because they will find the duster and know. Within seconds, she's down the hall and scooping up the rug by the entrance to the service stairs, then slipping out through the side door and running through the garden to the kitchen door. Rug still under her arm, she hurries through the kitchen and into the hall, arriving just as the vizeadmiral's putting on his hat.

"I'm sorry, Vizeadmiral Braun." She pauses, trying to steady her breath.

He turns to her, impatient but also curious. "Are you out of breath?" How he is around others has always been different than when they're alone. Irritated, he doesn't wait for an answer, just shrugs on his coat.

"I remembered I left this outside." She holds up the rug. "Yesterday, when I washed it."

His eyes widen. Nothing that Allied aviators can see should be left outside. "All night?"

"It was under a tree so not obvious, but when I remembered, I ran out to get it and dropped my duster in your office—"

"My office?" Already he's turned, heading back down the hallway. "You were in my office?"

"No, I wasn't—I had just opened the door because I realized it never gets cleaned, and then I thought of the rug and—I know nothing's supposed to be outside, but it wasn't dry yesterday and I forgot—"

The vizeadmiral stops suddenly in the hall. In front of him is Weber, holding the duster. Weber, who looks almost joyful for the first time, honey shining in the corner of his mouth.

There is rapid-fire German as the two men converse, and then the vizeadmiral turns to her with her duster in hand. "This is what you were looking for."

"Yes. I'm sorry; I can clean the room now."

He studies her, then glances at the rug. "You missed a spot."

"Pardon me?"

"You cleaned it yesterday, you said. But you missed a spot. That's unlike you."

He points to a navy stain. A splotch of incriminating dark on the fibers.

"That's ink," she says. "It's been there for years. The rug was in Mrs. Vanheule's sewing room, and she knocked over ink and it never came out."

He makes a sound like he's tasting his thoughts. "Maybe I've never looked closely."

"No, it's not a rug you see often."

"And yet you wanted to clean it. This is how you spend your time, doing things that are unnecessary?"

She wants to say *yes*, that half of what she does for a man who's barely home seems unnecessary, but the ego that's told him he needs someone full-time is also what keeps her from worse jobs for other people. Instead, she glances at Weber, whom she knows doesn't understand her. For a second she feels bad, but Weber is a man who finds reason to walk on her clean floors and leans his forehead against her shining windows. "There was something spilled on it. It smelled like beer. Strongly like beer, or I would've left it."

The vizeadmiral glances back at Weber and nods, irritated but accepting. "I don't know where he finds it." Then he glances at his watch. "My haircut. Evelien, the man should be here any minute.

Apologize and reschedule for tomorrow at eight. *Don't* tell him I forgot; he'll only be offended he's not more important. Tell him I was called away. The man's a tyrant but gifted with a pair of scissors." He swoops his arm toward the hall. "Go. I'm done." When Weber doesn't move, he turns to him. *"Du auch! Aus!"*

Weber, surprised to find the vizeadmiral's ire focused on him, looks only at the floor as he leaves.

~

Through the window, the sun now hangs low in the sky. A last glimpse of outside before securing the blackout covers; the mushrooms that grow by a woodpile against the wall are black in the dimming light. *Tippler's Bane*, her mother called them, because though edible, when mixed with alcohol, they can wreak havoc. Evelien has always called them *inkies* because the gills decompose into a black goo one can use as ink. Sketch pads are still hard to come by, but ink, courtesy of the mushrooms, is not.

All day, Weber's watched her, even more intensely than when she first started working for the vizeadmiral, back when it seemed that either he or a convalescing German—one on crutches, someone with an eye patch, another who was missing an arm—happened to be resting in whatever room she was in. Back then, the vizeadmiral may have trusted his cousin, but trusting her wasn't a given. *At least he disguises his suspicion,* August said, laughing, when he heard. *At the dock, they need manpower, so they've hired Belgians, but then they had to hire Germans to watch the Belgians. I heard there was talk of painting yellow stripes on our pants so they can tell us apart from the German workers. Like they would prisoners. Which we are, truly.*

Now, it's clear that though Weber doesn't understand how he got in trouble earlier, he knows it had something to do with her. The problem is that he's watching her, and this won't change by tomorrow. She has one more day to get the list, and to do that, she'll have to think of a way for him to *not* be there.

She wants the quiet of the ruined garden and the time to draw—and to get the carrots she'd forgotten earlier. Curfew is eight o'clock German time—German time being the mandated and official time zone, an hour difference that's a bone of contention for all Belgians. If she hurries, she'll just make it.

Emiel. His name barges back into her thoughts, along with the night, a year ago, when she was hit with the feeling that he was dead. As usual, August and Coletta kept up a steady stream of talk about him, *because when he comes back, you'll have children and you'll want to know stories to tell them as they grow and we're not getting younger; our memories aren't what they used to be.* Evelien kept her mouth clamped shut for fear that even a word would loosen a black grief within her that would spill out for Coletta to see. Coletta, who was supposed to know these things because she had the gift of second sight. Just barely, Evelien made it through supper and then stumbled into bed, where she whispered to him as silent tears turned the pillowcase wet along her chin. *She doesn't know you're dead. And I can't tell her, because then I'll lose her too.*

When he comes back, you'll have children. She thinks of this. If he's alive—which she prays he is—she will have to have children. Right away. For years, she's made peace with children not being in the cards—which was actually a relief, because she worries she wouldn't be a good mother. But if he returns, there will be no waiting, no adjusting and remembering each other. He wanted children before he left—it was why they got married the day before he reported. Wasting time wouldn't be an option. At this point, everyone has lost years.

"*Gib niemels auf,*" a soldier says kindly, urging her forward. He is a boy. No more than fifteen. His uniform hangs, and his pack is too big for him. The Germans have gone through their adults, and have no one else.

Keep going. Head down, feet forward.

And then she's in the house with the ruined garden, and light shifts and changes as a plane crosses the sky overhead. On a bookcase is a stack of proclamations from General von Emmich that she'd found, distributed throughout Belgium in autumn of 1914, just before the invasion, informing the Belgian people that the German army was forced to enter Belgium. Pages and pages of lies onto which she's drawn odds and ends, working on perspective and angles. Beside the bookcase is an old wood umbrella stand where she has five umbrellas, so that on rainy days she can try to protect certain exposed parts of the room.

The carrots. Two rows are in a deep drawer, and she pulls one—a nub. The next—the same. They didn't grow. They needed different soil or fertilizer. There is heartbreak to this. To their small, sad effort. Everything feels futile. That ominous feeling is returning, as if every move she makes is on a razor's edge.

Upstairs, in her canvas room, the feeling continues, because soon she will lose all this. Every wall, every image. The whole house will be knocked down and torn apart, and she's wondering if she'd still have done these drawings if she knew how deeply she'd feel their loss, when suddenly, from downstairs, she hears a noise.

She turns, just as the front door bangs shut. Forcefully.

Someone is in the house.

She needs to hide. The stairs are in bad enough shape that no one should think someone was up here—but then again, there's a garden in the parlor. A stack of proclamations she should not have kept. Everywhere you turn are violations. Speculating there's more upstairs wouldn't be out of the question.

Her only chance is to sneak out the front door, when whoever is there is occupied by the garden. If she waits too long, and that person turns back to the stairs, it will be too late.

Every step is a challenge, even in normal times, much less when noise is the enemy. Tentatively, she lowers one foot onto the first stair. Then her entire weight. Another one, this time trying to avoid a crack.

Then another. When she's at the spot on the landing where she's able to peer into the parlor, she keeps as close to the wall as she can. There, lying on the dark-green chaise by the garden, is a German soldier. His eyes are closed and his face is thatched with patterned light. Her heart is pounding, but she keeps an eye on him as she takes another step. And another. Just two more to go—but because she's watching him, she misses her footing on the last step and hits a cracked, loose spot.

Noise rips through the house. Just barely, she catches herself at the base of the stairs, right as he bolts up. Gun drawn.

She throws her hands into the air. A moment of terror-driven focus: she sees his finger ease off the trigger. But it's not over. The pounding in her ears continues, and he's squinting at her, as if the patterned light from above has affected his vision. Now she sees that he's leaning, heavily, against the chaise, and there is a cane resting beside him. It's the soldier from this morning, at the church. The moment she witnessed Father Louwagie in the rubble. As if up till now, the day's distraction held the tears at bay, here they are again. Streaming down her face. Two minutes, she thinks, feeling a familiar inner collapse.

He sees her crying and holsters his gun, fumbling for a handkerchief.

Knowing he won't understand, she spits out a rapid string of Flemish. "Don't bother. You've all done enough."

He looks at her, and must gather her meaning because he tucks the cloth away. Under one arm he holds his hat; with the other hand, he retrieves his cane. With a few steps, he's moved from the chaise to the tomato plant. He lifts his hand toward one of the fruits, only reddened on one side, and she speaks before she can stop herself. *"Don't."*

Now he turns back to her, slowly. He got her tone and appears less understanding this time, eyes narrowed.

"It's not ready." A feeble explanation.

Both are silent, as if determining course, and he looks back to the tomato, as if it's the deciding factor. There is a fractured allure about him, like something broken that once was beautiful. A man who appears decades past his heyday, though he must be only late twenties. War: the great accelerator. His hair is thick and murky blond, and when he looks back at her, his eyes are so light blue, they seem almost clear, like a thin pane of glass.

"You did this?" he asks.

In Flemish.

"I'm sorry," she quickly says, "for snapping—but the tomato—"

He flips his hat on his head. "You didn't answer the question. You did this?"

She looks straight at him, to eyes she knows will change based on what's above or below, like water, all reflection. In them now, a flash of bright green as something streaks overhead. He glances toward where the roof should be. As he does, she sees the stack of proclamations on the bookshelf right behind him.

"You speak Flemish," she says. He must have family here. With the countries as neighbors, many do.

"Again, I ask you if you did this."

"*Yes.* I did this. Because we're *starving*. Because my father-in-law went three weeks without vegetables and couldn't see for a day."

A smile. "And you know that was the vegetables?"

"If you're a doctor, I would think they need you on the front."

Now, dark blue in his eyes. His skin is tan from too many days fighting in the sun—everyone is darker with tans or burns, their lines deeper, youth smudged from their faces—but he flushes from what must be anger. She's being rash when she should be sorry. But she's not sorry. She's too tired to be afraid and now too angry to be sorry.

"I could arrest you," he says. "Where do you work?"

His right hand, the one not holding the cane, is in a slight fist, and she sees his thumb sliding against the bend of his index finger absentmindedly. It makes her think of pulling a trigger or loosening a grenade pin. *Do you know what the men call hand grenades?* the vizead-miral said last Christmas, his mood a pendulum, swinging to jokes that didn't make sense. *Nürnberger Lebkuchen.* He'd laughed, still talking of *Lebkuchen*, the sweet German cakes, as he left the room, tracking mud from his boots. Mud that smeared red as she cleaned it, slowing her arm and increasing her pulse because not once had she seen red soil, anywhere nearby, and she'd realized it was not just soil.

Now she looks up. "You *could* arrest me. And you might as well if you take this from me. It's the only thing I have."

He shakes his head, but his face softens. "A flair for drama is what you have. Where do you work?"

"The Potato Supply Center," she says, not wanting him to tell the vizeadmiral about this place or to know how to find her later.

He smiles. "All day peeling potatoes. You might be owed this."

She holds back her surprise, and he continues.

"You were careless. You looked up and down the street but didn't look *across* the street. I was there; I keep sentry nearby." He glances at the chaise, where just moments before he'd been lying. "I thought you'd snuck out."

"No. There's someone else who keeps sentry. You're not him."

"You like to argue. That man's gone. It's me now." He motions to the garden. "Get what you need. Curfew is soon."

It must be a trick. She waits, and when he nods her forward, she asks, "Really?"

"I seem in a joking mood?"

She thanks him, trying to be gracious. Quickly, she gathers the parsley and some lettuce. Out of the corner of her eye, she watches him inspect the room. Standing still, his eyes trace the light as it shifts on the wall, as if he's entranced with the play of shadows—and doing this, he no longer looks rough; he looks young, younger than the wear and tear of war has rendered him. Perhaps just older than Emiel. He takes his hat off again, rubbing his temple.

Was this the last time? The last time with the garden, and with her canvas room? Last times are rarely known in the moment—a blessing and a curse. She glances again at the man's hand, where he holds the cane, the strain of tendons in his wrist. The pain he's in is evident. *Explain your sympathy to the sheep,* her father once said, after she cried when he'd shot a rare lynx that killed their lamb. What he didn't understand was that she'd cried for both of them, but mostly for all the horrible necessity in life, for the fact that needing to eat for one meant death to the other.

For a while longer, he searches the walls. Finally, he turns to her. "You need to go."

At the door, she turns once more to the garden: the parsley, the curve of cucumber vine over the lip of brick, the tomatoes she's been studying, angling toward the sun. It makes no sense that the thought of plants being destroyed matters, but it's the fact that they are only here because she asked them to be that wedges within her. For them to be destroyed because she'd encouraged them to live where they should not breaks her heart.

"This garden—I'm sorry, but it was my fault, not—" She pauses, unsure how to continue.

But strangely, he nods. "It was not the fault of the garden."

She looks at him, surprised, and realizes her mistake. Another thing learned in a war: do not show need or want, or you will be caught, and a caught person is tied to their captor. Evelien knows this, and steels herself, not wanting the sympathy she craves.

"Go," he says. "Now."

Opening the door just a crack, she looks both ways to be sure no one is on the street. Then, quickly, she slips outside. A couple of houses down, she presses herself into the mouth of an alley and glances back in time to see the German do as she did—open the door slightly and slip out discreetly. Above him, a sliver of moon hangs in the sky, a shred of white.

Along the streets, all the windows are shuttered. No light visible from the outside, as is mandated. But the moment she turns onto their street, her eyes find the one bright spot—their window, uncovered, its yellow light an ember in the dark.

Inside, she immediately goes to the windows, as Coletta appears from the kitchen, hair wrapped in a burgundy paisley scarf, a spoon in her hand.

"Did you get it? The list?"

"The windows," Evelien says.

At the last window, Evelien catches something in the fading light. Him. The German. Across the street, at the end of the block, watching her house.

He keeps sentry here, she knows, but something tells her that he followed her. But instead of being afraid, she sees the way he'd taken care when leaving the ruined house, how cautious he'd been, and with this, she extends that protection and feels, though perhaps illogically, that he'd followed her to be sure she made it home safely. Hope. That's what it is. Hope that maybe, in all of this, there is someone who is good, whose kindness doesn't hide the rest.

CHAPTER 6

At supper, her mind returns to him. Even as they go over options and logistics and plans, she's pulled to the German in an illogical way. She blinks and sees his eyes flare with green—a bloom of chartreuse—as something soared above. His shoulders were broad, and though every man is too thin right now, there was a sturdiness about him, a solidity.

"Evelien," August says. "The haircut will be at eight, you're sure?"

She closes her eyes, trying to shake the image. "I set it. But it won't matter. Weber won't leave me alone."

"He will if something else has his attention."

The plan, then, is that August will take a half-broken wheelbarrow, filled with bricks, to the vizeadmiral's house. The bricks, spilled in front of the door, will demand attention—and if Evelien makes herself scarce, and the vizeadmiral is home getting his hair cut, Weber will have no choice but to help. While this is happening, Evelien can copy the list into her sketch pad.

August sits back, alarmed. "You take a sketch pad with you? Into a German house?"

"It's small. I sketch little things, flowers or a staircase or a chair. The vizeadmiral's seen me do this. He said I had promise." He was in a good mood that day. A battle they'd won.

Coletta nods. "What matters is that he saw the sketches were of nothing, that this has been established. Now, how do you smuggle out a list that can't be seen?"

"My hairpins," Evelien says. "I'll dip the ends in wax. If I write with them, colored water will reveal it."

"Very smart," August says. "Two smart spies and one old buffoon with a wheelbarrow. Wonderful."

Coletta ignores him. "Did I tell you, Mrs. Vereecke, down at the Lace Committee, told me that two women were caught smuggling letters in their underwear, painted red like sanitary napkins?"

"Is it true?"

"Anything *could* be true. My guess is it's an excuse, to give the Germans permission to search. Nothing is off-limits if we horrible Belgians are capable of even that." A pause. "Evelien, there's something about this list. This list will bring justice, but I see you with it, crying."

Insights, Coletta calls them. Premonitions and information that slip into her mind like notes beneath a door. Sometimes voices that come to her. Over the years, Evelien has learned to trust them.

"*Coletta,*" August says. "It's bad enough they're asking her to do something that could land her in prison or worse. But to say that?"

In prison. At the very end of the war. Everything for nothing. She's been so occupied with *how* that she's forgotten *why*—or that perhaps she has a choice.

"Me?" Coletta says, seeing the look on Evelien's face. "You're the one who just filled her head with thoughts of prison! You know how she worries—and that would never happen. She's perfect for this. She's been there so long, the vizeadmiral *wants* to trust her."

"Anna De Beir," Evelien says, referring to a widow and mother of three, who passed along submarine details from the inner port to the Allies and was caught with two letters from Belgian frontline soldiers. "She was sentenced to death."

"But she's alive! She got clemency."

"Alive but *imprisoned*. At Belitz. It's the end, does it matter what's on the list?"

Coletta shakes her head. "No, no, no. The list gets you the letter."

"But if the war is almost over, we'll get answers. Do we need the letter if—"

"*Yes,*" Coletta says, and with the speed of her reply it occurs to Evelien that if Emiel is dead, this letter could be his last words. Coletta must understand this as well, though she'd never admit it.

"First," Coletta continues, "the list brings justice. I know it will. And second, of course we need the letter because who knows what answers we'll get or when. What if he wrote to say he was injured, and we never go to him, and he's alone? What if he needs us?"

August looks from his wife to Evelien. "Evelien. A man will get rid of whatever causes him trouble. Needing a German in each room to watch you again is trouble. So you need to find a way to get back on the vizeadmiral's good side again, fast." A pause. "I think we forget to say this, but thank you." With that, he eyes his wife.

Later, in her bedroom, after an hour of practicing picking every lock they have, Evelien realizes that the worst part is that it's true; she is the perfect person for this. Though not because she's worked there so long that the vizeadmiral no longer hears her footsteps, but because she has no one. No children, very possibly no husband, no one who truly relies on her. If something were to happen to her, the absence of her life would cause no collapse.

Above, a plane chews through the sky. Her room is on the top floor, in what is essentially a bridge as it crosses over the street to the other side and connects to another house that's long been abandoned. On foggy days, mist hangs at the sill. At one point, it was a spare room where Coletta did her work, but when the war began and Emiel enlisted—even though then, as a student, he didn't need to—Evelien moved from the Vanheules' residence into the bridge room. Coletta and August and most of Bruges were sleeping in their cellars at that point, but Evelien couldn't, not even when they offered her a semblance of privacy by fashioning themselves a wall, a cordoned-off far corner that they called their *chambers*.

There's a knock on her door before it opens.

"I saw the light from Emiel's room," Coletta says, motioning to the flashlight Evelien has on. Heavy, black, with silver-and-tungsten-filament bulbs. Valuable, since they've only got two. Beside it, she has the Vanheules' diamond ring. The *earth's tear*, they call the round, seven-carat diamond. On the bedside table, a candle is lit.

"I couldn't sleep." Worry over the plan and guilt over each delay that kept Father Louwagie waiting jolted Evelien awake, over and over. Bolts of remembrance. Studying the colors in the diamond was soothing. "It's better in candlelight."

"Most things are." Coletta's eyes go to Evelien's wedding ring. Thin gold. A small blue-topaz stone. Beautiful in its own right. "Maybe we'll have a wedding for you, when he returns."

Evelien and Emiel married the night before he left for war, hoping to send him off an expectant father. *Lovely, just lovely,* the man who did the ceremony said, looking up only once from his papers before rushing off for more work, *everyone marrying everyone, making wills right and left.*

"Mrs. Vanheule couldn't remember her mother," Evelien says now. She does not want a wedding. The thought is tragically ridiculous. "But she remembered this ring on her hand."

"Consumption?"

Evelien nods, thinking of when Mrs. Vanheule spoke of her mother's death. "Mrs. Vanheule was three or four, I think. Anna," she adds, using her given name. *Children are drawn to shiny things, aren't they?* Anna Vanheule said that day. *I tell myself that's why I remember the ring but not her.* A pause. *When I have children, there will be nothing on my hands.*

"They could have children," Evelien says suddenly. "Now. In Paris. They could have an entire family."

"Who, the Vanheules?" A laugh. "You better hope they don't. That's work, is what that would be."

Evelien doesn't want to share them with anyone, though that's wrong to admit. They're her employers, but they talk to her in a way Evelien suspects they wouldn't if they had children.

Coletta nods to the flashlight. "Time for bed."

When Coletta leaves, Evelien waits till she hears her mother-in-law step a bit down the hall, then turns off the light and blows out the candle. The footsteps stop, as if Coletta's pausing to study the darkness, then start again. After a bit, Evelien turns the light back on and relights the candle.

Immediately, the diamond soaks in the light. Colors flare.

Like the real ring, she keeps the decoy in a Meritol La Perle Kiss Face Powder tin that's tucked into a space behind a loose board in the window frame. The tin that hides the fake, however, is dented. Now she goes to it, prying off the lid. Even this stone, a crystal, flashes with colors. Made by Pierres Taillées du Tyrol, a company with a man named Daniel Swarovski at its helm, the ring is also set in platinum and has a heft and legitimacy that would fool most. *Petrus, the waste,* Mrs. Vanheule said when her husband commissioned the decoy. *Not a waste at all,* he replied calmly. Always calm. Always logical. *It's for travel. For uncertain situations. So we can enjoy the beauty of the ring, while knowing its sibling is safe.*

Evelien always thought she'd prefer the decoy. It, too, sparkles and gleams, flashing its colors like an internal rage, but she could wear it every day, relaxed and enamored by its beauty rather than fearful of its worth. Though Mr. Vanheule didn't ask for Evelien to take the decoy when the war started, she had, only because she loved it as well and knew an unscrupulous German would gladly confiscate it, thinking it real. The thought of it stolen, taken by someone who wouldn't love it as she does, who could eventually discover its truth and toss it aside, breaks her heart. It's not the ring's fault it's an imitation.

Outside, something hits her window.

Immediately, she switches off the flashlight and goes to blow out the candle, her elbow pushing into the mattress as she props herself up. The rings tumble against her arm. Panic, as she knows they're mixed up. But it doesn't matter. She'll compare them later and return both to the Vanheules, who will know the difference. What matters is what's outside her window. Frozen, she listens. A remnant of a distant explosion, she figures. But then, faintly, another tap.

She gets out of bed, and with the flashlight off, she adjusts the shutter just slightly. In the moonlight, a face looks up at her. The German, a pail by his feet. Quickly, she closes the shutter, heart racing. Was he pointing at something? She goes to her other window, hoping to look again without him seeing her. Slowly, she takes another peek. Now he's closer to the front door, but finds her in the window. He points toward their door, and when he sees her notice this, he turns around and walks back down the street.

Then it hits her—more Germans, coming. He was telling her there'd be a raid, Germans about to pound on the door. Switching the flashlight on, she grabs the rings. One is slightly heavier, its hues deeper, prouder almost. She places that ring in the unmarred tin and the other ring in the tin with the dent. Then she works them into their spots in the windowsill, mentally ticking off the other items. The paintings, hidden, safe. The books August has brought home—were they banned? Or just rescues? Then she thinks of his political cartoons, illegal to possess and circulated covertly; last she saw, they were under the loose board on the stair landing. One depicts Admiral von Schröder, known for his fear of dogs, as obese and terrified on horseback while his gaunt-faced soldier shoots a tiny terrier. The others are bad enough, but given that von Schröder is in charge of Bruges, that one would be particularly offensive. Evelien's trying to recall the last time August had them out when she sees the German again in her mind. When she first glimpsed him on the street, below her window, there was a pail by his feet. Yet when she'd looked again, there was not.

Careful to avoid the creaking planks and steps, she makes it to the parlor. Though all the lights are off in the house, she still holds her breath as she opens the front door, nervous though she's done nothing wrong.

There, on the front step, is an aluminum pail, a stained linen at the top. Cautiously, she lifts the cloth and is shocked at what she finds: two onions, three tomatoes, one red pepper, and potatoes. She looks up at the empty street, like a world carved from coal, all top-lit darkness. Quickly she takes the pail inside and shuts the door. Once in the kitchen, she sits at the table, her heart beating, thinking of him looking up at her beneath the window, the lines of his face drawn in the moonlight. Her heart races faster.

Within seconds, she's on the stairs, hurrying to the sketch pad she keeps under her bed, a larger one that never leaves the house. No one will ever see what she puts on these pages. *Painting,* Picasso, the well-known Cubist artist, has said, *is just another way to keep a diary.* Inner thoughts and hopes splayed in picture form.

Loose images appear beneath her hand: the path of the street behind him, the length of his coat. Sometimes it feels as if drawing calms her, and other times it feels the opposite, as if her heart recognizes what it loves and goes fast with frenzy. Her heart, that muscle that overpowers her mind.

This angle, from above, is a challenge to her, so she takes her time, seeing every line before she puts it on paper. Everything she's learned, she's taught herself, repetition and insistence and fixation all honing what she knows is an imperfect skill, but one that's vastly improved over the years, thanks to the drawing manuals Mr. Vanheule gave her and her love of observing paintings. It was only just before the war broke out that she admitted she wanted formal training. *If that's what you want,*

Mr. Vanheule said when she came to him with her request, *we'll find an instructor. But promise me that you'll always pull the painting from within yourself. Never let someone else move your paintbrush.*

After a while, the rhythm has her, her hand seeming to move on its own. The world around her could be gone and she'd never know. The only thing that matters is what's on the page.

Then she stops, rising from her image long enough to think of the shadows. All that lit the German was the moon, and to mark this now, she shades in part of the night in the corner. Then back to him, the pail at his feet. Then his shoulders, wide, the folds of fabric at his elbow. His jaw, shadowed cheekbones. *Gauguin said to draw a curtain over the model while painting,* Mr. Vanheule told her, *in order to paint from memory and make it your own.*

Now she stops, holding the German's image in her mind, turning it, smoothing it, letting the details filter through, to emerge into a reality that is hers. After a while, she sees him clearly, his almost imploring look, the shine in his eyes and the two lines above the bridge of his nose. It's been minutes since she's put the pencil to paper. Ten minutes, fifteen. She looks down at her drawing. It's nowhere near done, but she sees him. He's there, as if an extension of her hand.

And then she realizes her mistake: to connect to him this way is wrong. A German. Never should she have drawn him.

CHAPTER 7

October 11, 1918

Morning. Dawn spills over rooftops and hits the second floor across the street, leaving the roads cool, still soaked in night. She dabs on her perfume sparingly. Penhaligon's English Fern. Geranium and lavender and clover and oakmoss and sandalwood. A soft, green smell of renewal and invigoration, opposite of everything around her.

As she examines the rings, the light through the window is still red from the smoke-infused sunrise, but she holds each one to the glass. One ring is slightly heavier and seems sleeker, a bit flashier. Or is it? Even the weights are similar. Back and forth, she debates before making a decision.

In the kitchen, August appears in his most threadbare sweater. "Do I look old and helpless?"

Coletta smiles. "You look like the hero of the morning."

He laughs and then is gone, off to wrangle the wheelbarrow and ready it with an *almost-break* in its support. Coletta sits at the table, holding a pepper like a fallen bird.

"What *I* want to know is why Alixa would sneak you food now, of all times. The dress wasn't worth that much."

"She thought it was. I won't say no to food." This is the story Evelien's concocted, to explain where it came from. "She said it was the first new dress she's had in years. Maybe she wants to be on our good side?" The lies are fluid. "I think she's missed me." As she says it, she wonders if it's true.

"Careful now. She had an iron cross, you know."

Evelien looks up, confused. *The Allies are stealing iron crosses off the bodies of our men,* the vizeadmiral once said of the German military decorations. Through the window, she focuses on a rectangle of light that yellows the bricks across the street. "You saw that?"

Coletta nods. "In her hand. In her pocket, when she went to pay for a tram ticket."

"Maybe she found it." A memory of the soldier who'd smiled at Alixa, smoke tumbling from his lips.

"I was warned about them, you know. By a voice. Her and her family. The collaborators. The voice said the Germans can't keep going as they are, and the new ones aren't strong enough to carry their own packs. Then it went on to say to watch out for the Germans in our lives. So, careful as you go with her."

Your voices are always general enough to be right, aren't they? an old woman said before the war began, back when Coletta was just beginning to do séances with a few like-minded friends. *Fool the others, but not me,* the woman added, getting up slowly from the table. It gave Evelien pause, but there was enough that Coletta relayed that was true for her to believe. *This is the beginning of a great rise for you,* Coletta told Evelien on her first day in Bruges, recounting a voice she'd heard that morning. *The voice told me that you, more than most people, will soar.* At the time, the words were electrifying. Evelien, who had never cared about soaring, only about existing. She, who grew anxious with alteration and found comfort in the familiar, somehow she'd transform into someone who took chances and braved uncertainty. But that hasn't happened. Until now, she's blamed it on the war, but has the war been an excuse?

"Did I tell you about Agnes Liefooghe?" Coletta asks. "Prim and proper as you ever, but there she was at my shop with her son's knit hat so I could hold it and see if anything came to me. Do you know what I saw? Her son cut and ran and left his men out to dry, then was shot while hiding in a barn."

"Did you tell her that?"

"Of course not! She came with beef—beef that became our carbonnade, I'll have you know. She wouldn't have paid for bad news."

"But she wanted the truth."

"You *think* you want the truth. Most people don't want the truth. And no one needs to hear that their son is a coward. I spared her. I was *meant* to spare her. Oh—do you remember my cousin Amelie? Typhoid, it was, that's how she died. But she lived in Paris, and the other night I was washing the dishes and there was her voice in my head. She said she saw Emiel in France. At a farmhouse. She even said he was milking a cow. Maybe he's stationed there, but she said, *He's not crossed over.* A *farmhouse* in France. *Milking a cow.* I wouldn't doubt it, that he'd help out wherever he billets. Of course he would. Milking a cow. My boy."

~

In the distance, the Church of Our Lady's steeple pierces the gray sky, and blackbirds spin in the air, swooping and diving like something falling. Below, on the road before her, a priest steps out of a building, and Evelien forces herself to continue, to not stop and cry and remember. Already the carved faces on the buildings are brightening, the morning in a hurry to take hold.

Evelien hurries to work, thinking about the first part of their plan: when the vizeadmiral is occupied, she'll signal August by standing in the upper bathroom window.

As hard as it is, she tries not to wonder about all Coletta has told her, all the predictions and warnings and hope, and how much, if any of it, the woman filtered through her own discretion. For a distraction, she thinks of the German. The rinse of moonlight on his face. His slow, angled gait. She also sees him in that first moment, yelling at a fellow soldier after Father Louwagie was killed. And then the food. The help. *You* think *you want the truth,* Coletta had said just moments ago. How much of her is being hopeful that he's different, to appease her guilt from thinking of someone she really, really should not be?

At work, Weber wrinkles his nose as he searches her bag. She glances at the empty kitchen table, where the vizeadmiral is supposed to be getting his hair cut.

"He's getting his hair cut, isn't he?" she asks Weber, who stares at her blankly, even when she moves her fingers like scissors at the length of her hair. "I know you understand," she says as he goes back to chopping celery. "I know you do, and I just want to know if he's still getting his hair cut in"—she glances at the clock—"four minutes."

"Yes, he is."

Vizeadmiral Braun. A towel on his shoulders. He takes a seat at the kitchen table with a newspaper. "The man will be here. He knows what would happen if he's not." He turns a page.

Evelien stares at the clock. Somewhere out there, August is killing time with a rickety wheelbarrow. Each minute he runs the risk of drawing the attention of Germans who will notice him loitering and tell him to move on.

"You have somewhere else to be?" the vizeadmiral asks her.

She's being obvious. Fidgety. Forcing a smile, she retrieves the porcelain cleaner from under the sink. "The bathrooms," she says. "May I?"

He glances at Weber, who would never want to follow her into a bathroom. "Fine. Yes, go."

And then, a knock. Evelien hurries to the front door, lets in a man with a waxed mustache, and then hurries upstairs to scrub the sink. When she thinks the vizeadmiral is fully into his cut, she stands at the window to signal August.

The sound of bricks tumbling and August yelling in Flemish. Knocks on the front door. More knocking. Louder. Then Weber's angry voice.

When she hears August start to thank Weber in Flemish, though Weber won't understand, she steps lightly down the hall, keeping to the floorboards closest to the wall to avoid the planks that wail—which, in a house that's more than four hundred years old, is almost impossible. She hurries to the back service stairs. Thanks to the electricity that flickers off during heavy rainstorms or bombardments that are too close, there are lanterns left in various locations throughout the house, including at the end of the hall. There, on a table, is a deck lantern, used on ships, complete with shade to black out the light for times when cover of darkness is needed. Using this, she can have the light on and ready for when she gets to the vizeadmiral's office.

When she's at the door, she sets the lantern on the floor. Tucked under her scarf, she's got several hairpins, a couple with bent ends. Carefully, she inserts the bent portion of one into the bottom of the lock, deep into the barrel. Just barely, without straining the lock, she moves it as if it were the key. With her other hand, she removes a brass stick pin from her bun and inserts that as well, jiggling it about. With steady pressure on her makeshift lever, it moves. *Click.*

The door is open.

She's done it. It takes a second to understand it worked. Then she's inside, and shadows lengthen and spill. Outside, August yells out, *Just seven more minutes of your help, I promise.* Seven minutes.

What she's listening for: *You've saved me.* When he says that, she knows to run.

The only thing with drawers is the desk. Immaculate. Nothing on top but a paperweight, a cast-iron inkwell with pen rest, and a Hutton & Sons sterling-silver picture frame that used to display Mrs. Vanheule but now houses a wedding photo of the vizeadmiral and his wife, the date of their nuptials below in black calligraphy. *Don't worry, I left Anna there,* he'd said of Mrs. Vanheule. *She's right there, beneath us.* Beneath us. *Petrus's German family looks down on us,* Mrs. Vanheule once said to her. *They think we don't see it.* One day, Evelien thinks, she'll tell Mrs. Vanheule about his comment, and they'll laugh at the irony.

She's careful to remember where everything goes and to put the items back once she's inspected them, since the vizeadmiral prides himself on his attention to detail. Letters from his wife, a photo of a baby, playing cards, and even an empty chocolate tin. One drawer contains stacks and stacks of German magazines. The list, with *166* at the top, could be tucked inside any of them.

Outside, a horn blares. She looks up and waits, frozen, till she hears August. *This wheel never worked right. Five minutes more and you'll have your day back.*

As fast as she can, she rifles through each magazine. But there's nothing. No loose pages, no writing in the form of a list, nothing.

She's gone through everything, and with the contents of one drawer still on the desk, she realizes that's it. There's no other drawers to look through. Not once did she consider it wouldn't be here.

And then she sees a poster. Small, laid out on an end table in the far corner. Even from here, she spots golden sun and ocean water bright with reflection, the silhouette of the Statue of Liberty rising from the burnished horizon. Evelien's there in seconds, holding it to the light. The image is beautiful, painted as if looking out from the French shore—which is darker, in shadow, a brackish green—facing an America that's practically beaming, lit with hope and promise. The Statue of Liberty was made with a thin copper exterior, she remembers. *I've heard she's begun to oxidize,* Mr. Vanheule said before the war began, *but at the start, she was radiant and shiny and brown.* France gave the United States the statue more than thirty years ago as a symbol of friendship, and the words on the poster are in French: *Pour la liberté du monde. For the liberty of the world.* France and the United States, united in the war.

No wonder the vizeadmiral has hidden the poster. The Germans would never let something like this be seen.

Then her gaze falls on a little wood stand by the door. The brass pull on the front is decorative—or so she's always thought. Setting the poster back as she found it, she hurries to the stand, pulls, and watches as the entire front opens. A drawer. And inside is one item: a slim leather notepad. On the first page: the numbers *166*, written in the vizeadmiral's tight scroll. Below it, a list of names.

A door slams. She turns.

You've almost got it, August says loudly.

The list isn't alphabetical or written in the same pen or ink, as if it's been a work in progress over time. Something he's done offhandedly, now and then. Only ten names. Ripping out the page would be obvious; her only option is to copy it. Quickly she removes a couple of additional hairpins, these with wax formed around their ends, and starts to write the names into her sketch pad. One by one. *Gunter Wagner. Josef Strauss. Johan Fischer. Peter Koch. Johan Eulen.* Suddenly, horses. Clopping hooves against the cobbles, echoing in the street. And under that, a voice. August? She closes her eyes, straining to listen. And then she hears it . . . *Really saved me.*

Five names remain.

She starts to form the first letter of the next name but then hears August say it again, louder this time, desperation edging his voice. She repeats the remaining names in her mind, then slides the leather notepad back into the stand's drawer. But the second she's got her hand on the doorknob to leave, she sees the contents of the last drawer she'd gone through, still on the desk.

A blast of fear. She races to the desk and puts everything away, trying to remember the order. Was the chocolate tin beneath the playing cards or on top? On top, she decides, and has just shut the drawer and is almost at the door when she stops.

They're gone. The names.

Slipped from her mind while her attention was elsewhere. Or, rather, they're there—for the most part—but jumbled. A collection of first and last names that may or may not go together.

She feels a pummeling wave of nausea and glances at the little stand again.

But then there's German. Spoken from Weber at the front door. A man with a rich baritone responds, and suddenly the vizeadmiral calls her name.

"Evelien!"

She needs out.

She shuts the lantern off and closes the door behind her. *The same, but in reverse,* August had said about locking the lock.

Heart hammering, she jiggles the pins. Weber's voice goes louder, as if he's yelling at someone as he heads down the hall—toward her.

"Evelien!" The vizeadmiral, calling to her from the front door.

Click. The door is locked.

But there's no time to relax—they have to think she's been upstairs this whole time. Racing back to the second floor, she fights to keep as close to the wall as she can, knowing that there's a good chance Weber is right below her, and everything is fine until she hits the wrong spot and the wood groans loudly. She stops. Downstairs, right below her, a door shuts. Frozen, she feels Weber beneath her, looking up.

Once in the bathroom, she flings open the window, to further sell the lie that this is where she's been. "Vizeadmiral? Are you calling for me? I'm up here."

Vizeadmiral Braun takes a few steps out onto the street, shielding his eyes as he peers up at her. The sky above him is half-smoke, half-sun. Like the day of the storm, danger pressing in. The hair on her arms rises.

"The woman who was supposed to mend my shirts is out with that flu. She's next to the butcher, so I told Weber to get them. Take care of them when he returns. Enlist the help of your mother-in-law, if you have to. I need them done." He slides into a waiting motorcar but then stops. "Oh, and make Lieutenant Klaus comfortable, if you would. He'll be with us while he mends."

A man with his arm in a sling steps into view, looking up at the window as if confused as to where the voice was coming from. A chaperone.

Whatever portion of the list she has, that's it. All there will be. The vizeadmiral, she understands, no longer trusts her.

CHAPTER 8

The line in front of S&P Market stretches four buildings down, and the air looks scattered, broken with a slight mist. As Evelien passes, she sees Martine Lemahieu, shielding her face with her hand, and Emma, leaning against the wall, her bad leg so straight that Evelien knows it must be in a brace. Slightly under the girl's sweater is her doll, protected from the mist.

Now and then, Evelien touches the sketch pad's hard corner to make sure it's still in her pocket. Checking on it has become habitual, born from a fear of losing something important during a time when losing what you love is expected. Each page in the book is like a crowded map of the years she's spent in occupation, all she strove to perfect or dared to escape into. With even a quick glance at an image, she knows where she was, what was happening, and what worried or enthralled her.

Just as Evelien's about to pass Martine and Emma, a group of soldiers rounds the corner, rifles held with their left hands, barrels up and against shoulders. She shoves her hand in her pocket, holding the sketch pad as if it might escape, while each person in the line looks down. Everyone but Emma, that is, who stares at the men straight on, terror-stricken. One of the soldiers glances in her direction and must see Emma's fear, must actually be entertained by the reaction, because all at once, his face twists into a frightful expression.

Emma startles. The man laughs and moves on.

Evelien approaches the girl. "There are paintings like that," she says, pointing to the doll, to a black ribbon tied around its neck. "Of a little girl with a ribbon around her neck."

Emma nods, face down, as if afraid to look up.

"The artist's name is Matisse and his daughter is Marguerite, and one night she couldn't—" Evelien stops, realizing that telling an already scared child about an emergency tracheotomy—*without anesthesia, and on the kitchen table,* Mr. Vanheule told her—would not be a good distraction. All of her instincts with children are wrong. She looks to Martine, about to apologize, when a man steps out from behind a wagon and stares straight at her.

The Irishman. The one who'd requested the list.

Quickly, Evelien turns. Her heart races.

"I don't know where all the children will come from," Martine says.

The Irishman. Did he mean for her to see him? She still has a night left. When she glances back, he's gone. "Sorry. Children?"

"The future ones. We've lost so many men. Who's going to marry the women? We'll have so few children, for years and years."

"I didn't think of that."

"Really? You, at the age to have children?" When Evelien says nothing, Martine continues. "You and Emiel planned on a family?"

Emiel, the way he'd looked up at her on their wedding night, expectant.

"I apologize," Martine says. "I shouldn't ask these questions."

"I don't mind, actually." Flemish people are private, and Evelien's own mother considered questions outside of directions or general information an invasion of privacy. The war, she thinks, has changed this. When every day could be your last, there's little incentive for talk that only skims the surface. "We'd just married. There wasn't time." The truth, in a way.

"Maybe I shouldn't say this, either, but *I* thought he'd marry Becarren Dupont."

Becarren Dupont, a girl whose family was from Namur in the Walloon region—the French-speaking other half of Belgium, different in many ways from Flanders. Becarren was whom people saw Emiel with, before Evelien realized her feelings for him. "I thought that too."

Martine smiles widely. "Even though she was a Walloon, you thought that?"

"He wouldn't have cared."

"Not him, no. Coletta. I figured she wouldn't allow it."

We can't let a Walloon have him, can we? Coletta asked. *Taking your place at the table?*

When the woman behind her pokes her shoulder, Evelien realizes the line is moving and takes a few steps forward. "Coletta wanted what he wanted."

"Of course she did," Martine says. "A good mother."

No wife would want another woman to be so close to her husband. You must know that. Coletta's words were like a few brushstrokes that changed the scene altogether. Suddenly, Evelien thought of life without Emiel, without Coletta and August, and what started as a flutter of panic grew until nerves took over: heart-pounding, thought-consuming, middle-of-the-night nerves, because she was about to lose him, and with him would go Coletta and August. The family she loved would belong to someone else. "But then we realized how we felt."

Martine nods. "That's the way it happens."

"It is." She turns to Martine. "For everyone, right? Or most people?"

Martine looks confused but then nods to someone exiting the market's side door. Lukas Schmidt. He's taller than the Belgian men and walks slightly hunched over, his hair flopped forward. Martine leans in closer. "If it wasn't hard for Emma to walk, we'd go somewhere else. What with that one there mixed in, so to speak. Messing with the scales and such."

"You know this?"

"Doesn't everyone?"

Someone's ration, what they'd been saving for, the nutrition that they needed, ruined. She thinks of Father Louwagie. The weight he'd lost in the last year.

Martine keeps her voice a whisper. "Children are losing their eyesight because they don't have vitamins."

His black pants that brushed against the ground and his worn shoes. Brittle nails. The way his clothing hung, as if he'd grown smaller since the start of each day.

"The limp Emma's got," Martine continues. "I think it's something to do with not getting the food she needs. Food that *I'm* supposed to get her."

"You can't get something that's not there."

Martine looks straight ahead but nods, as if accepting this one allowance. "She needs milk, and what we got was *gedoopt*," she says, the term for milk that's christened with water.

Evelien knows that not many cows are left, and those that remain have been dried off, but the water in the milk was added so more could be sold. So a profit could be made.

"Maybe you should go," Martine says.

Now Evelien sees a soldier on the other side of the street, watching them. Groups of more than five people aren't allowed, and Evelien's about to say this, to point out that they're doing nothing wrong, but then feels the list in her pocket, and quietly says her goodbyes.

Emiel. Did Coletta say something similar to him, that a wife would never allow a close friendship with another woman? What does it mean, if fear is what brought them together?

Overhead, gray clouds are tight and bunched. She keeps walking, unsettled with the feeling that she's just found a thread that could unravel everything, when suddenly there's the Irishman, rounding the corner. He turns, tips his hat to her, and falls into place alongside her. She tries not to look at him.

"You told me two nights," she says. "That's tomorrow night."

"I'm leaving a bit sooner than planned. It's an evolving situation. Behind that arch, there's a bench; I'll be on the other side."

"How do you know I have it?"

"Because you're looking at everyone as if they're about to arrest you. And you touched your pocket at least five times. It's for your own good to hand it off. Go to the bench."

As he starts across the street, she quickly steps under the arch and into a little green space bordered with boxwood hedges. A black-painted wood bench is next to a tree, and she's only just sat when she hears his voice.

"So, let's have it."

He's behind the tree, smoking. She rises again and stands a bit away from him. "It's in my pocket."

"And how do we make it *not* be in your pocket?"

"You mean the suspicious pad that I'm not supposed to be carrying?"

"Fine. I've got it. I'll hide you. We know each other, then. I need you to lean into me, like you're crying and I'm comforting, and I'll try to cover you while you get it."

"I'm not going—" But she stops, realizing it's the only way to do this in public. "I can be home soon. I can give it to you there."

"Like I said, it's an evolving situation and that means I'm leaving, now. Come," he says, motioning her to him, his cigarette waving in the air.

Reluctantly, she leans into him, and he lifts his arms around her. His coat rises just enough to cover her, unleashing a waft of smoke and dirt and body odor. She forces herself to lean her forehead against his chest and look down, at the pad. As quickly as she can, she rips the page out, gently folds it in half, and tucks it into his pants pocket. He jumps.

"A little forward, aren't we?" Before she can say anything, he's laughing. "I'm joking, I'm joking. You Belgian ladies are so serious."

"I am not."

"Oh, well, then I stand corrected." He laughs again. "I'm surprised you had it to begin with. You might be more cut out for this than you think."

Briefly, she feels a flush of pride. "You said you knew I had it."

"I lied. It's your face, I realized. You look that way, like you've always just stolen a biscuit off the counter."

She doesn't know what to say, so nods to his pocket. "You have to put colored water on the page. It's written in wax. We tested it, it worked."

"We?"

"My parents-in-law, the ones I live with."

"You told them? Other people, you told other people about this?"

"They're my husband's parents. It's his letter. Their son."

"I was wrong. You're not cut out for this."

Two young children, a boy and a girl, appear, picking sorrel from the grass. The boy sticks the end of a stalk in his mouth, and the yellow flower bobs as he chews.

"You should know, I didn't get it all."

Now it's his turn to be serious. "What's this, then?"

"Half. Just five names were left."

"You couldn't memorize them?"

In her mind, she sees the poster that lured her across the room. Remembers the shade of blue-green at the bottom, with more black toward the lower edge. The sky, yellow ochre, a brighter, almost daffodil yellow seeping in from the upper right corner. But the names, the names are gone. "I tried," she says, voice unsure.

"You'll have to get the rest."

"I can't. My employer—he suspects. It wasn't easy to get this."

"Then make him not suspect."

74

"He's back to having someone watch me."

"A guard?"

"A man who's recuperating. They have to be somewhere, he says. That's the excuse."

"And you can't outmaneuver a man who's recuperating?"

"The point is, it took four years for him to trust me, and now he doesn't."

"People don't *want* to be wrong about someone. I promise he'd only need a minute to trust you *again* because he *wants* to be right about you. You need to do one thing. Something big, and he'll go right back to trusting you and believing in himself because *that's* what he needs."

"I can't change it overnight. Now I need the letter."

"I don't have it."

Her eyes narrow. "How could you not have it?"

"Easily. I wasn't expecting to drop by tonight, until I got certain orders, and since letters could land me in heaps of trouble, I don't carry them around by habit. So, no. I don't have it on me—but I *will* get it to you when we get the remainder."

"I told you I can't."

"If you really don't care what's in the letter, where your husband says he is . . ."

She bites her lip, thinking. "So you read it, then?"

"Of course I read it. Those kids are eating clover."

"They're hungry, and I didn't *have* to tell you it was a partial list. You wouldn't have known."

"Are you trying to say there should be a reward for honesty?"

"Shouldn't there? After everything, I get nothing? That's half the list."

"Would you like half the letter?"

She stands straighter. "As a matter of fact, yes. I would."

Now he smiles, studying her. "Like I said, it's not on me, but you'll get it in days, or as soon as you finish what you're supposed to do. He seems like a good man, your husband. And you seem so yourself, so I hope you remember that good men don't always do good things. It helps, to see that's the usual."

He's a good man. Present tense. "So he's alive? Or do you mean, from the letter, that—"

But the Irishman motions for her to be silent, and glances at someone behind her. She turns to see two soldiers walk under the shade of the arch, toward them. One of them has a cane. She takes a step back, away from the Irishman, trying to see the soldiers' faces. Beside them, the kids pick up their baskets and leave hurriedly. Still, Evelien watches the soldiers—until the sunlight hits them and she sees that it's not the German who'd helped her, but another soldier with a cane and a skewed walk.

Quietly, the Irishman says, "Listen. Life has become complicated, I know. And no, I don't know what the list is, and maybe there's a chance it's a lot to do for nothing and they were just crossing their t's and dotting their i's when they asked for it, but that's not up to us to figure out. I'm telling you to *trust* that if they're asking for something, they think they need it." With a glance back at her, he touches her hair, as if lovingly. "It might be justice. It might be the missing piece. It might be a list for Christmas presents. And even if you do things that are wrong to get it, keep in mind there's a bigger *right* at stake. Your country needs you. So stop thinking about what *you* get out of it."

A familiar flutter in her chest. "You're making me sound selfish."

"Any of us who've not been on the front lines *should* feel selfish. You've got your life all to yourself. It's more than the lads can say."

He turns, watching the soldiers. Anger surges within her. Because he's right—but at the same time, her life has never felt like her own. Everything she does is for someone else. Staying in an occupied territory so she could care for her husband's parents. Subjecting herself to constant German scrutiny by working for the man she does, at the Vanheules' request. Cleaning for other people. Cooking for other people. Packing picnics and luggage—all so someone else can have fun and go places. And of course there's compensation that she's grateful for, but none of it is what she'd choose. The only thing in her life that's for her is drawing—eked out in stolen time, and something she feels enormous guilt over. "Do you know how easy it would've been for me to leave? Everyone I knew was going. If I was *selfish*, I would be gone. I'd be safe and happy in unoccupied France or even America. Everything—"

"Struck a nerve, I see." He shrugs. "And I don't know if anyone in unoccupied *wherever* is happy right now. But if you won't do it, you won't do it. I tried. That was my best spiel."

"Tell them, tell the person you report to that I tried. That I *can't* because my employer suspects. It's not that I don't want—"

"I have a secondary plan, for if you didn't have the list, which I figured you didn't. Six houses down, in your alley, there's a loose brick, four up from the ground. If you can get the rest, wonderful. Put it there and I'll be back in a week for it, on the eighteenth. I'll leave the letter then."

"It's *cruel* to not give us the letter."

He squints at her, as if seeing her for the first time. "I agree with you, you know."

"But you won't give it to me."

"No, I won't. Because what any of us agree with means very little these days."

As he walks away, a breeze catches a linden tree that's yellowed early, scattering leaves in a jaundiced drift.

CHAPTER 9

She needs to draw. Drawing is a reordering of her life, each stroke like a translation that helps her understand the world. Even as she walks to the ruined garden, she imagines stretching her arms and watching her fingers blacken with charcoal as worlds emerge.

Emiel. Could he really be alive? The thought is exciting and unsettling but, more than anything, confusing. It's being told that water isn't wet, that the sun isn't hot. And though she wants him back, there are layers to the thought of him returned, a few of which she can't seem to see clearly but *feels*, somewhere beneath all the good thoughts and hopes, a pervasive sort of panic. Panic to do with the likely possibility of him hurt and suffering but tied to her and this earth for years and years longer, but also a nervousness from the fact that his return will shape the mold of her future. Of course, this worry is from seeing things from her present perspective. Wait till she has a baby, she tells herself, and loves that baby more than anything—then the view of a life of family and children will look different, and the desire to paint and have time to herself will fall to the wayside. Passing through the market square, past a line of soldiers on horseback by the belfry, she decides that all she needs is time. Eventually, her distracted heart will come around.

You're making me sound selfish, she'd just said to the Irishman.

Do you think of anyone but yourself? her mother used to ask, back when she'd catch Evelien drawing. But, almost always, Evelien would have already finished her chores. Drawing was a reward, what got her moving quickly. Even the day of the storm, in fact, Evelien did her chores—but did them early and fast, so she could catch a certain light. Which is why her mother didn't know where to find her. Why Leona didn't have time to make it into the root cellar and to safety. Why Father Louwagie was where he was, when the plane crashed.

What she loves, the preoccupation that seems to encircle her heart, it causes problems. It upends her priorities and makes her different. But if Emiel returns, she'll change. She'll be better.

But now, tonight, she will allow it.

Inside the house with the ruined garden, all is as it was yesterday, before the German stepped foot past the threshold. The tomatoes remain, the proclamations still stacked on the shelf. And in her canvas room, the walls are as she left them, though the dark spill from the coffeepot has dried, and the rivulet from its spout now fainter, as if only an idea.

On two walls—the one with mostly intact windows as well as the wall with the door—she's drawn odds and ends, such as her mother's favorite vase, the rocking chair her father fell asleep in each night, a small lake, and a violin she once found in the attic of her childhood home, an instrument that was so beautiful and polished, it seemed to sing all on its own. Then, on the wall across from the door, the expanse one sees when first walking into the room, she's re-created the Braque painting, dunes and water and a faint horizon of buildings. But the fact that it's in black and white removed the very point of the piece, and each time she sees it, she feels its ache for life and color, its need for correction.

The same is true of the last, and final, wall at the back of the room. Also in black and white, this one is of the field at her family's farm, seen from the road, their house small and distant. But like the Braque landscape, it's wrong because there is no color. In real life, their fields were flax and rippled blue when they bloomed around her June birthday, turning the seemingly endless stretch into a wave of color, a sight that made her parents think of linen and income and promissory notes and pants they'd patched too many times, while Evelien took in the sweep of flowers and pretended the world had flipped and that a violet-tinged, dreamer's sky had landed on the earth. Even the hardest of men would pause at the edge of the field when the flax bloomed. *God's apology,* her mother once said of the flaxen blue. Later, when Evelien learned her mother couldn't have more children after she was born, the blue became a brilliant offering of sorts. *Take this color,* it seemed to say, *and forget what you really wanted.*

Emiel. Now she sees his hands, the tendons as he'd turned a page in his book, studying into the evening. Then the stretch of his hand when he'd reached for her on their wedding night, a finger on the strap of her slip.

She shuts her eyes tight. How does one draw a guilty face? What makes her face guilty? Under some leaves and splintered wood, there are a few broken shards of glass, and after a while, she finds one that's just big enough. She sees the way Emiel touched her chin, raising it to look at him. Holding the shard, she focuses on her faint, ghostlike reflection. What did he see? War has hardened and defined her face. He would've seen someone different. Someone guileless. Someone open, and trusting. She can almost feel his fingers lifting her chin as he tried to see into her eyes. *It won't be bad,* he said, and even then, in that heart-fluttering moment, she thought of how far *bad* was from *good,* and how much existed in between. She studies her eyes now. She's never been able to gauge her attractiveness because she can't see her entirety—all she sees are components, and taken on its own, a component is hard to judge. Her nose could be straighter. Eyes, brighter. Her eyelashes are possibly too curled, and the corners of her eyes seem to lift upward—maybe that's where the mischief is, the guilt. Her mother, though, she had the same eyes, and no one accused her of being impish or suspicious. She turns to the wall behind her: her farm, where there's the most open space at the top, in the sky. With one motion, she begins the line of her jaw, but then stops and picks up the shard again.

Movement. Out of the corner of her eye. A man. She whips around to see the German studying the walls, and when he looks at her, there is a pause before he lunges at her, fast. Terrified, she backs away, frantic as her foot twists on rubble and she starts to fall but then jams her left hand out for balance and sees the blood, and at last hears what he's saying.

"Wrap this around your wrist." A handkerchief is in his hand. Blood is slick around her fingers, dripping to the floor, pooling against her wedding band. "You cut yourself. Let me." He wraps it tight and raises her arm, his index finger and thumb circling her wrist. "Hold it up. It needs pressure." She feels sick, and he must see it in her face. "Lower your head. Lower, lower, or you'll faint. What were you doing with glass in your hand?"

He asks this with something like disappointment, and she realizes that he'd assumed she was about to use it as a weapon. "I was," but she stops, feeling her head begin to prickle, the world becoming a pointillist painting, composed only of dots, a Georges Seurat painting before her eyes.

"Put your head down more."

The paint is not blended. Mr. Vanheule's voice. She hears it, can almost smell the tobacco on his suit. *In pointillism, each dot of color is pure and unmixed, and it's the viewer's eyes that do the blending.* Blending. The world is blending and then firming. With her head lowered, the world slowly puts itself back together, and for a moment, she thinks of standing again, just to see the world divide and break apart and become a Seurat once more. Another example of her skewed and illogical thinking. She forces herself to focus on the German's feet, his worn, mud-crusted boots.

Still holding her arm up, he sees the black on her fingertips. "*You* did this. All this is you?"

She nods, not sure what she's admitting to. Drawings, hours of wasted time, a mess. Whatever rules she's violated with her work up here, she'll find out soon enough.

"You are an artist," he says, as if affirming something.

Her eyes widen. "I am not."

"It wasn't an insult. And the walls, by the way, disagree. You're an artist." He pauses. "I was a painter. I studied at the Academy of Fine Arts in Munich. I know art."

Even with the pain beginning to take hold, she wants to prolong the moment, to reverse his words and recall them over and over. *You're an artist.*

Emiel. The name conjured, her mind's reminder. Everything is wrong. The fact that a man is holding her wrist, that she's shot with nerves, that she wants this man to stay where he is and to keep talking. A soldier. The enemy. And yet she doesn't want to look away from him.

The ring on her hand. She glances up at it. There's blood on the gold. But then there's the German's hand, his skin tan. Emiel was smaller, with pale skin—though now, after years of his being outside, she no longer knows if that's true. Emiel, who never made her nervous. Why? Because they'd eased into life together? Theirs was a world of slow realizations and gradual understanding.

"I'm not an artist," she says. "I'm a housemaid. And I draw. And soon maybe not even that when my husband returns and we start a family."

Husband. The word seems to hold in the air.

There is silence, and when he's still not responded, she looks up at him. He appears confused, and for a while longer, he says nothing. But then, "You'd still be an artist."

"Would I? An artist who has no time for art?"

"Artists make time for art. And you can't *not* be an artist. It's how you see the world."

"Then why did you say you *were* a painter? Are you not still a painter?"

He looks down at her, as if pleased to be caught. But then his face changes, jaw knotting. "I won't paint again. I don't see the world how I used to."

The limp he has, the scar on his face. What they endure at the front: men shooting flames at other men, setting fire to strangers. Boys, made to be soldiers, tied to their machine guns so they can't escape, or ordered to leave the trenches and go over the top and into hails of bullets and cannons and gas—or face court-martial. Every day, somebody's son, forced to run toward his death. Millions of sons.

And here she's asking him to paint.

"I'm sorry," she finally says. Then, after another pause, "Why are you here?"

He focuses on the wall. "I wanted to see the garden again—I wasn't going to take anything. Then I heard someone up here." A pause, as if he's reconsidering what he says. "I knew you'd return. I could tell you wouldn't listen." For a second, he eases the pressure on her wrist, but then tightens again. "A bit longer. It's still bleeding."

"I guess I have a look about me, if you could tell I wouldn't listen." She explains, "I was recently told I look like someone who has always just stolen a biscuit off the counter."

He laughs. "A man told you this? He was being forward."

"He wasn't being forward; he was being mean. It's horrible, to look like that. You shouldn't laugh."

Now he looks down at her. "It's not horrible."

"To look guilty? That's not horrible?"

"To have a *secret*. Have you seen the *Mona Lisa*?"

Her two trips to Paris: first, with her mother, so Leona could sign documents for a will after her aunt passed, a trip that involved the impromptu visit to the art gallery, the day Evelien met her painting, when art took residence in her heart. The second trip was just before the war, when Coletta was meeting a woman from Provence who was transporting bolts of fabric, but at that point the *Mona Lisa* was still gone from the

Louvre, stolen in 1911. There was a line to see the empty spot. *Picasso, a suspect!* Mr. Vanheule reported to her when it happened. *He and his good friend Apollinaire, the poet. All because they ended up with some stolen statues a while back. Picasso denied everything, even that he knew Apollinaire—can you imagine?* Laughter. *Their testimonies were histrionic and emotional and the judge dismissed them both.* Later, in November of '13, the real thief was caught when trying to sell the painting.

"Yes. I've seen her," she lies.

"Why do you think people love her?"

"Because she was stolen and her face was in all the newspapers and because of that she is the painting everyone knows. So people love her, because they know her."

"I disagree. People love her because they *don't* know her. It's the look on her face. Mysterious. Her face tells you she has many stories."

"One being that she just stole a biscuit?"

He smiles. "Perhaps. But to have something about you that can't be known—that makes people curious. Men, especially."

"Why?"

"You wonder what that person is like, when the doors are closed."

She pulls on her arm, and he lets go. "I don't think that's what he meant."

"It's what men always mean."

Her heart pounds. "And you talk this way to a woman?"

"*He* was being forward; I was explaining. Maybe better to shock you than to leave you thinking someone had been mean to you." He looks down at her, and she feels heat in her cheeks as well as a tingling in her head. "Or maybe not. Keep your arm up."

"I'm not *shocked*," she says, though clearly she is. She holds her arm up with her other hand, trying not to look at the blood-soaked handkerchief. "Thank you for the food, by the way. I should say that before I sound ungrateful."

He smiles to the window, and she watches him, realizing he has no intention of leaving just yet. Given how lightheaded she is, she's thankful for this, but nervous all the same. Just last year, the vizeadmiral held a paper and laughed as he said, *We are informed that marrying Belgian ladies is prohibited.* Evelien had just watched a woman known to consort with a German soldier walk into the market like Moses parting the Red Sea, with every Belgian stepping aside. *I don't think we're allowed to marry Germans either,* she said. Now she thinks of Alixa, the smile on her face she tried to hide. Alixa's German, so it's different, but still contrary to what she's said, to their claims of being pro-Belgian. Her involvement with a soldier casts their allegiance into doubt. Now, she looks at this German suspiciously.

"Why do you speak Flemish?" she asks.

"My mother was born here. She made sure to teach me, so we could speak about my father. In front of him."

Despite herself, she smiles. "He would've been wise to learn."

"He would've been wise to do much he never did." He turns to her. "Do you need help getting home?"

"A German helping me home would not help."

He pulls a pocket watch from inside his uniform coat. "Curfew is soon."

She stands, woozy at first, and sees him watching her, his hand out as if ready to grab her. And it's this, more than the food, more than his sparing the garden, that makes her feel as though she might cry. It's one second and just one person, but it's concern. He's worried about her, and ready to help. Everyone, it seems, expects *her* to help—never the other way around. After a moment, she holds up her hand, still wrapped in his handkerchief. "It's ruined."

"I'm only glad it's your left hand." She's confused, for a second, till he nods to the walls. "So you can keep working."

So you can keep working. The words repeat in her mind as she carefully descends the stairs, as she closes the door behind her, and as she hurries home, the night crouched against the city as if patiently waiting.

CHAPTER 10

Coletta fusses over her hand, cleaning and bandaging while Evelien fills her in about the list and the Irishman. August stays in bed, and when Evelien asks where he is, her mother-in-law claims he's tired. He's never missed supper before. The empty chair across from Evelien feels like an admonition, and the cut in her hand throbs, though it's her wrist, where the German held it, that seems to burn.

"He's all right?" Evelien finally asks, motioning toward August's empty chair. "It's not the flu?"

"No, not the flu. Might be easier if it was."

Evelien's eyes widen, so Coletta explains.

"They took him and ten other men to a field outside of town, where their job was to collect the bodies."

Evelien glances toward the hall. "Bodies."

"Soldiers. It was all day. You can imagine what he saw."

"But he was taking tickets for the tram."

"Until he asked a question, which they didn't appreciate, apparently, and changed his job. Claimed he mouthed off. Claimed a few of them mouthed off. One man August liked was sent to Dudzele," she says of the village north of Bruges, the site of the nearest prison camp where they send recalcitrant workers. A step beyond that is Sennelager camp, in France, where civilians join British and French POWs.

"August can barely walk," Evelien says. "He can't do labor like that." *Labor.* The word doesn't begin to capture the activity, in this case.

"You see what one soldier can do. One man with power is all it takes. Remember that. Don't make light of this—you have to get in good again with the vizeadmiral. Not just so he feels comfortable enough to look the other way, so you can get the list, but to keep you safe."

"You still think I should get it?"

"What they're doing to an older man, in a war *they* started and inflicted on us? You don't think justice is in order?"

"But if I'm caught—"

Coletta takes Evelien's hand. "Who's always looked out for you?"

And though Evelien knows her mother-in-law is just saying this as a reminder that she should be trusted, suddenly Evelien feels as though her love has come with an unseen price.

"My God," Coletta continues. "To know where Emiel is. From what the Irishman said, it sounds like Emiel must have *explained* where he is. Like he was giving us information about his situation. Is that the way you heard it?"

"The way I heard it was that the man read the letter, a letter Emiel wrote a year ago."

"Which very well could apply to now." Coletta takes a deep breath. "Evelien, the *Allies* have asked for this. Tell me you understand how important it is, that you'll get this list."

Everything inside her tells her to retreat, to go back to playing it safe and make it to the end. But instead, she nods. Coletta clasps her hands.

"You're meant to do this. I've always known you'd find greatness. From that first day."

That first day. Alone and terrified and in Bruges for the first time, Evelien stood at the train station, holding a map that had smudged, confused, until Coletta spotted her. Even though Leona had only mentioned the time of Evelien's arrival as an aside, somehow Coletta had known to go meet her. *Just this morning,* Coletta said, *a voice said,* Find her.

"You're meant to do this," Coletta repeats. "I feel it."

Evelien's hand throbs. She needs to trust. *Don't listen to her,* Leona said about her old friend before sending her off. *She talks a lot of nonsense.* But even then, it was irresistible. *This is the beginning of a great rise for you,* Coletta continued that day. *You, more than most people, will soar. The voice also said that you should know your mother loves you more than anything, and that her sending you here doesn't mean she didn't want you.* Then, a sidelong glance as she grabbed Evelien's one bag. *You're much, much bigger than when I last saw you. But Christ if you're not still a child. No one should've let you do this alone.*

Unexpected kindness. Protection. And a little bit of hope.

For years, Evelien's held the prediction within her, a tiny beating pulse of a secret. And for all this time, she's thought she cherished the words because they not only promised some semblance of an important life but because they made Evelien feel truly cared for.

Now, hand aching and mind racing, she sees something else: she needed those words, because she needed to believe her mother wanted her.

~

That night, she dreams of the German. When she wakes, she remembers only the feeling of him watching her—an unctuous feeling, thick with longing. Learning he's an artist has intensified his attractiveness, and now she imagines telling him about her painting—a risk, but he doesn't know where she really works, or where she used to work. When she met him, she said she worked at the Potato Supply Center, so there'd be no reason for him to suspect she took anything from his vizeadmiral's house.

She lets a future conversation play in her mind. *Did you know Braque was a boxer? And an introvert, a bit of a hermit, really.*

A thump on the wall from downstairs.

And he's close friends with Picasso, but the two are so different, even in how they look. Polar opposites. I think Picasso gets the credit for Cubism, but even Matisse said it was Braque.

Another thump on the wall. Breakfast is ready.

She's wondered about Braque. If he's fighting. If he's even alive. A Frenchman—if he didn't enlist, he'd have been drafted, unless he had an exemption.

"The palettes will change," she says at the table. "After the war. No artist will paint the same."

Coletta slides an egg onto August's plate. "They'll be lucky to paint at all."

August stares blankly at the center of the table. When he doesn't move, Coletta takes his hand. "August, you can't let them get to you this close to the end."

He looks up. "*They're* not getting to me. It's the boys. All the dead boys."

"Seeing them like that, I can't imagine."

"I've seen bodies. Of course I've seen bodies. This is different. This is gore. But it wasn't even that. It was that every time I turned one over, I thought I'd see him."

Everyone falls silent. Quietly, Coletta says, "Emiel? You thought you'd see Emiel?"

August nods.

"Well, he's not there. He's not on the field. I've told you."

"Tell that to my hands, when they'd pull on a shoulder, to turn a man over. My hands were shaking, like I had a disorder. And I collect more again today. The whole day, looking for someone I hope not to find."

Coletta stands beside him. "You won't find him because he's not there. I told you this. He's not there on that field, so stop it."

"What they're making me do," August says, pushing away his plate, "will break me."

Coletta shakes her head. "No. You won't let it."

"No one chooses to break."

"You won't, though. Your mind is so strong—"

"One of the boys, he had a fork in his mouth. Because he was eating when he was shot. He was hungry, and he'd taken a bite—"

"August, this isn't helping."

"Another, practically a child, he was smiling like someone had told him a joke, but the top of his head was gone. Just gone."

"You don't need to tell us this. We've seen—"

"Not like this you haven't. The earth, in some places, it's made more of men than soil. And sometimes it's just body parts. A hand. Remember holding Emiel's hand, when he was little?"

"August, *stop*. I will not think about his hand! There are weeks to make it through—"

"To make it through to *what*? To some magic point where these boys come back to life? When I unsee someone's child? When someone unsees *my* child?"

"August," Coletta says, drawing out his name. Tears stream down her face. "Please. I beg you."

He squints at the table before him, as if making sense of what he sees. "I didn't want to become this person."

Coletta kneels beside him. "You're not. You'll make it through this. And I promise you, he's not on that field. In less than a week, we'll have a letter that's written in our son's own hand, his own *living* hand, where *he says where he is*. We'll have answers."

August looks up, and it breaks Evelien's heart because she's seen this look before, when Emma was on the bridge. Someone terrified, but trying to be brave. *You should be with your father,* August said to Evelien years ago, when the German invasion began, when the Vanheules' cook and houseboy left, falling in line with the stream of refugees who were fleeing, everyone piled into their finest clothes. At first it seemed reactionary, when the Mullers, a German family down the street, claimed the tide was turning and showed Evelien where they kept the spare key. *Check on things, if you would,* Ava Muller said as she dragged out her last bag. But then she added, *Now it's not safe for us, but soon it won't be safe for you. You should go.* But Coletta wouldn't leave her shop, and August's knee was no good for a long journey. August echoed Ava Muller's words: *You should go. Go to your father,* he told her. Evelien's father, remarried and with the infant sons he'd always wanted, lived farther inland, in a safer, less strategic part of Belgium. At that point, she could've gone. And though she'd promised Emiel she'd care for his parents, it was more than just the promise, as she explained to August. You *are the only father who matters.*

"Evelien is going to get us that letter," Coletta says.

For the first time all morning, August turns to Evelien.

"I will," Evelien says. And she means it.

CHAPTER 11

October 12, 1918

Everyone is hurrying—heads down, feet quick. Evelien will get the rest of the list somehow. A new determination is bright within her. *What they're making me do will break me.* And she will get the vizeadmiral to trust her again. Make him remember that in all these years, she's done nothing to earn his mistrust, that in fact they've had a good relationship, in a way. As good as can be when his mood flips just like that, and when a smile can mean anything. She's seen it before, the way his anger almost makes him giddy, like a dog whose tail wags not because it's happy, but because of the excitement of attack. But there is also an outward kindness and a consideration from him that at times has caught her off guard. This past Christmas, she was cleaning the parlor when she saw a gift basket with three oranges and an enamel brooch shaped like a butterfly, and a tag with her name on it. Luckily, he'd been gone, and so at home that night, she tried to think of what to give him, attempting to recall any stories he'd told her, and then remembered that he'd had an aunt he loved who hung dried lavender in the windows. Carefully, she drew a sprig of lavender, and then used the cherry root dye Coletta kept in a jar to stain the blooms lavender, then placed the sketch in a little tin picture frame that she most likely should've handed over to the Germans long ago, when they requisitioned metals. The next day, before he gave her his present, she gave hers to him, and he went silent. It was then she'd realized the mistake. The small frame in his big hand looked childlike, her drawing juvenile, the contraband tin accusatory. Silently, he studied the flower, and then, suddenly, breathed in deeply, as if he could catch the fragrance. Relief fanned out within her. When he found her again later, he gave her the basket and let her know she could leave early for Christmas. Later, she noticed the frame in the parlor, on the mantel, where it is to this day.

Kind. Appreciative. Until he's not. *He ordered the execution of five prisoners today,* August told her months ago, after he'd been assigned soup distribution in a yeast factory. *He was touring and gave the order while winding his watch. He never even looked up. Just stood there, winding his watch.*

What she needs to remind the vizeadmiral of is this: as strange as it may be, they've had each other for years.

Now, an explosion somewhere too close rattles panes of glass in storefronts, followed immediately by another one. Evelien stops walking. Though no one seems too alarmed, a woman pulls a sign in from in front of her shop and quickly closes her door. The lock clicks into place. Evelien looks behind her. People walk, perhaps faster, heads down. No one has the luxury to stop working, even now.

A few streets are blocked off, and she takes a detour that has her walking past the bridge that leads to the *beguinage*, the area that houses religious laywomen, white houses clustered around a grassy expanse that in spring teems with daffodils that even in war don't know any better than to bloom. Just as she's turning up Walplein, she sees the tall figure of Lukas Schmidt, smiling at someone at the door of a house before he ducks inside. It's his smile that gives her pause. A smile, just moments after her morning conversation with August and Coletta. A smile, as boys call for their mothers and men clear fields of bodies. A smile, as children ache for their fathers and chairs at the supper table remain empty. A smile, because Lukas is safe and whole and impenetrable, since he is German and working for them.

Impenetrable. She thinks about this. An idea forming.

On Mariastraat, there are stretcher bearers in white masks before Sint-Janshospitaal, a medieval hospital, one of the oldest in Europe. The air is pungent with the iron scent of blood. She stops walking when two soldiers pause to rest, lowering a stretcher to the ground. A hand hangs from beneath the white sheet. Fingers bent, skin wrinkled at the knuckles.

There is something about the simplicity of this hand. The loneliness of this hand.

It's too much. The world feels damaged, beyond repair. She misses Emiel. She misses the past, the ease of life she didn't know to appreciate. She misses a time when no one was suspicious, when thinking of friends brought a smile to her face, and not a sense that she'd never truly known them. And though she tells herself that a plan like this is justified and necessary, the person she used to be would never have done what she's considering, and because of this, she adds herself to the list: she misses herself.

Consider it pure joy whenever you face the trials of many kinds, Leona used to quote, *because you know that the testing of your faith produces perseverance.*

But Leona never saw this world.

How will it change? This whole time, the goal has been for the war to be over, but though they will be free, their country will still be destroyed, the men they love still gone, and their faith in others—and themselves—left in smithereens.

At last, two men pick up the stretcher in front of her. Eyes down, they walk slowly, trudging, one foot in front of the other, as Evelien hears August's voice: *To make it through to what?*

CHAPTER 12

At the Vanheules', the vizeadmiral is in the parlor with the pocket doors slid shut, and his German is loud and clipped and angry. A man responds, high-pitched with nerves. In the hall, the soldier with his arm in a sling sits dazed, his eyes tracking her long after she's moved, as though there's a significant delay between his inner and outer world. She tries to not think of Emiel like that, barely clinging to reality.

Inside the kitchen, there are a few turnips on the counter and an onion that's cut in half, a bowl of split peas, and a handful of mushrooms. Without looking up, Weber slices another piece of his war bread and places it on a plate before drizzling it with honey. Then he sets it on a tray, where there's already a cup with steaming tea, and turns to stare at the vegetables he has to work with.

"I'll take it," she says, already reaching for the silver handles, needing an excuse to approach the vizeadmiral. "Pea soup," she adds. "*Suppe.* With the turnip, onion, mushrooms, and I think there's parsley in the garden."

Dismissively, he waves her off, but she sees him glance toward the window. The peas will take hours to cook, and if she knows him, the soup will be the vizeadmiral's supper, and whatever's left will be Weber's breakfast and not once will he consider sharing it with her.

When she goes to find him, the vizeadmiral is no longer in the parlor, though an officer with red hair waits for him there. A glance down the hall shows a wedge of light beneath the office door. She looks back at the soldier, whose arm is in a sling, sitting in the chair. His right boot is untied.

"Your laces," she says, nodding toward his feet, knowing he won't understand her words. He stares, uncomprehending. She says it again, and though his face remains expressionless, he now looks down, at his foot. As she starts toward the vizeadmiral's office, the soldier is still looking down.

The office door is ajar. Pushing it open, she startles the vizeadmiral, who turns to her with the picture frame that holds the photo of him and his wife in his hands.

"What are you doing?" he barks. Angry. He fumbles with the frame, setting it back on the desk too quickly. It falls over, and he rights it.

"I brought this."

"You're doing Weber's job." It's not said as praise.

"He looked busy."

"Didn't you see the uniforms to wash? They're outside the door. Set it there, set it there," he says, motioning to a table by his reading chair. When she does, he squints at the tray, as if seeing it from a great distance. And then he seems to have an idea. "You have some."

This, she understands, is not a kindness. His mistrust of her is clearly still a factor, which is why she's about to do what she is.

"Take it," the vizeadmiral says, motioning to the second cup she brought in, intended for the officer who's still in the parlor. "I don't have time for this." But then, suddenly, he softens. "Your hand."

The bandages on her left hand are no longer white, and she puts her arm behind her, ashamed.

"Do you need it looked at?" he continues.

She shakes her head and pours a small bit of tea. The steam billows. "It's nothing I can't handle."

There is a slight smile as he watches her. She takes a sip of tea and still his eyes are on her. It's strong, and too bitter for her without sugar, like a tannic scrape of her tongue, but she can't show any distaste or he'll interpret it as more. Fighting to keep her face pleasant, she remembers the Irishman's words: *You need to do one thing. Something big, and he'll go right back to trusting you.*

She swallows. "Who should I report to, about food tampering?"

His eyes go straight to the bread.

"At a market," she says quickly, which takes everything past the line from which there's no turning back. A market will have to be named.

Now his words are slow. "You want to report a Belgian?"

Behind her, a noise. She turns and sees the redheaded officer, who must have grown tired of waiting alone in the parlor. Careful not to lie, she turns back to the vizeadmiral and says, "It's owned by a family I've known for a long time."

"And you would report them?"

"Only because what they're doing is not right."

The vizeadmiral studies her. "But these are people you know."

"They are. And they know us. Which is why I hate them, because they don't care. They don't care that a little girl who gets her milk from them has hardly grown in a year." Even as she feels anger over what they've done, she sees Lukas caring for his parents, his father who has trouble walking, and the torment she feels over naming their market brings a sweat to her skin. As she wipes her forehead, she reminds herself that since they are in fact working with the Germans, nothing will happen.

Unless, somehow, whoever Lukas's working with isn't there to help?

"What if I'm wrong?"

"Have you gotten tampered food or haven't you? It's simple." And now he must see the actual debate on her face, because he continues. "An investigation would take place, and if you're wrong—which I don't sense you are—nothing would happen. And if they *are* tampering, then a hand-slapping. A fine. That's all. But think of the people you'll help by bringing it to an end. Why should they profit while you suffer?"

She needs his trust. Just a little trust, and just temporarily so he eases up on her chaperones and so Weber is the only one to keep an eye on her. Weber, whom she can handle. And if there's a moment when Lukas feels some pressure or worry, would that be so bad? Lukas, who never married, who claimed to not have time for women, since he had to work at the store and also help his parents, one with hip trouble and the other with a bad heart. *Though maybe that's why I need a wife,* he once laughed, swatting Alixa's shoulder, *so she can take care of them when you're off and busy with your own husband's family.* The comment made Evelien indescribably sad, as if her heart beat in sync with this random, faceless woman who'd finally be able to leave her own family only so she could dedicate her life to someone else's. It was only later that Evelien realized why the comment affected her: because she *was* that woman. From her parents' home to her employer's home to her husband's home.

The vizeadmiral tries a softer approach, with an obviously forced smile. "Honestly, I'm impressed you've brought this to my attention." Still, she says nothing, and just like that, his face changes. Patience gone. "Enough. Who?"

She made him see her resistance, her apprehension, which were both real and embellished. And with this, she names the market. And as she does, she remembers what the Irishman told her. *In war, none of us is what we do.*

CHAPTER 13

The day continues, painful with creosote in the wash to combat lice, her hands raw and her nerves frayed. She's clipping shirts to the line outside when she sees a hole by the collar. A pause as her mind catches up.

As if scalded, she drops the shirt.

Because it's a bullet hole. Right at the neck. Of course soldiers have worn these same shirts. Many soldiers. There are entire floors of women whose only job is to sew closed any gashes, holes, or tears, so a man can wear the uniform without feeling the death or injury of his shadow soldier, the one who came before.

The shadow soldier. Another painting she will do, she thinks, setting the shirt aside. Whole lines of shadow soldiers. Fields dark with echoes of the past, all the men who came before. An arm that lifts a rifle, shadowed by other arms, like faint pencil marks on an oil painting.

When she looks up, at the parlor window, she sees her chaperone, who is perhaps gazing at her or perhaps seeing something else entirely. But then her attention refocuses. In the reflection of the glass: a pale, ghostly army of white shirts. Her breath catches. When nothing that Allied aviators can see should be left outside, including laundry, she's strung up an entire row of white. At a top-ranking officer's billet, no less. A prime target if ever there was one.

Then, in a far window, movement. Weber. If *he* sees, he will for sure raise the alarm bells. Joyously and immediately. Hurriedly, she goes to work, heart racing as she unclips the shirts and drops them into the basket, praying Weber doesn't end up anywhere near a window.

And then the last shirt is down—and she's relieved, until she realizes that though the vizeadmiral's own clothing will fit on a line she's hung in a spare room, there are far too many shirts to dry for that space. The only option is the cellar, where three long lines crisscross.

Electricity, thanks to the war, works as often as it doesn't, but the cellar was never wired. At night, she'd never go down there. But during the day, she can stave off the fear of being trapped below with bright lanterns, and by latching the top door of the cellar to the wall in order to let in sun from a world that carries on as usual. Even so, she only goes down there when extremely necessary.

She walks inside the house, dread slowing her steps. Outside, Weber's opening the back kitchen door, then heading to the patch of parsley. The pea soup, she thinks, must still be cooking on the stove. Often Evelien suspects that he cooks what he himself craves, since the vizeadmiral is rarely home to eat at night and yet Weber always has food ready for him before he leaves each night—food Weber ends up eating for breakfast the next morning. It used to be that he'd force her to taste it, just to be sure it was still safe and hadn't been tampered with, but either time has loosened his vigilance or his hunger has increased, because now he keeps every last bit for himself.

By the top of the steps is a lantern. She hooks the door to the wall, to keep it open. *Dregs of canal,* the vizeadmiral has said of the smell down here, which he detests. Things also don't dry as fast down here, either, which has worked in her favor.

There is a daydream she has, one that's ready for moments like this, times she needs to escape. Paris. Her own *chambre de bonne,* or attic servants' quarter, with a slanted ceiling and green walls. Stacks of canvases in the corner, all waiting. A view of rooftops. Now, in her mind, she paints, choosing soft colors. A sunrise on water. A candy-coated Monet. Then a thought: if Emiel is alive, where will they live? Would they leave

Coletta and August? She can't think about that, and tries to return to the painting. But then she sees the German's hand wrapped around her wrist and the painting is gone altogether and her heart is pounding as she stares at the shirt in her hand.

"Here you are," the vizcadmiral says, the stairs creaking beneath his steps.

It takes her a moment to surface.

"Evelien," he says.

"I'm sorry." She searches the room for any indication of the time. How long has she been down here? "You're home."

"Just for a minute. But on the way here, I had an idea about a supper I think we'll have."

We. She catches the word and tucks it away, deciding she'll think of it later. Beneath her feet, the cellar floor trembles from an impact. She quickly looks to the stairs, wanting out. At their base, the vizeadmiral is turned in the direction of the impact, moving his fingers as if tapping a sort of code or marking an internal notation of distance.

"Is Weber gone?" she asks. "I'm not good with food."

"Really? I don't imagine this."

Maybe it's the *we* he just used, or the slight shaking that trembles the room, but suddenly she's unnerved. "I think he was making split pea soup."

Unfazed, the vizeadmiral explains. "I didn't mean tonight. Tonight will be late—I won't eat here. No, this is a nice supper. At the end of the week. You won't need to cook—Weber will. But you'll be needed for the preparations."

"Preparations. A party?" she asks, trying to understand.

He runs his foot through a layer of brick powder at the base of the wall, squinting as if bothered by how much there is. As he should be. Bombardments sift the dust of everything—brick, stones, wood—onto every surface. How much there is is an indication of the increased activity, the onslaught just outside their city. The thickness is a reason why a party should be the least of his concerns.

"Not a party. A gathering. The men need to eat," he adds. "Why not here? Why not have a nice meal and nice china in a room that doesn't smell like what they're trying to forget?" A thread of logic, wound around fantasy. He nods to the corner of the room, where Mr. Vanheule's wine rack has remained untouched. "You realize I haven't touched Petrus's wine. Not just because I rarely drink, but because I'm protective of my cousin. If I wasn't, I would've turned over his collection, like I should have."

"That's true."

"What would one bottle hurt? The 1890 St. Julian?"

The Germans are supposed to list everything they "requisition," to pay back later, but lists are half-hearted if at all. *How does one pay for four years?* August once asked. The situation is worse for farmers and those outside of Bruges who endure armies that are not stationary, units that appear one day and destroy fields and burn barns and then are gone, as filing a compensation claim involves specifying *which* army unit was responsible—but anyone who tries to get that information is deemed a spy. That the vizeadmiral is asking about taking a bottle of wine is only because he's related to the owner.

With another tremble, she eyes the stairs.

He starts up the steps. "You know you're safest here."

"I don't like being underground when"—she thinks of her wording—"when things are happening above."

He pauses and glances back at her. "You'd rather be in it?"

"I don't like not knowing what's happening. Surfacing to a different world. So if *being in it* means being aware, then yes, I'd rather be in it."

"We are not unalike, the two of us. It was good that you told me about the market." He smiles and turns again. "Oh, and don't mind Lieutenant Klaus, the statue in the hall. He'll be gone tomorrow."

With this, she knows she's passed the test.

~

Lieutenant Klaus, her chaperone, stands when she passes. Somewhere in the house, a door slams, and he tenses, his fingers white as he clenches his fists. She tries to give him an understanding smile, but he doesn't seem to see her. Not in this moment.

Even though he'll be gone tomorrow, she'll have Weber to contend with. Weber, who is rarely confused, even when his cheeks flush with alcohol. Alcohol. The word seems to brush against her, an idea nudging her. At the window, she peers at the overgrown garden and the brick wall and the haphazard woodpile below. Mushrooms sprout through the grass, some already edged in black. Mushrooms that are mild and harmless, unless alcohol is consumed, even within a day.

And in the kitchen is the pea soup, with mushrooms.

Distantly, she hears a plane approaching. The soldier hears it as well, but his expression changes as the sound seems to thicken and grow. Rapidly, his eyes move back and forth, as if he's reading a transcript of how the moment will go. It's not one plane, she realizes. It's a squadron. Most likely on the way to the front. And now she knows what she needs to do—fast.

The noise is growing, a chaotic churning in the sky. With every second, the soldier's panic increases—his mouth moving as he steps back, against the wall. Momentarily, she wants to abandon her plan and comfort him, because she, too, knows what it's like for your mind to lead you to a place that isn't there. But there's no time. Already she's in the parlor and then out the back door. For cover, she snaps a few flowers, and then is at the woodpile, shoving as many mushrooms as she can into her pocket.

Getting them into the soup isn't hard. Even after she's cut them up—crudely, but just enough—and stirred them into the pot and returned to the hall, even then the man holds the doorframe with his good arm, his eyes still shut. Lightly, she touches his shoulder. He opens his eyes, still panicked, and she points to his laces, muddied and untied, before kneeling down to tie them herself.

Then she waves to him as she leaves, and he lifts his hand just barely, but just enough.

Outside, she is hopeful about the plan.

Even if the vizeadmiral returns home hungry, she's not worried. He rarely drinks. The last time she saw him with wine was toward the end of the Battle of Verdun in '16, a battle that lasted almost a year. Desperately contested soil that claimed boys and men whose lives and homes were nowhere nearby. Though the Germans didn't speak of their losses, word later came through to the Belgians: almost 350,000 German casualties. Even more than that for France. That day, as the vizeadmiral poured himself a glass of wine, he told her of the flame-throwers the Germans had introduced.

"In the trenches, where can you go?" He took a healthy gulp of wine, and when he spoke again, his teeth were tinged purple. "You can't escape. It's like a stream from a firehose, only it's fire itself. Rounding the corner, spilling toward you."

"You're setting men on fire," she said.

"Not me. I've been here, haven't I?" With that, he downed the rest of his glass, and Evelien couldn't help but wonder if the drink was from sorrow or celebration, and then decided it was best not to wonder.

CHAPTER 14

At the house, she goes straight to her canvas room. There is the rust red of her own blood, and with it, she sees the German and how he held her wrist. Starting to draw, she thinks of Coletta, her irrational disappointment when Evelien wasn't pregnant after the rushed and hurried wedding ceremony, a disappointment that grew as the months went on and the war didn't just hold steady but actually bloomed, fed and wild. Evelien could see it on the woman's face, a longing for the continuation of her only child. A missed chance. Perhaps the only chance. If the worst happened and Emiel never returned—something no one would say, but felt with every breath—Coletta might've still had a part of him.

Evelien's working on a swan and its reflection, the delicate fold of water and air, when she hears a noise. Hand frozen, she listens, waiting. When no one appears, and she hears nothing else, she realizes that what she's feeling is disappointment. Disappointment, because she was hoping to see him—a man who is not her husband, and is also a German.

Right as the war is ending, she does this. Right as her husband is about to possibly return, she's hell-bent on sabotaging her marriage. Treachery from her heart, something she knows all too well.

～

They eat supper as the night deepens and the pounding outside picks up, as it tends to do in the evening.

"Imagine being closer to that," August says, referring to the sound. "Being *in* that."

"August." There's a warning edge to Coletta's voice.

"You wouldn't sleep. No wonder the boys go mad."

"I'm happy you're speaking, but I kindly request a new subject."

"Both sides, they attack at night. This would be relentless. *Every night.* The pounding. The shrieking."

Coletta pushes her plate back. "I said stop."

Evelien's jaw clicks as she chews. The potatoes the German brought are dry and stunted, but better than nothing, yet the meat Coletta found is tough and hard to swallow. Still, Evelien chews. All night she's sat with her husband's parents, talking about punishing the Germans and helping the Belgians—yet thinking of an enemy soldier. Not to mention praying, for all these years, that her husband would return, yet now worrying that he actually *will*, and realizing that maybe what she'd really meant to ask was that he return, but not to her.

After a moment, August says, "Do you think Lexi turned on the light on purpose?"

Coletta gives him a hard look. "I think you're trying to provoke me."

"Lexi Peeters," Evelien says, referring to the woman who'd lived in the house beside the one with the ruined garden. Only days after learning of her husband's death, she'd somehow forgotten to cover her windows. "From three years ago. That Lexi?"

"I think she wanted to be done," August says. His voice is soft and distant. "To join her husband."

Coletta shakes her head. "You're being morose."

Evelien knew Lexi from the school the Vanheules insisted she attend—a treat for her, since Evelien came from a rural community where most just attended in the winter. "She was nice. She wouldn't have done that."

August turns to her. "Done it to whom? She didn't have neighbors. Everyone around her had left. A direct hit—that's a fast way to go. If only there were Germans around."

Now Coletta shoves her chair back and stands so quickly, the water in her glass spills. She makes no move to clean it up, so Evelien mops the spill with her napkin. Again, August falls to silence, though now he appears to be holding himself in, hunched over at the table with his arm against his stomach.

Coletta stands before the covered window. "Mrs. Delie says she no longer believes in God. Father Louwagie being killed did the trick, I suppose."

"I still believe," Evelien says. "Even after that."

A glance over her shoulder, and Coletta smiles appreciatively. "I had a feeling you did."

August watches them with a flicker of interest.

"Not like my mother, though," Evelien adds. Leona, at confession multiple times a week, sometimes more than once in a day. Evelien found God in nature. Or—as she discovered that day at the gallery in Paris—in art. It wasn't until Evelien moved to Bruges and became close to August and Coletta that she realized that her version of belief might be something other than shameful. The only one who urged her to return to her religious roots was Emiel. *When we have a family,* he once said, *that's when you'll need to attend. If only for our children's sake.*

"Imagine," Coletta says, "if we all saw things the same way. What a boring place it would be." After a moment, she says, "I did always think it was one reason your mother was so down on herself."

"Because of her belief in God?"

"No. The belief is good. I'm always happy for anyone who has it. I do as well. No, I mean where it got hard for her is that I don't think she believed God *liked* her. And that didn't make for an easy time."

"God was up there giving her all the thought, was He?" August asks.

Evelien remembers her mother, praying for her. "She said it would be easier if I believed like she did. If I could be like her. She said it's where I went wrong."

"Well, I think she saw something of herself in you," Coletta says.

"In me? I'm nothing like her. That was the problem."

"At the end, you weren't like her. But you didn't know her always, did you?"

"People said *I* had it easier," August says, "because I *didn't* believe in God. But I ask you, how can that be easier? To not have a reason? To know that there is no reason for all of this?"

"Oh, August." Now Coletta goes to him and crouches by his chair, taking his hand. "We're your reasons. Me, Evelien. Your son, who is coming back. I see the beyond and I believe in God, and if you don't, then that's just fine and I love you, but look here, at this table. If it's all for now, and nothing for later, then look at *us*." A pause. "And remember how we met. What brought us together and the toll that day took on me. Because I felt the same way—you know I did. I needed reasons too. They would've helped. But I'm telling you, you can't see the valley when you're in the middle of climbing the hill."

Evelien watches her mother-in-law. *The toll that day took on me.* "You met when your train was diverted to the wrong platform, didn't you?" It's what she's always heard. A mistake that brought them together.

"True."

"But there's more."

"Also true."

Now August is paying attention. "Coletta. The girl doesn't need to hear this."

"She doesn't *need* to hear anything. But maybe I want to say it. And we've lived through a war, August; women are exposed to much worse than sad stories." She turns to Evelien. "You know your mother and I wanted to move to Paris."

The trip she took with her mother to Paris, when she was young. Roasted chestnuts, oysters, and cigarette smoke. Baking bread and the reek of the river. Her mother had hated it all. Had stopped at the door of a cabaret, the notes from the piano raucous and loud, frozen as her eyes took in everything around her, the sooty surfaces and the crowded sidewalks.

Coletta continues. "Leona and I talked about it all the time. Back when we were young and full of dreams. I saw it so clearly, my life as a famous designer." A quick laugh. "But it was all talk. Until one day I decided to do it, and raced to get on a train. No plans, no money, it was the least thought-out decision of my life. So I was on my way there when a signalman diverted us to the wrong platform. We hit another train and our engine lifted right on top of the car behind it."

Evelien's breath catches. This was an accident her mother spoke of. "You were there?"

"There? You've heard of this?"

"My mother talked about it. It happened when she was in her teens, she told me." Twisting heaps of metal. Bodies, burned. All from a split-second choice. Like a wrong turn down an alley. Or a decision to go upstairs and draw. *Two minutes.* The slim, narrow path they cling to. "It was why she hated the train. Why she said she knew she was meant to stay where she was."

"Why *she* hated the train? Did she, now? Leona, who was nowhere near the train that *I* was on." Coletta bites her lip for a second, as if trapping another comment within, and continues. "The point is, because I was the last on, I ended up in the worst spot at the far rear but, as you might have heard from your mother, it turned out to be the best spot, because we in the back were spared. Fourteen people died that day. Many by scalding. That was when I started hearing the voices."

"You hadn't before?"

"No. Dreams and feelings and such, I was used to all that. But not the actual voices of spirits. Not till that day. I think I was brought closer to the other side, I don't know."

"You never told me this."

"Because I don't talk about it. If I tell someone, they pass it off as me being damaged from the accident and discredit the voices. People love to write off what they can't explain. So I keep it to myself. August knew, though, only because the accident happened in his town, and we met when I was recuperating. That was the point of the story. And it's not about fate, which I believe in, you know I do, but I can't be worth fourteen people. It didn't happen *for* me. It happened for everyone. All of our fates are one. Do you understand?"

Evelien nods, though she's not sure. Still, in her mind, a web shimmers beneath their feet. Everyone, connected. At a time when everyone is so divided, she likes the thought that perhaps they're all on the same side after all.

Coletta continues. "At the time, I struggled with being alive. The *only* thing that changed it was Emiel. Because every choice I'd ever made, and every loss and every disappointment, all of it had to happen exactly as it did to lead me to this moment and to Emiel. Evelien, everything you do is so life places that child in your arms. It doesn't matter what you've done wrong, because you're gifted the reason for the wrong. It's all for that."

Sitting at the table, as the world rumbles and cracks, Evelien feels a bright, unnamed anger within her. "So having a child is seeking forgiveness?"

Though she wasn't sure he was still listening, August smiles.

Coletta shakes her head. "No. What you've done wrong is still a wrong, and an opportunity missed is still an opportunity missed, but you understand it was *necessary*. If life hadn't happened the way it did, I wouldn't have had Emiel. You see the shape of the road you took and you're *grateful* for every twist and turn, because it led to where you are. Cause and effect or fate, it doesn't matter what you call it, because you hold your child in your arms and you'll take *whatever* led you to that moment. It's *acceptance*. I've never regretted not living in Paris and my life as a famous designer, not from the moment he was born."

"And what if you don't ever have a child?" Evelien asks. "Is life meaningless then? No acceptance? My mistakes never justified?"

Coletta reaches for Evelien's hand. "You will have children. Many children. And since you brought it up, I want to clarify that I never looked at you like you'd failed, after not being with child. It was one night, and if it had worked, it would've been something of a miracle."

"But you expected the miracle," Evelien says.

"I was confused. *Not* because I expected a miracle but because I *felt* a grandchild. I'd had a dream with a little boy with Emiel's brown eyes who was waiting in the other room, as if he was on the way, and when it didn't happen, I was . . . I was confused. I had the timing wrong, that's all. And now he'll be back and you *will* have a family. The little boy. And a girl, I think."

Children are a gift from the Lord, Leona used to quote. When she said it, it was at moments when Evelien exasperated her. A reminder, not an affirmation.

Quietly, Evelien asks, "But what if other things do matter?"

"Trust me when I tell you there is no love like that between a mother and her child. Nothing. Other things matter, of course they do, but not like that." She smiles and then adds, "Your time will come. One night was one night. It was no one's fault."

So Evelien doesn't tell her that it *was* her fault. That with her heart beating from fear and sadness and worry, she stood at the window, long enough that his hand drifted from her shoulder. Long enough that when he asked her to come to bed, she'd already stopped crying, firm with a sad resolve. Emiel, her best friend, the man she'd grown with and loved more than anyone, and yet everything felt wrong. Her mind held a picture of him gone, and her left behind with a child, and in the image she was distraught, and undone, and no matter how she tried, she couldn't stop seeing it, couldn't change it to something good. So she told him that she couldn't take the chance of having his child while he was gone, and, good man that he was, he accepted it. Never could she admit that she'd selfishly taken the last chance he might've had, only to protect what tenuous grip she had on her own life.

Selfish. Inexcusable.

"Never mind all this," Coletta says. "I only brought it up to show August that things will become clear later." She turns to him again. "What I went through, what I was devastated by, if it didn't happen *exactly* the way it did, there'd have been no Emiel. And Evelien would not be at our table. And I would never have gotten to love you."

After a moment, he nods.

Coletta smiles, but then her expression shifts to sadness. "I never told Emiel that story. It always seemed too sad—so he never knew that about me. How important that day was."

"You'll tell him soon enough," Evelien says.

Coletta brightens and then is back to clearing the table. "Yes. Yes, I will. Now hand me that plate and let's talk about Weber getting his comeuppance."

CHAPTER 15

In bed, Evelien thinks of the train accident and Coletta's belief in spirits. Though she's aware she's doing exactly what Coletta worried people would do, she wonders about the guilt from having been spared when fourteen others were not. Did Coletta *need* to believe those spirits continued? That she could help them, somehow, and be their voice? She's never doubted Coletta, but also never truly questioned the predictions.

A tap at her window. Drowsy, she opens her eyes, adjusting. Then another tap. Hurrying to the sill, she adjusts her shutter enough to see the German below, a bag at his feet. Then, behind him, at the far end of the street, two soldiers on horseback. Though she can't hear them, he does, and indicates a U with his hand as he nods in the direction of the alley, as if letting her know that he's about to loop around to their back door. Then he's gone, walking below the bridge of her room.

In the kitchen, she opens the door to the alley without thinking, wanting to see him before he leaves. Immediately, she spots the bag by the door, and then sees his back, claimed by shadow as he walks away. "Wait," she says, too loudly. She knows better, but wanted to stop him. Coletta and August, both downstairs, are each a bit hard of hearing, and with the constant din of war above them, they're essentially sealed up and tucked away, but still, she looks toward the cellar door, grateful when she doesn't hear them stir. Turning back, she catches him watching her. Then a quick shift in his eyes. She's in a nightgown, she realizes. Her hair, always up and tied back, is down. All of it, improper. He opens his mouth as if about to speak, and she points in the direction of the red milk door and steps back into the kitchen to close the door. Feeling her way through the dark, she sits before the spot.

"Thank you," she says in a loud whisper.

She hears movement in the alley as he must be walking toward her voice.

Quietly, he asks, "How's your hand?"

"It could be worse. It could be my right hand." As she says this, she realizes she's hoping to talk. In a war, life is put on hold. Conversations and chances to meet new people. Meeting a new person—just that. The possibility, the excitement of standing before an unexplored life. How long has it been since she's felt that potential?

"You were there again?" he asks. "At the house?"

"I was."

"It's dangerous if you're caught. You didn't listen to me."

"No, I didn't."

She's said it quickly, automatically, and only then realizes she shouldn't have told a German soldier that she didn't listen to him. But he laughs. "I'm impressed that after four years of occupation, you some-how have no respect for authority."

She smiles. "I can't *not* be there."

"Well, good," he says. "Good to keep working."

In the dark, she leans back, the bones of her shoulder blades against the wall. "What should I work on?"

"I meant in general."

"You'd be doing me a favor to tell me. Since you've studied. Unless you need to go back to where you're supposed to be, if you can't stay?"

"I'm on sentry close enough; I could say I thought I saw something. No, the problem is that art's subjective. There is no right or wrong, despite what a class tells you."

Her conversations with Mr. Vanheule. Talk of art. Of color. Subjects. All of it—gone these past four years. She feels a rush of unsaid words. Kinship with someone when for too long she's felt only differences. "Did you know Vlaminck never studied formally? And has never stepped foot in the Louvre?"

There is a pause before he speaks. "You know Vlaminck?"

"Someone I knew did. But Vlaminck, he said that because he translated by instinct and not by method, he was a tender barbarian." A pause. "I thought that was beautiful. A tender barbarian."

When he says nothing, she turns toward the wall, wondering if he left.

"That is beautiful," he finally says. "You surprise me."

"Why? Because I know Vlaminck? My employer, the one I worked for before the war, he was an art collector." Instantly, she regrets her words. Wishing she could let her knowledge of art stand on its own.

"And he liked the Fauves? Even though they went out of style?"

"Is it about what's in style? What a person responds to?"

"It shouldn't be. But collectors are their own breed."

"Maybe. But I still love the Fauves. Perhaps I don't know enough not to."

"That's ridiculous. You love what you love."

"I meant I haven't taken a class to learn any better."

"Classes shouldn't make you love less, though they can."

"I was about to start with an instructor when all this began." She thinks of her drawings, the walls in the canvas room. "What I've drawn. Do you have advice?"

He laughs. "You'll make me say it, will you?" A pause. "In my opinion only—the violin, for instance, is too dark and needs more contrast. Restrain how often you use the darkest of the dark—which yes, is hard in charcoal. And now and then, squint. That will help you simplify."

Somewhere in the city, there is gunfire. Tapping like the beginning of a song. She realizes he might feel as she does—a need to pretend life is normal, even if through a wall. Above them now, a volley of booms.

"Those classes might happen soon," he says.

He's admitting the war is ending. The end, she knows, will bring vastly different outcomes for the two of them. "Now it would be harder," she says. "A waste, unfortunately. Things have changed."

"Because of the war? Money?"

"All of that. But I'm older now. And I got married, right as it started."

Though he says nothing, she hears the grinding shift of his cane on the cobblestones as he must be turning. She imagines him facing her, picturing her through the wall. Even the thought makes her flush, his imagined gaze a warmth. She glances in the dark toward the cellar door, knowing they hear nothing but still worried that Coletta and August are somehow picking up on her words, or worse, her feelings.

"And your husband," he finally says, "he doesn't approve of art?"

She closes her eyes. Sees her mother, worn. Sleeping when there were breaks, a seldom occurrence. "In the order of priorities, art's not high on the list. I wouldn't have time with children. But I'm happy to take your advice, for now. For fun."

"My advice is not to listen to someone who says your only option is to be a wife with children."

She stiffens. *No one wants a woman with big plans,* she once heard a man say when speaking of Marie Popelin, a Belgian advocate of women's rights and education. Marie studied law, but was initially told she could never practice because she was a woman. She died just before the war began. *Never married,* the man continued. *Because what man would want to be saddled to that?* "I meant advice for art."

"So did I."

"Yet you yourself said you won't paint again. To that, I'd say that the change in how you see the world might make your art more—" She stops, looking for the word.

"Important?"

"Affecting."

"Maybe it would. But it doesn't matter. I won't find out."

"*Art is a wound turned into light.* Georges Braque said that, or so I was told."

When he says nothing, she worries she's overstepped. What does she truly know of wounds compared to someone who's spent time on the front?

"I agree with that," he finally says. "But when you paint, you're alone with yourself, and I don't want to be alone with myself." A pause. "There was a man I killed, who was smiling because in his last moments, he thought he saw his mother. If I painted, every face would be his."

Evelien takes this in, about to respond when the sound of a plane above the house grows loud. A single airplane, churning into the night. She can almost feel the golden burn inside the church, and see the dusted white of Father Louwagie's hand. Only moments prior, sunlight through his thinning hair. *Maybe what we think of as wrong really isn't.*

"Did I offend you," he says, "talking about only being a wife? There's nothing wrong with it, if it's what you want." A pause. "If I offended you, I'm sorry. Talking to women isn't something I get to do often. I've forgotten how, I suppose."

"I can tell."

A laugh. "The men and I—we're ruined by the front. There, we say whatever we want, since there's not much chance of seeing the person again. Everyone, priests on the other side of the confessional. So you *do* want children, then?"

She smiles. "I think war has reordered conversations. Now we start with what's important and work our way to the weather later. And everyone wants children."

"That's not true."

"Men, maybe not."

"Women too. Maybe they just don't say it."

"Fine, then." She weighs her words. "For men, it's different. It doesn't speak to the core of who they are and why they were put on this planet. Being maternal, it's what a woman *is*. Or what she's supposed to be. Maybe there are women who don't want children, but you're right, they wouldn't say it. Why admit there's something wrong with you?"

"You think there's something wrong with you?"

She wants to answer honestly and say *yes*, that she's always known there was something wrong with her, just to throw this at him, to see how he'd react. But that would be sabotage. Her way of turning someone against her. She knows better than to admit the truth. "I didn't say *I* didn't want children."

"You didn't say you did."

She says nothing. For years she's told herself this feeling was temporary—but what if it's not?

Maybe it's her silence, but he hastily adds, "Forget I said anything. In fact, if you'd like to offend me, you can, so it's even."

"I'm not going to offend you. Not on purpose, at least."

"You know we were told that Belgian girls collected German eyeballs in a pail?"

"What? Why?"

"Why were we told that? Or why collect them?"

She leans into the void where the inner milk door used to be. The wood of the cubby smells dank. "Both."

"Why we were told that—for the same reason the Allies started rumors of German soldiers eating Belgian babies and hanging nuns between church bells and ringing them to death. To turn people. But to the second question—why collect them? Maybe for a stew."

She laughs. The rumors are fierce. More at the start of the war, when posters appeared depicting Germans as brutes and beasts. Since the occupation, since the Germans control what's seen, she's spotted only a couple in the vizeadmiral's office, before he used them as kindling.

"We might be nearing dangerous conversational territory," she says.

"True. But the need to be right—to *insist* you are right—has caused more problems in the world than actually being wrong. We don't need to agree on a beginning to admit we're in the same middle, do we? We started for different reasons. True. We might each believe our countries were right once. But can't it *also* be true that we're somewhere else now?"

"So you don't agree with your country," she says. He's never come right out and admitted it. She's pushing him, she knows. "Now, I mean."

In his silence, she understands she's seeking a sort of permission.

At last, he speaks. "It's been quite a while since I've believed in what my country is doing. That's one of the reasons I'm here, in Bruges."

She smiles. "Where the nonbelievers go?"

"Where I can rehabilitate and not be a problem."

"You're not an exemplary soldier?"

"Did you not notice that I steal food? And that I'm sitting in an alley talking to a woman, when I should be working?"

A jump inside her. She's smiling.

"The food is something I can help with, now and then," he says. "And if someone did the same for my family, I'd be thankful."

"Your family," she says, aware she's prodding.

"My mother, my sister."

"They're not doing well?"

"They're starved by the British blockade." He gives a small laugh. "We're not supposed to say that to the locals, because they might gain confidence and make the war go longer."

"You were told that?"

"Every month, they remind us. *Silly or overanxious women tend to paint the situation in exaggerated colors.* That's what they say. Meanwhile, the truth has more color than even I care for. In Dresden, the people are so hungry, they ate the horses and had to use the zoo animals to work and pull the wagons. The zebras and elephants and camels. But the blockade continued, and the people were still hungry, so they ate them, too, the zebras and elephants and camels. That's what my sister told me."

Silence. Faintly, she hears his cane grind against the cobblestones, as if he's shifting, turning to leave.

And then, "I need to move on. Wear a glove."

"What?"

"Your hand has oils. No medium will sit correctly in those places."

There were times, she remembers, when she had trouble getting the dark to spread the same way in certain areas. "Thank you."

She thinks she hears him say something in return, but then there's silence. After a moment, she goes to the kitchen door and opens it, just enough to see him walking down the street, leaning on his cane, tipped in moonlight.

CHAPTER 16

October 13, 1918

How do you say you feel broken, for being a woman who might not want children? Or explain that you can love someone but feel panic when thinking of being with them forever? But all this will change, because it has to. Because no man would want a wife who doesn't want children, and no child wants to belong to a mother forced into parenting.

She thinks of all she said to him, but the one thing she really wanted to say went unspoken: *Tell me that I'll see you again.* She realizes now, she doesn't even know his name. How could she not have asked his name?

Sleep comes and goes. Small moments of escape.

In the morning, Evelien dabs on her perfume and gathers her things to leave, trying to only focus on the plan to get the rest of the list.

"Wish Weber sweet dreams," Coletta says when Evelien steps outside.

"The mushrooms won't put him to sleep. He'll be violently ill."

"And unable to do his duties. God bless the inkies."

At the corner by a bridge, four men huddle over a bundle on the ground. As Evelien draws closer, she sneaks a look and sees a water-soaked shoe, the sole split away, revealing a socked foot inside. Quickly she averts her eyes but then moves forward to look. *Perverse,* her father once called her when she'd looked at part of a bird that had fallen from an owl's nest. *What is wrong with you?* It was shameful, she knew, that insistent curiosity and appreciation within her that didn't just leave her enraptured by all that was beautiful in the world, but sometimes widened her very definition of the word. Years later, she saw sketches on Mr. Vanheule's desk. *Da Vinci,* he said, referring to the drawings. Exposed muscle. The tendons of a shoulder. *How do you think he knew the human form so well? He studied. Even what's not visible to the eye. Life is made of layers, and artists need to be aware of those layers. Everything is informed by what came before.*

One of the men moves to help with a stretcher board, and there's the person on the ground: a German uniform, blue eyes fixed and still. Evelien pauses; the face is familiar. When she looks up, she sees Alixa Schmidt, leaning against a light post. She's staring at the man with her fist held at her mouth. And now Evelien realizes who it is.

Alixa's eyes flicker to Evelien. "Don't say anything."

Evelien glances back at the German uniform, the wet field-gray fabric. "Do you know what happened?"

"A fight. They were drunk last night."

"Are you all right?"

"I don't have a choice, do I?" A deep breath in, and Alixa looks away from the man on the ground. "On top of this, Lukas's gone missing."

Now Evelien feels a rush, like a kick in the ribs. "Missing. Since when?"

"Yesterday. Evening."

"Something to do with—" Evelien looks toward the dead man on the ground.

"No."

"How can you be sure?"

"Because I was with—" Alixa tips her chin in the man's direction. "When Lukas didn't come home. I shouldn't say it, but Lukas was mixed into things he wouldn't tell me about. I'm not surprised this finally happened."

"Messing with the scales and such," Evelien says quietly.

"You knew?"

"Our flour was mostly sawdust this last time."

Alixa nods. "I'm sorry that it went to you." Her eyes fill.

"Not just me," Evelien says, thinking of Emma Lemahieu and the watered-down milk, the fact that the girl's barely grown.

Alixa wipes her eyes. "Yesterday, there were some German soldiers looking for him, for questioning."

Evelien's breath catches. Just yesterday she told the vizeadmiral Lukas's name. And now he's missing. "They're the ones who took him?"

"I don't know. They asked about him and left."

"So he could be all right."

Alixa tilts her head. "When has someone gone missing and been all right? No, and he's always at opening, every morning, before anyone. He doesn't like me to lift anything heavy." A pause. "My guess is those soldiers found him."

"But you don't know," Evelien says, feeling faint. She lowers her head.

"Miss," a man is saying in Flemish. "Look away, miss. The Lord's with him now."

"I've got her," Alixa says to the man. "You can go."

The man nods, unconvinced, but turns away, passing an elderly woman who stands in the doorframe of her house, watching. This woman must have noted the uniform, that it's a German soldier on the ground, and determined that two girls are more upset than they should be. Glaring at Evelien, she makes the sign of the cross, and Evelien understands it's her soul she's worried about—not the man on the ground.

Evelien turns from the woman. "Did the soldiers say *why* they wanted to talk to him?"

"About the store." Alixa must see something pass on Evelien's face because her eyes narrow, but then she's smiling. "I never saw it before now."

Evelien's face flushes, her heart pounding. "Saw what?"

"You love him, don't you?"

"Who?" Evelien asks quickly.

"Lukas."

"Alixa, no, I'm just worried for him, that's all. He's my—" She stops, unable to say the word *friend* because of what she's done. But that's what he is. Or was. For years. Until she told herself he wasn't, because he was German. He may have done something bad, but, she realizes, she did something unthinkable.

~

A hand-slapping. A fine. That's all.

As Evelien walks to work, she recalls what Alixa said about her brother being mixed into things he shouldn't be, but no matter how she tries to get around it, she can't: this has to be the vizeadmiral's doing.

Inside the house, there is no guard by the front door. The vizeadmiral was true to his word about one thing, at least; Lieutenant Klaus, the statue in the hall, is gone. There's one less set of observing eyes.

In the kitchen, Weber stands at the stove, stirring the soup from last night. Immediately, he hands her a teacup with a small, meager amount and a spoon. It's been a while since he's done this, since he's decided that verifying that his breakfast is safe is worth losing even a bite. Clearly his suspicion of her holds. But it's all right; the mushrooms won't affect her, since she doesn't drink, and so she gladly scoops the spoon into the soup, blows on it, and puts it in her mouth. Her tastebuds fire, rejoicing. It's food not just for the sake of eating, but for enjoyment, and it feels like years since she's had anything this good.

Beneath her feet, a rumble. She glances out the window and sees a dark cloud that plumes above buildings. Even Weber watches the spreading black but then turns to observe her as she swallows.

"Delicious," she says, washing the teacup out in the sink. "You might be a horrible, horrible man, but you are an incredible cook."

When she looks back at him, he's smiling. Her stomach drops. Did he understand?

Then, gruffly, he waves her from the room. As she grabs the mop, he's already bringing his spoon to his mouth.

It doesn't take long. Most likely he already had alcohol in his system, or nipped from the bottle in the pantry. Whatever the case, a few hours later, she hears him heaving in the kitchen.

His face is flushed and blotchy. Angrily, he waves her away, leaning toward the sink to retch once more before sitting, right on the floor, eyes watering as he stares at the ceiling. Calmly, she grabs a copper stockpot from the shelf, one of the few remaining in Bruges, she would bet, since the Germans requisitioned even copper door and window fastenings. She sets it on the floor beside him, and he looks up at her, searching for symptoms. She gives him a small, sympathetic smile. In the pantry, where she keeps the rags, she lingers near his bottle—hidden behind a canister of rice—and waits till she sees him notice. His drinking is known, but never addressed. If the vizeadmiral saw him in this state, she'd just have to nod her head in the direction of the pantry and he'd know Weber overdid it. In doing this, she's letting Weber know as well, that his secret is not secret. Should he feel the need to publicly question why he's sick, he now knows her response.

When she leaves, he's still on the ground, staring at the cabinet in front of him, confused—a drinker who's realized the rules of his world have changed. There is actual fear on his face, as if his future has come loose. Briefly, Evelien feels regret, that she did this to him. Then she thinks of Father Louwagie and Lukas, and what the vizeadmiral most likely did and what he's been doing, this whole time, just outside these walls. All that she's ignored, because it suited her to keep a job that was easy and known and beneficial to her family.

You're nice to him. The enemy. And yet you sleep well at night?

Now she has a chance to make this right. Soon there's no room for remorse, only bright, inspiring anger.

CHAPTER 17

Weber is asleep on the kitchen floor, worn out. She brings him a pillow, to help keep him sleeping, and is at the vizeadmiral's office door
within minutes, picking the lock with a strange sort of bravery, her heart
calmer than before and her mind focused. Inside, she heads straight to
the little table by the door, opens the drawer, and takes out the small
pad.

The first page is blank.

The list is not there.

She turns, scanning the room. He could've put it anywhere, taken it
out of the house or even destroyed it. Though she goes to his desk and
rifles through the drawers once more, she knows she won't find it. This
is the end. He suspected her, he moved it, and now her list will remain
incomplete and they will never get Emiel's letter.

Reeling, she tries to go about her day. Wiping down surfaces, she
sees the silver frame with the drawing of the lavender sprig, still on the
mantel. Is it possible he isn't as bad as she's started to assume? *A fine,
a hand-slapping.* No one *saw* the Germans take Lukas away. And why
would they, if Lukas was working with them? Unless, she thinks again,
whoever Lukas was working with wasn't there to cover for him. Now
she feels sick. Because he used to be her friend, and she gambled with
his life. Her anger, she understands, should be directed at herself.

Before the war, life was so easy. So good. And they never knew. They never knew how lucky they were, that they could walk, just to walk. To feel the air along the canals. To see their friends and stop to admire lacemakers and chocolatiers. Restaurants were packed, sauces rich and thick. Plates left behind, piled with food. So much food, scraped into bins. And they didn't know. They didn't know what a privilege it was, to throw things away and to linger on bridges. To not be asked to do impossible things, or to live in a world where turning on a friend makes any sort of sense, however briefly.

Lukas Schmidt. Before the war, he was only ever commended for helping his parents, his father, who once was strong but could no longer make it up a flight of stairs, and his mother, who was worn thin and exhausted, but who lit up when she caught him in the market, whistling. *Boys who whistle get a girl with a fortune!* she'd informed them. Evelien still remembers that night, because Alixa had an earache, and Lukas tried to help by holding an onion poultice to her head. Face turned to the ceiling, his eyes watering as he tried to take away his sister's pain.

~

She doesn't deserve a stop on the way home and passes the street with the ruined garden without a glance. In her bedroom, she watches the cobblestones trick with light, pink and orange, purple and gray, brown and black.

When Coletta calls that supper is ready, Evelien closes her shutters, bracing herself to admit that in five nights, the Irishman will return, but there will be no list to give him, no letter handed over in exchange.

"To the list," Coletta says at supper, lifting her glass of water.

Evelien doesn't raise her glass.

Softly, Coletta says, "No?"

"It wasn't there. I got in the room, but it wasn't there."

127

"It wasn't there," Coletta says, trying to understand.

Those five names. Five names she had until she let herself be distracted, and they were gone. Once more, she feels sick, and catches August watching her. He's still not said much, though now and then he seems to force a smile, as if to reassure whoever might be watching, or maybe himself, that he's trying.

Coletta sets her glass back down. "But the Irishman, you can convince him to give the letter regardless."

"I don't think it's up to him."

"Then *make up names*. How would they know?"

Now August speaks. *"Coletta."*

"Not real names," she explains.

"Not real names that *you* know of. Over ten million Germans have fought in this. *Every* name could be real. And if there are repercussions to someone innocent—"

"Fine, fine." She sits back. "This isn't over. I want that letter."

Silence, the distant barrage of the front a low drumming.

"Lukas Schmidt is missing," August says.

Evelien turns to him. "You heard that?" Something about this makes it more official. "What time did you hear this?"

"On the way home. Why?"

And so Evelien admits what she did. That she'd given the vizeadmiral the market's name. Coletta is nodding, but August stands, taking his plate to the sink. Evelien watches his back, his stillness at the covered window.

"There was a rumor he was skimming off the Germans," he finally says.

"No, he was skimming off us," Evelien says quickly. "The profit he was making was off the Belgians. It's why we got the flour, why Emma Lemahieu's been drinking *gedoopt* milk." She looks to Coletta for confirmation.

"Absolutely," Coletta says. "I've heard that too. And we had the tampered food. Though the Lemahieus were shopping at the market on Dijver. I saw Martine there, more than once."

"She wasn't shopping at S&P Market?" Evelien asks.

"Not till now."

Had Martine said *where* she'd gotten the tampered milk? "I heard he was making a profit off the Belgians," Evelien says again, less certain. Had she heard that? *He got mixed in, messing with the scales and such.* What if that really had been just to punish the Germans and had nothing to do with making a profit off the Belgians? He'd always claimed Belgian loyalty, but then he didn't enlist, he was German, and his store was doing well. Everything pointed *against* him being loyal to the Belgians. Still, though, what if it really was an innocent mistake that she got tampered flour? *I'm sorry that it went to you,* Alixa had said.

What if nothing was as it seemed?

"Maybe he's all right," Evelien says. "He could be just fine."

No one responds.

"What this war has done to us," August says, and Evelien knows what he's saying.

What this war has done to her.

CHAPTER 18

The night is loud. Louder than it's ever been.

"A taste of what's to come," Coletta says, standing at the top of the cellar stairs. Her eyes are on the glass in her hand; the water's rippling.

Evelien glances toward the back door. "Will there be fighting on the streets? Here?"

"I don't know. I don't know what's involved in taking a city back. But I think now is when I'd like a country house to hide in."

Entire armies billet at farms, sugar beet and hop fields turned to battlegrounds. Harvests left to rot and barns set ablaze, cattle bellowing inside. "The country is worse," Evelien says. "I'm sure of it."

"You shouldn't be in your room."

"The parlor, then, I promise."

"But you're going up to your room, right now, to draw, aren't you?"

Caught, Evelien smiles. Her room is where her desk is. Where she can set a light and spread out. "Only for a bit. And then the living room, I promise."

"Not long, please. I'm telling you, this is different. I don't want to jinx it, but what we're hearing isn't about maintaining ground. A week and it's over."

"We've thought that before."

Another rumble. "Don't you feel how close that is?"

And though she does, and she intends to only work in her room for a bit, time loses shape when she draws. She studies and sketches the small stack of three bricks she keeps in her room, there so she can observe their color throughout the day. Blues at dusk, greens in late afternoon. At midday, a dry sepia shade that makes her thirsty. Her favorite, though, is evening light, when the bricks deepen to purple. Eggplant purple, rich and bruised. *After seeing a brick as purple,* August said when she showed him the shade, *people will still say red. Bricks are red. Life is easier if you deny the nuances.* Then he laughed. *These bricks are your version of Monet's haystacks. Always the same, but different.*

August. The same, but different.

It's only when she reaches for her pencil and finds that it's not there, that it's rolled to the edge of her desk, that the world slams back into focus. Sounds suddenly unmute, the world so loud, she's not sure how she'd tuned it out. Shaking threads through her feet. Without wasting time, she races downstairs, pausing at the cellar stairs to listen for Coletta and August just in case they've been calling for her. Silence. Heavy sleepers, they barely woke when the bomb hit Lexi Peeters's house only blocks away.

Then Evelien's in the kitchen and about to head to the parlor—to a corner far from windows and with sturdy walls, the corner where she sometimes sleeps—when she sees an emerald-green line form under the shutters. There and then gone. Followed by a strip of blazing white, then nothing. Green again. Then red. An orange-red, like currants. Frozen, she watches the flashes and streaks from the bombardment fill and empty in this one space, this thin line of reflection.

Never has she gone outside in something like this; never has it been like this. Just for a second, she wants to see the sky. If she stays against the door, it will be fine—the eave and the roof will protect her, and the impacts themselves are still far enough away. A quick look up, that's all she wants.

With that, she's outside.

The alley is electric, lit from explosions around the port and just beyond the city, the air wind-fed and acrid, pungent with smoke and the sweet rot of decay. Her heart races as she presses her back against the door, watching papers and straw swirl on the cobblestones. All at once, a squadron tears through the air. It's wicked and entrancing, the light and the wind, the howlings and growlings. *War creates its own weather,* August has said, but this feels like something more, like lightning bolts and retribution. Or, she decides, taking in the shadows of manganese violet, like a painting.

Above, the iron-gray sky flares with a shock of lime green, then bursts with white. From outside the city, the artillery barrage beats like distant drums. Then, over a rooftop, there is a flare of light that blooms from a location that doesn't make sense, that should not be a target. That is much closer than it should be.

Maybe it's a hit that doesn't make sense, but she's jerked from her role as an observer. She needs to get inside, but in her turn, she spots a shape at the far end of the alley: Emma's stuffed cloth doll. Already the wind's carried it away from the Lemahieu house, and even as she watches, it lifts into the air, catches on an empty flower box, and falls, momentarily braced against the stone base of a house. Whistling sounds shriek into the night like screams.

In her chest, a quickening. Emma's lost so much: her father, her childhood. Here, in this moment, Evelien has a chance to do something right. To spare someone pain. To make something better. For once.

She lets go of the doorknob. And runs.

She's at the mouth of the alley when a spray of something hits the rooftop up ahead. Pebbles, maybe. Bits of brick. Earth from a distant explosion. Quickly, she tucks herself against a wall, which trembles against her back. The doll is right there. Three houses down. Barely hanging on to the stone base of the building.

Right as she's about to move, the wind picks up again. Burned, charred bits of ash begin to swirl and lift up, twisting and turning. Her heart slams against her rib cage. A pounding that might be only in her head takes over, and she hears her mother's voice: *We'll know soon if God finds me worthy and fit to see this out.* A June night, back when the flax was most brilliant. Evelien can almost feel it, the pulse of blue, those blooms that were glory itself and would be gone the next day, shredded and torn. She was ten years old. It was the green light that fell through the slats of the barn that made her look up. Then she heard the noise, and her mother calling her. Her mother, who couldn't find her because Evelien was not where she was supposed to be.

The wind. The sick smell of decay. She watches as the doll starts to lift up and in a flash, she's there, grabbing it, just as something hits the corner of a roof a few houses away and a cascade of bricks spills into the alley. To her right, a riderless horse bolts past, its hooves sparking against the cobblestones. She needs to shelter somewhere—now.

Quickly, she tries the closest door—locked—but then spots faded red trim with C+M+B barely evident above the door, the initials of the Magi as well as a German blessing of the house, a tradition that her old neighbors, the Mullers, adhered to. Behind a stone in the sill, they kept a spare key. It's been years since she was inside; the last time was when the Germans started in with their requisitions—metals and wood and clothes—and Coletta declared the Mullers' items fair game.

Doll under her arm, Evelien jiggles the stone. Back and forth, back and forth, as the wind lifts her hair and pushes her dress against her and the stench of battlefields builds. Then the stone is out. Trying not to think, she stretches her fingers into the dark and then has the key and the Mullers' back door open—but then there's a dark silhouette with a cane at the mouth of the alley. The doorknob trembles under her fingertips as she lets go and runs out after him.

The sky casts him in flashing green, white, yellow, and red. She calls to him, but he doesn't hear, till there's a momentary reprieve and he spots her. Waving him toward her, she runs back to the Mullers' and waits in the doorframe. He's seconds behind her, and as they get the door closed, a plane trails fire in the sky above.

And now Evelien sees her mistake. Because inside, the room is pitch-black. She can't be in here. Not with the noise and the dark, not in a place that might as well be a black cellar, cut off from the world as blue flowers are torn from the field and her mother goes silent and time unhinges.

Then, light. His flashlight. Evelien takes a ragged breath, her hands in fists. Slowly, painfully, she straightens her fingers. Crescent-shaped indentations cut into her palms from her nails.

She needs to pull herself from that day. Trying to latch on to details, she surveys the room. The beam from the flashlight is yellow, like once-damp newspapers. The empty space where the player piano once stood now holds drifts of dust against the baseboard.

"The cellar," he says, motioning toward a door.

"I can't. You go."

He looks confused.

"I don't like cellars. I won't."

He must see it in her pallor, because he doesn't ask again. She remembers where the candles are, and the matches Mr. Muller used to light his pipes. Finding them, she sets two candleholders on the kitchen table and lights the wicks before taking a seat, the doll on her lap. When he sits across from her, he shuts off his flashlight. He leans back against the chair, and the wood creaks.

"You're afraid of a cellar," he says. When he speaks, he angles his head down, as though he's looking at a spot on the ground, but then peers up, from under his brow. "Yet you were sightseeing in a bombardment?"

She won't think of her mother. Or that day. "You're lucky I was."

He gives a smile, then turns in his chair when the walls rattle from an impact. Shadows are thick at the edges of the room. For a moment, they listen to the chaos outside. Then, with a finger, she starts to trace a pattern in the dust on the table, creating swirls like paisley. The candles' flames jump and tremble.

"It's never been like this," she says, and adds, "here."

When he turns back, he spots the pattern on the table. Studying it, he then uses his right index finger to trace the same pattern on his side of the table. "This is the worst. So far."

Things are different without the barrier of a wall. It feels strange to watch him like this. With his hat off, his hair is thick and full and falls to one side. And he's younger than she thought. Most likely only a few years older than Emiel.

Face lowered, again he peers up at her. The impression is bashful, and she can't believe she never noticed that he does this. Unless he hasn't. Unless now he, too, is nervous.

"Do you know," he says, "that even an hour from the front, it's as if there's no war?"

"Imagine the tables of food."

"Imagine a sky without smoke."

"The silence."

"Birds. I'd rather hear birds."

She nods, watching his hand move against the table, the pattern emerging. When he's done, he traces a border around the edge, but stops when he gets to the middle. Again, he looks at her from under his brow, expectant. Picking up where he left off, she continues the border on her side. She watches him as she speaks. "Am I wrong to trust you?"

He looks surprised. "Would you trust someone because they told you that you could?"

"No."

"Then does it matter what I say? Or maybe only what I've done?"

"But that's it—I don't know why you'd bring us food. And be nice. I don't even know your name."

"Because I have access to a small bit of food that I don't need, and you said you were hungry. Like I said, I'd be happy if someone did this for my family. And it's Joseph."

Joseph. Strong and simple. She tells him her name, and he repeats it perfectly, with the Flemish pronunciation. There's a thrill from even watching him say it, and she looks down, blushing, to the table. "Well, thank you again. For the food."

He wipes the dust from his hand against his pants. "My sister's a little older than you. Now that her husband is gone, she's staying with our mother, and I know they're hungry. Even with what connections my family has, they're hungry."

When she and Coletta let themselves into this house, years ago, toast was on the table. Two cups in the sink. Though they'd said they planned on leaving, when the Mullers actually left, they did so in a hurry and didn't say goodbye. *They will understand,* Coletta and Evelien said as they tried on Ava's coats—better than their own—and slipped jars of mustard and pepper into their dress pockets. The Mullers were Germans, after all. They would be fine, they thought.

"What about your father," she asks, "the one who didn't speak Flemish, is he fighting?"

"You remember that, the Flemish bit."

"Talking to German soldiers is not a habit that I have."

"That's wise. No, he passed away before the war."

"I'm sorry."

"Don't be."

"You didn't like him."

"My father was military, and in steel. Opposite of me in every way. That was our issue." There's a shine in his eyes with the candle. He smiles. "No, that wasn't it. My sister and mother hated him as well."

She smiles. "So you went to art school to spite him?"

"I went to art school because I loved art. And I thought that was all that mattered. And it meant my sister had to marry when we ran out of money."

When the table shakes, the candlelight jumps and quivers. He rests his arm on the table, alongside the border he'd traced, and she glances at a tendon in his wrist. Remembering the doll, she sets it on the table, on top of the pattern, as if laying it on a bed. "I saw this. It belongs to a neighbor girl. She must have dropped it. The wind had it; I couldn't wait. It's all she has."

His jaw is dark with stubble—a sign he's not on the front, as the men there are clean-shaven to allow the gas masks the best fit. One corner of his mouth lifts, just slightly, as if he suspects there's more. When she looks up, she sees that he, too, is looking at her mouth. Quickly, she looks down, at the doll. "You were on sentry?"

More shaking. Dust sifts through the slats of wood on the ceiling. "I am. I should still be out there, but I've done enough for my country. Whose house is this?"

"Neighbors who were friends. They left a long time ago."

"They were German."

She sees where he's looking, at a framed German postcard on the counter. "Yes, we had German friends. Before they became the enemy." She meant it to be funny, but it comes out heavier than intended.

But he just nods, then looks up at her. "You ran out to get a doll?"

"I was outside, just at the door, when I saw it. I wanted to do something right. For once."

"*Something right* would've been staying inside. People are *trying* to stay alive. It's a luxury to stay alive. And you put yourself in danger. Why?"

On the wall, a cuckoo clock hangs, unwound and still. It's an excuse to look away from him, to gather her thoughts. *Sabotage,* she thinks. Here it is. A wall she's dropping between them. She feels her words come through as a challenge, and as she speaks, she watches him, defiant. "Sometimes I watch the shellings. They're distant, when I go out there, just streaks in the sky. Tonight, I could tell it would be different, and I wanted to see. But I thought I'd be out there for seconds."

She waits for him to chastise her. But instead, he shrugs. "I've been with men who looked at the sky and clapped. I'll never judge someone on how they make it through this."

"You don't think it's wrong?"

He shakes his head. "The only thing that's wrong was that tonight the danger was closer, and real. Not sailing over our heads or on the horizon. But it's not wrong because your mind works differently."

She wants to laugh. He must see it on her face, because he continues. "Different doesn't mean wrong."

"Doesn't it?"

"I hope not."

She thinks of Emiel. Of children. Of how she'd spend her time, if it was up to her, and the future that her mother envisioned for her: to be good and faithful and hardworking, a dedicated wife and mother who never thinks of herself. A noble life that Evelien fears. It's unforgivable, this reaction. Her heart holds everything backward. "Everything I want is wrong." Silence. He watches her, and she rubs her arms, cold. "Let's talk of something else. You tell me something."

Another booming, this one that rattles the windowpanes against the shutters and shakes the acorn weights that hang from the clock on the wall. "I tried to desert."

Surprised, she waits for the rest.

"With that, you could turn me in."

"So why tell me? You want me to trust you? Or do you *want* me to turn you in?"

"You're very suspicious." He smiles. "I don't want anything. That's the problem. I don't care anymore. But you were being honest, so it was my turn."

"What happened? When you tried?"

"It didn't work. I was caught."

"But they didn't punish you." If they had, he wouldn't be here. A firing squad would've seen to that.

"Someone who knew my family covered for me, and others, who knew the truth, are gone and took my secret to their graves. I should've been shot. If it wasn't for my family, I would've been. Now it's spun as if I deserve a medal when what I deserved was a court-martial."

"Stopping fighting—that doesn't seem wrong."

"I don't agree with my country. I told you. But how I went about it *was* wrong."

"Because you left?"

He considers his words. "I might not want to be a part of Germany, or what they're doing, I should say. But I'm still part of the men I stand next to. And they needed me. So yes, in that moment, what I did was wrong."

The table rattles, candlelight quivering, the weights on the clock swaying. Then the deep-throated booms of cannons, followed by a reprieve, filled only with the stretching, aching howl of the wind. "Someone told me that we are not what we do in war."

With his finger, he picks at a gouge in the table. "We always have a choice."

"You say that because you're a man."

He looks back up at her, and there is something like a smirk on his face. "Possibly. But with men forced to fight, now's not the time to wish for equal treatment." A pause. "Each sex has their burdens. I had the ability to make the *wrong* choice. My father died, and my mother never mentioned there was no money until I'd spent what we had left on myself and schooling for something that doesn't pay much, even if you're lucky. Because of me, my sister had to marry. So I had a choice, yes, but as the man, it was up to me to provide, and I didn't."

"Now you bring me food, because I remind you of your sister. And you feel guilty." She tries to smile, to lighten her words, but the truth is she wants him to say no. To tell her there's more.

He looks at her curiously. "You don't remind me of her. She's soft-spoken and reserved. You're not. But I prefer that, so don't be insulted. Not that it matters what I prefer, but I'm used to the art world, where women aren't wallflowers. And yes, I would want someone to feed my sister, if they could. And yes, I feel guilty. I won't paint again, not just because of that man I keep seeing in my mind, but because of what it's cost my family."

Something hits the front wall of the house. A loud tap and then another. Evelien stands, about to make sure the door is secure, but Joseph's already up and stopping her, his rifle in his right hand and his left arm out, holding her back. The pain on his face from not using his cane is evident. Eyes trained on the door, he holds his hand against her.

"The tree, I think," Evelien says. "A willow." He lowers his arm, and she takes a seat. "So you don't agree with what I was told, that we're not what we do in war?" Because this is what she needs, she realizes.

Slowly, he sits. "All I know is I have been at my worst when my best was needed."

"In war?"

"In everything. Now, back then."

"Is he a good man? Your sister's husband."

"He was." Again, he seems to weigh his words against the cost of being understood. "Not one of us is getting out of this intact. But he loves her, that's true."

"Then it could be worse."

"But it also could be better. Their marriage wasn't for love. At least not for her."

"Not everyone marries for love."

She sees his eyes widen, and in a beat feels what he's about to say. "Don't—"

"You didn't marry for love." He's sitting back, observing her from under his brow.

She hears herself breathe, a pounding in her ears. "I absolutely love my husband."

"I used the wrong words, then. Because I absolutely love my dog, but it's not the same, now is it?"

Frustrated, she meets his eyes. "You can grow to love someone. It can happen that you start to think of them that way."

"*That* way?" he says, smiling.

Everything inside her jumbles. "You know what I'm talking about."

"I do. You're saying you can marry someone you don't think of *that way*, and after years you might not dread a kiss. But wouldn't it be better if you wanted it? Really, really *wanted* it?"

His eyes are steady on her, the quiver of light from the candle at their center. The word *want*, it's pushing against her. She can't get away from this word. Trying to refocus, she glances at the clock on the wall, the weights still. Out of the corner of her eye, she sees him do the same. "Of course," she says. "If—"

"It's stopped." He's standing. "They're reloading. We need to go."

He's right; she places her hand flat on the table and there's no vibration. In what feels like a daze, she stands and tucks the chair into the table. Holding back her hair, she leans in to blow out the candles just as he switches on the flashlight.

He goes first, and cautiously peers outside, while she stands behind him. With the door cracked open, she can barely make out the dimmed gray of his uniform, the ends of hair beneath his cap, and the space of skin on his neck. That skin—impossibly smooth. A deep breath in and there's something like amber or wood, pepper, and an element that's deeper, like leather.

"It's clear," he says and turns, surprised to find her right behind him. His mouth opens and shuts, and his jaw tightens as he swallows.

She watches his eyes lower to her mouth. Her skin goes hot, the air between them heavy. When she looks back up, into his eyes, he seems to make a decision, and his hand, still on the doorknob, slowly draws the door so it's almost shut, so no one can see them.

Only a thin sliver of light remains.

Want. That word. Never has she felt it from someone like this. Never has she felt it like this. And here they are, alone. It feels as though she's jumped and is falling, her heart catching up, still caught on a different momentum. But suddenly she sees Emiel—his brown eyes and his kindness and the way he looked at her, protective and appreciative and loving. Emiel, who only did what was right, marrying her because he loved her and wanted to keep her safe, and because it made sense and was good for everyone.

Then there is a brightness. He's pushed the door open again, and is watching her, waiting.

Relief. Curiosity. And disappointment. Sharp, biting disappointment.

She forces herself to walk, unable to look at him, not trusting what he'd see on her face. And she's almost out the door, has almost made it past him, when he puts his hand on her arm. A pause as he leans in to whisper, his lips against her hair.

"For once," he says quietly, his words a heat on her skin, "I did my best. But I'll have you know, all I wanted to do was my very worst."

CHAPTER 19

October 14, 1918

In the morning, ash is like a thin layer of dirty snow, but the war has lessened its grip on the city. No longer are they shaken, squeezed, and rattled. The chaos is once again farther away. All part of the deadly tug-of-war, sometimes over mere meters of land. Evelien sits at the kitchen table while Coletta talks of the army trousers she's been assigned to mend at her shop, and August sits in the corner with a book. When he blinks, he does so heavily, as if forcing his eyes closed, and Evelien realizes that though he's staring at the book in his hands, he's not reading it.

Now and then, Coletta stops what she's doing, hand on her forehead, as if trying to extinguish a headache. *Five names,* she says. And though it's said to point out how close they were to fulfilling their agreement, to support the idea that the Irishman should just give them the letter in exchange for what they've done, what Evelien hears is an accusation. Five names, and she let them go.

"How are you getting back in?" Coletta asks.

"I don't think I can."

Coletta shakes her head. "No. It doesn't end this way. I do *not* see it ending this way. There will be another chance."

"Coletta," August says now, lowering the book. "She'll do the best she can."

For once, I did my best, but I'll have you know, all I wanted to do was my very worst.

Evelien reddens with a quick flash of what that *worst* might be, her skin conjuring the feeling of him backing her against the wall and the rough tips of his fingers.

"Of course she will," Coletta says. "You don't have to tell me she will; I know that." She stops, taking a deep breath. "I'm sorry. I don't mean to snap. August, can't you bring an exemption, about your knee? Would that get you off the fields?"

"No."

"No, it wouldn't work? Or no, you won't try?"

Now he shuts his book and places his palm on the cover, as if trying to absorb something from its words. "It's better it's me. Not someone who hasn't already seen the things I have."

Coletta stands before him. "Oh no you don't. If you can get off the fields, you do. They're not safe. Littered with mines and who knows what. Don't go being noble and sacrificing yourself for someone else. If you won't think of yourself, then think of me, and of Evelien. What would *we* do without you?"

He remains silent.

"You need to trust me," Coletta continues. "Didn't I tell you Emiel wasn't there?"

Just barely, he nods.

"We *will* get this letter. Evelien will convince the Irishman. I feel it. We'll get news of Emiel in just days."

August gives her a thin, worn smile, and it hits Evelien that he's appeasing Coletta. He knows, she thinks. He knows that Emiel is dead, must feel it like she did. Or does? She's unsure now, her instinct muddled by the recent events.

Then, a moment of clarity: soon this will be over, and if her husband returns, her life will continue, like a train car righted on the tracks, and it will be these last days that she misses. An illogical, horrible longing.

~

The plan is to drop the doll off at Emma's on the way to work, but as soon as Evelien's stepped outside, there's Joseph, standing at the mouth of the alley. He catches her eye and disappears around the corner. Smoothing down her hair, she follows.

On the next block, piles of brick and timber, a corner of a house exposed, as if someone sliced off the edge of a cake, the layers revealed. No one else is around.

There's exhaustion on his face. Quietly, she says, "They don't let you sleep?"

"They don't care about sleep, no. Actually, now's my chance, but I wanted to bring you something." He notices the doll under her arm. "I'm starting to think that's yours."

She smiles. "I'm about to drop it off."

He holds out a worn book. *Der Blaue Reiter.* The Blue Riders, an art movement in Germany.

She flips through the pages. "I've heard of them."

"My mentor was one of the founding members. Franz Marc."

"He did a painting of horses."

Now he barely attempts to hide his enthusiasm. "Several. Which ones have you seen?"

"Just the one. The horses were red, I remember. And there was a shade of blue he used that was like a sunlit grape."

"For him, red was danger."

To spin in the same orbit as these artists . . . there's a thrill of connection. And if Marc was his mentor, then Joseph's art could be along a similar vein. *What's your art like?* Though irrational, the question seems incredibly personal.

Hedging along what she really wants to know, she asks, "And you worked with him?"

He nods. "We both painted animals, but he put them in land-scapes, and I painted them in urban jungles, so to speak."

What she's feeling, she realizes, isn't just a satisfaction from talking about art, but from thinking of *him* and art. What he knows. What he's capable of. The thought of *him* painting, his ability and his eye and his taste and what captivates him, all of it—she wants to know that part of him. She's never felt it before, the magnetism of a shared passion.

He takes a step away, peering around the corner. When he turns back, he catches her watching him and smiles.

"Is he still painting?" she asks.

"He enlisted. Cavalry. A hell for him, I imagine. To see the horses he loved, used like that. Then they assigned him military camouflage, which we all wanted. Even that was beautiful—his camouflage. He used a pointillist style."

"When I almost fainted, my world broke into a Seurat."

At first, he looks surprised, and then, strangely, he looks almost upset. Even over the distant rumble of the front, she thinks she hears him breathing.

At last, he says, "I can't think of a better way to describe fainting."

A rush. Not just from having something in common with someone, when usually she's the odd one out, but from the chance that he might even *appreciate* the way she sees the world. She hides so much, or tries to. Swallowing down words, lodging them beneath what's proper and acceptable. But with him, there's a feeling that the filter through which she sees life could actually be good.

But then he looks away. "Franz was reassigned, for his own safety, but he ended up at Verdun."

Verdun. The night the vizeadmiral spoke of that battle, his teeth were stained with wine. The one time he drank, that she knows of. "There were flamethrowers there."

"And gas. And mud, clay mud that sucked you down. It's a necrop-olis. Buried alive or dead, the ground doesn't care; it takes them all. And

Franz. He was struck by a shell splinter and died instantly, before the orders reached him."

She should've expected this, but still it catches her off guard. *Before the orders reached him.* An added tragedy, an enhancement of the injustice. And though now she aches to ask about Braque, she holds the question back. Joseph actually knew Franz Marc. She will not take from his loss by inquiring over someone she's never met. "I'm sorry," she says. Two words anesthetized by the war.

Then, footsteps. He lifts his hand, indicating to be silent, and she backs against a door, tucked into the slight shelter of the doorframe as he steps forward to see who's there. The sounds grow louder but then fade, and he signals that it's okay.

She holds up the book. "Thank you. For bringing this."

"It's not really why I came," he says, and for a second, she feels stupid, that she'd assumed she was the reason he's here, when off duty.

But then he continues. "I keep thinking about what you said last night. You think like an artist. That's not wrong. Being *different* is not wrong. It's interesting. If it wasn't, we'd all paint the same thing and see the world the same way and there'd be no movement, and no chance at understanding."

You think like an artist. Already the words have scooped out a place inside her.

"I won't lie; being a woman makes it harder," he adds. "But male, female, you're either an artist who does their art or one who doesn't. And there might be a price for doing it, but I'll tell you there's a greater price for not."

Above, there is a plane. The sound a backdrop to a feeling she wants to remember.

He peers up. When he looks back down, there is a second when his eyes seem faded, a parched, thirsty blue. "Degas said that art is not what you see but what you make others see. So don't be ashamed. Be excited. And inspired. And be thankful, because what you have is a gift."

~

You think like an artist.

  Different is not wrong.

Walking to Emma's house, she hears his voice saying the words, and at one point finds that she's stopped, hand on a lamppost as she relives the moment. It's hesitant, like a place glimpsed, but there's a sense that eventually she might not feel awkward within her own skin, and it's the first time she's felt this. With it, a sense of hope. And relief.

But his words go against what she's been told to strive for, what she knows she should strive for. Everything is a horrible, exciting confusion, as if someone's tossed the pieces of her life into the air and the world's gone bright with possibility—all the different ways they could land, all the pictures they could create.

Before she knows it, she's at Emma Lemahieu's house, the doll under her arm, the book in her bag. When the girl answers the door, she stares at the doll as if afraid to believe it's real.

"She must have taken herself on a walk," Evelien says.

In the background, Martine Lemahieu sees what Evelien has and braces the wall with her hand. "Four years of war, and that doll got her through it all. It's her only escape."

"Escape is good," Evelien says. If Emiel returns and she's good to him, these days of escape will stay hidden like a note slipped between the last pages of a book. No one will see them, but knowing they're there, knowing where to find them to relive them and savor them, might be enough—to provide for future escapes as well.

"When it went missing—" Martine stops and shakes her head. "The things that undo us. They're never what we think they'll be, are they?"

CHAPTER 20

At work, the vizeadmiral is gone, and Weber seems uninterested in following her around the house, his days as a chaperone over. She debates over trying the office once more to search for the list, but she'd already gone through the desk. Her only choice, she thinks, is to convince the Irishman to have mercy on them. *Truly,* Coletta whispered to her when away from August, *making up names wouldn't be the worst thing. Maybe we can find a list of Germans who were killed. What would it matter to them?* Evelien watched her, trying to determine if she were serious. *The people left behind bear the brunt,* Evelien finally said. *Imagine if someone did that to Emiel.* And that was all that needed saying.

Just to check, Evelien tries to turn the vizcadmiral's office doorknob. Locked. She can't take the risk again, she tells herself. Not when the list is no longer where it was. Not when it might not be there at all. Instead, she rehearses her plea to the Irishman, inserting arguments and shifting words until she returns to the kitchen and finds Weber, leaning against the sink, eyeing smoke that lifts from the corner of the city. There's exhaustion on his face, as well as something that looks like incredulity—perhaps at the fact that the vizeadmiral is asking for something like a supper party, now of all times. *He's not right,* Evelien wants to say, but say to whom? Maybe no one is right in the head anymore. She, herself, went outside during a bombardment just last night, and now has no choice but to prepare for a supper with china and fine wine for men who could be killed shortly or taken prisoner. She pauses. A last supper. Maybe that's what it is. Maybe the vizeadmiral knows it's over and is giving them this one last thing: a small kindness before the end. Before there are consequences.

Weber turns and eyes her, wearily, before quietly murmuring, *"Danke schön."* When he sees her confusion, he puts his hands together as if in prayer and then brings them to the side of his face and closes his eyes to indicate sleeping.

"For the pillow," she says. He nods. "You're welcome."

Moment over, he lifts a folded lace tablecloth and points to a gaping hole. It's been years since she's seen the cloth: beige lace, intricate and delicate, Mrs. Vanheule's favorite. Then he's shaking it in her face while pointing to the door. *"Jetzt!"*

"Fine, yes, all right, I'll fix it. Or my mother-in-law will later."

He shakes his head, not understanding and not caring, and she returns to her work, composing a painting as she goes. The *vlaskapellen*, the flax as it dries after water retting, swooped upright into what looks like hundreds and hundreds of knee-high golden huts. *Flax chapels,* they're called, due to their resemblance to the turrets on the chapels in the Flemish countryside. The landscape at their farm would be filled with them, and Evelien sometimes saw the scene as a field of long-skirted women dancing beneath the sun. Now she places them in her imagined painting. But the vision shifts, and there's her mother, her back hunched in the field, stooped over and working. Always working. Always looking down.

On the way to Coletta's shop, Evelien thinks of running into Joseph at the ruined garden later. *You didn't listen.* That, right there, her tendency to not listen, tried Emiel. Emiel, who followed rules and spoke when spoken to and was always someone people felt safe to be around— the good guest, the one who brought hostess gifts and told entertaining and appropriate stories. No one ever worried he'd say the wrong thing or take an unnecessary risk. And though she loved all that about him, often it made her feel worse. Because she was the one who didn't measure up. Lucky to be with him, and never the other way around.

Somewhere, the German military band plays, jaunty and nonsensical. *An hour from the front, and you wouldn't know there's a war.* At this moment, not too far away, a man might shuck oysters for a laughing woman, and the air would be clear, their beaches not strung with barbed wire. Children wouldn't be scared to wander from their mothers, and artists would stand at their easels, not afraid to study faces.

She pauses in front of Becarren Dupont's house. Several windows are bricked over, something done long before the war, when the government declared that taxes should be determined by how many windows a building had, and the Belgians responded in kind. *There's something tragic,* August once commented, *in an unseen view.* Becarren and her family left to France, to be with her grandparents, and now Evelien wonders, if Emiel had married her instead, would Becarren have stayed to watch Coletta and August? Evelien likes to think that she wouldn't have, that the longing to be with her own family would've won out, and that this is another reason why it was good Evelien decided to be with Emiel. Yet another thing to remind herself of when hit with the feeling that she took another woman's life.

A few more blocks and she's at Coletta's shop. Only two stories, the tiny building is eclipsed by all those huddled around it, like the shortest family member in a photograph. Inside, Evelien peers behind a dressing screen: jumbles of upholstered busts, pincushions with needles, and stacks of garments to be repurposed and reused. But no Coletta. In the corner, there's a mess of parachute silk Coletta will turn into whatever she can, the red-stained segments cut away and left in a basket on the floor, alongside the treadle Singer sewing machine. *If I had money, I'd buy them all,* she'd said when they passed a pawnshop window filled with sewing machines, countless abandoned since the cost of fabric had risen 400 percent. *All the little orphans.*

And then the floorboards upstairs creak. Evelien takes the stairs two at a time.

Sitting on a velvet couch is Martine Lemahieu, who smiles before catching herself, before perhaps realizing that she—a pious and proper woman—should not be seeking Coletta's help.

"You know Mrs. Lemahieu," Coletta says to Evelien. "Her daughter's got a limp that Claude said I could help with."

Claude, Martine's dead husband.

"I had a dream," Martine explains slowly. "He said to come here. I think."

"You didn't tell me."

Martine nods, eyes down. "I wasn't sure what I'd do. But it's Emma; shouldn't I try what I can? You saw her—she can't even run when she needs to."

"That was fear, I think," Evelien says.

A wash of regret on Martine's face.

"But a limp as well," Coletta quickly says. "We've all seen it. And we do whatever we can for our children; that's the first rule of being a mother." With that, she glances at Evelien, as if reminding her of the importance of getting the list and in turn the letter.

"Now," Coletta continues. "I think amethyst. Healing crystals. But I need a night. There's a full moon, and I'll leave them out to soak and ask that the spirits bless them. Then they go in a pouch she needs to wear, around her neck or in her pocket. But she's *never* to open it. We need to keep the strength inside. Can you do that?"

Martine shakes her head. "No. It won't work. Children are curious."

"I'll sew it closed, of course. Tell her it would be a sin to open it."

Maybe it's the word *sin*, but Martine's face caves. To have gone from a staunch Catholic to this, pious and dedicated and now handing over a gold bracelet in exchange for something she once deemed sinful.

"Do you think the amethyst will help?" Evelien asks Coletta when Martine's left.

"I wouldn't suggest it if I didn't. What's that? Give it here." She spreads the lace out and makes a clicking with her mouth. "Rats. Chewed clean through."

"I thought it was a tear."

"A tear? Torn by little vermin teeth, perhaps. I'll need three days."

"I can give you two."

"Fine, then I need a hand mending the pants downstairs so I can get to this later."

Evelien agrees, as light dims in the windows, and any chance of the ruined garden is lost to shadow.

CHAPTER 21

That night, she uncovers and studies the painting. A reminder of colors, destiny, and purpose. Even a reminder of her own childhood—when she'd first seen it—that wild, untamed hope.

Behind her, Coletta leans against the wall. "It's like a love affair."

It takes Evelien a moment to understand the woman is referring to the painting. She takes a step back. "Yes. It's beautiful."

"Only a young person would describe a love affair as beautiful. No, I mean it's skewed. It's a boring scene in Antwerp, really. But through his eyes, it's magic. Like how one sees the world when first in love. Beautiful, but in no way accurate."

Heat rises in Evelien's cheeks. She never felt that way with Emiel. With them, love was a slow burn, something that evolved over the years. "I suppose what I really see is fate."

"Absolutely."

"If the painting was always meant to be mine, and there's an order that led to that, then everything that's a part of that order—the war, the sadness, me missing my family when I first came here, all of it, every bit was meant to happen. Like you with Emiel."

"A painting is not a child, but I agree with your assessment."

August emerges from the hall. "You need fate because you don't trust yourselves. Both of you."

Coletta turns to him. "Ah, the old naysayer himself."

Unfazed, he continues. "Fate is a crutch. You can't feel wrong if you think what you're doing is fated. Where's the importance of choice? Where's your moral responsibility?" He glances at Evelien and then takes a seat in the parlor, leg extended as he rubs his knee.

"Is it wrong to believe in something because it makes you feel better?" Evelien asks, thinking of all the ways she's escaped in her mind, and even the painting hidden in the wall close by, a boring landscape seen as magical.

"Depends on what that belief makes you do. If it doesn't hurt someone, then why not? But if you relinquish responsibility, in the name of your belief, then I say it's a wrong packaged as a right."

"The amethysts," Evelien says, remembering. She turns to Coletta. "For Martine."

"Right, right," Coletta says. "First, the painting. Above the mantel? Is that where we'll put it when the war's over and it's officially yours?"

Evelien tries to focus on the painting. "The mantel, yes. That's where it will go." One more lie, stacked upon the others.

"Emiel will love it," Coletta says.

Another lie. Because Emiel did not love it. The couple of times he saw it, he thought it garish and untrained. The last time they spoke about it was a year before the war broke out. Even thinking about life *before* makes Evelien feel ashamed at their luck, their lives they didn't know to cherish.

"All your Fauves," he'd said when she told him Mr. Vanheule had just had the painting reframed, "are so childlike and bright. Now van Eyck and Memling," he continued, listing off two of the Flemish primitive artists, "*they* had talent."

She'd only meant to tell him about the man at the frame shop, a man whose monocle appeared like a door to the blue cave of his eye, and it felt personal, this attack on what she loved. "Are you defining talent by realism?"

"By the *ability* to capture things realistically, I'd say."

"And the people who have the ability but *choose* not to paint realistically—what category do they fall into?"

He considered his answer, and she pulled out a chair to take a seat. Their tastes were different, it was clear, but the conversation they were about to have seemed to hum with promise. However, he shook his head, and she stayed standing.

"It's a waste is what it is," he said. "And I'm not alone in saying that."

"People hated them. You're right. They still do. Which is why what the Fauves did wasn't easy. To move from true imitation, to incorporate emotions into color—"

"Emotions into color?" He laughed.

"Derain said that for the Fauves, colors became charges of dynamite. An attempt *to free the picture from all imitative and conventional contact.*"

"You're standing in my light."

She shifted over and her shadow moved from his book. She wanted to defend her favorite artists. She wanted to explain the relief from seeing that lifting from reality was not only all right, but could actually enhance a world that sometimes needed enhancing. She wanted to engage her best friend in a debate. She wanted *more*, and so she continued.

"I think he was reacting to photography, which changed everything, of course, because once the world could be captured exactly, what became interesting was to capture it *differently*. But *I* like to think he was saying we should take what we know and blow it up."

Now Emiel glanced at her, and she thought she saw something in his eyes, a new understanding, perhaps.

"Braque's Cubism is worse," he said, and she realized she was wrong. What she'd seen was an end to the conversation. "That I really don't understand. And maybe I'm old-fashioned, but I'd rather have art that doesn't make me want to blow things up." Then he was back to studying, his face so close to the page, she saw the reflections of words in his glasses.

They're different. That's all. Or is it?

In bed, the world thunders. She conjures the painting in her mind and thinks of Joseph, wondering what his work is like. The fact that she can't see it feels like a huge injustice, like never hearing the sound of someone's voice. In her mind, there are deep blues and dark, furtive greens, and she only realizes she fell asleep when she wakes to a tap on her window. Quickly she pulls open the shutter to see him below, nodding toward the alley. She hurries to the kitchen, to the milk door, still gripped by the conversation she'd had with Emiel before the war.

"Do you like Braque?" she asks when seated.

"Braque?" he asks, thrown. "I do. The shift he made. His experimentation." Another pause. "He was fighting, you know. A lieutenant."

Was. Past tense. She stills, waiting for more.

"I heard from an artist who knows Picasso. Picasso dropped Braque and Derain at a train station in France and never saw them again. That was in '14."

The room's silence comes down heavy. All the art that won't be made. "They haven't been heard from since?"

"*Somebody's* heard from them, just not Picasso, according to my friend. But from someone else, I heard there was a head wound. For Braque, I mean. I don't know about Derain. But Braque was badly injured and left for dead. Blinded, even."

She opens her mouth to speak, but doesn't know where to begin. An artist without sight.

"He got it back, though, his sight. They drilled a hole into his head to relieve the pressure. Though maybe that caused the blindness. It's all rumors, really."

"And?"

"He'd be unfit for duty, I assume. I don't know what the French would do, but even if you're discharged, it doesn't end, does it? Oh, I got flour. I'll leave it by the door when I go. What have you told them about where the food comes from?"

It takes her a moment to adjust, to leave her wounded artist. Wounded, but if discharged, safe. "The food—it's from a girl I know who's trying to help."

"Good."

She laughs. "Good that I'm a liar."

"You're not a liar; you're a white liar. That's perfectly acceptable."

"Maybe," she says, thinking about the lies she just told Coletta.

After a moment, he says, "Do you remember I told you I shot a man who thought he saw his mother?"

She takes a breath. "I do."

"In his final moments, what would the truth have done?"

"We're still talking about white lies?"

"Yes."

"Then I guess the question is, what would the truth have done for you, or for him?"

Silence. "Who benefits from the lie? That's the question. I think I want to tell you this. If you want to hear it."

She straightens her legs. "I want to hear anything you want to tell me."

"That might not be true." A pause, during which there's a low, deep-throated rumble. "I was a sniper. I suppose I still am, even without my rifle."

She unclasps her hands. Thrown. A sniper: possibly the most feared person on the battlefield. The reason men are terrified to lift their heads from their trench.

"You're horrified," he says. "I don't blame you."

"But you didn't want to be a sniper, did you?"

"*Of course I didn't.* I would've done anything but that. But choice isn't something you're given."

"But a sniper," she says again.

"That's not who I am. It's what they made me do. You understand that, right?"

"I do." *A white lie,* she thinks.

"I thought I had it figured out. I'd be bad at it. What could they do? So I shot wide. And the first man I did this to, he lived. I was relieved. Because I'd gotten away with something, I thought. But then he made it to a trench, and by that point it was too late and I couldn't do a thing. He killed three men I was friends with. Six others too. From then on, I shot well. Not because I wanted to kill, but because I wanted to save. Which makes sense and doesn't make sense, and is all part of this battle of logic, and the only thing you can do, the only thing that works, is to stop thinking. And to see targets, not men. If you can."

"Targets." That this man, an artist, someone who paints animals and brings her food because her family is hungry, that he sees men as targets—she's reeling. Maybe she's numb to the sight of the uniform, after all these years. Maybe she's forgotten what it truly means.

"I've said this wrong," he continues. "I didn't *want* to see them as targets. No one wants to see men as targets." She says nothing, and after a bit, he adds, "You're shocked."

"It's war. I shouldn't be."

"It's good you are. That says something about what you've held on to. Me, I lost all that. Though I'm trying to get it back—if I can, I don't know. Telling myself to see men as targets—even that. Justifying that life for this life. Christ. I see it, I do. And that's what I mean. Those lies, they're a kindness. The man I brought up? The one who smiled when he thought he saw his mother? I was set up in the attic of this house when he came in. And it's instinct—his and mine, we both reached for our weapons but mine was out, and in the turn I didn't aim as I needed to." He gives a short laugh. "A marksman without aim. But I was used to shooting from six hundred meters out, not at someone standing by a door, breathing my same air. I really got the man, but he didn't die."

Him, with his hand that had wrapped around her wrist, with his bashful way of looking up at the world. Him, a man who loves his sister.

"Up close," he continues, "you only see the man. Not the target. Shooting him was instinct, because he had a weapon on me, but when he didn't—the truth was I had nothing against this man. I didn't know him. Most likely they dragged him into this, just as I was. He was hungry, like me. And tired and scared and homesick. And so I kept him alive. For two days, I thought I could make him live. Not just because I didn't want him to die—but because I didn't want him to die because of me."

Above, there is the churning roar of a plane turning in the air.

"He called me by his friend's name and thanked me for a Christmas present I never sent, obviously delirious. I told him he was welcome. In his coat pocket, he had his wallet and letters and photographs. Every soldier does. They're all we have, and we keep them close. But he talked about his son, asked if I'd met him yet. And I told him of course I had and he was a fine boy and he should be proud. Every word of it, a lie. And I'd do it again. The lying part. *That* lie was right, to let him feel that connection, that he was with someone who loved him at the end. But I was still lying to myself as well. Like when I said they were targets, or when I said that I had to do it because if I didn't, more people would die."

"But it was true. If you didn't kill someone, that person would go on to—"

"But *I* didn't have to do it. It didn't have to be *me*. I could leave is what I realized. Desert. That's when I decided. Because the lies were never a kindness. They were always cruel. A trick to feel better about doing horrible, horrible things. Really saving that man would've been me putting a bullet in his head. But I didn't do that. And he must have suffered."

This, she understands, is his true confession. Facing the wall, she leans toward the empty spot where the little door used to be, waiting to hear more.

At last, he says, "I told you that you might not want to hear this."

"Then why did you tell me?"

"I have no one else to talk to."

She takes this in.

"But that's a lie too," he continues. "I tell myself that to justify coming here. I think the truth is I want you to see that part of me. I'm trying, though, to make up for it. If it's possible to make up for something when you can't change the past, when I can't unkill a man, or men—"

"You need forgiveness. You thought you could make him live. He might have suffered, and it's true you can't know how badly he did, but *you're* the one who had to keep going. You needed to"—she pauses to correct herself—"you *need* to do whatever you can to help yourself live, and to live with what happened. And maybe the lies aren't right, but maybe what's right isn't always an option. You have to keep going, and you deserve one less regret. So this is all you need to remember: you wanted him to live. Tell yourself that and believe it because it's true."

She waits for him to respond, but the only sound is the front, steady and soft. Gently, she asks if he's there, but there's no reply. Maybe he's gone. Someone might have passed by the mouth of the alley, forcing him to leave without a word.

After a moment, she stands and quietly walks to the back door. Opening it just enough to peer outside, she looks down and to the right, and there he is, still sitting on the cobblestones. Back against the wall, he has his knees up, his head bent so she can't see his face. The folds of his uniform stretch dark beneath the haze of the moon, and now and then a sporadic shock of light brightens him, honing lines and colors. Without saying a word, she quietly closes the door and takes a seat. And when, a few minutes later, he asks her if she's there, she tells him that she is.

CHAPTER 22

October 15, 1918

Morning. A rain-washed sky. She's bleary-eyed but awake. It's the first time she doesn't want to be dreaming, that her mind is the last place she wants to be.

"Will you go to the house?" he asked last night.

"As soon as I'm able to leave work. Will you be there?"

"If I can. Someone I know has fertilizer. I'll try for some."

She'd wanted to tell him not to bother, that the war was ending and she wouldn't need the garden soon, but she liked the excuse. Maybe it was an excuse for him, as well. When he finally left, it was long after midnight, and only because of the rain.

"It's getting closer," Coletta says, referring to the day the Irishman is supposed to return.

Evelien has worked on her argument, for why he should give them the letter without the rest of the list, but she essentially said as much to him in person. Coletta's hope feels cruel, like flattery to a person who knows the truth.

"You'll tell him again what you've gone through," Coletta says. "There has to be a reward for that."

Evelien lets her say this. Disappointment will come on its own. No point in hurrying it along.

Five names.

Outside, pigeons scatter as she rounds the corner. A glance at their legs—none are homing pigeons, the unsung heroes of the war, able to carry messages through hails of gunfire. *We ate well,* the vizcadmiral said a few months back, when they discovered a hidden basket of pigeons. Evelien tried not to think of it, but most were probably pets. Outlawed since the war, when they were on par with weapons, but pets nonetheless.

Then a battalion of soldiers marches past, knees lifting into reddened sun. She needs flowers for the supper tomorrow, she decides, remembering days when flower carts lined the market square. Bursts of buoyant yellows and zealous purples. The lush exuberance of peonies and the dark-centered, watchful eyes of tulips. *Tulpenmanie,* her mother told her about. In the 1600s, people spent all they had on bulbs, a year's salary even, abandoning everything to immerse themselves in the tulip trade. Nobles to footmen. Farmers to mariners. *Three hundred guilders for a tulip bulb—can you imagine?* When the tulip craze ended, the Dutch economy was all but destroyed; fortunes of great houses crumbled, noble lines clipped short. *All a myth!* August said when Evelien repeated her mother's story. *Satirical poetry taken as literal hundreds of years later!* But Evelien likes to imagine it true, that if even briefly, the world had suddenly understood true value and gone desperately mad for flowers.

At work, the house feels ominous the moment she walks in, and a torrent of German floods from the vizeadmiral's office. He's home but not alone, which is never good. She's heading to the kitchen, determined to stay out of sight, when there are the sounds of planes and gunfire.

Racing to the parlor, she presses against the glass. *Your instincts are all wrong,* Coletta has laughed. But Evelien needs to see. *It's better to know, isn't it?* she asked. *No,* Coletta said, and there was more laughter.

A languid trail of smoke rises from the direction of the port. Then two biplane bombers, German Gotha G.IVs, draw in, just as a British aircraft emerges from behind a cloud. At the bottom of the Gothas are black dots: bombs. *The Royal Family changed their name from "the House of Saxe-Coburg and Gotha" to "the House of Windsor,"* the vizeadmiral said last year. *That's their country's anti-German sentiment for you; one swoop and their heritage is gone.*

"What are you doing?"

The vizeadmiral, flanked by his men.

"Are you stupid?" he barks at her. "Away from the window. To the cellar, *now*."

To the cellar. His words ring in her ears. She only starts to move when he waves his arm, ushering her forward, thinking he's protecting her.

If they keep the top door open, so they're not sealed in, she will be okay. If there are many sources of light. If there's not much noise. She thinks these things, searching for reassurance, but with two steps into a cellar already filled with men, she feels the air tighten and hits a stair wrong. Her arm juts out. Her fingers grip the banister. Laughter erupts behind her.

Then she's in a corner. Daylight continues to spill from the top of the stairs, the door left open. She faces the comforting brightness, refusing to look away, but then one last soldier appears on the stairs, and the second he places his hand on the doorknob, she knows he will shut it, and the reminder of the outside world will be lost. Breath held, she watches as the light narrows. Smaller, smaller, and then gone.

Confined. They are confined. Though two men have flashlights, and the vizeadmiral fumbles with a gas lantern in the corner, they are officially sealed in. Sitting on a crate, Evelien tries to be calm while above the noise grows and fades as the planes circle and swoop. The reek of unwashed uniforms and men grows, everyone sweating and nervous and stuck in a stagnant room, and she holds her hand to her nose, trying to smell only her perfume, the faint hold of the base notes, sandalwood and oakmoss. Someone passing by must have grabbed a dried cluster of lavender, because now there's a medicinal stink mixed in, and it's worse.

She can't escape. All the sounds and scents anchor her to the present and prevent her from crawling fully into her mind. Bootheels hit sharp on the ground as a few men pace. The noise above gets louder, and one of the men backs against the wall, his eyes wide.

And then, a booming. The walls shake. The man nearest her fumbles his flashlight and the light disappears and there is darkness. And though it's momentary, and not complete, that smash of dark is enough, and with it she hears a rasping she realizes is her own breathing—too shallow and quick—and suddenly she's sweating, her heart thundering. This wasn't supposed to happen. She looks to the vizeadmiral, who's calm with his lantern despite the fact that they could be trapped, that they must be trapped, that it's probably already happened and they simply don't know it. The noise is now somewhere at her center, inside her, all the chaos and guilt and fear, all of it swirling, pushing against her skin. She can't stop sweating. Everyone must see this.

The vizeadmiral is speaking German. The men are speaking German. She doesn't know what's happening outside or how long they'll be down here and what she needs is to escape into her mind, to be somewhere else, so she closes her eyes and tries to see Bruges in better days, the sway of vines off a bridge, but then the water becomes the river at her family's farm, light shuffling on its surface, and above the blue bowl of the sky suddenly darkens and splits in two and there is noise, so much noise, and then everything is splitting, coming apart, splintering. *When I almost fainted, my world broke into a Seurat.*

Distantly, she hears the vizeadmiral, from across the room or right beside her, she can't be sure. Though her eyes are open, her vision has completely darkened. Her arms and legs feel as though they're tingling, swarmed with a million pinpricks. "Evelien," he's saying. Someone's holding her shoulder. "Lower your head."

Lower, lower, or you'll faint.

~

Sleeping. Her mother was sleeping. Always sleeping when her father was gone.

It was the noise that woke Leona. Evelien herself didn't hear it, not right away. She was supposed to be cleaning the chicken coop, but she'd rushed through everything so she could draw, and was in the barn, drawing one of the escaped hens who was brooding in a nest of hay. She was ten, and her drawings were primitive and untrained, but the hen was still and a good subject, and so Evelien didn't notice when hanging tools began to clank, or even when the wooden walls began to groan.

What she noticed was the light on her page. Suddenly, it was green.

And then her mother's voice. Angry. Frantic. Leona had wasted time looking for her, and there was one horse she still needed to get. She flung accusations and instructions in equal force, and when Evelien stepped outside, she saw the brilliant blue of the flax and a sky that had inked half-black. Wind pushed her hair and dress, shoving at her back like a parent in a hurry. Though she was sure she was running, it felt like years before she was at the root cellar. Slower still was her mother, who'd gotten the horse inside but now seemed shocked still, staring up at the sky behind Evelien.

Curious, Evelien turned.

Later, she heard it called a tornado. They weren't common. Her uncles would tell of one long, long ago: *God's pinkie, testing us.*

Underneath that hook—that lowering, curving, swaying hook— Leona slowed and stared straight up, hands balled into fists. At the root cellar door, she stopped completely and glanced back to the house.

When she spoke, she spoke against the wind. "I must have done something."

Above her, the sky growled, and that hook, God's finger, scooped toward the beautiful blue of their field and tossed color into the air. No amount of pleading worked. Her mother wouldn't move. Evelien inched down the stairs and back up, over and over, retreating when the wind became something almost guttural, like a deep-lung scream, and then back up when she tried to reach for her mother.

"We'll know soon if God finds me worthy and fit to see this out," Leona said, voice faint against the screaming of the sky.

This. Life, she meant.

Leaves swirled furiously in the root cellar. Once more, Evelien retreated down the steps, when suddenly Leona flung the door shut and latched it from the outside.

In the black, with the noise and the shaking, time untethered.

Terror. Both from being in the dark and the shaking, but also from the thought of her mother, outside. As hard as Leona was on Evelien, as disapproving and sometimes downright mean, she was her mother. The one person Evelien loved more than anyone. Love, marrow-deep, was something Evelien later understood to be created by the heart, not the mind.

At the time, there was no understanding, no words, only a relentless rumbling black while outside there was a rage, an unknown. Her mother, fit or not fit. Taken or spared. Alive or dead. Outside because of her.

When, finally, there was silence, the door was still latched. Evelien heard herself breathe and felt the dirt floor beneath her hands. There were splinters under her nails—at some point, she must have clawed at the door—and her dress was sodden. She had no grip on time, but when the door finally opened, there was a blast of light—intense, though it was now dusk—and her mother was alive, but with a leg that would never work the same again.

Neither mentioned the details to her father, who returned the next day after his trip to bid on farm equipment, and surveyed the torn fields, nodding as though this was something he'd expected. A month later, when their neighbors were water retting their flax, to separate the fibers from the stems by throwing bundles of golden stems into basins on the river, Evelien's parents were still picking through their field.

Along with some trees against the road, they were the only ones hit. *God's finger.* How could they—and everyone around them—not see it as something they'd brought on? A test that her family had failed.

Or had they? Because Evelien knew that God *had* found Leona fit to carry on. He'd spared her. Despite this answer, however, not much changed. Maybe her mother still found herself worthy of punishment.

Punishment. It felt aimed at Evelien—punishment for the way she was. When Leona wasn't tired she was angry, and she'd hurl this at Evelien, to remind her that it was her selfish need that caused the delay, that made it so she couldn't go into the root cellar.

And then one morning she softened it, and added another element to the day, one that Evelien clung to: Leona claimed she couldn't be sure the door would stay shut. She had to lock it from the outside. *I had to, to keep the wind from tearing it open.* In some ways, it made sense. And in others, it did not. But love, felt in the heart and not thought out in the mind, accepted that as the reason, and Evelien tried to close the door on the subject and that day.

But like a wind, fault and fear and memory tend to slip just beneath the crack.

~

When she comes to, there is light at the top of the stairs and her mother, standing there. But no. Not her mother. A soldier. Latching the door at the top of the steps to the wall, to keep it open. The shaking has stopped; the sounds of the planes are gone.

"You fainted," the vizeadmiral says. She's on the ground. Someone's coat is beneath her head, and the fabric stinks. Quickly, she sits up, but the motion is fast, and the world splinters again.

A laugh as she lowers her head.

"This is why women don't fight," the vizeadmiral says, and then repeats it in German. More laughter, louder now. Embellished. Then legs going up the stairs. "That was a Tommy plane, a Handley Page, one of their night flyers. Now there's one less, which is good for us, but it sounded like it went down in the direction of my men."

She won't be left behind, and struggles to her feet, holding on to the stair railing with both hands as she goes, desperate to get upstairs. Once there, she blinks in the light. There's a flurry of activity as the vizeadmiral and his men pile into cars and take off and again her vision breaks off, splintering, so she sits where she is in the hall, on the floor. The house has gone silent. She looks up. Before her is Albert Marquet's *Bay of Naples*, a painting Mr. Vanheule bought not long before the war broke out. Boats and a blue sky and Mount Vesuvius. Tumbling clouds. *The water*, Mr. Vanheule said, *the way he's captured shine on the water. When I go, I want to be in that shine, that glossy serenity.*

She studies the brushstrokes. Impressionistic. Short but languid, not frenzied. Each one simple and yet perfect. The gleam of water conveyed with an absence of color. Her pulse is beginning to slow, her breathing becoming even. Then she hears what the vizeadmiral said—*it sounded like it went down in the direction of my men*—and her heart once more begins to race.

CHAPTER 23

A stone of worry within her. Even if the vizeadmiral were to return before she left, he'd never tell her about the German losses. Very rarely do any of them hear about German losses, which is a part of an optimistic picture that's painted for the troops as well. *A few months ago, we saw British soldiers up close,* Joseph said last night. *Since the beginning, they told us the Brits were starving. But there they were, better fed than we were.*

She tries to comfort herself with odds. That Joseph has survived actual battles and isn't fighting right now means he should be all right—but the same could've been said about Father Louwagie. War throws rules out the window. As a distraction, she concentrates on preparations for tomorrow night, polishing silver as if King Albert will be a guest. Soon she has a blister on the base of her thumb, silver polish under her nails, and dust lodged in her nose. When the workday is done, she steps into the simmering fade of early evening light and hurries to the ruined garden.

Sunlight threads the wall, the parlor empty. Above, the canvas room is silent and abandoned. *It sounded like it went down in the direction of my men.* Back downstairs, she brushes dust off the tomato leaves and reminds herself he was coming only if he could; she shouldn't read into his absence. Trying to stave off nerves, she pulls weeds and imagines that instead of walking away the other night, she'd kissed him. She sees him pull the door shut and keep it shut. In her mind, she finds him in the dark.

She surveys the ruined garden. Not kissing him was right. She will be happy when Emiel is home and she did what was right. *Do what's right*, her mother used to say, *and what's right will happen*. But did it? And what's right for whom?

Climbing the stairs to her canvas room, she wonders if she really believes the correlation between doing what's right and what's right happening, or if she only repeats it in her mind because her mother believed it. Leona found links everywhere—*you helped Mrs. Snyder with her roses and suddenly Mrs. Goosens stops eating sugar and gives you her* sneeuwballen—cause and effect. Sacrifice and reward. But also, the opposite: wrongdoing and punishment. *I let myself sleep too long, and God punished me with that storm. Let it be a lesson.*

The storm. That day. The smell in the air: gunpowder at first. Followed by a lit-match, sulfur smell. Then torn land: grass, and burned wood, and open earth. She picks up the charcoal. Before her is her field, the farmhouse in the corner. With the black and white, the storm is perfect, and it feels as if this entire time it's been waiting for her to come to this realization, silently biding its time in her mind. She starts to sketch. The swirling hook, the darkened sky. The roiling, churning clouds. The side of her hand turns black.

Her mother was not happy. She'd known this, but not known this, in that way that childhood memories exist undefined and unlabeled until one day the words emerge and change everything. *My mother was not happy.* Evelien had assumed it was her fault. That she was the reason her mother was tired and angry and slow to smile. But maybe it was more. Maybe it started before Evelien. There was talk that her parents' marriage was arranged, that there were farms involved and water access and rail access, all possible with their union, but as a child, she never considered what that meant.

And children. Evelien knew they'd wanted more children—every family on a farm hopes for many children, many workers—but the way this translated into Evelien's mind was that she, an only child and a girl at that, was a disappointment. Worth more sent away and hired out than kept at home. Love never figured into the equation. Yet still, Evelien never thought of the blame her mother might have felt from the fact that she couldn't have more children. That day her father returned, Leona had apologized for the fields, for the torn blue and the destroyed crops, as if she herself had upended everything. In her mother's mind, Evelien realizes, maybe she had. *I must have done something.* Cause and effect. Punishment.

What if she ends up like her?

Evelien draws herself in the black cellar by drawing around herself: the form of a girl huddled on the ground, evident only in the absence of the charcoal dark. Though from the inside, Evelien had no idea what was happening or where her mother was, she sketches what, on better days, she imagines: Leona lying on her back against the root cellar doors, to keep them closed. Though Evelien knows, even as the scene spreads and grows before her, that this might not have been the case, that this is one of those kind lies, still she draws, deciding it doesn't matter. What she needs is to think of her mother this way, doing what she could to keep the door shut, to keep her daughter safe.

She realizes she's stopped drawing only when he takes the charcoal from her hand. How long he's been standing there, she's not sure. His thumb finds her cheek, and she blinks to clear her vision. Then his head turns as he studies the wall, and she watches him—his eyelashes dark against the light of his eyes, a scar beneath his cheek, the way his hair falls onto one side of his forehead. When he looks back at her, she sees it—that though he doesn't know the details, he understands. Undefined and unlabeled, it's there for him to see.

When he kisses her, her shoulders drop. There's an inexplicable, tremendous relief. Then his hand is in her hair, and her fingers curl against his shoulder blade, and in his mouth is the sweet of pipe tobacco, and a touch of pepper, and she realizes there will be black left from their fingertips, incriminating traces marking where they touched. But then he's pulling her closer and she's pressed against him and she doesn't care what's left behind.

He pulls away to survey the room, the debris, the shards of glass. Then he meets her eyes, questioning. She doesn't look away. When he pulls on her hand, she follows, down the stairs, careful and slow, to the green chaise amid the plants of the ruined garden. Lying back, she watches him and then closes her eyes. Against her eyelids is the lace of smoky, moving light. The shifting sun, faded through the destroyed roof. And his lips, trailing to her neck.

Everything is a current. Her lips, collarbone, waist. When he pulls off his shirt, the fractured sun hits his chest, but by the time she presses her fingertips deep into his shoulders, she looks up to realize that now the light is only on the tops of the walls, the last kiss of the sun before it's gone.

CHAPTER 24

Lights are out. Windows shuttered. She hurries home, trying to make it before curfew.

Her lips feel raw, and she touches them as she walks, worried it's obvious. The betrayal. The want. *You won't be with child,* he told her, *the army gives us something.* Despite everything—the gathering of the end and the rising of risk and the dreadful, forward motion of life—she feels lighter than she ever has. Streets are a blur, and the regulations posted on the city walls that inform people not to stand about only make her stop and stand about, smiling.

They did the best they could to wipe clean the traces of what happened. The charcoal from his uniform, the marks from her skin. But first, they lay in the slivered light, and he asked about what she'd drawn. So she told him, using the words she'd found. He listened with an expression on his face as if he'd arrived at some place of understanding that she was only nearing, and then he kissed her fingertips.

"You're right that she was keeping the door shut for you," he said.

And she let him say it. Even if the accusations her mother hurled rendered it likely untrue. Either there was no time to get in the cellar, because Evelien had been hard to find, or there was, yet her mother chose to stay out and protect her daughter. What her mother claimed happened all depended on her mood.

Running a finger down his thigh, she touched the rough, raised skin of a scar. "Was this from when you—" A pause as she tried to find her words. "From that time in the attic?"

"No," he said, eyes on the broken roof above them. "I wasn't injured then. In war, every day is a new day to die. There was nothing special about when I was shot. Only that I was."

"And then they made you come here, to do sentry?"

"To recover. A man with a limp isn't the best at the front but is a good set of eyes. I was lucky I could request Bruges."

She thought of all the men in splints or casts who ended up in the Vanheules' house, convalescing while essentially doubling as security, watching her and protecting the vizeadmiral.

"Back to something pleasant," he said. "Tell me about the landscape you drew."

Her black-and-white rendition of her painting. And so she told him: the trip to Paris, the rain, and the gallery that seemed to beckon them inside. She told him of standing before the painting, entranced and still, the stillest she'd ever been, while beside her, Leona fidgeted and looked to the door, waiting for a break in the clouds. And then, later, years later, when she felt failed by life, there it was, on her new employer's wall, and she realized it was a part of her, like a curve in the palm of her destiny. In a way, she said, she knew she'd survive this war, simply because the painting was meant to be hers.

"Yours?" he asked, and so she told him she'd been asked to care for it, and another two, and that at the end, it will be hers. A risk, she thought, to tell him this. But he didn't know where she works or where she worked before the war. And at this point, everything with him was a risk.

There was a moment when she saw her future through his eyes: a messy, loud house. Children running. The painting, hidden in a room, unseen and quiet. It seemed unfair, to the painting, to end up like this, and so she told him of her daydreams, if only to give the painting an imagined better life: in Paris, she'd live with it, in the area where she'd stayed with her mother.

"Rue du Mont-Cenis. We stayed in a hotel that used to be a mill for a porcelain factory. There. That's where I'd live."

"In Montmartre?" he asked as he picked a yellow oxalis flower from a clump of clovers by the chaise. Moving her hair back, he placed it behind her ear.

"I loved it. But it was too bohemian for my mother. She spent the entire time shocked. All the cabarets. The smell of bad red wine and shanty houses at the top. Someone told her windmills when they recommended the area."

He laughed. "Someone had a joke at her expense. But to your benefit—Renoir and Degas lived there. Monet, Toulouse-Lautrec, Max Jacob—do you know him? A poet and a writer. Everyone was there. I visited once. Braque—your painter, he had a studio at the foot of Montmartre. Near Picasso, I believe."

Picasso signed his early works Pablo Ruiz, Mr. Vanheule had told her, *his family name. Picasso was his mother's maiden name.*

"I might have seen him." She smiled. "There was a café on the stairs of Rue Muller. You climb and climb and climb and then the view. And all these men and women with their drinks and hats, and painters with easels and writers with ink stains. It breathed. The whole area breathed. I wanted to live there."

"So you will."

"As a housemaid? A widowed housemaid?" She stopped, her skin chilled. "Because otherwise, I'm here."

"Those are the only options? I think you're right and your painting deserves to go back to Paris. As do you."

Now, at home, Evelien opens the door and feels for the yellow oxalis flower. Seeing Coletta in her chair, she tries to fill her mind with random thoughts, worried the woman will sense what's happened. But Coletta is fixing the lace tablecloth, bobbins clacking along with the distant thundering, and barely looks up. In the kitchen, August reads while standing, stirring something on the stove. These are the people she loves. These two, right here.

Guilt leadens her steps as she heads to her room, to the point where at the top of the stairs, by Emiel's door, she can't move another foot. Hand on the wall, she pulls in a breath, and then another one. Would they ever understand? One day? With a glance at Emiel's room, she knows he'd understand. He was her best friend. She can't help but think in some way he would want this for her, but then she shames at the thought. An attempt, she thinks, to lessen her guilt.

In her room, she allows herself to return to how she'd felt with Joseph. Under her bed is her big sketch pad, which she pulls out to find the drawing she did that night when his face was cut in moonlight as he looked up at her. One day, she thinks, she'll turn this into a painting. On the side of her wrist, there are faint traces of charcoal, and that's it, all she needs, because now she's relishing in her memory of the evening. Thick, syrupy memory. She's wading through it. Conjuring the press of his fingertips. The way he'd watched her. How it felt to curl under his arm.

Never would it have been like this with Emiel. She doesn't even need to wonder; the answer was there that night, the night they married, the night she'd only felt a tense worry and a desire to turn away. She'd blamed it on a fear of having a child while he was gone and trepidations over her ability to be a mother. And while that was all true, beneath her words was something she couldn't admit: she did not want him that way. She'd arrived in a place where she loved him, loved him always and forever and since the day they met, but not how she needed to. Not in a way that involved *need* at all.

Now, listening to the bombardments start up again, the beating pulse of their nighttime lullaby, she wonders, *What is it to love someone you're afraid to see again?*

CHAPTER 25

October 16, 1918

Early in the morning, August screams. The sound rips through the house, and Evelien is halfway down the cellar steps in seconds.

"Only a nightmare. Only a dream," Coletta's saying.

Evelien stands on the last step, heart pounding.

In their corner, August sits in bed, hunched over, his face against the blankets. His words are muffled, and Evelien strains to hear. *A nightmare,* she thinks he's saying. *But real.*

"You will get through this," Coletta says. "We'll get the letter. I know we will. We'll get news of where he is—"

Suddenly, August sits up straight. "Stop! Stop with the letter. We're not getting it. We're not getting *him.* Why persist with this lie?"

Coletta appears struck by his words. At last, she turns to the stairs, her voice shaking. "Evelien, leave us please."

Five names, Evelien thinks, wedged in that horrible territory of no-man's time—neither night nor morning. No distractions, no justification. Just middle-of-the-night brutality that clears the way for this question: After everything the Germans have done, to Emiel, to Father Louwagie, and to August, how could she have done what she did with Joseph?

Hours later, there is sea on the morning air. Salt and brine and gleaming water. It's so incongruous with the war and the dark cloud above that Evelien stops with the back door open, breathing in. Then, a knock on the other side of the house, at the front door. From the sink, Coletta glances at Evelien, and Evelien steps back inside, worried.

"The pouch," Coletta suddenly says. "Martine Lemahieu. I forgot. You reminded me and I forgot. Stall her."

At the front door, Martine holds out a small bouquet of orange mums, tied with twine. Awkwardly, she hands them to Evelien.

"Please," Evelien says, "come in."

Martine's blue eyes flicker toward the fireplace. "She's done a nice job of keeping the house up. Ours is—" She pauses, then adds a shrug. "Too much is gone. I can't find the will to put what's left back together."

"No one needs a perfect house right now."

Martine meets her eyes. "This will help, won't it? What she's giving us?" When Evelien starts to say *yes,* Martine continues. "When it hurts to walk, she holds that doll and you can see her pain. Her fingers are white with it." A small, embarrassed smile. "I never thought I'd be the one here."

When Evelien goes to get Coletta, she finds the back door ajar. A glance out the door, Coletta is bending over, gathering something that she puts inside a pouch. Two nights ago, Joseph sat right there. Was he beside a little pile of amethyst? Shining purple, soaking in the moon. Wouldn't he have said something?

"How did no one see it?" Evelien asks when Coletta comes back inside.

Coletta grabs a thread and needle from a drawer to seal the pouch shut. "If you don't expect to see something, you won't. And if you expect to see it, it's what you find. In our hearts, Evelien, we want to be soothed. We want to believe. Our minds do everything they can to force our worlds to make sense. Amethyst in an alley in a war? It makes no sense and so the mind skips right over it."

"You had it in the open?"

"Not in the open, but enough to be touched by the moon."

Evelien fills a glass of water for the spray of orange mums, a bouquet of little suns.

"He's better," Coletta says suddenly. "August. It was the middle of the night; you know how that is."

Evelien nods, well familiar with the anxiety of dark hours.

"I still feel there's some way to get the list."

"If it's not there—"

"But maybe it is. Between books. Pages of books. Under a rug. Try again. You saw how much he needs hope." She pats Evelien on the arm. "We all do."

~

Try again.

The sky holds rain back in a vague threat. In town, more soldiers are leaving. A field-gray stream of them, lined along the street with their packs, some wearing shoes that are new but too big, others wearing shoes that fit right but were recently pulled from a dead man's feet. Everyone has hollowed cheeks and sagging pants. Even the helmets are too big. Another street: the entire road is filled with them. Germany's focusing its energies elsewhere, and soon there will be only a bare minimum of soldiers left here, but those who stay behind will be forced to fight, she knows. There is no surrendering. Not yet.

She scans the faces for Joseph. Is he leaving too? The thought of him gone is like everything right now: a confliction. A torment. A confusion.

"I wish there was—" she said last night and then stopped, swallowing down the words *more time*. To wish for more time was to wish for the war to continue.

"What do you wish for?" he asked.

She answered honestly. "I wish we could've arrived here differently."

Because every choice I'd ever made, Coletta said, *and every loss and every disappointment, all of it had to happen exactly as it did to lead me to this moment.*

Would it have been possible, to meet some other way?

Though she didn't ask it out loud, he answered her question. "I think we would've met in Paris. You, living in Montmartre. An artist. Me, visiting."

"Visiting?" She laughed. "Not living there?"

"You only say it that way because you've never been to Berlin. But Paris. I'd walk up the hill, maybe at dusk. That purple-gray time, when lights come on. And you'd look down from your window, from your apartment, where you do all your painting. And I'd look up, maybe lost, maybe just looking at the buildings."

"Like the first night I saw you outside my window. You looking up."

"But no war. No hunger. Just curiosity."

Would it have happened that way? Could it have? She sees no path that would've led her to Paris, and it makes her sad, that so much is just beyond the wall of her life.

She turns in the direction of the Church of Our Lady. Red bricks that seem to build into the sky, leading to the spire. Below, at a corner café, a waiter drops a bottle. Glass shatters against cobblestones. Laughter from men at a table.

And then a confusion, because somehow her memories of last night have seeped into the morning and there is Joseph, straight from her mind and sitting in a chair. She stops walking, trying to understand. But it's real. He's there. At a table with four other soldiers and plates of breakfast.

By himself, he is only Joseph. But now, among the others, he is one of them.

She feels sick. How is what she's done any different than what Lukas did? Or Alixa? In fact, it's far worse than Alixa, because Alixa is

German and unmarried while Evelien's betrayed her country *and* her husband.

She can't let Joseph see her. Not now. Face down, she hurries across the street, but out of the corner of her eye, she sees him turn toward her. She keeps walking, not breaking stride, and when she finally glances over her shoulder, he's gone. Her pace slows with confusion until she approaches the opening to an alley and sees him, leaned against his cane, out of breath, a map in his free hand.

"Excuse me, Saint John's Hospital?"

Despite herself, she smiles.

He hands her the map, and she feels his eyes on her. "Here," she says, and points to where the Sint-Janshuis Mill is, built in 1770 and grinding flour until the war. In a completely different part of town than the hospital.

He grins, recognizing the location as incorrect.

"You're not sleeping," she adds, a comment that sounds more like an accusation than she'd intended.

"No. A bite to eat first." Then, studying her, he asks quietly, "Are you all right?"

"You mean do I feel horribly guilty?" She feels a surge of boldness. "Or am I wishing I was there with you now?"

He smiles. "Both. Especially the latter."

"Then yes, to both."

"Your perfume," he says, and breathes in deeply. "I left something for you in the house." And then, as someone passes by, he points to the Belfry on the map and says loudly, "And this is the hospital?"

Rain, held back till now, sends its warning shots in haphazard drizzles. She looks up, into the sky, which has broken into a spreading mist, then catches sight of herself in a shop window's reflection, smiling beside a German soldier. In a flash, her expression changes, which makes it worse, because it becomes disappointment, remorse, and judgment. It becomes familiar.

"You look like you've seen a ghost," he says.

"My mother. I look just like her." She looks away. "I keep wondering, what if I am like her?"

"Then she must have been imaginative," he says. "Wickedly talented. Beautiful."

He's being kind, she knows. But he didn't know Leona. Leona, angry with life. Sad and tired. "Just off from center."

The rain picks up, and the map darkens. Without caring who's watching, he takes his hat and holds it above her head, shielding her from the torrent. Then he looks at her curiously, water on his lashes.

"When you look at a painting," he says, "your eye is drawn to the focal point. Light and dark together, the juxtaposition, *that's* what draws the eye. The contrasts. Don't let anyone tell you otherwise—because all of it is necessary. The highs and lows and the brights and darks." He smiles. "And you don't put the focus in the middle. So it might not be what you mean, or maybe it is, but *off from center* seems best to me."

CHAPTER 26

Tonight: *the doomed supper*, as she's started to think of it. But now, pounding rain and rattling thunder and flashing lightning. All of it, as if the battle has at last arrived at their doorstep. Is this how it will be? Will the fighting be in their city, on their streets? All she knows is the end, when it comes, will be twistedly welcomed. Dreaded but necessary.

The second there's a break in the clouds, she rushes to Coletta's shop to get the lace tablecloth. Everywhere she turns, the city appears rinsed clean. Red tile roofs slick with moisture. Canals shivering with reflections. Soot and ash washed away. The world shining with a temporary reprieve.

Listen at your window for me tonight, Joseph said before she left him today. He'd held the map over her head when the rain came down harder. *And remember, I left something for you in the house.* Fertilizer, she assumes, which she'll have to hide. If someone came into the ruined garden, it would be one thing to find plants but another thing to find something so coveted. Questions would be asked. Houses searched.

Coletta's holding the lace to the light when Evelien enters the shop. "Try to find the spot. You can't. I impress even myself." A smile, and she lowers the cloth. "I meant to tell you—I heard a voice. I don't know whose it was, a man is all I know, but he brought up tonight and that the vizeadmiral's only bringing in men with tin on their shoulders. He wouldn't bring in the lowlies, not for an event like this."

Evelien studies her. "A voice knew of the supper?"

Maybe Coletta heard the drag of doubt in her voice, but she tilts her head curiously. "Not a meal, specifically. But that something is happening tonight and that *you* have a role to play. There's importance surrounding you and what you could do. An opportunity to bring justice. Maybe the list, I don't know. But a risk you should seize." A pause, and then she lifts the lace once more to the light. "I was also told you were too close to a German."

Now Evelien fights to keep her eyes lowered, studying the basket with the cutaway, bloodied parachute silk. "Alixa?"

Casually, Coletta responds. Almost too casually. "Could be. The opportunity that was mentioned, that seemed key."

If Evelien avoids her eyes, the woman will see her guilt. Or has she already seen it? What else did the voice say? "Opportunity to land myself in prison?"

"My personal opinion is that a little wrong that prevents a lot of wrong is worth it. It might not be popular in the eyes of the law or the Lord, but to prevent cruelty—wouldn't it be *right* to do something a little wrong? Something that helps a greater good?"

Coletta removes a ledger from the shelf and jots down numbers. Evelien watches the swirling lift of her 7s. "What are you saying?"

A pause, and Coletta scratches out a 7, then writes in a 9 above it. "Here's my thought: I don't know what you're walking into tonight, and I certainly don't want you doing anything dangerous; you've done enough. But the borders of what's right and wrong were scratched out long ago. There's not one person left without sin who can judge after a war like this."

Not one of us is getting out of this intact.

Evelien watches the sunlight spread through the unshuttered window on the far wall. The storm is gone. "Sometimes I wonder what my mother would've thought. If she were alive during this. If *I* have a hard time thinking things will get better—that they even can get better—imagine her." For a second she's quiet, listening to what sounds like a bird outside, until she realizes it's a squeaking wheel. "Everything seems broken. I don't know how we go back from here."

"Well, you don't go *back*, do you? At least you hope you don't." Coletta jots down another number. "You might take comfort in this, and you might not, but life is repetitive. Maybe it's the journey humans need. But every so often, a war or a plague or what have you. A hundred years pass, and our streets look different, so different that we think we're nothing like the people who came before us. Our situations, our circumstances, they're all new. They must be, we think, because *we're* so different. We want to be different. But at the core, everything's the same. A hundred years ago, two hundred years ago. The same lessons learned differently. And no matter when it is, you can guarantee *something's* waiting in the wings to make us feel broken, but more importantly, to force us to find a way through." A pause. "Your mother was the one who told me that."

Evelien laughs. "No she didn't."

"She did." A smile. "With different words, I'll grant you, but the sentiment was the same."

"That's far too optimistic for her."

"She had hope. Not as much when you knew her, that's true." Coletta starts to fold the cloth, matching corner to corner. "Even after her wedding. There she was, furious with her family for selling her off, mad with life for not being the way she thought it would be, but *even then* she thought there'd be love. That it would form or evolve or what have you. The first time she heard your father play the violin, she said she could love him."

The violin Evelien found back at their farm, shining and pristine in its case. Tucked away and out of sight. Not once did she consider that it might have been her father's.

As if seeing the connections in Evelien's mind, Coletta smiles. "It's too bad we're not able to be friends with our parents before becoming their children, isn't it?" Another smile. "He played the music she wished she could've. That's what I always thought. And when he stopped, the way she saw him changed. Maybe because she lost herself completely. And then the rest came unraveled."

"But she didn't care for music."

Coletta looks up sharply. "Didn't *care for* music? Why do you say that? You mean she stopped even *listening* to music?"

Knives and forks on plates. The sound of chairs scooting against wood floors. A door latch clicking into place. "In my house, there was no music."

Now Coletta nods slowly. "Maybe it was easier that way. She had the ear, your mother did. There was an organ at the church, of course, but she wasn't allowed to touch that. But her aunt had a piano. That's the one who died, the one who ended up in Paris. You probably never met her. She was a bit of a nut, and ultimately your mother's family decided she was a bad influence. But she was the one who loved music. And let me tell you, when Leona found that piano, it was as if she'd been looking for it her whole life. She couldn't even read music, but somehow it came straight out of her hands."

"She never told me."

Outside, the furious gallop of horses. Coletta moves to the window. "More and more," she says, "I'm realizing that it's safe to assume that *everyone* wanted something they couldn't have. There's always something just outside our grasp."

Leona in Paris, back when Evelien was a child, when they'd gone to sign documents relating to her aunt's death. Struck still at the open door to the cabaret, the piano raucous and loud. The way her eyes searched the street. The way she seemed unable to move. Evelien thought it was because she hated it. A challenge to all that was prim and proper.

"She was sad," Evelien says.

"I imagine a life without what you love is hard. I've always been lucky that way."

Absentmindedly, Evelien feels for her sketch pad in her pocket. "I knew she was sad. But I didn't *feel* it for her. If that makes sense. I think because so often her sadness came out as anger."

"Your mother was not an easy egg to crack. I think it was easier for her to think she *deserved* the bad things, that *she'd* brought them on—rather than understand that perhaps those things weren't right. And maybe she needed it, that belief that she could prove herself and be made happy." A slight, sad laugh as she returns to the basket of parachute silk and riffles through the scraps.

Punishment. The day of the storm. For the first time, Evelien sees it without the obstruction of guilt. What happened with Leona wasn't because Evelien was off drawing when she should've been somewhere else. "She had time. The day of the storm. The door locked from the outside, that's true. But she could've come into the cellar right then; it would've taken seconds. Either it was because she was trying to prove herself, like you said, or she really did want to keep the door closed. For me."

"Or both. But nothing to do with you drawing."

Evelien tries to feel only this, a sort of twisted forgiveness. "She said she was given a second chance. But nothing changed."

"Well, there are all sorts of second chances, now aren't there? Look at it this way: if she sent *you* here after the storm, maybe the second chance was for you."

CHAPTER 27

Preparations continue—napkins ironed, already shining plates wiped down, candlewicks trimmed. As Evelien works, her mind races. Her mother. Guilt. An opportunity tonight. The list. Opportunity to get the list? But where? She needs it, if only for August. For all of them, of course, but especially August, who needs something, anything, to give him hope. Then her mind loops back to her mother and her parents' marriage. Arranged. How did she never think of what that meant? The ramifications and all that Leona was forced to give up for a union that benefited her parents more than her.

Music. Paris.

In Evelien's mind, her mother's alternate life plays out. A life snatched from existence, but mourned all the same.

And her father. Why did he stop playing the violin? Why was it tucked away and out of sight? So many truths kept hidden. So many unknown starts to the stories around her.

"We won't have champagne."

Vizeadmiral Braun. Standing in the threshold to the dining room, staring at the ice bucket.

"It's food and wine. Not a celebration. There's no celebrating at a time like this."

Evelien blinks, trying to leave her mother behind. "This would be for ice, for water."

He continues, as if he didn't hear her. "This supper doesn't make sense to you. You think I'm not right in the head."

He's goading her. Instigating. There's an edge to his voice, a clip that tells her she's balancing on a precarious edge. Carefully, she says, "The men are hungry, like you said. They need to eat somewhere. Why not here?"

He nods, appeased. "Life is too short to not eat your food and drink your wine and—" He stops, and his eyes drift from her face to her hands. "I have to be out for a bit, but then I'm back for the supper. You stay. When the guests arrive, you can go, but you're needed till then."

"That will be after curfew."

Immediately, she regrets her words.

"Whose men enforce curfew?"

"Yours. Of course."

"I've been too good these last years. Protecting this house. And he won't even notice."

There are some who need God to be good, because their morality comes from being watched, August has said. *Those people are dangerous the second they stop believing. After all, if no one's there to punish them for a sin, why not be bad?* Evelien studies the vizeadmiral, who is religious, who does believe—but somehow she knows he wasn't referring to God.

"Who won't notice?" she asks, hesitantly. "God?"

"No." A bitter laugh. "Petrus. I wish I knew he wouldn't notice—I wouldn't have bothered being so good." He glances towards the hall. "I brought up more wine. The bottles need dusting."

Two officers appear outside the door, waiting. One of them looks anemic, pale and gaunt. Spittle webs in the corners of his mouth as he says something to the man he's with. And there, on the floor beside them, are the bottles. Almost a dozen, crowded together like bowling pins. She takes in the labels and remembers Mr. Vanheule adding them to his cellar, reciting future plans and parties. *New Year's Eve, to ring in 1920,* he said, holding up the Bordeaux that now sits on the far left. Then the Burgundy beside it: *For your wedding night. Whenever you decide to say* I do, *this will be ready to drink. And I'll have six more ready for your guests.* To have gone through the war without touching the stars of Mr. Vanheule's collection and then to drink this many in one evening, right at the end—it feels like an affront. A passive way of lashing out. The vizeadmiral is mad at something—the German loss being obvious, but there's something more.

"You're not hiding anything," the vizeadmiral says. His eyes, those wheat-shaded eyes, bore into her. "I see what you're thinking. So I'll remind you that these bottles have only stayed in this house because *I* kept them. Anything that's here is because I made it so." He pauses. "Including you."

This side of the vizeadmiral, *this* is what people fear. The self-importance. The entitlement and anger. The paranoia. And now, a recklessness. Has she never fully seen this side of him before? Or did she excuse it because seeing the truth would've undone too much? What's clear is that something's changed, and only a fool would've thought that this man would keep his word. *A hand-slapping,* he said about Lukas, *a fine.* Only one of countless lies she believed.

"I agree." She can't fold now. "And I want to help. Like I did with the tampering."

His eyes narrow. She's about to ask him about it, to find out what happened—*Has it been taken care of or should I still avoid that market?*—when he turns from the room. "If you want to help, get the wine clean and quit feeling bad about it. Tell yourself what you need to, but you and I both should've known Petrus would never notice them gone."

There's venom in his words. She needs to remind the vizeadmiral that *she's* not the enemy, and glances at the man in the hall again, ashy skin and glassy eyes.

"Vizeadmiral," she says, and he turns, angrier now that she's stopped him. She approaches so she can whisper, and watches his face turn with confusion as she nears, clearly unused to people voluntarily engaging with him when he's in a mood like this. "That man. I think he's sick. Stay a bit away from him if you can. To stay safe."

She sees the whites of his eyes as he glances over his shoulder. Slowly, he smooths a napkin on the table, as if needing a moment. She can almost see him settle—the set of his jaw loosening, the skin around his eyes relaxing. But it goes further—to something that looks like sorrow. And for a moment, she thinks he's going to apologize to her, to explain, but instead he stands straighter, steeled against whatever he was feeling. Silently, he turns to leave.

~

His words leave a wake. She repeats them in her mind, hearing a jealousy that seems to grow and firm. It's true that Mr. Vanheule has racks and racks of wine, even champagne that he used to turn diligently, so it's possible he might not miss a few bottles. And the vizeadmiral was correct—what's here *is* only here because of him, since all wine was supposed to be handed over to the Germans long ago. But there was a cryptic element to his words that has her on edge. *I wish I knew he wouldn't notice—I wouldn't have bothered being so good.* She doesn't want to think about what that meant. What it could still mean.

In the kitchen, lids jump against pots and fragrant steam lifts and spreads above the stove. How Weber has done it is a mystery; he must have called in favors and spent a fortune on the black market. When he sees her, he waves her out of the kitchen. Everything feels wrong. All she wants to do is stop moving and rehash conversations and statements, to lie on her side in a quiet room and let her mind go loud. But she has to keep going.

Just then, a hit that's too close shakes the room. In the parlor, a man with a pinched face looks up, toward the ceiling, and then pours what she knows is his second or third glass of wine. Two soldiers glance at each other, as if sharing an unspoken concern: no one should be here. But, like her, none of them has a choice.

Room to room, she puts the blackout covers in place. Curfew comes and goes. It's been years since she's been here when it's dark. Stepping outside, she looks for flowers for a vase and then up to the night sky that holds the Church of Our Lady. Even that, the church cast in dark tones, takes her back. This was her home. Where she lived from when she was thirteen until her wedding day, right before Emiel left. She knows this house. Loves this house. The creaks in the stairs, the stained glass windows that need to be jiggled to open, the stepping stone behind the boxwood that always stays cool, even in the dead of summer. The house felt like hers, until she was abruptly told it wasn't. A loss she couldn't even claim as her own.

When she's back inside, she pauses before a window. What if she were to leave one uncovered?

A direct hit—that's a fast way to go, August had said about Lexi Peeters's death. *If only there were Germans around.*

It's a fantasy, but she entertains it. Just one window, in a far corner room not visible from the garden and not obvious from the street. The back service stairs, she realizes. Flush against the canal, the stairwell has three narrow windows that aren't set up with shutters, since no one uses that hall and those stairs in the evenings. It would only be a matter of turning on a light. An innocent mistake. If questioned, she could say she didn't want to interrupt the guests when she needed more tapers from the upstairs closet. She glances at the electric lamps in the parlor; both are working, so at the moment the electricity is steady. Turning on the light in the service hall is an actual possibility.

Her arm slows as she dusts the back of a chair. Those thin rectangles of brightness in the stairwell—would the Allies see them? And if they did, would they see them before any Germans across the canal? She thinks of Lexi, when her house was hit. *They'll go for any target in the dark,* the vizeadmiral said when it happened, when Evelien was still reeling from a bomb dropped on a civilian's house. *Don't think there aren't spies here, sending signals just that way.* Evelien wanted to laugh at the idea of poor Mrs. Peeters as a spy. *She was just sad,* Evelien told him. To that, the vizeadmiral laughed. *Then it's worse. Her death benefited no one.*

But here, she thinks, that wouldn't be the case. A house of high-ranking Germans. A gift to the Allies.

And then Coletta's voice. Saying that the vizeadmiral was *only bringing in men with tin on their shoulders.* For her to have known Evelien was too close to a German was convincing—but now this. *An opportunity you'd see, to help bring justice.*

CHAPTER 28

Filling crystal decanters, angling mother-of-pearl knife rests, starting fires in the parlor and dining room fireplaces. She tries to keep busy, working faster, watching her hands and trying to empty her thoughts, to squelch her earlier fantasy and to stop thinking of her parents and all the off-limits subjects her mind returns to. The violin in the attic. It was always polished, she remembers. Did her father go up there when no one was around? She imagines a lone note, sighing in an empty house. As she swipes a dust cloth along the sideboard, her mind conjures Braque, who was a classically trained musician. Then she remembers, it was his painting of a violin that Mr. Vanheule intended to purchase, right before the war. The day they departed for Paris, in fact, he told her of the Cubist still life. *A violin. Fractured. With a dizzying sense of motion, all different angles of views at once—can you imagine?* Mr. Vanheule's words were a rush, as they often were when he found something he loved. *But you'll hate it. The colors. Browns and grays and a little green. Neutral in their associations, I think he said.*

She never got a chance to see the work in person, because Mr. Vanheule never returned.

A year ago, though, she'd thought of that last conversation and made a sketched attempt of how her mind interpreted the painting. Now, without thinking, she reaches into her pocket for the pad. Flipping back, it's like slipping through time. There it is, her fragmented drawing. Like shards of a scene. The violin. The fret, the segments of strings.

"What are you doing?"

She looks up. The vizeadmiral is standing beside her.

Quickly, she shoves the sketch pad back in her dress pocket—but he's faster, and snatches the pad, ripping the edge of her pocket as he yanks it away.

"Now, of all times," he hisses, fingers practically a blur on the pages, "to be drawing. Or wait—were you writing something down? Is that what you were doing?"

"No. I wasn't," she says. "I was—"

"Everything I've done, and you make a fool of me in front of my men."

He's racing through the pages: weeping willows, a rocking chair, an old man, a clutch of flowers. Faster and faster, her years fly past. All she's seen, thought of, and escaped into.

"Please. I won't do it again," she says, begging. "I promise."

When he looks up at her, it's with such intensity, such anger, that when the fire in the fireplace shifts and flares orange into the room, she sees it in his eyes and knows what's about to happen.

"No. You won't." His arm extends, and her sketch pad sails, pages splayed, into the fire.

The pad crinkles. Orange rims the edges and spreads and builds until it's completely engulfed. The fire, fed and satiated, brightens, and her heart pounds against the cage of her chest.

He is talking to her. His mouth is moving and his eyes are furious and what she loved, what she planned on treasuring forever, is ashes. She takes a breath and tears her eyes from the flames, needing to focus, to think of anything else to try and remove herself from this moment. "Were you ever able to find the market?"

"The market?" he asks, thrown by the shift in conversation.

"The market that was selling tampered food."

And now he smiles. "Reminding me that you've done something admirable makes it far, far less admirable."

"I only want to know if I can shop there again."

A pause. He believes her. His boots are sharp against the floor as he brushes past her.

"It's been taken care of."

Once more, the fire flickers and shifts, the walls inflamed, and his words echo in her mind.

~

It's been taken care of.

In a daze, she's in the parlor. Shoulder boards and dark-blue frock coats. Gold buttons, flaring with light.

There was nothing left of her sketch pad, as if it never existed. How quickly so much can come to an end.

And Lukas. Whatever happened is because of her. Because to justify working for this man these last years, she told herself she could trust him. *You're nice to him,* Alixa said. *The enemy. And yet you sleep well at night?* She understood it was in her best interest to be good to him—but never saw that for what it was: Delusional. Selfish. Wrong.

Tell yourself what you need to, but you and I both should've known Petrus would never notice them gone. There's the whirring spin of the victrola before the needle hits, and a scratching as someone holds it in place too long. Then a swinging rush of orchestral music. *I wish I knew he wouldn't notice—I wouldn't have bothered being so good.*

His sudden anger today. His words, actions, and the brief flashes of something that looked like sorrow.

Her breath catches. Understanding like a punch.

Yellow flames on a candelabra duck and weave. There are men in the room, but she needs to know. She's behind him before she can think better of it.

"What did you mean, that Mr. Vanheule would never notice the bottles gone?"

The skin near his eyes slackens. Because he's not just tired—he's sad. And in a horrible beat, she knows she's right.

In another world, they'd comfort each other.

"Please," she says. "I need to know."

His mouth opens. He's about to speak, to tell her, but that drunk man with the pinched face turns toward them, his reddened, loose gaze witnessing a Belgian woman demanding answers from a German officer. The vizeadmiral's eyes harden.

"The impudence," he says. "Why would you think you can question me?"

Shadows on the wall lengthen. Mr. Vanheule, like a father to her. "Please just tell me."

"You didn't answer my question." His words slow to a verbal crawl. "Why . . . would . . . *you* . . . think . . . you . . . can question me?"

The focus of the other men is on them. His audience has grown.

She lowers her gaze, staring at his shoes. "He's dead, isn't he?" A drop of water hits the floor, and it takes her a moment to realize she's crying.

"Go," he says, and the sudden softness in his voice is the answer.

CHAPTER 29

In the hall, she braces herself, arm against the wall. In front of her is the last painting Mr. Vanheule brought home: Albert Marquet's *Bay of Naples.*

When I go, I want to be in that shine, that glossy serenity.

When I go.

Why didn't she think of it? He was in France when the war broke out and impervious to the fighting, she'd thought, lifted above its reach by his wealth and exemption. All the worrying she's done over these last four years and none of it was over Mr. Vanheule. Was he killed in battle? Did he die from some other cause? Millions of civilians have been killed, through violence or starvation or disease or simple lack of care. Whatever the cause, it was the war, that thief of futures, the robber of hopes and chance. Mr. Vanheule, gone. The man who taught her everything she knows of art, the man who was more of a father to her than her own ever was. *The colors of the water,* he'd said of the painting that's before her. *They're whites and grays and green and ochre, but very little blue. Nothing is simple, Evelien. Never be one of those people who just thinks the ocean's blue.*

Above her is a spot from when he dragged in a Christmas tree and scraped the ceiling. And just down the hall, the swinging door he ordered permanently propped open after their chef suffered a bruised cheekbone. There, in the entryway, the corner where Mr. and Mrs. Vanheule left their luggage on that last day, so they could have a quick bite to eat before leaving for the Paris apartment they'd just bought for what was supposed to be only a few weeks. Mr. Vanheule ate a *pistolet*, a small round bread, smothered with orange marmalade, his favorite. He had a sweet tooth, a dedicated and demanding sweet tooth, and more than once Evelien woke to find him in the kitchen in the middle of the night, eating chocolate and watching the moon through the window.

He's everywhere, and nowhere, and nothing makes sense.

All the loss they've endured these past years and even this past week, everything pummels her at once, relentless, leaving her raw and reckless and, above all, angry.

She turns, and there, at the end of the hall, is the door to the service stairs. Fury takes hold and spreads. Fury that Mr. Vanheule was taken. Fury over Lukas, Father Louwagie, and her mother's thwarted life. Fury over all the lies everyone's told, including the ones she's told herself, even fury for the five names that would've bought her the letter they need from her husband, a man she's failed to love properly. As she walks, she can feel her finger on the push button, her hand drawing shut the door. Fast. A room condemned with light. What had Coletta said? *A little wrong that prevents a lot of wrong is worth it.*

It takes a second to open the door a crack and feel for the metal switch plate. She presses the button. There's a shaky surge of electricity, and the stairwell lights up. Swiftly, she closes the door behind her.

Done. How easy it is, to condemn a houseful of men.

She has to get out. Before the light is spotted—by anyone. But then there's Mrs. Vanheule, the image of her, and the fact that Evelien's entire job has been to protect this house. This house that Evelien loves as well. A sacrifice, she thinks. Worth a greater good. At least what's most important to Mrs. Vanheule—the earth's tear diamond and the paintings—are all safe at her own house, but the thought gives her pause. Would Mrs. Vanheule approve of this? Mrs. Vanheule, who never liked the vizeadmiral. *Petrus's German family looks down on us.* Evelien remembers that day in his office, the vizeadmiral and his ironic statement as he'd held the photo frame in his hand: *She's right there, beneath us,* he'd said about the photograph of Mrs. Vanheule.

Down the hall, there is laughter. It makes her sick, their enjoyment. Drinking Mr. Vanheule's wine, holding his crystal glasses to their lips. These German soldiers who have done God knows what in a war she knows led to Mr. Vanheule's death. Mrs. Vanheule would blame them as well. Her country, stolen. Her life, taken. Her husband, killed.

Yes, Mrs. Vanheule would approve.

Evelien's halfway down the hall when she remembers the photo frame in the vizeadmiral's hands—*not* that day when he'd told her Mrs. Vanheule was *right there, beneath us,* but only four days ago. When Evelien brought tea to him, and he hastily put the frame back on the desk. When he was at the height of his suspicion of her, the day before the list was suddenly no longer in the drawer.

The list. The photo frame.

Getting into the office is easy, now that she's done it before. A muscle memory of some sort, instincts of where to apply the pressure on the lock, how to jiggle the pins just so. What's harder is tuning out the sounds of a houseful of men who wouldn't hesitate to shoot her for what she's doing, and then to ignore the fact that the light is on in the service stairwell, and thus she is essentially remaining inside what could be a target. But this is it. The last chance to get this list and to get Emiel's letter. To do her part in this war after years of doing only what served her.

She'll be fast—if it's not there, she's gone.

When the door's open, she registers the darkness and knows he covered the windows—thankfully. Quickly, she shuts the door behind her and locks it with the key that's always left on the inside. Carefully, she turns on the sconce beside her. Gaslight, soft and delicate, not as blaring as electricity, graces its way into the room.

Then it hits her: anyone walking in the hall could see the strip of light beneath the door. It would be obvious someone's in the office. She glances at the desk—she needs to do this fast.

201

In seconds, she's got the frame in her hand and is fumbling with the latches on the back, then sliding out the velvet board that serves as a stand. The list, if it's here, would be sandwiched in between the two photographs.

Breath held, she lifts up the back photograph.

And there it is. The list. Torn off from its pad and hidden.

She doesn't waste time. She finds paper and a pencil and jots down the names. *Ernst Schaefer, Karl Richter, Walter von Unger, Joseph von Essen, Hermann Schreiber.* Done, she folds the copy and tucks it into her brassiere.

Then, a sound. Steps. Deliberate and fast. Drawing closer.

Heart racing, she turns to the door just as the doorknob begins to slowly, almost imperceptibly, turn. There is no thought, no hoping or praying, as if the clamor of her mind would be heard by whoever's in the hall. Her breath is held as she watches the doorknob—but then the lock must catch, because the turning stops. The doorknob shakes. Whoever is on the other side is rattling it, trying to get in. Panic bolts through her because the lock on this side is only a key that could fall out. If it did, would the door unlock? Frantically, she glances around the room, looking for a place to hide, but then stays frozen. If she moves, whoever is there will hear.

It's not the vizeadmiral. That's all she knows. If it were, he'd have unlocked the door by now. Does someone know she's inside? Did they see her slip away and then spot the light beneath the door?

Just as suddenly as it started, the shaking stops. Now there are different steps, heavy steps that seem to lack rhythm, also drawing closer, as if someone is lurching, pausing, and then lurching again, walking unevenly. The drunk man in the parlor. She knows it's him. And while whoever is on the other side of the door is calm and quiet, the drunk man will not be. He will be loud. He will knock and bang and make a scene, him and his pinched face, his indignation that she, a woman, a Belgian, dare ask the vizeadmiral a question.

Breath held, she listens as the drunk man calls out loudly, *"Ist das das Badezimmer?"*

Whoever stands there doesn't respond, but leaves. Thankfully. She closes her eyes, reeling, as footsteps recede down the hall, and the drunk man says something else as his voice fades. Someone, thankfully, is escorting him back toward the party.

All she wants to do is hide until tomorrow when she can sneak out. Every ounce of her bravery is gone.

But she's come too far to fold.

She opens her eyes. She *will* do this, because there's no other choice. Putting everything back in place, she's back at the door, listening. Hearing nothing, she moves fast, locking the door behind her. Her steps are fast down the hall. At her back, she can almost feel the light she left on, that lure in the night sky. Danger from above seems to push on the house.

The parlor. Voices. She's hoping to make it past the room, to get to the kitchen and get her bag and get out, but the vizeadmiral spots her. "Plates for the hors d'oeuvres," he calls out, and his voice is heavy with disappointment, as if this entire night were a test he'd helped her prepare for, as if he's only just realized he's put hope in the wrong person.

Her heart pounds, and she eyes the front door.

Then the vizeadmiral is in front of her. He puts his hand on her shoulder. Quietly, he says, "I'm sorry."

It catches her off guard. His kindness. The acknowledgment of what happened, this shared loss. She lets herself look up at him, unsure what he sees in her eyes.

"I don't know *how*," he continues. "Not yet. I'll find out what I can. But you and I, we must work together, now more than ever. We've been a team all these years, have we not?"

And that, right there, is the sick truth. He thinks she's on his side and has no reason to believe otherwise. Shame rises in her throat. She feels the list against her skin, a comfort against this horrible fact. She can fix things. "We have."

"Good. For now, the plates." He nods her forward.

Her head is heavy, and a buzzing is growing. She's almost to the kitchen when she realizes the sound is not in her mind but is actually a plane. She looks up at the ceiling. It's happened so fast. She won't have time to get out. Yet somehow, this makes sense, that she'd lose in this as well.

But then the sound continues and builds and it hits her that it's part of the record that's playing. It's been so long since she's heard music in this house, but there it is, a string instrument. Her ribs expand with a deep, calming breath. *Do what's right, and what's right will happen.* But what's right for whom? She remembers when her father shot the lynx for killing his sheep and how she'd cried for the horrible necessity in life, for the fact that needing to eat for one meant death to the other.

Whose story is this, she wonders, and who is the villain?

~

She's pushing open the kitchen door when she hears voices in the hall, the vizeadmiral introducing people.

"Korvettenkapitän Walter von Unger," he says, clipped and proper. "*Und* Fregattenkapitän Hermann Schreiber."

She picks up the stack of plates but then stops, as if having felt a tap on her shoulder. The door swings shut.

"*Ich bin* Kapitänleutnant Johan Fischer," says a voice. Familiarity now a slow creep, a gradual dawn.

Another name: *Karl Richter.* And with this, she is certain. Because she just wrote the name Karl Richter when copying the last part of the list. The list that included every man just mentioned.

She returns to the entryway, plates in hand, glancing at a short man with a mustache who's just arrived and is meeting the other guests.

All the men have black iron crosses at their necks and uniforms that do not look too big, that are instead tailored and fit, and in a rush she understands that though she was not asked to do this, it's something the Allies would dream of. Coletta's voice was right—there is importance surrounding what she can do tonight, what she *is* doing. The list, the paper held against her skin, feels hot. Maybe she can do it all.

Quickly, she turns to the dining room, careful to not look at these men she's doomed either by plane tonight or, later, by the fallout from the list.

"*Und immer zu spät und* Scharfschütze Joseph von Essen," the vizeadmiral says, just as she ducks away. Out of the corner of her eye, she sees the vizeadmiral introduce the short man to a guest who's standing in the parlor. It's when she hears the punctuation of a cane against the wood floor that she stops, frozen. And then looks back, to the man who's now stepping out of the parlor, hand extended.

Joseph. Her Joseph.

~

The plates tremble when she sets them on the sideboard. Everything she does is with shaking hands and an absence of thought. Wiping the rims. Smoothing napkins. Slowly, her emotions solidify. First, confusion. Incredulity. Then anger. In her mind, the iron cross at his neck blazes. The smile on his face taunts. His name screams from the list.

He's a soldier, she's always known that. But so are countless men, and at this point, most were forced to fight, their actions mandated, not based on who they are or what's in their hearts. But to be invited here—a regular soldier wouldn't get this invitation. This entire time, Joseph's lied to her.

She thinks back to what he's told her, his guilt and regret over what he's done, and the fact that he was able to think of men as targets. Though she doesn't know the details of his actions, she now understands that whatever they were, they were bad enough to earn him a place on this list. Like with the vizeadmiral, she should have known she wouldn't see the truth of him, and for her to have thought any differently was where the true wrong was, where the real lies were told. She's sick, recalling his smile to the vizeadmiral and the other man at the door. Because being forced to fight is one thing, but to do whatever he must have done that led him to this house and to that greeting and to the list—that's something else.

And then she thinks of what he knows. The garden, and the paintings. He knows that she has art that once belonged to her former employer, and if he sees her here and realizes that this is where she works, he will know she lied to him and will wonder what other lies she told. He will understand she took things from this house, and that she deceived his vizeadmiral. And worse, Mr. Vanheule will be revealed as mistrusting of his cousin and the Germans. The fact is, anything could happen, because—like with the vizeadmiral—she ignored the uniform and saw what she wanted to see.

She needs to leave. She needs to get out before he sees her.

But it's as if he senses her there. Some rearrangement of molecules, the faint hint of her perfume, geranium and oakmoss. Because he turns. In a beat, his eyes have caught hers, and there's the start of a smile, and Evelien feels everyone watching them, an entire room full of men who have just been informed of what's between her and this German, these two who are not supposed to know each other, who should never have met. And then Joseph must realize where they are and what this means, because his face clouds. There's a twinge of shock and a flash of anger.

Immediately, he looks away, and she trains her eyes to her feet as she walks, but at the last second forces herself to glance back to the men who in fact did *not* notice, who are shaking hands and speaking German and not caring that her world has just cracked wide open.

All the men except one, that is.

The vizeadmiral studies Joseph. Dark, golden eyes. A twinge in his neck. He saw it, she realizes—the recognition, the familiarity.

And then she remembers the light.

~

Maybe it's seeing Joseph, but suddenly she feels as if she's snapped to. Because she doesn't know. She doesn't know the truth of the situation—truth, murky and many-limbed. She doesn't know the people in this house or even that the Allies would want these men dead or that Mrs. Vanheule would want her house damaged or worse. Perhaps the Allies want these men *alive* and accountable. Maybe these men have answers, information. And maybe none of this matters, because all she needs to know is *herself* and who she is, and that condemning a house full of men she knows nothing about, without all the facts and information, is wrong. While men in this war have been forced to kill, *no one has* forced her to do this.

She will not do this.

Hurrying into the kitchen, she grabs her things and is back in the hall, rushed and trying to not make eye contact. If she races past them without a glance, maybe they won't notice her. No one will stop her, and she can hurry to the service stairs and leave through the back door.

And in fact, it works. No one stops her, and she's past the threshold to the parlor, past all the men whose fate could hang in this one task, hurrying down the hall and listening for any sounds from above. And though the war maintains its distant rumble, there's no plane above—not yet, at least. Incredibly, she's there, and has the door open, is about to feel for the switch and end that horrible, incriminating brightness, when there's a voice behind her. Joseph.

"You work *here*."

She lowers her arm and turns to him. The light behind her still blazing.

"You lied to me," he continues.

"I'm not the only one who's lied."

"If I had known you worked here, of all places," he says, not listening, his face tight with anger.

"What then, you wouldn't have risked the food? I wasn't going to *say* anything."

But now his gaze is directed behind her, at the light. "You turned a light on."

"I was turning it off," she says, reaching past the door and feeling for the switch. When she finds it, the corridor goes dark. Turning back to Joseph, she sees confusion on his face.

But then, distantly, the vizeadmiral's voice, calling for her.

Without a glance, Joseph turns and starts back down the hall. Brisk. Still angry, she follows at his side. "I may have lied, but so did you."

Horribly, he doesn't deny it. Instead, he stops, struck. "Evelien—"

Again, the vizeadmiral's voice from down the hall, louder. "Evelien!"

Eyes down, heart racing, she returns to the sounds of music and voices of men who are no longer doomed. At least not by her hand. Or, rather, at least not tonight.

"The safe conduct pass," the vizeadmiral says when he sees her, and he's taking out a paper from his coat pocket when he sees Joseph exiting the hall as well, Joseph who promptly ducks into the parlor. And this, she knows, just made everything worse.

The vizeadmiral's voice is calm. "Would you like an escort?"

"No," she says. Too fast.

The vizeadmiral smiles. "Thank you, again, for being here tonight. It's what I've always appreciated about you, Evelien. The loyalty." With that, he glances at Joseph.

To have her morality called out by the vizeadmiral, of all people. And worse, for him to be correct. She forces a smile. "You were right. The pass should be more than enough—coming from you."

And he nods, and lets her go.

CHAPTER 30

Patrol stops her three times on the way home. Each time she is unfazed, if only because there is too much worry within her to allow for more. The last German who stops her is kind, and tells her it's not safe for her outside.

"I will walk you home," he says in French, handing back her pass. "I won't harm you. I have sisters."

Haze and smoke have stripped the moon's power, and the man's eyes look black in the dark. When she tells him she's almost there, he looks relieved. Even his shoulders drop. He's nodding, as if encouraging her to stick with her choice.

She lied to Joseph. He lied to her. They both should've expected as much.

Her street is empty, but her front door is dark with a shadow that seems to deepen and move. A spark of nerves. Is something there? Someone? Then, above, a sudden showering of stars. Twisting flurries of light. Closer, closer. She watches one of the few that makes it to the ground: a fire-rimmed paper that soon extinguishes. All around, the orange-and-yellow specks drift and disappear. Momentary and bright. Here and then gone. A message, perhaps. An announcement that no one will read.

Letting her eyes refocus, she peers back through the murk of dark to her door, where there's nothing. A trick, she decides. The result of a mind that's guilty and nervous and always far too inventive.

The house is silent and the room pitch-black, but the moment she pushes open the door, she sees something on the ground, something that brightens with a series of flickering streaks overhead. An envelope. One that must have been wedged between the door and the frame. She glances back outside—someone *was* here. But now the street is empty. Picking up the envelope, she takes a step inside and kicks the flashlight, which Coletta must have left on the ground so Evelien would have it the moment she walked in. Shutting the door, she switches on the light.

In her hand is the envelope with Emiel's name on the back.

She's at the cellar stairs in a flash, calling out for Coletta and August even as she hurries down the steps. A light in the corner comes on, and Coletta's up and confused. "Is it over? Is it done?"

"No—*it's the letter*. Emiel's letter. The Irishman must have left it."

Now they're both up. August drags another chair to the little table where they have a chess game set up, and Coletta holds the envelope like something that could fly away. "He posted this from France."

"Let me have it," August says. He's got a letter opener in his hand but pauses before opening it, blade poised at the edge. "It's been resealed. Someone read this."

"Of course they did," Coletta says. "Open it."

"When we do, there's no going back."

"Why would we want to? My God, just open it."

With one stroke, he slits open the envelope. As Coletta paces, he holds the page close to the lamp.

"June 29th, 1917. Seconds to sleep, seconds to eat, seconds to write. Though in all fairness, I do not think the hours in infinity would help a man not gifted with words find a way to say what he has seen or what he has done. It is an awful mess. I won't waste my ink on that. Suffice it to say there is not one among us who does not grapple with sin. In my better moments, I wonder: What is one more

upon the rest? In that respect, I apologize, profusely, for
my last letter and for laying everything upon your feet."

August stops reading. "Last letter?"
"There's another one?" Coletta asks. She looks to Evelien.
"I don't know. The Irishman didn't say."
August flips over the page. "There's only one here."
Coletta urges him to continue.

"I hate that I wrote you as I did, but there was drink
involved, the devil's own courage, which is why I wrote to
begin with, I suppose. Regret aside, everything I said was
true. Please try to remember that I found a way to live,
and for that I cannot apologize. One thing too many of us
have learned is that being alive does not mean living. It's
better to learn that before it's too late, and though I hate
the way you found out, I am glad that you did."

"Christ," August says, lowering the letter. "What did he tell us?"
"August, *keep going.*"

"Mother, perhaps if we had been allowed to take our leaves
on Belgian soil, my heart would not have gone the way it
did because I would have liked the reminder of home. For
now, please know that I have found escape and joy and
for that I hope you are happy, however wrong it may be. I
am told this letter will also go with a man who will help
it find you, and I hope when it does, that you'll forgive me.
I worry about you all, from the horrors I have been told
and have seen in the newspapers. I have met quite a few
British soldiers who said that at the start of the war, every
family in the United Kingdom wanted to host a Belgian, as

if happily bringing home a new pet. Now he says there are new villages that are considered Belgian territory and are run by the Belgian government and even Belgian currency is used. It is this thought that gives me hope, thinking that perhaps you will not receive either of these letters because somehow you found a way to leave and are there, under a cloudy yet free sky. More when time and health allow and please tell Evelien that I owe her a lengthy letter as well and will always love her and I hope she also forgives me. Forever yours, Emiel."

August continues to examine the letter, then the envelope, as if searching for clues. "Look here, at the address in France. His name, care of a market in Chantilly."

Something catches Evelien's eye, and she asks for the envelope before holding it to the light. Faint pencil marks in the corner. She looks closer: *Honesty* should *be rewarded. Another will come, if agreements are kept. Leave what's requested for pickup in two nights.*

"The other letter," Coletta says once Evelien has read it aloud. "If you get the rest of the list."

Evelien smiles. "I got it."

They both turn to her, shocked.

She continues. "I did. It was horrible and—"

"So we'll get this letter," Coletta says, "the one Emiel apologizes for? You've already put the list out?"

She thinks of Joseph's name, included with the other four. She's not sure what to do but knows the Irishman doesn't need the list till the night after tomorrow. "Not yet—"

August looks concerned. "*Where* are you putting it? This isn't safe. I don't like this."

"It's fine. Six houses down, four up from the ground, behind a loose brick. Far enough away that no one would even *think* it has to do with us, and I'd never do it if someone's watching—"

"Even to keep it here, Evelien." August starts to pace. "If someone finds it—"

"They won't. It'll be safe, I swear. In that spot in my room at the baseboard. And tomorrow I'll put it out, when it's not dangerous."

Coletta reaches for the letter. "The other one's the one we need, it sounds like."

Something edges forward from the back of her mind. Distractedly, she hands August the envelope. And then she remembers. "The Irishman, he said Emiel was a good man, but good men don't always do good things. I thought he meant in general, that that's the nature of war."

Coletta is nodding. "The nature of war and sin. Yes."

"No." August drops the letter on the bed. "Emiel said, *I have found escape.* He *escaped.* That's what he must have told us in that letter. He deserted."

Deserted. A dreaded word, one that leads to public humiliation and punishment—but one that comes up more and more these days. *Cowards,* the vizeadmiral has said of the deserted Allied soldiers they've caught. Widows unable to receive their pensions. Children left ashamed of their fathers. You might keep your life if you desert, but lose everything else.

Tears sink into the lines on Coletta's face. "August, do I care? If he's alive? My cousin saw him—"

"Your cousin is dead! Stop with this!"

"She saw him milking a cow in France and says he's alive and there! And then this letter was posted from France! It's proof—"

"He's saying he deserted! Left his countrymen to die! Left his country to die!"

"*So he could live.* So he wouldn't be one of those boys you're pulling from the mud. *It's how he found a way to live*—he said that! You've seen what's become of them. What's left of them. You want that for our son? Our boy? First, he was forced to fight—"

"He wasn't forced."

"Oh, he was. It doesn't matter that it wasn't mandatory when he signed up—what man would forgive him if he didn't volunteer to go? What *father* would forgive him?"

Through the muffled din of war, Evelien can hear August's breathing. And then she realizes where she is. In the cellar. So excited about the letter, she didn't notice. Immediately, her breath comes up short, and she eyes the lantern, trying to ground herself.

"If he deserted," Coletta's saying, calmer, "it means he *lives*. There's a much greater chance he's safe and alive."

Mr. Vanheule. It wasn't just Evelien's fear she'd forgotten. There's a slight burn in her eyes from staring at something so bright, and her vision begins to blur.

"Mr. Vanheule's dead."

Both Coletta and August turn to her.

"The vizeadmiral told me tonight. He just found out. He doesn't know how, or anything else, I suppose." Coletta tries to take Evelien's hand, but Evelien pulls back. Too much has happened tonight—she only wants to think of the letter. "I can't. Not now."

"Evelien," August says. "He—"

"Not now. Really. This is good," she says, motioning to the envelope. "We need something good. Let's leave it at that."

"Deserting is not good—" August starts to say, but Evelien interrupts.

"August. This war, you've said it yourself—it doesn't make sense. It's not black and white. God knows it would be easier if it were. If there were something true to be fighting for, a real villain—"

"*You don't let the Germans win.* Not after this long. Not after all we've lost."

"If there's a man who's not *blindly* doing what he's told, if he questions things because he doesn't know *why* he's fighting—"

"*Emiel* knows."

"*No.*" Evelien's never yelled at her father-in-law, but now she does. "Emiel knew. He knew, everyone knew, *at the start.* Or they thought they did because we were sold a laundry list of wrongs so we'd *want* to be involved, because we *need* a villain. But is that what happened with the Germans too? With everyone? All I see now are miscalculations and nationalism and alliances, countries dragged in when it didn't even affect them. Germany, you ask them, and they didn't *want* anything to do with Belgium—"

"I'm not asking them! Who cares what they *wanted*, when what they *did* was destroy us! We *cannot* stop," August says slowly as he stands. "We've been ruined. We cannot fold. To desert is to fold and to let others die, because why, my son deserves to live when others don't? The boys I pulled from the mud—if we stop now and say there's no point, then *why* did they die?"

No one speaks. There's no answer to give.

Finally, Evelien says, "All I know is that continuing on with a mistake doesn't make it right. It only makes it bigger."

August is crying. Slowly, he takes a seat at the table again, drained. "I cannot let this be needless."

Coletta takes his hand. "Who's to say it is? We don't see the big picture. There could be a reason. There could be a reason we are meant to *feel* there's no reason."

August smiles and shakes his head. "Coletta. You speak in riddles."

"Then ignore that, but what Evelien said is right. And if we tie ourselves to the start of a problem, we never get to the end. Who cares why it started? *We're not there anymore.* And it had nothing to do with the citizens of any of the countries; I'll tell you that." Coletta sits back. "Emiel is a good man. And if he found a way to live, does it really matter how?"

Good men don't always do good things.

"Coletta," August says. "How someone lives *is* all that matters."

CHAPTER 31

October 17, 1918

After midnight. Three hours since she left the Vanheules' house. Two hours after reading Emiel's words. One hour after leaving August and Coletta in the cellar, both taking turns with their son's letter, holding it to the light, looking for traces of his life.

Now, list in hand, she remembers Coletta's words: *This list will bring justice, but I see you with it, crying.* And she is. Even as she finds one of the three envelopes she has left, reserved for letters she never got to write Emiel, even as she folds the list and tucks it inside and seals the flap. Even as she wedges the envelope into the gap where the baseboard doesn't sit flush, and as she tells herself she'll decide what to do later, that for now she only needs to make it through the night.

Joseph. Emiel.

Guilt radiates from her disloyal heart, spreading through every bit of her body. In the dark, she lifts her hand and feels the shame in her fingertips. Especially in her fingertips. The way they'd touched someone they should not have. She closes her eyes, sick. But even this, this familiar feeling of having done wrong, is preferable to the other emotion she feels when she eases up on the admonitions: grief.

"I want to go to sleep and wake up when everything's done," she said before she climbed the stairs to the parlor.

August shook his head. "Don't go up tonight. Stay down here. It's too dangerous."

But how could she explain that she no longer cared? That she was exhausted and tired and even the one thing she did right—getting the list—now feels wrong, and she no longer knows whom to believe or why. She couldn't stay down there, what with Coletta and August arguing about desertion and the dust sifting from between the bricks and her guilt burying her alive. She told them she'd be fine, that it wasn't as bad as the nights before, and she'd come back down if that changed. And then she went upstairs, and then up another set of stairs, and up into her room that was waiting and vulnerable beneath an angry, flashing sky.

Can she be the woman she's supposed to be? The one her mother knew she could be, the one her husband saw and the one Coletta and August believe in? She loves Emiel, she always has, and though it might not be the way she'd like, it will be good, and time will file down the sharp edges of her errors, as well as Emiel's shame from deserting, if that's what he's done. These years will go unspoken. A collection of days that no one needs to look at. She will never ask him about life in battle, and he won't ask her about life in occupation. Their worlds will be back on track.

Then a thought: What if it was the wrong track to begin with?

But it's pointless to wonder.

In the dark, she listens to the whizzing and screeching of the bombardment, fainter than before, the location of the front changing often. And though she thinks she hears a tapping on her window, she doesn't move. Somewhere far off is a deep bass explosion, distant enough to not be a danger but close enough to put a slight tremble in the windowpanes. *Don't be afraid of the sound,* August once told her. *If you hear it, you've not been hit.* August and his strange, lopsided comfort.

Again, a tapping—definitely on her window.

She knows it's him. And she hates that she feels this, but she does: hope. She wants for her gut to have been right in thinking that beyond all odds, he is good. Because though he was a sniper, he was forced into it and fought against it, only acquiescing when he grasped the twisted truth that people he knew would die if he didn't do his job. And the man in the attic? Joseph kept him alive because he couldn't bear to be the cause of his death. Not right, but also not strictly wrong. Everything, braced against shadow stories, the rarely seen histories and reasonings that led to the facts, because facts do not exist on their own. Every moment roots out, created by all that came before. The whole world, thick and layered and intricate.

Everything is informed by what came before. Mr. Vanheule's voice. She hears it, so clearly it's as if he's in the room.

Again, a tapping. Slowly, she gets up and drags the shutter to the side. When Joseph spots her, he points toward the alley.

Once there, she waits for him to speak.

"You gave a name to the vizeadmiral."

She sits in the dark, reeling in confusion.

He continues. "To investigate. You told him a market was tampering with food."

"This is what you want to know?"

"I don't know what you're doing. Have you been loyal to the vizeadmiral? Because he says you've been good to him and even helped him."

She won't admit to anything. Won't give Joseph any other reasons to arrest her or to condemn her. "I *have* been good to him."

"But then tonight, you turned on the light."

"That was a mistake."

"You're lying."

She laughs. "Am I? What you've done, who you really are—there's more than you've told me."

In the silence, she thinks he's going to apologize. She actually feels it, so strongly she aches for the words. And it makes her mad, that after everything, here she is, desperate to forgive—though maybe, she realizes, the need is to forgive herself. Because to have been so wrong in what she's done fills her with shame—but if he's not so bad, then maybe neither is she.

As if he's found her anger, his voice emerges with a cutting edge. "*Of course there's more.* What do you think caused the regret? You can't be in this without being guilty."

"And bringing us food—me, do I appease that guilt?"

"No. The opposite. You've made it worse."

She closes her eyes against the dark.

He continues. "The vizeadmiral says you've worked for him for years. Has he been horrible to you?"

She considers this. The complex relationship she has with a man who in fact has *not* been horrible to her, whose kindness may have obscured the rest. A man who's either a respected officer or a monster, depending on which side you ask.

And then she remembers her sketch pad. "I carried a sketch pad with me everywhere. I had it for years and it was full and I was going to keep it forever, like a diary. And I know this won't sound like much, but it meant something to me, and he caught me with it and threw it in the fire." Even as she says it, she regrets her words. The loss of a sketch pad, in the face of true loss. The way it sounds, as if losing her drawings should in any way justify endangering even one life. "And that market, the one I named to the vizeadmiral? I only told him because he promised there'd be a fine, a hand-slapping, and now a man is missing."

A pause. "He didn't do anything to the man."

"He was a friend of mine. I know he's gone."

"A friend of yours—"

"When I asked the vizeadmiral what happened, he said it was *taken care of.* I know what that means."

"So do I, because he *took care* of it by asking *me* to handle it. I went to that market to question them."

She turns to the wall. "*You?* And then what?"

"The man in charge wasn't there. He was already gone."

"He's missing, coincidentally?"

"No, I'm sure it's not a coincidence. People get word we're about to investigate them, and they hide. Information can fetch a price. Someone leaked it to him, I'd bet. But I was there to question them, that's all. Per the vizeadmiral's orders."

She leans back against the wall, hesitant with relief. This means Lukas might be alive. "How do I—" But she stops herself before the words come out. She shuts her eyes, hoping he maybe didn't hear. But he did.

"How do you know if you can believe me?"

He sounds incredulous. As if all the wrong is on her end, while she still reels with the feeling of being lied to, of thinking that she's never really known him. Him, who showed up at a high-ranking officer's house. "*Yes*, how do I know I can believe you. You, a German soldier—"

"*You handed your friend to the vizeadmiral.* Why would you do that?" He sounds exasperated.

All her anger seems to pool out of her. Why did she do this? It made sense at one point. She tries to think of a way to explain that there was only to be a fine and yet a greater good was at stake—but whose greater good? Everything is clouded and confused.

But he continues. "Tonight, there was a houseful of people, and *you* left the light on. You say you've been loyal to the vizeadmiral. But I want the truth. Will you give me the truth?" He's almost pleading.

In war, none of us is what we do.

Reasons scroll through her mind, but suddenly everything, every justification, every reason and excuse, feels flimsy. Is August right? Is *how* someone lives all that matters? Do the ends justify the means at all?

Finally, she says, "I made a mistake."

She waits for his reply.

At last, he speaks. "Don't go back there."

In the dark, she turns to the wall, her heart hammering. "Why? Did you tell him about the light?"

When the silence from the alley continues, she goes to the door and opens it to find him gone.

CHAPTER 32

In the morning, there's a change in the house. Hope, both from Coletta and from August, whose face clouds when Emiel's whereabouts are brought up, but whom Evelien caught standing in the threshold of his son's room for the first time in years. Downstairs, Coletta sings "De Vlaamse Leeuw"—"The Flemish Lion"—in the kitchen, a regional anthem that people are forbidden from even humming in public. Her voice goes quiet when near the windows, but louder, deeper when in the center of the house—*time devours cities, no thrones will ever last*—and then soft again in the kitchen. All of her—from her voice to her red curls to her skin to her movements—all of it radiates hope and belief.

Meanwhile, the list and its implications are still tucked behind the baseboard in her room. The Irishman comes tomorrow night—she has till then to decide what to do.

"You're not ready for work," Coletta says when she sees Evelien.

Evelien turns, half expecting August behind her—but no, Coletta was talking to her.

"I can't go back there."

"Evelien, it's your job."

"The vizeadmiral was already mad before I left, before—" She stops. *Before a German found out I'd tried to get them all killed. And before the vizeadmiral realized I clearly knew that German, too well.*

Coletta shakes her head. "The vizeadmiral was upset that his *cousin* died. Nothing to do with you."

"No, he was mad at me." She sees the seam of orange burn her sketch pad, the ashy shrivel of pages. "I can't go back there."

"You don't have a choice! You *have to go* until he tells you not to report. That or you work your way onto his bad side and, Evelien, imagine what he can do. He's not a man you want to anger."

"Which is why I can't go!"

Coletta stands before her, frustrated. "If you were in trouble, there'd be men at our door. You're fine now, but if you don't show up to work, that changes. We can't have you shipped off to Germany, not now. Have you seen the trains? The condition of the transport? Never mind the prison they send you to. People *die* before they even *get* to Germany. No. No, you can't risk getting on his bad side and inviting his wrath here, to our door. I'm telling you, he was only upset about his cousin. Nothing to do with you."

And so, taking a seat at the kitchen table, Evelien tells her about the light in the service stairs, the needless risk Coletta will chastise her for. And though she says someone might have seen, Evelien leaves out Joseph and his role.

Silently, Coletta walks to the window. Evelien waits, watching the woman's back, the pull of fabric at her shoulders when she crosses her arms. The hues of red in her hair shift in the already inflamed light. Then, suddenly, she turns. "*Why?* Why would you do that?"

Evelien's about to explain, to offer up all the anger and blame and remorse and even grief that went into the idea of turning on the light, when Coletta continues.

"In one swoop we could've been rid of them! The men in that room—one can only *imagine* what they've done. Evelien—to have missed that chance!"

Evelien looks up, shocked. "You think I should've done it?"

"Of course you should've done it!"

"But it's almost over, days maybe."

"*Days maybe?* Think of what a day is! It's thousands of men! Their lives! The Germans will not go peacefully. They're moving their planes and ships and anything big, anything that can help their next defensive line, but they *will* leave men, men they find disposable who will have *no choice* but to fight to the end. And who are they fighting? The Allies! If he didn't desert, if he's fighting, Emiel himself could be killed!"

Evelien opens her mouth but can't find the words.

Coletta continues. "This is unlike you, to think of yourself like this."

Now Evelien finds her voice. "Maybe it is unlike me, to protect myself. But someone needs to."

Coletta ignores her, wiping down the table as she speaks. "I knew it. I *knew* it was an opportunity—the tin on the shoulders of the men there, every one of them—"

"The voice knew it."

"What?"

"The *voice* knew that it was an opportunity. You said it was a voice you heard, but *you* disagreed because you wanted to keep me safe."

And though at first she appears thrown, at last Coletta nods. And reaches over the table, scrubbing at a spot. "That's what I meant."

Suspicion is taking hold, grabbing at everything. "Did you put amethyst in that pouch?"

"What are you on about?"

"The pouch for Emma Lemahieu, that you said should never be opened."

Still Coletta scrubs. Not looking up. Fingernails scraping at something sticky. "And it shouldn't. And that's not what we're talking about. We're talking about a missed opportunity the likes of which—"

"Why shouldn't she open it? Because she'd see what's really inside?"

If you don't expect to see something, you won't. And if you expect to see it, it's what you find. In our hearts, Evelien, we want to be soothed. Martine, desperate to be soothed, for her daughter to be better.

But instead of countering with anger, Coletta stands up and turns to face her, exhausted. "Does it matter? Amethyst or bits of brick—who cares if you believe and that belief *helps?*"

Everything is unraveling. "Do *you* even believe? In your sight and your dreams and—"

"*Of course I believe.* You want to know the truth? I believe that what is meant to happen *will* happen. Yes, I hear voices and have dreams and feelings and sometimes they're right and sometimes they're not, but if they're wrong, I believe I am *meant* to be wrong, because even *that* is part of something. If I hear a voice, I'm meant to trust it. *Full stop.* Even if it's wrong. We are *meant* to help each other however we can, and if Martine needed to believe that her daughter would get better—no matter *how* she gets that belief, even from bits of brick—then I helped her. I *helped.*"

"But you lied."

"Oh, come now, I don't think *you're* one to lecture *me* on lies."

Slowly, Evelien asks, "What do you mean?"

But Coletta ignores her. "Evelien. I'll ask again. What if Emiel has *not* deserted and if he's one of the men who's forced to enter the city and fight the Germans and *you* had a chance to spare him? What then? What if he makes it to the end only to die now? And *you* could've prevented that?"

"But we don't know. A German soldier could've spotted the light and I'd be arrested and shot by a firing squad. For something that made no difference. *I'd* be the one killed now, at the end. And even if not, I can't live knowing I've killed people."

Coletta stands tall, and in the motion, Evelien can almost hear the words gathering, coming together and taking them past a point of no return. *Please don't,* she thinks, but already Coletta's mouth is moving.

"Unfortunately," the woman says, "now you might have to."

Evelien can hear her breaths. Exhalations that sound ragged. Trying to stay calm, she turns to the door, stepping away.

"Evelien! You cannot tell me that you are worth all those lives."

Somehow, she manages to keep walking. Outside, into a red morning air that feels wounded, humid, and bursting. Smoke damp and clinging. It seems as if the sky itself is breaking up, little bits and pieces that zigzag and scatter.

CHAPTER 33

The world's been kicked off its axis. Everything she's done wrong, all the loss, all the blame and fault—she could've made it through everything, until now, when she sees how easily Coletta would sacrifice her. Even getting the list—would Coletta have asked Emiel to put himself in such a dangerous position? Evelien understands how desperate the woman has been for news of her son, and for what she won't admit could be some of his last words, and, naturally, that he's her child makes it different—but, logic aside, Evelien expected she was worth protecting. But then her thinking vines out and changes. Because Evelien *should've* given her life, to save so many. Even for the *potential* of saving so many—shouldn't she have done it? Though, for all she knows, each one of the men in the house is like Joseph, with a shadow story that may or may not make the facts look different. Maybe the real casualty of war is *right* and *wrong*. Even the belief that there *is* a right and wrong.

She's walking, but doesn't know where to go. Father Louwagie gone, Joseph not who she thought he was, the Vanheule house filled with loss, the vizeadmiral potentially waiting for her, irate. Was Joseph warning her to not go back to the house to protect her? Or to protect the vizeadmiral? Even her sketch pad, her escape—she feels for it before remembering it's gone. Everything has been shattered.

"Gehen! Gehen!"

She didn't realize she'd stopped walking until a German soldier ushers her forward with his hands. For the first time, she doesn't know what her goal should be. To make it to the end of the war—for what? Though maybe August is right. Maybe the goal, the end result, isn't what matters, and what's important is the path to get there. If that's the case, and if *how* one lives is what's important, what does she do next?

A nun slips through a door into a building, black habit trailing. Evelien only needs to make it a few more days. Head down, feet forward. But then she notices that the same soldier who just yelled at her to move is keeping pace right alongside her. A quick, sidelong glance. He's watching her, lips slightly parted.

"You walk to work?" he says in French.

She answers "yes," automatically, and he nods, his arm swinging. She looks at her feet, the cobblestones, anything but him. Soon, he starts to whistle. A jaunty, happy tune: "Old Comrades," a German marching song she's heard too many times. He lifts his knees higher and bats her arm, as if indicating she should do the same.

The Church of Our Lady is tall before her. She's two blocks from the house she both wants to be at and to avoid, because though it might be escape from this soldier, stepping inside also could mean walking into the trap of a man who's much, much more dangerous.

"Up," the soldier is now saying in French, motioning she should lift her knees. "Up!"

People turn their heads, then quickly look away.

"*Up,*" he says, angrier. Harder now, he bats her shoulder with his hand until she lifts her knees. Her vision swims with tears.

And then, a voice, barking something angrily in German. Immediately, the man beside her stops walking. There, coming out of a store, holding a bag of rice and a bag of rutabagas, is Weber, who berates the soldier as if having waited his whole life to yell at just this person. Shoving the bags into Evelien's hands, Weber continues his tirade, his German clipped and furious.

"Danke schön," she says quietly, as he starts to walk away. Just slightly, he nods.

When he glances back at her, she knows the only option is to follow.

~

Don't go back there.

Yet here she is. Studying the windows of the house, trying to determine if the vizeadmiral is home. Irritated, Weber holds the door open. In her mind, she sees the German soldiers waiting for her just beyond the threshold.

But there is no choice. If they're going to arrest her, they'll do it wherever they please. With that, she steps inside.

The halls are ghostly, and immediately she forgets her present situation and is overcome with Mr. Vanheule's death. A pulse-spiking flare of grief, in every vein and every ounce of her body, a grief so powerful, it throws her off-balance. What about Anna, his wife? Is she dead as well? This house will forever be thick with their lives, their laughter, and the sounds of their steps. And yet.

Halfway down the hall, there is a slender line of light where the vizeadmiral's office door was left cracked open. Quietly, she approaches.

"There you are."

Caught.

Leaned back in his chair, he's got a telegram in his hands. She averts her eyes, waiting for him to acknowledge her. Spread over the arm of his reading chair is a poster of a crazed, drooling giant gorilla in a spiked German *Pickelhaube* helmet, carrying a distressed woman. Her blue dress is torn, her chest exposed. A violation, all of it. DESTROY THIS MAD BRUTE, it says. ENLIST. The US Army.

"We are the mad brute," the vizeadmiral says, after translating. The beast holds a club in one hand, the end red from what must have been a brutalized killing. "They like to dehumanize us. Apes, dragons, monkeys. I think she's meant to be their Statue of Liberty."

Without intending to, Evelien looks toward where she'd seen the other, smaller poster, but there's nothing.

"Newspapers, magazines, and radio," the vizeadmiral continues. "Even films now. All the places they put their lies."

"They," she says, watching him. He can't know about the light. If he did, she'd be arrested. The last thing they'd do is talk of posters. She glances toward the frame on his desk. *Thank God you got those names,* Coletta said this morning. *This other letter is what we need.* And then, *I'll yell at Emiel one day for sending such a cryptic note—even if he did think it was just a follow-up.*

"The US Committee on Public Information," the vizeadmiral says. "The Wellington House, the British War Propaganda Bureau. They put images like this in newspapers and magazines, because they've found that when a person pays for something, they have the illusion that it's what they believe, or that they're forming their own opinion. Entire departments are dedicated to the science of spreading lies."

She looks straight at the vizeadmiral as she speaks. "And Germany's War Office Press Bureau?"

He turns to her, his eyes shaded, jaw knotted. He smiles. "You are bold, in these last moments. But possibly not incorrect." He taps the telegram with his finger. "You'll have your house back. Or she will."

Mrs. Vanheule. "She's alive?"

"I don't know. I only assume she is. I have inquiries out. About both of them. And I still don't know how he passed, so please, let's not talk about that."

She nods, trying not to cry. "When are you leaving?"

"Evelien. You know better than to ask me such questions." Then, a glance at the window. "Tomorrow, I think."

And it's strange, because her instinct is to ask him if he's all right, to tell him that she's sorry. But she's not sorry. She wants the fighting and the fear to stop. She wants him gone and for Bruges to have its streets back, to sit outside in the sun and paint along the canal and speak their own language and sing their own songs. She wants the trees to grow again and the leaves to stay on branches and things to not be so broken, for people to not fear losing their children, for boys to not be forced to run toward death. She wants all of this. She wants the war over and the Germans to leave. But with them will go a small taste of something she'd never known to crave.

"I'm only here for a few minutes," the vizeadmiral says. "I had to get something. Then back to work."

A moment more of silence as he studies the telegram. Without looking up, he asks for coffee, and she starts to head toward the kitchen. *It wouldn't taste so bad,* Coletta once said of the ersatz coffee made from chicory beans, *if we never knew the real thing.*

As she steps into the hall, he continues. "I could use a few more minutes in peace before—" He pauses, as if searching for an appropriate word, and then looks at her and smiles. "Before the end, I suppose."

The end.

In the hall, she tries to breathe, deep and steady. She can do this. Life will go on.

And then, as she places the kettle on the stove, she realizes she doesn't want it to.

Not that way, at least. And not just for her sake, but for Emiel. For him to return, after all he's been through, and be with a woman who only is trying to endure each day, only hoping to forget that for a brief moment she'd had what she wanted—even if it turned out to be a lie—it's not right. It's not fair to him, and it's not fair to her. He deserves something real and deep and true. Something that's not born from obligation or a desire to be someone's daughter. So much, she realizes, began with a fear of losing the woman who's most important to her.

"Thank you for working last night," the vizeadmiral says now, appearing in the threshold of the kitchen. "I may have let the desire for the evening to be good—and what happened with my cousin—well, I might have let those things shorten my temper." When she says nothing, he continues. "The men who were here, they've all gone beyond the call of duty for Germany. It was one evening, but I'm glad I could do that for them. We have plans, when we get back. Ways to make things right."

Beyond the call of duty. Ways to make things right. Again, she sees Joseph's face, smiling as he greeted the vizeadmiral. When she says nothing, he continues.

"Joseph said he knew you."

Her skin chills. Hearing his name, spoken by the vizeadmiral. "We've spoken. That's all. He's assigned sentry near my house."

He waits, allowing her to say more, but when she doesn't, he nods, as if accepting her omissions. "You should know that he's lied to you about who he is."

Everything inside her slams to the surface. She can't let the vizeadmiral see the effect of his words, the pronouncement of what she's feared, so fights to keep her eyes on the flame beneath the kettle. Joseph lied to her about who he is. Is that why he told her not to go back? So she wouldn't discover his lies? "What did he lie about?" Her voice comes out small, and the hope she detects makes her mad.

But he ignores her. "Tell me the truth. The two of you have only spoken?"

Strangely, she hears hope in his voice as well. But the very fact of the question tells her he either glimpsed the truth last night, or that Joseph said more than he should have.

"I'm *married*," she finally says, as if this partial statement should preclude the rest. And when she turns to face him, what she sees is sadness. Grief, she thinks. Grief that she wasn't the person he'd thought she was. Acute, sheer disappointment in who she truly is.

CHAPTER 34

You should know that he's lied to you about who he is.

So desperate for an alternate reality, she created it. Fooling herself and letting herself be made a fool. All day, she works, as the noise outside begins to build, the chaos of the dark hours starting early. Packing the vizeadmiral's things, she wonders how, in all of this, *she's* become the villain. How could she have come this far? But then she thinks of the shadow stories, how much more there is to each truth. If they apply to Joseph, then shouldn't they apply to her as well? Is anything she's done excusable?

When the day is over, the house is empty. Will she ever see the vizeadmiral again? He told her to get him ready, and that's what she did, organizing and folding, leaving little stacks of him around the house, traces that can easily be removed. At the last minute, she realizes he'll need things for tonight, if he's able to return and sleep, and so quickly folds pajamas and places them on the bed, then makes sure his toothbrush is in a cup at the sink. Anticipating his needs like a good wife, she thinks. And it makes her sick that she's done this. She glances back down the hall, thinking she will move his pajamas, hide them in the oven or place them at the top of a shelf, but suddenly it's all too much, the energy it takes to be angry.

Giving up, she turns back to the door and steps into a singed evening of smoke and rumblings, the loudest it's ever been. A few blocks away, she stops as a little boy, maybe ten years old, tears around a corner and keeps going. He jumps over a patch of broken cobbles and almost falls but then throws his arm out for balance, and that's when she sees what's in his hand: a German soldier's hat.

"You don't want to be caught in this," a woman's voice says.

Evelien is smiling, thinking of the little boy who's spurred with rebellion and awakened by hope, and so when she turns to the woman, she's confused, and for a second she forgets everything and glances at the sky. As if the relentless, squeezing grip of war and all its horrible sounds only mean that soon there will be rain.

The woman, holding her coat tight around her throat, sees this and laughs. A round laugh, chest-deep and full.

"I meant the end," the woman finally says as she starts to walk away. "I meant you don't want to be caught in the end."

And Evelien loses her smile, hearing it a different way. *You don't want to be caught, in the end.*

~

At home, Evelien tries to ignore Coletta, who watches her from the counter the second she walks in.

"You won't talk to me now?"

Evelien stops, one foot in the hall. "I think we've said too much."

"No one wants to hear certain truths. And maybe I shouldn't have said them."

"That was your mistake? Telling me the truth?"

"Evelien. You know how I feel, that there's no way to justify *one* life being spared in the face of losing so many. That train crash, did I tell you I got there late? I only decided that morning to go, so I didn't time it right. And I was running on the platform, chasing the train, and it stopped. I got on but because I was late, I was in the back."

"You told me this."

"No. *Because* I was late, the timing—" She stops. "That time made the difference. The other train would've been gone." She continues. "Did I think it was my fault? Of course I did. Like you and Father Louwagie. But you have to believe that everything is a part of the next, and if that's true, how can timing be our fault? Because *when* does that timing start? I was late because a horse threw its shoe. Is that where the blame begins? Or with the man who took the horse down a muddy road? How far back does it go?"

When does the story start? Evelien doesn't realize she's crying until Coletta wipes away a tear with her thumb.

"I didn't just struggle with the idea of fate," Coletta continues. "I struggled with guilt. You and I, we're—"

"No. You're right," Evelien says, gathering herself. "You're right, that one person is probably not worth it. But what matters to me is that *you* didn't think I was worth it. You would never have said that to Emiel."

"Emiel's my—"

Evelien watches Coletta catch herself.

"That's not what I meant," Coletta says.

"It is," Evelien says. "It's all right. It's different. He's your child. But I guess I hoped that you loved me enough to not"—she pauses, looking for the word—"sacrifice me."

"Evelien. That's dramatic." Coletta follows her as she heads for the stairs, but then August is behind her, his hand on his wife's arm.

Upstairs, in her room, Evelien thinks of Joseph. She eyes the spot where the baseboard hides the list, the list the Irishman is supposed to get tomorrow night. *Beyond the call of duty,* she hears in her mind. *You should know that he's lied to you about who he is.*

~

There is no tapping on her window that night. No face looking up from the cobbled road. But then, right as she's falling asleep, there's a pounding on the door. By the time she's raced down the stairs, Coletta and August are both there, sleepy and terrified and talking to two German soldiers, who hover at the threshold like wraiths.

"A search," Coletta says to her. "I think. We were almost asleep." She adds the last part as if sleeping would've been the protection they needed.

The men are speaking German and inside the house before questions can be asked. As the door closes, Evelien squints—across the street there was a shape, another soldier. But then Coletta has her hand on her arm and is talking to her in a furious whisper—*nothing is amiss, I hope*—and Evelien is trying to remember the last times she had the paintings or the jewelry out, hoping she put them back properly. In all this time, they've never had a raid. Complacent. Foolish. They thought they'd made it.

The list.

Five names that are decidedly German. That might be known as important men. That could get her arrested, and worse.

She racks her brain for excuses, explanations she can offer, as she follows the soldiers through the rooms. They're opening drawers and removing cushions, tilting back chairs and sweeping rugs aside to look for trapdoors.

"It's a way to scare us," August says calmly. "Nothing more. They're hoping for bribes, for whatever we have. Money, that's what they want. Trust me—they've got nothing in mind."

"The list," Evelien whispers. "If they really look, they'll see it."

"You put it out," Coletta says, "this morning, you said—"

"No, I didn't. Not yet."

And then Evelien hears the creaking stairs, and silence. Again, the creaking, as if someone is stepping on that one spot to test it. The spot where August has hidden his Belgian political cartoons. Illegal to possess.

"August," Coletta says.

He turns to his wife and nods, accepting. "We almost made it."

Evelien rushes around the corner, toward the soldiers who already have the plank up and the cartoons in their hands. And what she sees is that neither of them looks happy, as if maybe they were hoping to not find anything at all.

August steps toward them as they reach for his arms. "It will be all right," he says. "It's almost over and I'll come home."

One of the soldiers holds Coletta back. "You don't know that," she's saying. "August, you don't know that! You could be on a train tomorrow! They don't feed you—they, no—August, tell them I'll go! Tell them it was a mistake and *me*," she says now to the soldier holding her. She gets out of his grasp and turns to him, pointing to herself. "Me, take me instead! I'll go!"

Bribes. If they want bribes, they have the small ring at Coletta's shop that Evelien took for just this purpose.

"*Bitte,*" Evelien says, one of the few German words she knows. They turn to her. "A ring," she continues, pointing to her finger. The one in charge looks at her hand and then is speaking, and the other one looks irritated, as if the night has gone on too long. But pointing to one's ring finger is enough to hint at her meaning, and the men are intrigued. After all, this is almost over. Prisoners will be released in a matter of days, weeks, or a month, but whatever loot they get will be theirs and could finance a future.

One says a few words she doesn't understand and then steps outside. He's gone for only a few minutes, and when he returns, he indicates someone behind him should follow him inside, and there, walking into their parlor, is Joseph.

He doesn't look at her. The men fill him in, and the entire time he studies the floor, nodding now and then, but not looking up. When he finally does, it's August he looks to and addresses, in Flemish.

"They are saying you have mentioned a ring that could persuade them."

"We don't have it here," Evelien says. Now he looks at her, steady. It's gutting, his eyes holding hers. "It's past curfew. I can't get it now, even if I wanted. But it's worth much more than a man who can barely walk. First thing in the morning, I can get it."

For a second more, he holds her gaze. Then coldly, he replies. "Then tonight, they will take him."

And that, they do.

~

When the door closes, Coletta starts pacing, fist held at her mouth. "Why now? Why now, at the very end?"

Joseph was the last to leave. *You brought them here?* she wanted to ask, but the look he gave her silenced her.

"There has to be a reason," Coletta continues.

Evelien takes the lantern and heads to the kitchen where she starts making tea. Coletta, right behind her, places two cups on the table.

"What if something happens to them?" Coletta asks. "To the soldiers. What if they're hurt overnight and no one else knows the agreement and August gets sent off tomorrow?"

The lamp throws shadows. "We'll fix this. As soon as curfew lifts in the morning, get the ring from the shop."

"I don't have it."

Coletta doesn't say more, so Evelien explains. "The little ring you were to keep for emergencies. The Vanheules' ring. That ring."

"Haven't these last years been an emergency? Wasn't it an emergency to eat? To get meat on the table?"

Suddenly, there's a shrieking above, followed by a booming. The floor trembles. "The ring is gone?"

Coletta pulls out a chair and sits heavily. "I don't even care to go downstairs, without him here. *Yes.* The ring is gone. I could've said it was lost. I could've lied. But the truth is I did it for us, about two years ago, to keep us fed. And we never missed it."

"Until now, when we need it! And it wasn't yours to give away. It didn't belong to you."

"Evelien. Be realistic. I didn't know if we'd see the Vanheules again, but *we needed to eat.* And they owed us! All the rich, gone, off drinking wine and mineral water, safe with their paid-for exemptions. And what did they leave us with? Occupation. Germans breathing down our necks. Mansions we're forced to care for while we should be looking after our *own* lives."

"They didn't leave *us* to care for their house—they left me. *I* was in charge of it. Of everything. It's one thing if the ring is gone, but I can tell them it saved a life—"

"You think it didn't? Again, I ask, how do you think we've had meat on our table?"

"But it should've been a discussion! You should've asked me!"

"You're mad at me. From before, you're mad, and I understand and I don't blame you, but tonight let's only address the issue with August, please."

"I thought that's what I was doing. Until the ring we kept to bargain with went missing."

Coletta pours the water into the cups. "What about the other ring?"

"The earth's tear diamond?"

"No. The fake. The copy of it. The decoy."

"They'll tell."

"These men, tonight? No." Coletta stirs her tea, though they've no sugar. It's an absent-minded motion, *the sound of yesteryear*, she calls the clinking of metal against porcelain, the memory of sugary dissolve. "No, these men will see sparkle and feel the weight of the platinum and see the stamp and then they're gone. Out of our house and out of our city and that will be that. And they'd get a deal. The platinum itself is real and worth more than they deserve."

"It's dangerous, if they realize."

"Then give them the real one!"

"*Coletta*, the trouble I'd be in. That ring was Mrs. Vanheule's mother's— one of the few things she remembers—*and* what she might need to live on, now that her husband is—" She stops, unable to say the word.

"Aren't you the one who just accused me of not valuing you enough, and yet here you are putting a ring over August's life?"

"That's not fair." A bright-green light flares under the shutters. Though the night is loud, for a second Evelien thinks she hears something. She looks toward the kitchen door, waiting, but there's nothing more. "It's different," she says at last, quietly.

"Is it?"

"Espionage and endangering a high-ranking officer—*they'd kill me.* August had political cartoons—they won't kill him for that."

"Of Admiral von Schröder! Cartoons of the highest-ranking man here! We don't know what they'll do. And it's not just them we have to worry about—he'll be on a German train bound for Germany with the Allies bombing anything German. You tell me how safe that is." She takes the spoon out of the cup and sets it on an ivory linen. Liquid seeps into the fabric, a wash of dirty color. Finally, she looks up at Evelien. "It was him, wasn't it?"

Thrown, Evelien's heart pounds. "Who?"

"The German soldier. The man translating tonight. He keeps sentry here; I've seen him. He was across the street when the soldiers came in. He brought them here."

"I don't think so," she says, unsure. Because he couldn't have, and yet it makes sense. An entire war without a raid, until a German soldier learned she'd turned on them and put them in danger. *You should know that he's lied to you.* What does she really know about him? He was here, and then so were the other soldiers.

"You don't think so." Coletta sits back in her chair. "You upset him, maybe?"

"How would—"

"I don't have it in me to play this game. Evelien, I recognized him from your sketch pad upstairs. The one under your bed. I found that *drawing.*"

A wave of nausea. *I don't think* you're *one to lecture* me *on lies.* How long ago did she see the drawing? "He was helping me."

"Helping you—and what else?"

There's the accusation. The woman waits, unflinching.

I was also told you were too close to a German.

Coletta's words come back to her, and all at once, Evelien realizes that Coletta *knew*. She wasn't told; she *saw*, with her own eyes, proof that Evelien was too close to a German, and she used that to sell the authenticity of her "voice" and to convince Evelien that she should take a risk and do something dangerous. Now she wonders if there were ever voices, or only manipulations. "You made it up. All of it."

"What are you talking about?"

"Your voices, what you've heard. Your dreams."

"We talked about this."

"You plant things in people's minds. You make them think that they're meant to do certain things."

"Oh, come now. I'm not that powerful."

"But you are. Last night—you had me thinking I was meant to take a risk. I was on the verge of doing something horrible."

"To Germans!" Coletta says, standing. She pushes the chair in to the table, fast, and Evelien's tea spills over. "Something horrible to Germans benefits *us*! Or have you forgotten whose side you're on?"

Evelien sits back. *"But there was no voice."*

"That's what you want to hear? That's what makes a difference to you? Fine, then, this time it was *my* voice. *I* knew it was right. I knew there was opportunity—because I *felt* it. But who would put faith in a feeling *I* have? Who would put that faith in me?"

"*Me.* I always have."

Lips pressed together, still angry, Coletta gets a cloth to clean up the table. "I don't want to know about you and the German."

Evelien nods, aware her silence speaks more than she intends. Finally, she says, "It was him, who gave us the food."

Coletta nods. "So you, too, crossed lines you shouldn't have, so we could eat." When Evelien says nothing more, Coletta nods. "And here we are."

CHAPTER 35

October 18, 1918

As usual, the morning is quieter, as if war were a nocturnal beast that raged through the night but sought rest at dawn. Evelien has her windows uncovered, and though the air is still hazy, she uses the light to study the rings. With confusion, she sits back. The ring she has in the dented tin, the ring that she'd determined was the decoy, is shining brighter. Somehow, it's more alluring. Secretive. Everything tells her *that's* the real one, and that she'd actually mixed them up before.

It's a nightmare, for this to unravel now.

Trying to feel a difference, she holds the one she suspects is real in her right hand and the other in her left. It's hard to tell, both due to the similar weight and the shaking in her hands. Just barely, the one on the right is heavier. Maybe.

She switches them.

And puts the one she thinks is real into the tin, and hides it once more. The other, she puts in the blue velvet box that the real ring came in, when she brought it over from the Vanheules' house.

Then, through the window, there he is. August, walking alongside two Germans who are on horseback. Just the sight of him is a relief. But then, from another direction, there's Joseph, his cane the giveaway, and right next to him is a short, white-haired man who walks with his head down. She squints. She doesn't know who that man is or why he's there, but when the two groups meet in the middle, to confer, and then start in her direction, she understands she's about to find out.

Downstairs, Coletta waits for her. "You know I love you."

And the truth is, Evelien does know this. Everything Coletta does, she does with her full heart and the belief that she's helping—even if she's wrong.

But then Coletta continues. "And I forgive you. For whatever you've done."

Evelien turns to her. "For what *I've* done? You wanted us together, even if we shouldn't have been." She thinks of Becarren, the woman Emiel was seen walking with. *No wife would want another woman to be so close to her husband.* "You made me think if I didn't marry him, I'd lose him as a friend. Is that what you told him too?"

"I *encouraged* you both because I love you and saw—"

"*You saw what you wanted to see!* He was my best friend, and you made me think I'd lose him, and that I'd lose you. And Emiel—he'd have done *anything* for you—even broken his own heart by making a choice he didn't want to."

Coletta starts to open her mouth and Evelien sees a mother's pain, the realization that she hurt her child, and she regrets her words. But before either can say anything, there's a knock on the door, a bit lighter than last night but not something to ignore.

In seconds, August leans against their wall, his hands tied, and Joseph, who Evelien refuses to look at, stands beside the other two soldiers. The smaller man she'd seen on the street enters the room slowly, slightly hunched over, wearing a dark sweater much too hot for the day. His hair is all white, but there are still charcoal-colored strands in his eyebrows, wiry and disheveled.

Joseph addresses them in Flemish. "I will translate. But you should know there are three of us now. I'm not sure one ring will suffice, but we will see what remains due."

Now Evelien looks up at him. The paintings. He doesn't know about the rings because she never told him—but he knows she took paintings for safekeeping. He knows because she told him, proud that she could share her own exposure to art. Now that stupidity will whip back to bite her.

Coletta's voice comes out strong. "No. It's changed—in your favor, yes, but we have terms as well."

Joseph looks to Coletta, surprised.

"What we thought of originally," Coletta continues, "we couldn't find. But it's no matter, it was small. It wouldn't have done. What we *did* find is a different ring, and it will cover all three of you—more even. But we only present it to you if you take it and go. *Nothing* further due."

Joseph confers with the soldiers and then motions to the little man. "Obviously we can't agree until we see what it is you're offering. And its value. For that, we have brought an appraiser."

An appraiser.

The clock ticks. Evelien hears the rasp of her eyes as she blinks. It takes her a moment to realize that everyone is looking at her, her with the box in her hand and a fake diamond that's about to be discovered. She steps forward. This will be the end. To lie to these men, to make them waste their time. There's no telling how angry they will be.

The little man takes the box from her and sits beside the window. From his pocket, he produces a jeweler's loupe. Evelien's eyes follow his fingers. Hangnails, ridged nail beds. He opens the lid and takes out the ring, and there's a sharp intake of breath from one of the soldiers, who then smiles, eager. The other soldier, the one in charge, watches from the corner, wary and reticent. Just barely she glances at Joseph, whose eyes meet hers in a question. Even he thinks she's reckless, for bargaining with this.

The appraiser's eyes narrow. His brows bend together. He sees that it's a fake. It was a matter of time, she knows, till someone caught her. There's too much she's done, too many limits she's tested. But it doesn't matter. There's nothing left to lose. She'll tell them it's her fault. That neither August nor Coletta knew it was fake. She won't let them take August. Not again.

She steps forward, about to speak, but Joseph puts his arm out, stopping her.

"Don't interrupt. Please."

The man continues his inspection of the ring, turning it this way and that, taking in each color and each facet as he rotates it, leaning in so close that she thinks he's smelling the stone, searching for hints of time and pressure and earth. She watches, soon entranced in his passion, feeling a strange calm.

When he finally looks up, she startles, surprised to find him looking at her. Then he looks away. Almost sadly, he puts the ring back in the box, closes it, and hands it to the soldier in the corner. Evelien waits for the chaos, for the anger, the fingertips pressing into her arms as they pull her from the house—but the little man nods, and the wary soldier's face breaks into a smile, and now all the calm is gone and Evelien's legs suddenly feel taxed, her muscles unsteady.

A quick glance at Coletta, who also looks confused, but then must remember what this means because suddenly she's across the room, in front of August, trying to untie him. Joseph goes to them and stands awkwardly on his bad leg so he can help with both hands, and then August has his arms around Coletta and Evelien is still standing there, blinking in the dim morning light, trying to understand as suddenly the door is shutting and the Germans and the little man are all gone, gone to do their work, to fight a losing fight with what Evelien is realizing is a diamond worth more than any of them would dream of in their pocket.

A nightmare come true.

She can't breathe, and drops into the nearest chair, her vision beginning to splinter.

"Evelien," August is saying. "I don't know whether to scold you or kiss you but my God, one night with them was enough. I don't know German, but I can tell you with certainty that I did *not* want to be a part of what they had planned for me."

Evelien nods. Too stunned to speak. She glances toward the stairs; she needs to see the remaining ring, but without the other to compare it to, it won't do much good.

"I'll get you water," Coletta tells August. "You go sit. Did they feed you?"

The appraiser. The look of sadness—why? Because he'd known what she was giving up.

"Not much. But don't trouble yourself," August says, going to a chair in the corner, walking slowly and weakly, despite the fact that he'd had supper in this very house just the night before.

Evelien stands and makes it to the base of the stairs when she feels a hand on her shoulder. Coletta, behind her, has tears in her eyes.

"There are no mistakes," the woman says quietly. "I won't tell him that you didn't mean to give that one. But you were *meant* to. You see that, don't you? *An appraiser.* How could we have known? Thank God. *Thank God.* Somehow, you saved us."

Evelien's not sure who Coletta thinks did the saving—God or Evelien— but already Evelien feels the drag of time, days long and monotonous, life in a little room where nothing belongs to her. She will be indebted forever. Never able to leave. The ring, gone. Without her husband, Mrs. Vanheule could've been relying on that ring for the money it would fetch.

"I will owe her, forever. I won't be able to leave."

"You wanted to leave?" Coletta asks.

"Coletta," August calls from his chair. "I believe you said you were getting food?"

Now Coletta smiles. "Gone for twelve hours and he's forgotten where the kitchen is. Not that there's much there." She takes a step, but stops when a deep booming seems to throttle the room. Her smile disappears. "Cannons?"

Another hard rumble. The frames on the wall rattle, and the reflection in a hanging mirror jumps and blurs. Evelien crosses the room to take it down. "The vizeadmiral's gone. There could be food left. I'll check."

Coletta takes the mirror from her and sets it flat on the floor. "No, you won't. You're not going out in this."

"It always sounds closer than it is."

"Not now, it doesn't. Now it *is* close."

"We could be stuck awhile. We need the food. Any food."

Relenting, Coletta leans in for a hug. It's quick but strong. When she stands back, she looks Evelien straight in the eyes. "You might not agree with how I've done things, and that's up to you, but I need you to know that my intention was always good. You believe that, don't you?"

She waits, and then continues when Evelien nods. "Lord knows we're all so different. Each one of us. And it's exhausting and it's trying, but you ask anybody and our truths are the same: we want what's best for the people we love. We just get there differently."

And though Evelien knows Coletta meant well, what's happened has put a spotlight on the truth of their relationship, because Evelien is *not* her daughter. She never has been. Marrying Emiel didn't change that, and it wasn't right to Emiel. She remembers the distance that grew between herself and Alixa when Evelien informed her of their marriage. Even her friend had glimpsed it—the way Evelien was forcing herself into a role that was not hers. And yet Evelien, determined to be blind, instead blamed differing nationalities for their falling-out.

The tapestry of her life has come unwound. The family she thought she had. The knowledge of where she'll be tomorrow, and who she'll have with her. Even the job that kept her employed and surrounded with art, the thinnest connection to what she loved. All of it, upended. Right at the end.

More than anything, she is terrified.

And though Coletta is saying something, Evelien is already at the door, a drone of worry in her mind. Then, a single crash and impact, too close. It sifts upward through her feet like a nerve gone wild. Stepping outside, she stands beneath the beautiful tragedy of the sky, bruised clouds lit with sun and stray ashes that drift like snow.

CHAPTER 36

What church bells remain jangle on their own, and windowpanes shiver in their sills. The onslaught at the front is steady, and closer than ever. In the air, a sense of impending, inevitable conclusion.

The city itself feels exposed, caught in a vicious gaze. All the citizens must be hiding, battened down and praying, though now and then, Evelien catches movement in a window, and a face that stares out at her, curious. The only people out are soldiers, and only two check her pass. The others watch the sky or street corners, nervous, as if staring down the barrels of their future.

Then, a noise. Low grade and growing—and not from the sky. A deep rumble that vibrates the ground beneath her feet. Yellow flowers growing between the bricks of a crumbled wall begin to shake, the petals trembling. She looks up and freezes.

A tank. Armored and battle-weary.

Maybe it's the steal beast's slow lumber, but she has the irrational feeling that if she doesn't move, it won't see her, that it will continue on its hulking way. It starts to cross a street, a wake of crushed cobbles in its tracks. Seconds spread out. The steel treads grind. And grind. And grind. Frozen, she lifts her gaze enough to see that the German iron cross on its flank is dinged from bullets. Maybe it's because it moves so slowly, but somehow she hasn't registered that bit by bit the barrel of its gun has been moving—*is* still moving—until its black eye is staring her down. A leap in her throat. Futilely, she holds up the pass in her left hand. Then she puts her head down and starts walking, feeling the pummel of her heartbeat.

One step. Two steps. A block away and she still feels it at her back. Even when she rounds the corner, it's there. Even when she knows it's not, when she's walked far enough away, still the burning continues, like a red-hot target on her back.

She doesn't know if she can do this. She wants to curl into a ball in a forgotten house and disappear. But they need the food and she made a promise, to take care of Emiel's parents, and that's what she'll do. The one vow she won't break.

Two blocks from the house, she sees him. Joseph. Standing on the center of a bridge with a map in his hands, now and then marking the page with a pencil. A pause in her step as she decides what to do, and at last goes straight to him. His head turns. Standing behind him, she faces the other direction, hands on the stone wall of the bridge.

Squinting into the day's red light, she says, "You brought them to my house."

There is the grinding of his cane as he turns toward her. "Look at me," he says. Reluctantly, she turns. His eyes are tired. He clearly hasn't slept, whatever schedule he has most likely thrown into chaos by the end. "I did *not* bring them to your house."

She wants to believe him, but the timing is too much. "You're outside and suddenly they're there—"

"*I keep sentry here.* Of course I was outside. I saw soldiers going to your door—"

"Then the most important thing I was to keep and protect, the ring, is lost."

"You didn't lose the ring."

"Bartered, a payment. The word doesn't—"

"It wasn't the real ring."

Now she's yelling, not caring who hears. "Of course it was! What appraiser wouldn't spot a crystal?"

It wasn't the real ring.

Quieter now. "How do you know there was a—"

"*Because you talked about it.* With your mother-in-law, in your kitchen. I went back to find you. I was in the alley, and it was clear as day. You're lucky it was me—talking of fooling Germans, it's not something you want overheard by anyone, even other Belgians."

She's reeling, trying to understand. "But the appraiser—"

"Who found the appraiser?" He's frustrated. But then, out of the corner of his eye, he must see someone watching them, because he turns, again, to face the water. "I didn't know what it would look like and thought an 'expert' opinion would help sell it. I told him to expect a fake. He's a family friend—someone my mother knew, and he hated my father as he hates most Germans. And if you care, you should know he won't be in danger. Those men are gone. And were more than happy when I said I'd find them later for my cut, which of course I won't, just as they won't be found."

She hates that it happens, but she's crying. Overwhelmed by relief and forgiveness and even hope, as stupid as it may be. She swipes at her tears with her sleeve. "I have the real one? You're sure?"

When he turns back, he faces the corner of the bridge, though his gaze is steady on her. "The man, the appraiser, said it was a good imitation. But an imitation."

"I had it right." As she continues, she watches him, wanting to be right in this as well. "Why did you do this?"

Giving up on pretense, he faces her once more. "Is it not obvious?"

Heat rushes to her cheeks. "No—I thought—" She pauses. At the start of the bridge, an older man has seen them and stopped. Assessing the situation, he turns the other way. To Joseph, she says, "The vizead-miral said you've lied to me about who you are."

"I don't think I'm the only one—"

"*Of course* I lied to you! I didn't want to get in trouble, for the garden!"

"You worked for him the whole time and I didn't know, and then you turned the light on—"

"I was wrong."

"*No.* You weren't. You should've left it on."

Thrown. She doesn't understand.

He continues. "I would've deserved it. The men in there, they would've deserved it. All of them. What we call valor, what might earn us medals and awards and honors, your side could call war crimes. And the same of your soldiers."

"You're saying I *should* have left the light on. You're on the side—"

"Stop," he says and then shakes his head, as if sobered with a reassessment. "*He said you were working with him,* that you could be trusted, and *you turned in your friend.*"

Now she stays silent. Like him, unsure of what she *can* say. All their words, hedging truth. At last, "I want to speak plainly."

"*Can* we?" he asks. Either imploring her to do so or questioning if it's even possible.

She feels the push of all she wants to admit, along with the one thing she knows she cannot say: *I have a list with your name on it.* Nothing else matters, because she can't get past that fact.

At the start of the bridge, the old man is now obvious in waiting for them to leave, facing them and not looking way.

"The truth is," Joseph says, "I can't come back from what I've done."

"From the men you've killed?"

Though he nods, he looks down, unable to meet her eyes.

"Did you"—she pauses, not wanting to ask the question, but needing to—"did *you* commit a war crime?" The closest she can get to asking what she needs to.

Now he looks up, his eyes shining. "Never."

Never. Emphatic. "Then, Joseph. Everyone—"

A sound. He holds up his hand. Motorcars and horses. The world with one foot in the past and one in the future. The present nothing but a confusion.

He takes a step back from her. Even the old man at the mouth of the bridge turns, hurrying the other way. "Go home. The streets won't be safe." A pause as the men on horses emerge down the street. He takes a few steps back. "I wish," he starts to say, but then stops as the sound of the motorcars grows.

Frustrated, she asks, "What do you wish?"

He looks at her. "Like you, I wish we could've arrived here differently."

CHAPTER 37

She leaves him there. The choking day thick around him, the white noise of battle constant. As she walks away, she realizes that was it; she will never see him again. With the thought, she misses a step and juts her hand out to stop from falling, but then keeps going. She will not stop. She will not turn around. She will think later. Feel later. Head down, feet forward.

Confusion. If his name is on this list, then even if he regrets what he's done, does that matter? He very plainly said he did something he can't come back from. And if he tells her that he and all the men in that house deserved to die, shouldn't she believe him?

Yet everything he's done is contrary.

What's clear is that he wants to trust her, but doesn't. Not fully. The same way she feels about him.

But none of it matters. Because that was it.

The streets are empty, and she lets the tears fall, not caring. She needs any food left behind at the Vanheules' first. Then she can shelter at home and steep in a sadness that's starting to take over.

At the front door, she stops, afraid of what she'll find inside.

But what she finds is a sense of release. The first claw of war pried away. The hall is empty. The rooms dark. The vizeadmiral must have come home one last time for his belongings and closed all the shutters and curtains, sealing off the light. Standing in the hall, she knows she should check all the rooms, but with another deep bass explosion, she decides she needs to be with Coletta and August. Get whatever stray bits of food remain, go home, and stay there until it's safe.

Beside the front door is a gas lamp. Moving down the hall, she sees that the vizeadmiral's office door is slightly open. Inside, all is as it was. The same newspapers, even a coat slung over his chair. But one thing has changed: the photo of him and his wife is gone. Once again, Mrs. Vanheule is there, smiling into the room. The list, she knows, is gone as well. And though she's happy to see Mrs. Vanheule back in her rightful place, she'd always liked the photo of the vizeadmiral and his wife. Such a serious man, so softened when he spoke of her. Two years ago, on the day of their anniversary, he'd offered a linzer cookie to Evelien. *June 16th is my Christmas,* he said. *My day to celebrate.* Out of everything here, she's glad he remembered the photo.

The floor trembles. Hurrying, she goes to the kitchen, where she spots two canvas bags on the butcher block and an envelope with her name on it. Cautiously, she looks inside the first bag: Food. Cans and jars and tins of meat. The second bag: potatoes, onions, rutabagas. Everything packed and ready for her.

Another explosion. The windowpanes rattle. She tosses the envelope inside the bag and grabs both the handles, slipping them on her wrists so she can hold the lamp as she heads back to the front door. Quickly, she eyes the entrance to the parlor. All looks as it did when she was last here. Paintings still in place, the victrola silent in the corner. Another explosion booms somewhere too close, and the crystal coupes on the enamel tray rattle.

Time to go.

It's only as she's stepping into the hall that she glances back at the mantel. One thing is gone: the gift she gave him, the small silver frame with the sketch of lavender.

CHAPTER 38

The jagged gable of the house with the ruined garden is at the end of the street, roof edges carved into the reddened sky. Parsley, chives, whatever herbs are growing there—already she's justifying a stop, but the truth is she hopes he might be there.

A quick jiggle of the doorknob, four times while pushing to the right, and she's in. The light is hazy, speckled particles bright in long motes, like a ghostly Roman world of misty ruins and pillars. Right away, she can tell the house is empty.

Leaves are dusty. Another patch of wall has crumbled, and new rivulets of water seep from the corners of what windows remain, as if the house itself is mourning its imminent end. She touches a tomato leaf and sees the start of another bloom on its branch, bits of yellow about to unfurl. Even if the house isn't torn down right away, the weather will turn and the plant won't have time to bring the flower to fruit. It's sad, to put so much energy into something so futile. Then a glance at the green chaise, spliced in a broken shaft of sun. Now she wishes she'd never stepped inside. So much over, right as it begins.

Then the noise of planes. Within her, there is the illogical idea that this house wouldn't be hit twice, though she knows it's not true. Everything, she thinks, all of life is woven with lies necessary to take another step. Soothing white lies.

Then she remembers: Joseph said he'd left something for her here. Looking around, there's no fertilizer, no plants out of place. He thought better of it, she realizes.

Turning to the broken staircase, she's nervous. How do you say goodbye to a place into which you poured your heart? One broken step at a time, she thinks.

Immediately, she takes in her odds-and-ends walls. All the items she's practiced drawing, little bits and pieces from her life, an evolution of her work these past years. Then her version of the *Landscape Near Antwerp*, the Scheldt River and the hush of dunes, dark and dull with lack of color, as if caught in an eternal night. When this is over, she thinks, if she can get back before the house is torn down, she'll slather these walls with color. Fevered, blissful color. Even if only for an afternoon, these walls will surge with life, brimming and seen.

Then the last wall—she feels it. Letting it go will mean leaving it once again: the field and her old house, the storm that raged and churned, her mother's torment stirred to life. She doesn't want to see it and wonders if maybe she should just leave, walk down the stairs and avoid her mother's pain and her own pain and everything that was once wrapped into her childhood, even the violin from the attic she'd drawn and the idea that her silent father had once played music so beautifully that her mother thought she could love him.

But she can't leave it. Not like that. So she turns, and when she does, her breath catches. Because it's her, Evelien, drawn in the upper corner. Her face, continued from that one line she'd drawn before hurting herself, done in profile as someone gazing down, taking it all in, observing and understanding. Her hair swirls with the storm in curving, sinuous lines. Bits of flax flowers and petals appear caught in the current. And the lift and angle of her eyes, that feature she'd thought turned her suspicious or guilty, instead looks knowing, and intrigued, as though she's entertained and enticed by the world, as though she has a secret. She smiles. Combined with the magic swirl of her hair, there is the impression that when she closes her eyes, her world only grows brighter.

Standing back, she takes it in as a whole. Through his eyes, she is beautiful.

She drops the bags of food onto the floor and sits heavily. Worn. This, before her, is the glimpse of his work as an artist she craved, one that makes her feel she knows him a little better, which leaves her more confused. She thinks of what he'd said to her on the bridge, his insistence he couldn't come back from what he'd done. And though she doesn't know the details of his actions, everything tells her that she was right about him, and at his core, he is good.

And then she thinks of the letter the vizeadmiral wrote to her, and fishes it from the bag. Unfolding it, she sees a page of his tight, ordered script.

Evelien,

First, I must apologize. After I saw you last, I learned that Petrus was killed in action, fighting for the Allies. A man who'd pledged German loyalty, fighting against Germany? Of course they forced him to fight, but I realized that too late. In my anger and suspicion, I set into motion a search of your house, which of course yielded nothing. I do apologize. But the real reason I write . . . you should know that Joseph will not leave until he knows you are safe. He has told me as much, not only because he clearly has affection for you but because he feels it is his duty, and I fear he has lost all sense of self-preservation and could be seeking punishment, though he should not. If you see him, please try to impart on him the urgency of leaving. The Allies will shoot before they ask questions, and then, if by some miracle he survives their arrival, he will be taken prisoner and may be tried for things he in truth did not do and which I cannot explain in a letter. I will have too much on my shoulders and cannot add his fate to that burden.

Please know that I am sorry for what I did. I do not pretend this food will make up for the visit to your house, but it's my hope it may at least make for one or two nights without worry. Again, please tell him to leave, if only for my wife's sake. Tell him that he should think of her, if no one else, because she cannot lose her husband as well as her brother.

Sincerely,

VAdm. Braun

CHAPTER 39

Joseph. The vizeadmiral's brother-in-law.

This fact has pried everything loose, all her assumptions and understanding. Even the photo the vizeadmiral had on his desk—that was Joseph's *sister*. Her eyes. Evelien sees it now. How light they were in the black and white. The set of her jaw. Even the slight arch in her brows.

He will be taken prisoner and may be tried for things he in truth did not do.

What did Joseph say before? That for trying to desert, he should've been shot. *Now it's spun as if I deserve a medal when what I deserved was a court-martial.* Whatever it is that the vizeadmiral said he did, all that matters is that Joseph did *not* do it, and that the favor a man was trying to do for his brother-in-law might turn out disastrous.

What's also clear is that they've reached the end.

The second she walks out the door, she feels the change, the intensity of an imminent culmination. Planes swoop in formation and giant machinery rumbles through town, mounted with howitzers. No one is on the streets save for soldiers, all hurrying north. Everywhere, gray-green uniforms; gaunt, unshaven faces; and worried eyes. She rushes through the streets, trying to get home while looking for him.

But he's not at his usual spot. Nor the block over. Maybe he left. Maybe he was forced to go.

Then she is on her street. Above, a noise. She peers up. One British plane is cut off from the others, like the smallest of animals separated from the pack.

A woman shouts from her door, waving Evelien inside.

Evelien yells back that she's almost home before the woman shakes her head, as if angry, and the door slams shut.

The plane is so slow that it seems suspended, frozen. Her heart aches for this plane, this pilot, abandoned but trying to catch up. And then there is the loud, angry churn of a German bomber coming in. She forgets herself, watching them shadow each other in a dance. Something falls from the plane on top. Pilots toss bricks or grenades, ropes even, whatever they can to hit or entangle other planes, but whatever it was doesn't matter because within a split second, the air is pulverized with gunfire and she's running, fast.

Everything becomes sound. A soaring sound that grows and envelops her and ends in a smash of thunder. Then a carmine bloom over the rooftops. Tails of wagging smoke.

Above now, only one plane. Before she can tell which one, she starts to run.

~

The door slams behind her, and she scrambles for the flashlight on the ground before racing to the paintings. She will get them, the jewelry—including the ring she now knows is real—and the remaining sketch pad from under her bed. She will store it all in the cellar where it's safer, where she may have no choice but to shelter.

At the pocket door, she feels for the string and pulls it toward her. She needs to hurry, but the thought of the painting snagging, jamming within the wall, has her heart racing. A little farther. Her hand shakes. She hears herself breathing, and somewhere behind that Coletta's voice, calling for her.

At last, she has it. She holds the Braque with both hands, walking as if the ground were unstable, and takes it to the top of the cellar stairs, where Coletta meets her. Then she gets the others, and informs her mother-in-law she still needs her sketch pad and the ring.

"The ring's useless! Trash! Forget it!"

And so Evelien quickly explains that the appraiser lied, and Coletta studies her in confusion.

"The appraiser lied? Why?"

"So we'd get August."

"And the ring . . ." Her sentence trails, as if she's not yet found the words. "Get it, then. Hurry."

Upstairs, Evelien pries loose the board in the window frame and grabs the tin with the ring. Then she's turning to the bed, to get her sketch pad, when she sees the baseboard where she hid the list. Though the likelihood of anyone searching their house tonight is slim to none, she's begun to glimpse the implication of these names—and the fact that Joseph's is on there, for what she's realizing is something he didn't do. She can't leave the list where there's *any* chance it might be discovered.

Quickly, she goes to the spot where the baseboard gapes from the wall, but there's nothing. Getting as close as she can, forehead against the plaster, she tries to see if the envelope slipped farther down, then tries to shove her fingers painfully between the wood.

Still nothing.

The noise outside is increasing; the edges of their city must be under attack. She hurries to Coletta. "I can't find the list."

"The *list*?" Coletta says, taking the ring from her. "The list that you were supposed to put out for the man tonight? He won't come, not in this, but—"

"I took care of it," August, standing on the bottom step, calls up.

Evelien peers down the stairs. "What do you mean?"

He looks up proudly. "I knew it would be bad tonight. I told you. They've blown up bridges and water towers and set fire to the Oude

Gentweg, all their lovely kraut parting gifts. I figure no one's coming to get it in this, *but* to be safe, I put it behind the brick, where you said. So you wouldn't have to." He smiles.

"It's out there, now?"

"That's what I said. So get down here where it's safe."

Her ears pound with her heart and the sounds of the chaos outside. She feels sick. "I can't be the one to do that."

"To get down here?" he asks, confused.

"*No*, to hand over those names."

"But they're German names."

"What if the man comes, even tomorrow morning, before I can get it back? No one can get that list."

"Evelien, he *asked* you to do this. You were *meant* to get the names. These are bad men if—"

"Not all of them," she says. "At least not one. One was a mistake."

Now Coletta looks down at August and then at Evelien. "Oh," she says softly. Understanding. She glances at the door and then takes a deep, shaking breath. "I'll do it."

Coletta's already got her hand on the front door when Evelien realizes what's happening.

"*Coletta,*" Evelien says a few times, and then louder. Coletta lets go of the knob. "This doesn't have to do with you." She touches the woman's shoulder, forcing her to turn. "You don't need to prove yourself to me. I know you love me. I do."

All around them, the world sounds as if it's breaking to pieces.

CHAPTER 40

A flailing reach at the end of a rope, the high arc of the crescendo: Evelien feels the culmination the second she steps outside. Above, the sky is crowded, flashing lights, shelling and antiaircraft, along with the acrid bite of smoke and the bone-deep booming of cannons, closer than ever.

In the alley, outside their kitchen door, she feels the length between where she is and where she needs to be as impossible. But it's only six houses. That's it. Six houses to get the list. Running, that's six seconds. Then she'll get the list and maybe even save him, the German who doesn't wish to be saved.

Now is the time. She glances up, and then down, and it begins.

One. She takes off, staying close to the buildings as she runs, hoping that what's left of eaves or rooflines might protect her. *Two. Three. Four. Five.*

She stops. Fast. A pain in her back from the jolt. There, on the ground, by the back door of the fifth house, is a cylinder the length of an infant. An unexploded shell. Even in the flashing light she sees it clearly, her fear becoming that precision tool that focuses and clarifies. Shells are found in the city and outside, in roads and streams and fields, so many in fields that people say when this is over, the country will have years of iron harvests. Many never go off, while others are just in need of a touch, a nudge, or even the vibration of a rolling tank.

But how do you know which shell is a dud and which is waiting?

She's one house from her goal, mere steps. Above the roofline, a distant explosion unfurls in the night sky.

There's a tug, an awareness, that she does *not* have to do this, that Coletta was right and no one would come out on a night like tonight. But another part of her understands the risk Joseph took to save August, and knows that should something happen to her and the list is out here, anyone could get it tomorrow, or the next day, or the day after that. For all she knows, it's already gone.

Underlying it all: a feeling that if she's survived this long, she is not meant to die now.

Slowly, carefully, she starts walking. Sticking to the edge of the building.

Chances are the shell is a dud and no danger. With each step, she watches its dark gleam. Around her, the battle's screech and clamor are steady and relentless.

Then she is beside the shell, and only now does she look forward. Cautiously, she walks straight ahead.

She's there. At the house. Counting up, four up from the ground. The brick moves in place.

"Stop!"

She turns. Joseph stands on the other side of the shell, his eyes on its gleam, his hand out as if to order her to halt.

"Don't move," he continues.

"I'm being careful. I saw it."

Again, he tells her to stop. But he doesn't know, and so she continues.

"There's something I need to get back," she says as she slowly wedges the brick out. Holding it in her left hand, she reaches with her right into the darkness, until she feels the envelope beneath her fingertips, but then hears another whizzing soar above her and a booming. Then, with horror, she feels shaking. Slight, but enough.

And in this moment, she understands it's inescapable. This end. *And here we are,* she thinks.

She braces herself. For the whoosh of wind and the blast of heat, for the noise and the fury and the callous claim of this one moment, this one crack in time that will not let her past. And in this, she is suddenly overcome with a wordless yet loud desire and anger. To have made it this far. Both of them. To have struggled and survived and fought and prayed, and then to die, right now, in the eleventh hour—it's not right. Because she *wants* to continue. Even with loss and confusion. Even with everything she thought she knew and understood gone and a future that's solitary and uncertain. All that matters is that there *is* a future.

All of this in one beat. One pummel of resolve. One heartbeat of determination.

It's only when she moves her hand that she realizes she's still there. She looks to him. He's got one arm out for balance, as if he, too, was braced for an explosion. In between them, the shell is intact.

She smiles, disbelieving, and is about to put the envelope into her dress pocket when he yells at her again.

"Stop."

"I got what I needed; now I'll go around. I'll meet you on the other side." To avoid any vibrations from wedging the brick back in place, she sets it on the ground, gently.

"No," he says. "I mean put that back."

"The brick?" she asks, until she sees that he's looking at the envelope. "You don't know what it is."

"It's the list. Isn't it?"

Thrown, she's silent as he continues.

"I'm the one who ordered it. And it needs to go where you promised it would go."

Her first thought is he ordered its retrieval so he could destroy it, so he could absolve himself. But that's not what he's saying.

He's telling her he's the one who informed the resistance about it.

"The vizeadmiral told me about it," he continues. "Back when he trusted me."

"And you told the Irishman?"

"I don't know an Irishman. Everyone's separated. No one knows who's who. I only knew about the list, and that he wouldn't let me in his house, not after I tried to desert. But then he had us over." He pauses. "And there you were. And I couldn't be sure, but it made sense, that you were the one they asked to get it."

Have you been loyal to the vizeadmiral?

She'd thought, at the time, that he was trying to determine if she meant the vizeadmiral harm.

"I work there," she says.

"*I didn't know that.* I never would've—" He stops. "I was told it wasn't successful. That the person couldn't get—"

"That was *you.* That was you, trying to get into the vizeadmiral's office." The doorknob, the way it shook as someone tried to get into the room, while she stood there, frozen.

He nods. "You need to put it back. Put it wherever it's supposed to be. And we need to go."

"But—" She stops and holds up the envelope. "Your name is here."

And surprisingly, he nods. "I know."

He will be taken prisoner and may be tried for things he in truth did not do.

"But you didn't—"

"I've done enough to earn my place. It will help make things right. For everyone. Myself included. Please, if someone's supposed to get it, you need to leave it."

Above, three planes pass over. Shoving the envelope in her pocket, she turns and starts walking away from him, away from the shell.

"Evelien!"

She makes a U with her hand, indicating he should go around the building. "Go to the other side. I'll meet you there. For now, the list stays with me."

~

Slowly, she walks. Then faster. And faster. And when farther off, she begins to run. At the end of the alley, she turns onto the street to loop back around, to approach her house from the front, but then there's another blast, somewhere far away, and it's nothing, a slight noise and tremble, which is why she's not ready for what comes next: a blast that is here. Next to her. Around her. Everywhere.

A whoosh of air and noise as the street jumps up to meet her, followed by a moment where everything, all of life, pauses.

Silence.

She blinks in the dust. Feels her elbow against the cobblestones. Feels that she's on her back. Her ears are ringing and there is no other sound. She rolls her head to the side to see that the house just behind her is mostly gone, which makes no sense, but then does, but then doesn't. There is something hot on her face, and when she touches the skin by her temple, it feels wet, and then she's coughing and crawling, then standing and walking awkwardly down the road, waiting to see him, searching for him, scanning the thick smoke, but he's not there. How far could he have gotten with his cane? In her heart, she is already begging. Unspoken bargains swirl within her, all the sacrifices she will make if only he is okay. And Coletta and August—they're far enough from the blast, she thinks. She prays. She needs to get to them. She needs to get to him. She needs to move.

One foot in front of the other. Her eyes burn with dust. The powder and granules of bricks and cobblestones and who knows what else clog in her throat. When she sees her house, intact with its roof in place— even the bridge room a solid, undisturbed, hovering expanse—she feels relief like nothing she's ever known. Slowly she passes Coletta and August's front door, and notes that at the corner of the street, the air is clear and yet the road is empty.

He is not there.

~

She stops walking, arm out, hand against brick. Leaning down, her head swims. Then she's looking up again, her eyes taking in everything. Doorways, alleyways, the corner of the street where he should be, but where he is not. She forces herself to continue, and makes it to the corner, where she tells herself he will be waiting.

But when she rounds the bend, she is alone. Blinking and uncomprehending. There's no one.

She wants to sit and cry. To allow herself this one moment, to let everything spill over before the rest begins.

Then suddenly he's there. Emerging from the alley, one hand on his cane and the other reaching out to her, urging her to hurry.

He doesn't say anything when he's got her arm, and she's not sure who's holding whom up, as both are limping and neither is moving very fast. Then she's got the back door open and is stepping inside, calling for Coletta and August—at least she thinks she is; she's still uncertain what sounds are inside her and what are out. Joseph, however, has stopped at the threshold, unmoving. And then Coletta and August rush into the room.

"She's done nothing!" August yells, racing toward them. "Get! Go! Leave us!"

Evelien is saying "no" but she's not sure if anyone hears her over the noise and the din of battle or maybe just the din inside her mind. And then Coletta is at Evelien's side, wiping the cooling heat from her temple with her sleeve, holding her arm, holding her up, and Evelien sees her eyes flicker between her and Joseph right as he turns to go.

"Wait, stop," Coletta says to him.

"*Coletta,*" August says. "He's a German! Let him go!"

"He's the translator, the one who found the appraiser," Coletta says. "He's why you're back."

"He's German! Get him out of here!"

Evelien is yelling. Her mouth is moving, and they are all looking at her.

She's trying to usher out the sounds in her mind, to calm the rage within her. A count to ten, to clear everything. They're watching her, and the world begins to settle, sounds sifting into cracks and disappearing. When she speaks, she does so quietly, so quietly that they lean toward her to hear. "You cannot send him out there, and if you do, I will go too."

"Please," Joseph says. "I don't want to cause problems. I can go—"

"He's a soldier," August says, confused.

"Does it matter what he is?" Coletta snaps. "My God, August, let the man inside."

"But who," August manages to say, trying to make sense of things, but Coletta holds up her hand.

"August," she says. "He is coming inside." She turns back to Evelien and Joseph. "Both of you, into the cellar, now."

CHAPTER 41

It's ironic, she knows, that in the midst of war, the possibility of her own death was never something she felt acutely. But it wasn't real to her. Not with any sort of immediacy or consequence. The future was always so certain, the course so stiflingly set, that she was gifted the luxuries of *assumption* and *dissatisfaction*. But now, now that her future has unraveled and nothing is certain, now is when she understands how much she wants to continue and how easily she could lose the one thing that's truly essential: herself.

For once, she goes to the cellar without question.

Downstairs, Joseph stands at the last step as Coletta takes her aside to stare into her eyes, searching for signs of a head injury. "To be safe, you should stay awake. My mother always said a hat would make you warm, and if you hit your head you don't go to bed."

"My mother said that sewing white linen with black thread attracts death and picking poppies will bring lightning."

Coletta smiles. "Tonight, we're taking my mother's advice." Then, in a whisper, "Do you love him?"

Evelien is thrown by the question. She tries to find the right words, and then settles on the truth. "I don't know. It was the start. But it's different than with—"

"It's all right—I don't." Coletta stops, then sighs. "He *is* just over there. So it's not *was*. It's not past tense." Another pause. "But do you still believe Emiel is alive?"

If Evelien's husband returned tomorrow, she would tell him he deserves more. That she deserves more. But Coletta must believe that Emiel's death is the only way Evelien could move on, and so Evelien feels the lie form naturally. "I do. I still think he is alive." *In our hearts, we want to be soothed. We want to believe.* A world filled only with truth—sharp, grating truth—is, quite simply, not one that's livable.

There's shine in Coletta's eyes, but she quickly looks away, then tells Evelien she'll be with August in their chambers on the other side of the cellar. Evelien knows it's to give her and Joseph privacy, and understands what this costs her.

~

Above, through their floor and furniture and ceilings and walls, the war thunders on, louder than ever. Evelien sits at a small black table with two chairs. On top is the chess set—left mid-play—and a glass oil lamp, one that Coletta and August light only when absolutely necessary. Evelien knows they lit the lamp for her, so she'd feel safe, and though her view of Coletta has come undone, it now seems to be settling into something new.

"They're here," Joseph says. "Or they will be. The Belgians. In Bruges. I need to surrender."

She remembers the vizeadmiral's words. "No. They'll shoot first and ask questions later. Wait this out, then go back to Germany with no one shooting at you."

"It doesn't work like that."

"*He* knows how it works, and he wrote me a letter, begging you not to get caught. He said you could be tried for something you didn't do."

"I told you, it doesn't matter. I've done enough."

He takes a seat across from her, carefully moving the chess game to the side. When he puts the lamp in the center of the table, he studies her, then reaches forward to brush her hair from her forehead, to peer at her cut. She raises her hand to it, feeling the hardened blood.

"What is the list?" she asks.

He says nothing.

"I've risked a lot for it," she continues. "I deserve to know."

At last he nods, accepting. "It's a personal interest of Vizeadmiral Braun's. Something even people above him didn't approve of, which is why he kept it at his house."

"But what is it?"

"A list of what he called *celebrations*. People to celebrate. Men who weren't officially recognized for their actions. Men with promise. Who didn't like how things had gone or how they would go. Men with plans, who proved themselves by—"

"Going beyond the call of duty."

He watches her, steady. "In ways that should be brought to justice."

The vizeadmiral, she understands, included his brother-in-law on this list, in what he thought was a favor.

Celebrations.

June 16th is my Christmas, she remembers him saying of his anniversary. *My day to celebrate.* The title of the list—*166.* 16 June. 16-6.

Joseph glances toward the stairs. "There's no place to put it now. That house is gone. Give it to me, and I'll make sure it gets where it needs to go."

"I was promised a letter, from Emiel, in exchange."

He nods, taking this in. "All right. But the list needs to be seen, now, before the people named know to hide. I can find a way for that to happen. I *will* find a way. If you believe anything, I need you to believe this."

"But you'll be—"

"Punished. As I should be."

A deep rumble, and the chess pieces shake. "The men left here didn't have an option to leave. They didn't have a brother-in-law who'd move mountains to keep them safe."

A sad smile. "He told you. I thought he might." With his thumb, he scoots the queen on the board away from the edge. "None of it's simple. But I think we should use our time to talk about something else. Something pleasant. I want to see your drawings."

"My sketch pad." She forgot the remaining pad upstairs, under her bed. So alarmed when she saw the list wasn't behind the baseboard that she forgot to grab it. Already she's up, her hand on the banister.

"No," he says, standing. "You stay. Tell me where it is."

But there's something she needs to do, and already she's climbing the stairs. "No, there're a few places it could be—it's faster if I go."

In the parlor, the noise is louder. She takes the stairs two at a time and once in her room races to her bed, where the large sketch pad is still hidden beneath. It doesn't take long, this mission she's on, only a couple of extra minutes, and when she's back downstairs, he looks up, expectant.

"May I?" he asks, motioning to her sketch pad.

When she hands it to him, he sets it on his knees, showing a reverence even in the care he takes opening the first page. Then he nods, as if something's been confirmed. She watches his face as he studies each sketch, imagining she knows the image by the movement of his eyes. When he gets to one, he leans back in his chair and breathes in deeply.

"The drawing of you?" she asks.

He nods. Quietly, "You thought of me that night."

"I did."

"I thought of you, as well. I was surprised. I didn't think I would." He turns another page, then traces a form with his finger. "This all could be part of a series. Keep with this."

She's about to answer, *If I can*, when she realizes there's no reason why she can't. Not anymore. The fact is, it's not about being a good or bad mother. And it's not about her heart coming around; it's about accepting what's already in her heart. For years she's lined up justifications—a husband away fighting, the time it would take from her art—all to try to soften the edge of what she felt was wrong with her. But the truth is, she doesn't want to be a mother. At least not now. And she doesn't want to be married. And maybe that's all right. And if later she decides to have children, she knows she'll stand a better chance of being a good mother by honoring what she loves. By accepting what she loves.

"That's it, isn't it?" she asks.

He lifts his head, confused.

She thinks of her mother. Herself. All the strife that's come from thinking there's one right and correct way. "Acceptance."

"We could certainly use more of it," he says, looking down again at a sketch.

Then she tells him what she learned about Leona, that she once loved music and must have dreamed of a different life. That the mold of her world was too tight to allow for variance.

"They needed her on the farm," he says. "Your father, too, it sounds like. That's how it goes, for many people. Not just on farms, of course, but in life. People are told how their lives should go."

I imagine a life without what you love is hard.

Evelien feared ending up sad and angry, marked with blame and disappointment, like her mother. Yet now she sees just how close she was to that very path.

He leans back in the chair, and the wood creaks. "You know that loss played into the day of the storm. Her unhappiness. It wasn't because of you."

"I'm seeing that."

"So you don't still blame yourself?"

"Not as much," she says honestly. And already she senses a difference. As if fuel's been removed from a fire. Things are settling. Dissipating. Even the fact that she's down here, now, her breathing steady—something's changed, even if just from the realization that her bigger fear is losing herself.

He reaches to a pawn on the chessboard but doesn't move it, just turns it. Around and around.

"I'm not the only one," she says, and he lets go of the piece. "You, and your blame. If the families of the men knew you, if they met you, they'd see you're a good person who was put into something horrible. Just like their boys. Just like everyone. And they'd understand."

He won't meet her eyes, but nods, just barely.

"But you'll never meet those families," she continues. "And they'll never get a chance to look you in the eye and give you that forgiveness. *And you know that.* And that must make it easier."

Now he looks up at her.

"Because you have nothing to do but suffer through it. And that's what you want, isn't it? That's part of the punishment. You know they'd forgive you if they met you. You know that. The real issue is that you didn't need it from them to begin with. You need it from yourself."

CHAPTER 42

October 19, 1918

Past midnight. The cellar is cold, and they each have a blanket, hers a quilt Coletta made, and his a plaid throw. Sleep is a drowsy enticement.

"You can't," he says, brushing her hair away from her eyes. "Your mother-in-law said not to let you sleep, and quite honestly, I won't go against her."

All night, there's been a feeling that they need to cram everything—confessions, hopes, fears, favorite foods, favorite seasons—into these dark, booming hours. Now and then he takes her hand, as if trying to be respectful of Coletta and August, but unable to resist the touch.

Evelien smiles, drowsily, with an idea. "Stay here. Don't look. Keep your eyes closed."

On the far side of the room are the paintings, still wrapped and covered. First, she'll start with the framed Matisse sketch, Mrs. Vanheule's sentimental piece. It's small, a young woman smiling. There are only a few black strokes, and yet each line is definitive and powerful and done with such purpose that the look of the woman is clear and known. Above her eyes is a flurried line to indicate the fringe of her hair—just a few strokes, and she's a woman with bountiful, pinned-up curls.

Evelien tells Joseph to keep his eyes closed, and moves the chair so it's in front of him. She undoes the wrapping and sets the framed sketch on the seat.

"Now," she says.

There is a split second when he struggles to register the situation, that here, in a cellar, in a bombardment, they have art. "Matisse," he says and leans forward, slowly, as if not to startle the woman.

"Mrs. Vanheule said it was sentimental. I think it was an anniversary present."

With his hand hovering, he follows the lines of the woman's face. After a bit, she asks if he'd like to see the next one.

Wide-eyed, he turns to her, exhilarated. "There's more?"

When she unveils the Renoir, his mouth opens, unbelieving.

"Evelien. This is a Renoir."

The painting, of woods at the edge of the ocean, feels like a daydream one would have while inside the scene itself. Trees curved and delicate with a sense of dreamy swirl, peaceful and encompassing. Two women and children, distant, face the water, as if emerging from a leisurely walk only to find an ocean. A temperate day of blues and greens. Yellow lichen on branches, trees that seem to lean into shrouded secrets. This is a place where you can exist without being found.

He closes his eyes. Breathing in deeply, he opens his mouth slightly as if to taste the oils and fumes of long ago. Another breath, and another, as if placing a memory within him or igniting a past craving.

Then it's clear what the remaining canvas is: the one she's spoken of, the one she's owed for watching the Vanheule house and staying when she should have left. The painting she loves.

Carefully, she uncovers the Braque and takes a step back. There is no cellar, no war, no one and nothing else. All she sees is the painting and it is everything—bright in a muted room, elation in the midst of despair. Hope and promise and creativity itself.

As always, its beauty takes away her breath.

When he opens his eyes, he smiles. "It's you."

She laughs. "You see me in there?"

"It feels like an extension of you."

And it is. The colors. The pulse. What made her fall in love with art.

"You'll have this forever," he says, rising to stand. Beside her, he faces the painting.

With his words, she feels the painting in its future room, simmering with promise, a reminder of different worlds and brighter landscapes. But as well, she feels the clutter, the mess around her as she'd try to work and paint in slim, fragile hours, struggling to afford oils and canvases and instruction and time. All doable, she knows. And yet. And yet there it is, insistent and urgent, yelling with its colors to take a step from the safe perch, to fling wide your arms and break free and hurl yourself deep into the dream, and she sees herself in that room with the painting's small, brilliant promise, standing eagerly before it until life continues hard and unchanged and the years unspool and she enters the room only to avoid it, afraid of it, shying from its demands and hope.

Or.

"I won't have it," she says, and he turns to her, curious. "I'll sell it. The money will start me where I need to be. Taking classes. Living in Montmartre." A risk, a gamble, to take this chance on herself, but suddenly she understands the painting's purpose in her life: it was never to loop back into her world and her future to one day sit on her wall, but rather to open the door and *enable* her future. A future without it, but because of it.

"But you love this painting."

"I do. But I love the chance at making my art real even more."

He looks down, at her lips, then glances behind her, toward where Coletta and August disappeared. In one motion he has his hand out, fingers curled behind her head as he draws her to him. A kiss. Soft and delicate. After, he doesn't move. Just holds her, his eyes closed, lashes glistening, drawing out the moment.

When he finally pulls back, he turns to the painting. "May I?" he asks, his hand hovering above the canvas.

She knows you're not supposed to touch the surface of a painting, but she has. In a tiny corner, just to feel the brushstrokes and intention, to be struck with a moment in time, one motion of an artist's hand. The urge, the yearning to get closer, she knows it well. She nods, and watches him reach to a corner, just a small area, and as he stretches out his fingers, his hand is shaking until his skin brushes the contours and even that, the lightest touch, seems to steady him. Stilled with relief. Anchored and reminded.

CHAPTER 43

Though she fights against it, she sleeps, as does he, both on cushions they've arranged against the wall. Now and then she wakes to her head on his shoulder, their hands laced together. The faint shapes of the paintings lean against the wall, all carefully wrapped back up, and the noise and rumbling seem to reach an apex in the night.

In the morning, the world's gone quiet.

And though she's waited years for this wondrous silence, with it comes the end—and a space beside her that's empty.

She's curled on her side on the cushion, and he is gone.

She sits up. Blinking, she feels for the lamp, but then pauses, not wanting the confirmation. Above her, the steady silence tells her the city's been released. Reluctantly, she twists on the light. On the cushion beside her is a note. Across the room, on the chair where he sat last night, is the blanket he'd used, folded neatly, with something on top.

She pats the pocket of her dress. As she knew it would be, the envelope with the list is gone. Taking a deep breath, she unfolds the note beside her.

Evelien,

I had to go. I could not put you and your family at risk when my whole purpose was to protect and help in any way I could. He left behind family in Bruges, a place where I knew I could ask for a favor and be of assistance, and so that day in the attic I made a vow—

She stops. Heart racing.

In a beat she's up, hurrying to the blanket on the chair, hearing Joseph's voice when he spoke of the man he killed in the attic, the man whom he fought to keep alive for two days. *In his coat pocket, he had his wallet, and letters and photographs.*

On top of the folded blanket: a wallet, envelopes, and photographs. Emiel's wallet.

It was Emiel.

She's crying as she touches the top envelope, a corner stained with a rust-colored bloom. She picks up the photographs—one of her, and one of Coletta and August. *Emiel is gone.* She's saying the words in her mind, repeating them, letting them carve a little place in her heart. She knew he was, felt it, but seeing the traces of his end and having the confirmation, it's as if she's losing him again. Her best friend. The long shadow to her every step. The calm hand on her shoulder. A man who deserved love and now will never have that. Heavily, she sits back into a chair.

The devastation continues. A one-two punch. Because Joseph was the one who did this, and though she knows the story and who he is and what was in his heart, the fact that it was him blares with cruelty. There's the cushion on the floor, where she leaned with her head on his shoulder. There's the table where they sat, telling stories. Betrayal is everywhere and in a rush she's hit with anger at Joseph, for the fact that what he did to Emiel was so awful he was able to bestow cruelty to her as well, that he's made her complicit in the injury.

Minutes pass. She hasn't moved.

If they met you, they'd see you're a good person who was put into something horrible. Just like their boys. Just like everyone. And they'd understand.

And she does. Of course she does. She hates every second of this, but she understands.

And then, in one beat, she allows in feeling for him, as well. A tide of sadness. Joseph. His voice, after telling her about the man in the attic. *I want you to see that part of me.* The horrible burden he carried. *There was a man I killed, who was smiling because in his last moments, he thought he saw his mother. If I painted, every face would be his.*

Coletta. Evelien turns toward where Emiel's parents are still sleeping, unaware.

Quietly, she gathers everything, the letters and the photograph and the note Joseph left, slipping it all into her dress pocket. She picks up the cushions. Folds her blanket. Removes all traces.

"Are you all right?" Coletta. Just woken.

Evelien wipes at her face and then turns. "He's gone," she says. The truth.

Until she's looked at what's here, she will leave it at that.

"I'm sorry." A pause, as Coletta glances up at the ceiling. "We've been freed?"

Behind her, August appears, touching the walls of the cellar to feel for any vibrations. "My God, I think it's over—for our city at least." Then he looks at Evelien and sees that she's crying. He smiles, assuming her happy. "Go upstairs and open the windows. Then get changed and ready. We're going to run in the streets."

"If you can," Coletta says, laughing.

"Barefoot if we want," August adds. "Singing the whole way."

Evelien turns, starting back up the stairs.

"Evelien," Coletta says. "I am sorry. He was a good man."

Good men don't always do good things.

CHAPTER 44

Morning glazes the road below her window. The air is clearing, smoke and ash and dust all given a chance to settle. Everything has collided within her. Hope and sadness, dreams and reality, the past and the future. But the one thing she still does not feel is blame. There's too much sadness to allow for anything else. Sadness that Joseph went through that—is still going through that. Sadness that he will always carry this burden. And sadness for Emiel, to have died at all, but especially as he did. Both stuck in a war that had long ago stopped making sense. Both just someone's son, trying to find a way to make it through. How can there be blame?

You should know, the vizeadmiral said about Joseph, *that he's lied to you about who he is.*

I want to hear anything you want to tell me, she'd said to Joseph.

That might not be true.

One of the envelopes Emiel had is addressed to her, and a second is to his parents. The third is to Emiel himself. That envelope, she sees, was posted to Emiel from an address in France and has not only been opened, but appears worn, as if he'd read the contents many times. She sets that one and the one to his parents on her bed, then gets the letter opener from her desk. In one motion, she slits open the top of the envelope that's addressed to her, reaches in, and feels that tender seam of *then* and *now*. The last time someone touched this, it was Emiel and he was alive.

Then there is his handwriting, prim and neat. Heavily, she sits on the bed.

Evelien,

I apologize for the letters you must have read through my parents, especially the first one that revealed everything so boldly and with such little delicacy. As I mentioned, drink was involved in the writing of that missive. I owe you, more than anyone, explanations. For as long as I can remember, you have been my best friend, and I do know we were meant to love each other forever, but I think you'll agree that it was never to be as husband and wife. I truly hope I'm not adding to any sadness you might feel by telling you this, but I venture to guess that I am not, because I saw it on our wedding night that you felt the same. I was terrified to speak to you of this, but, as I wrote, I did find someone. While on leave (weeks of light amid indescribable dark) I was with someone I love, and I ask you to forgive me. I wish I had been able to discuss our mistaken marriage with you first, before pursuing this course, but time was not on my side, and if there is one lesson I've learned, it's that you should embrace love and life when you are allowed to, which is every second you are blessed with breath. Evelien, my friend, take big, selfish gulps of air when you can, because they are never guaranteed. And please know that it is my sincerest wish that you forgive me, and find love as well.
Love forever,
Emiel

Evelien lowers the letter. Through the window, there are soldiers in khaki uniforms: the Belgian army. For a little while, she forgets everything else, caught in the joy of seeing her country liberated. And then she hears something, faintly, and cracks open her window: bells, ringing from every church.

Coletta calls to her. Asking if Evelien wants to join them for a walk to see the city, to greet the soldiers, and to walk and wander and stop along the canals and in the market square, because they can.

Evelien tells her that she'll catch up. Then, through the window, she sees Coletta and August. Holding hands, they stroll right in the center of the street, their shadows thrown askew behind them. Another image she wants to paint. Life through this window. There could be an entire series, this view has captured so much. And one day, she thinks, one day someone will stand in this same spot and never know.

Joseph. She glances at his note on the bed. With a deep breath, she picks it up.

Evelien,

> *I had to go. I could not put you and your family at risk when my whole purpose was to protect and help in any way I could. He left behind family in Bruges, a place where I knew I could ask for a favor and be of assistance, and so that day in the attic I made a vow to do just that. My brother-in-law is many things, but I've always found him to be understanding. Rightfully so, after I tried to desert, his trust was tentative at best. But he knew I struggled with a death I'd caused, and he was not unsympathetic. Thus, when I asked for the favor of undertaking my convalescence near the man's family, he accommodated me . . . though never thought to ask which man or family I spoke of, just as I never thought to tell*

him. When all came to light, he was angry that I'd lied to you, though never as angry as I was with myself for omitting the very reason I was looking in on your family. How do you tell someone you're the reason a person they loved will never return? The truth is that I never wanted to be happy, not after what I did. I only meant to watch over you and his parents because I could, but meeting you changed everything. Though I'd intended to help, it was me, undeserving and guilty and lost, who ended up saved. Even for that I am sorry.

By now, you know I have taken the list. Time is of the essence, and I know someone I can give it to so that it will end up in the right hands, fast. In exchange, you will get the letter you are due. I will see to that. I owe you that, and everything more.

Now, I'm sure you understand why I am deserving of whatever punishment comes my way.

I admit to reading the open letter sent from France, and learned of the delicate situation at hand and gather that there is news in what your husband wrote both you and his parents . . . news that may break hearts and cause grief, but I hope, too, that it will provide answers and opportunity. You see now that I could not leave before getting you these items, but please know that even without another motive, I would've sought a chance to see you one last time. I know I do not deserve it, but it is my deepest wish that at some point you might forgive me. I do not pretend to be a good man, but if I am bold enough to think I am deserving of any favors, it's my hope that one day I'll see you again, doing what you love.

I am sorry.

Joseph

CHAPTER 45

Later, she will make up a story of a man she didn't know who found her in front of the house, a kind person who'd simply wanted to return a soldier's belongings to his family. *These are from him,* she'll say. Coletta and August never need to know the truth of how she came across Emiel's belongings, or whom they let into their home on the last night of occupation. Here, the white lie is best.

Now she opens her window, for once not trying to avoid acrid, sickening smoke. Then, hand shaking, she picks up the other two envelopes and takes them to her desk—but as she does, something falls from the open envelope that was sent to Emiel from France, the one Emiel must have read over and over. A small rectangle. It shoots from the envelope and drifts toward the baseboard, landing face down. A photograph. All Evelien sees is what's written on the back: *Benjamin, huit mois.*

Benjamin, eight months.

Her heart starts racing. *He talked about his son, asked if I'd met him yet,* she remembers Joseph saying of the man in the attic. Of Emiel.

Her fingers brush against the back of the photograph and she is already crying, already knowing what she will see—a boy with Emiel's eyes—and as she turns it over, her breath catches because the child is him, a little boy with dark swirls for hair and a dimple on one cheek only and eyes that are patient and thoughtful and will spend a lifetime looking for hints of a father he'll never know.

That persistent beat of loss. Loud and relentless. Loss for her, for Coletta and August, and now for this boy, loss that webs and streaks and continues, the war like a stone hurled into the fragile pane of the world. *Benjamin, huit mois.* How many times did Emiel hold this photograph? How many times did he whisper his son's name?

To keep the photograph from being lost again, she takes the envelope sent to Emiel from France and removes the letter, unfolding it carefully to place the image within. She won't read it, and is even trying not to dwell on the beautiful, elegant penmanship, but despite herself glances at the signature: *Becarren.*

Now she grabs the envelope. Above the return address are only the initials B. D. But that's enough. Becarren Dupont. The one Emiel had been spending time with before Coletta got involved, before Evelien became afraid of losing him and believed that fear meant her feelings were of a different nature. Becarren fled to France with her parents before the war began, and with this Evelien understands that they must have found each other while he was on leave. She's hit with a wave of tremendous relief, because he was right: he'd found light amid indescribable dark. And though he was killed by the war, in some way he was not beaten by it. More than anything, Evelien is thankful that by the time he died, he had loved, truly and fully, and that he'd had what he'd always wanted—and *whom* he'd always wanted—however briefly.

Coletta. Evelien knows that the woman acted out of love, a need to keep the ones who meant the most to her closest, and most likely she thought she knew best and was helping, but the interference and manipulation were costly. Though the words in the letter from France belong to Emiel, and Evelien will not read them, she will give the letter to his parents along with the photograph, and in one motion Coletta will glimpse the love she'd had a hand in hindering, and lose the child who meant more to her than anything—but will gain a chance to love again, to meet the little boy whose very face will be a reckoning and a dream come true. Was her dream of a grandson waiting in another room a premonition? Or a mother's hope? A simple coincidence? Though Evelien knows much of what Coletta said or did was a part of her own agenda, perhaps the woman was right and we each play a part of fate's hand. Was any of it real? There's no way to answer definitively, and for this Evelien is actually thankful, because alongside uncertainty is possibility, and a world constantly capable of surprise.

There is only one thing she needs to do, right away. Hidden behind the baseboard is the list, the one that Joseph thought he took, one that never should've included his name. What he removed from her pocket when he left was different, something she'd quickly jotted down last night on a blank corner in the sketch pad she'd run to retrieve, then sealed in one of the remaining envelopes before racing back downstairs. That list included only four names.

There are matches next to the candle on her desk. She strikes one, then reaches out the window, letting the flame touch the corner of the original list of five names. A seam of fire, it builds and grows and she watches Joseph's name, overtaken. Only when she has to does she let it go, watching the burning page shrivel and drift and extinguish. All that remains is a bit of gray ash, but soon even that blends into the cobblestones and is gone.

Downstairs, she opens the front door to sunlight splayed along the road. She will go to the ruined garden and move what plants she can to a safe place. With each step, she finds herself looking down the alley and around the street, searching for him, though she knows he's gone.

At the house, a quick jiggle of the doorknob, four times while pushing to the right, and the broken lock unlatches. She steps inside, tentative with the belief that he will be there. But the room is empty. Of course. Light falls through the broken roof and everything is silent, making it feel empty in a way it never has. She lets her hand trail on the dusty remains of furniture, furniture she usually covers this time of year as best she can but that she will leave uncovered now, to let the wood and stuffing and fabric collapse, to let everything go, to break and fade and disappear.

With a slight start, she pauses at the green velvet chaise. There, on the round pillow, is a little bouquet of yellow oxalis flowers, tied with a string.

What is it to want to be with someone whose life intersected so devastatingly with your own? Or maybe to want to be alone? Or, she realizes, to understand that there might be nothing wrong with a person who wants both. Uncertainty and questions and answers that unspool with each new day, truths that look different under changing lights and people who are always just slightly off from center. The hardest thing, she understands, is acceptance.

CHAPTER 46

In the eleventh hour, of the eleventh day, in the eleventh month, the Armistice is signed, and the war is officially over. Belgian flags lift into the air, the tricolors twisting in the wind. German troops are captured, and collaborators are attacked, their houses looted. Lukas Schmidt, no longer fearing repercussion, comes out of hiding, but is immediately questioned by Belgian authorities when other civilians complain of food tampering. Those who fled Belgium try to return, but part of West Flanders has become the *Verwoeste Gewesten*, the Devastated Lands, and return is anything but easy. Roads are gone. Fields pitted with craters and planted with mines. Chlorine, phosgene, and mustard gas wiped out livestock and vegetation alike, and now what's left is the desolate world of nightmares, barren land and broken trees and water that's still struck with poison. Cleanup is slow, and German prisoners of war are used for the effort. Farmers in the Netherlands help by donating animals, and local breweries assist by drilling deep for clean water.

When people return, they don't recognize their land.

And the dead, of course, stay dead.

~

Though she knew Joseph would turn the list in, as he said he would, when that first letter from Emiel arrives, she understands the list indeed made it into the right hands. Forwarded from Dublin, a note on the envelope simply reads, *As promised.* On the page, Emiel's handwriting is sloppy, the paper stained. A confused, drunken confession of sorts. Coletta and August sit at the kitchen table, reading it over and over again.

The one thing that comes across clearly, Evelien thinks, is that he found love. "This is *good*," she says after reading it, and August and Coletta are relieved. Though Evelien explained that both she and Emiel felt the same way, they still tread carefully.

"I hate to say it," Coletta says, "but I'm glad Emiel died when the war made more sense, when there was still a reason to fight."

This is the mantra that gets repeated: A reason. There was a reason. A reason for it all.

"That's true," August says.

Coletta smells the page. "Apples. August, I smell apples."

"Brandy, more like it."

When Coletta folds the letter, she adds it to a small wooden chest where she keeps her most prized possessions: the first letter they'd received from the Irishman, and the one Emiel had on him when he died, as well as a reply from Becarren Dupont, saying yes, she would love for them to meet their grandson.

"And I've said it before," Coletta continues, "but things *had* to go the way they did. If not, there'd be no Benjamin."

Evelien smiles. "That's true."

From across the table, August gives her a wink.

~

December takes on a sadly joyous feel, as it's the first Christmas in years without battle, but also the first Christmas when absence is felt in a more permanent way. Half the world, it seems, is in mourning. More than twenty million killed, ten million of which were civilians. Days are filled with sweet spiced biscuits and Christmas markets and poinsettias and wreaths of fir, but also loss and vacant seats at tables. When Christmas is over, there is almost a relief, to be able to sink back into unremarkable days, to not have to smile or try to feel generous or happy.

Time twists into late January. Bruges a fairy-tale world dusted in snow, bridges and cobblestone streets white along their untrampled edges. Even the ruined houses look beautiful, broken remains smoothed in white. There is an exquisite, muffled silence that Evelien will never take for granted again.

Today is the day that Mrs. Vanheule returns. Evelien has the house in order, the paintings back and hung in place, even the Braque, which she does not want to assume will be hers. *January 24,* Mrs. Vanheule wrote, *please have the bed linens ready.*

She steps into a cold morning, powdered snow shining and canals shivering with flakes that drift from branches. Everyone is bundled up, breaths steaming. And though it's refreshing to see so many people on the street, every presence is marked with absence, empty spots where someone should be, hands that brush only air. As always, Evelien looks to the corner where Joseph used to stand, and as always, there is nothing. Only sunlight, like a hesitant fire on the white.

Evelien,

It is presumptuous for me to hope you might care, but I want to let you know that I am alive and in Germany and trying to make things right. I think of you and wish you only the best. Again, I am sorry.
Joseph

The note she received was brief, but welcomed. Though the time his world brushed against hers was slim, it was important, and even though she understands that the changes she endured and embraced and created were a little to do with him and a lot to do with her, she would still like to know him now. But she needs time—how much she doesn't know.

The letter she sent back was brief as well; mostly, she wanted to let him know that she would reach out to him later, if she chose, because this, she realizes, is her story.

Joseph,

I do care, and I thank you for letting me know. I will not be in Bruges much longer, but I thank you for your address. Please remember: you were never to blame.

At the last second, she scribbled a P.S. onto the letter.

P.S. Maybe one day we should meet again, but differently.

Now, as Evelien hurries through town, she thinks of Mr. Vanheule and the emptiness of his office as well as the clothes she left hanging in his closet, not wanting to be the one to take them down. Worry intrudes, a low-grade panic over telling Mrs. Vanheule that the decoy ring is gone, as is the little ruby ring, and that Evelien will help as she can but won't stay in town, that she sees her life differently now.

Lights blaze yellow in the windows of the house. When she opens the door, Mrs. Vanheule is before her, arms wrapping tight around Evelien's shoulders. Even though she knows he's gone, Evelien can't help but search the stairs and the hall, feeling him there.

"Tea first," Mrs. Vanheule says, "then we'll talk."

When they're both sitting, drinking real tea, Evelien braces herself, then tells Mrs. Vanheule she's ready.

"It was simple," Mrs. Vanheule says. "Tragically simple. He enlisted, Evelien. He didn't have to but he did. Memorized an eye chart and was in. Then he got on the train and waved goodbye."

A familiar scene. Train cars full of bravery, faces pressed against the glass. She saw it with Emiel, who watched them until he rounded a corner. Steam chugged into a gray sky, held for a moment, and was gone.

Mrs. Vanheule continues. "He was killed in the Second Battle of Ypres."

"But that was in '15."

"I tried sending you a letter, but it never made it. It came back to me, and that seemed like God's way of correcting me, of saying, *Anna, you do what's right and tell her in person because she was like his daughter.* I knew telling you face-to-face was the right thing to do, but I had to wait years to do it. And then I learned that someone got word to his cousin. And I hated that that man was the one to tell you."

Though Evelien has been without Mr. Vanheule for so long already, the loss continues to pile on her. Mr. Vanheule, who once sat with Evelien on the floor in the parlor, looking up at a painting of an amaryllis he'd just bought from a Dutch artist named Piet Mondriaan, who would soon lose the extra *a* in his name, becoming Mondrian. Now she looks to that spot on the wall, which is empty. Mr. Vanheule sold it before the war. *Note how the bold colors complement each other,* he said. *What do you see when you look at it?* Evelien studied the painting. A royal-blue background, petals that were bright red, and a stem that was electric blue. *It's like closing your eyes in the bright sun, the image against your eyelids.* To that, Mr. Vanheule nodded, pleased. *He also did this same image in watercolor.* Then a pause. *I heard he had a miserable childhood and escaped into his mind. A marvelous ability, isn't it? To escape into one's mind.*

The next day, there were watercolors left by her door.

"But then," Evelien starts to say, thinking of the year of his death and what this means. If Mr. Vanheule was killed in 1915, then who, years later, let the resistance network know there was someone in place, someone who could help? Who passed along the arrangement and the numbers on the back of the Braque painting?

Mrs. Vanheule is watching her. "You assumed Petrus was the one who put this into motion?"

"I did, but it couldn't have been."

"Agreed. It could not have been." Mrs. Vanheule smiles.

Anna Vanheule. Patriotic and connected and determined and surprising.

"But *you* had Emiel's letters?" Evelien asks, to which her employer looks confused. And so Evelien explains.

"No." Mrs. Vanheule shakes her head. "No, I never knew of letters or I would've found a way to get them to you. I was only told that something was needed from the house. No one was ever told the full story."

Evelien does not tell her about Joseph, or his role.

"They said it was important," Mrs. Vanheule continues. "Or I never would've endangered you. Honestly, I don't know what Petrus had planned for you, only that he had the foresight to make sure you could trust a messenger. And later, that became important. In fact, they'd asked about something else, earlier on, and I said no. But this list, these men, they said these men knew the end was coming and were unhappy. Unhappy and vengeful and dangerous. So it wasn't only for justice that they needed the names, but for prevention. And they got that because of you."

Then Evelien asks a question she's been dreading. "Do you know what happened to the vizeadmiral?"

"Ah. Him. Not yet." A pause, and Mrs. Vanheule tilts her empty teacup, as if reading the leaves. "Petrus loved his cousin. None of this was easy for him. But the vizeadmiral believed us. He told Petrus we'd come out on top if Germany prevailed, and Petrus let him think that was what we wanted, that a German victory was our goal. In part, so you'd be trusted, since we vouched for you." She smiles at Evelien, and then adds, almost sadly, "They were close, the two of them. And Petrus trusted his cousin to be good to you, which wasn't a given with someone else. We put thought into it, I hope you know, before asking you to do what we did. Rather like putting you in the eye of the storm, I realize. But we knew you'd be protected, because of who he was and because Petrus's word carried weight with him. Really, the vizeadmiral had every reason to trust him. But me? If that man thought less of my husband because Petrus was only half-German, imagine what he thought of me, not German at all." She smiles.

Light snow has started drifting outside the window. When Mrs. Vanheule goes upstairs, Evelien takes a moment alone in the parlor, listening to her footsteps above. The sound is a hook into the past. With a little imagining, she could be back in time, with Mr. Vanheule about to walk in the front door. She wants to stay with this, with possibility and memory thick around her.

A marvelous ability, isn't it? To escape into one's mind.

At last, she goes upstairs to help Mrs. Vanheule put things away in the bedroom, and when she does, she sees the little Matisse sketch, off the wall and propped up on her nightstand.

Mrs. Vanheule, sitting on the bed, follows her eyes. "I want it here, where I can be next to it. It can't be worth much at all, but he gave it to me on our wedding night. Our first piece of art, on our first night, in our first home."

Behind Mrs. Vanheule, inside her armoire, is the jewelry box where Evelien placed the earth's tear diamond ring. "The replica is gone," she says quickly. "And so is the little ruby ring. We sold one to eat, and the other we used as a bribe—"

"Evelien, I don't care. The earth's tear, yes, I'm glad to have it back because it was my mother's, but the others—you did more than enough to earn those and the painting and more." She must see the relief on Evelien's face, because she smiles. "Of course the painting is yours. I don't know why you rehung it. He'd want you to have it; he always did."

Now Mrs. Vanheule lifts her hand to her mouth and bites on her thumbnail. It's brief, but a motion Evelien recognizes. *Always be wary if Anna has no nails,* Mr. Vanheule used to joke.

"What's wrong?" Evelien asks.

Mrs. Vanheule lowers her hands to her lap. "I should tell you, he was giving you the painting regardless. Even before the war started, it was our plan to give it to you when you left us to marry."

Evelien takes a moment. "Even if I left Bruges at the start of the war, you were giving it to me?"

Mrs. Vanheule nods sadly. "He told me the day you first walked into the house and saw the painting that it belonged to you. Then you worked hard for all these years, and you loved art as he did—all that was secondary. It was yours from the moment you saw it. I told him I didn't think it was fair to use it as incentive, but he said you needed it, to help you get through the war. He knew you wouldn't leave, not with your husband's parents here, but he told me the promise of the painting would be—I don't know. Hope."

Mr. Vanheule, who asked to see her sketches and then left certain art books leaned against her bedroom door, images and descriptions of technique that seemed to complete her untrained thoughts. Mr. Vanheule, who knew the painting was a comfort and a drive and a distraction. He knew it made her want to be a part of the future, just from the thought of it on her wall one day.

"He was right," Evelien says, also thinking of her canvas room. Last she saw, the roofline of the house with her ruined garden was different. The remnants of the stepped gables that once were over her canvas room were gone. Collapsed. The room no longer. "The painting was what I needed."

Mrs. Vanheule continues. "He always said he didn't know what he was getting into when he hired you, but you were a gift he'd forever be thankful for."

Quickly, without thinking, Evelien says, "I'm not staying. I'm going to Paris. I'm going to find a place in Montmartre and take classes and paint. And to do that, I might have to sell the painting, so you don't need to give me anything, but you have to let me go."

"There? With the cabarets and the bohemians?"

"And the artists and the writers."

Mrs. Vanheule nods, accepting. "He set aside money for you. I didn't know about it until only recently, but he intended to give you more than just the painting. So if you go *there*, which I don't recommend you do, but I suppose I understand—what I mean to say is your money could last you a good while. So maybe you can keep your painting. Though it's yours. Do with it as you will."

Evelien is reeling. Everything seems to be unfolding and rearranging. "And you would let me go?"

Mrs. Vanheule smiles. "My dear, we may have borrowed you for a little while, but you belong only to yourself."

CHAPTER 47

April 18, 1921

Light falls off the white stone buildings and splashes down the steps. The Sacré-Coeur, the second-highest point in Paris, crowns the city, and the height of its colonnade stirs the clouds. This is one of those days when the streetlamps turn on and the sky holds an ochre flush from a fleeting rainstorm and everything combines to honeyed gold, the steps and the bricks and even the ivy that hangs and reaches.

Two years have come and gone, filled with classes and oil paints and jars of soaking brushes, as well as part-time work at a bakery to stretch the money from the Vanheules. The painting is still with her. Already a few artists she knows have mentioned it to dealers and collectors, and there are standing offers, kept off to the side of her mind. At some point, she figures she might have to part with it, but until then, she keeps it close, blaring with promise from its wall, reminding her of everything.

She lives above a tobacconist with a green awning that casts a minted shadow onto a portion of her ceiling. When friends come to visit, she lowers a key on a string outside her window, a dangling lure in the light, and in the summer when the scents expand and lift, her room turns drowsy with the smell of wet canvases and wood and vanilla and sweet tobacco. Across the street there is always a line of hungry people in front of the clouded windows of the boulangerie where she works, the owner of which also gives her bread if she watches his ten-year-old. *I'm not good with children,* she'd said when he first asked, and the owner laughed. *If I wanted someone good with children, I would get another child. What I ask is that you keep her alive.* And so Evelien does, and has learned to cook many dishes featuring stiff and stale bread.

Montmartre, the higher the climb, the lower the rent. It's where she wants to be, with the artists and writers and musicians, the loud, drunken celebrations and the early-morning painters squinting into the sun. All of it a bright, fragrant, delicious chaos. *Anything you need,* Coletta had told her when she was leaving, *I will do.* And indeed, when August and Coletta visit their grandson, they always stop in to see Evelien, and August leaves new books for her to read, demanding she send letters with reports, while Coletta tends to "drop" a new dress on her way out, one that somehow fits Evelien perfectly.

It's now her second spring in Paris, and the city trembles with life. Chestnut and cherry trees in bloom. Irises and peonies and forget-me-nots. Entire trees covered in a confetti of flowers that Evelien finds irresistible. Every street is dashed with new-growth green, and there are markets with fresh peas and asparagus. She tells people she would live through a thousand winters just for one Paris spring. Even the dandelion clocks in the park are buoyant with light and promise.

Her mail goes out from the tobacco shop downstairs. Today she has a letter to send, and as she approaches, she spots the owner in the window, waving to her with an envelope in his hand. The bell clangs as she enters. The men inside turn and stare. With a smile, she gives the owner her letter to post, and thanks him for the envelope he gives her in return.

She is midway on her stair landing when she flips the envelope over and sees who it's from: Mrs. Vanheule.

In her apartment, the scent of paint enfolds her. Some pieces she did right away. Fast, a sort of expulsion of that time, a purge. Others sit within her longer, incandescent with importance, images that keep her company and turn with the passing days, memory-tinged and contoured with time before they make their way onto a canvas. The shadow soldiers. The ruined garden. And her most recent one, a painting that seemed to take her on a journey, every day bringing her a little closer, like she was nearing a land that had always been just out of sight. With this painting, it felt less like creating and more like discovering, as if beneath the white of the blank canvas was an entire world, only waiting to be seen.

Now, she studies this latest work, on an easel against the wall: the *vlaskapellen*, the waist-high swoops of flax in their field. But the golden shapes are not little chapels, they're women. Dancing women with long, flared dresses swayed with movement. And there, just off from center, is her mother. A few days ago, Evelien received an offer for the piece, only to realize that she'd never painted it to sell, but to see.

This one, as well, she will hold on to.

At the window is a little stool with a stack of art books, on top of which she's placed a slender glass bottle with one fiery orange tulip, its stem bent in its chase for light. Next to it is her favorite chair, a gold upholstered wingback with wooden feet. On the arm, a smear of Prussian blue and a vermilion fingerprint.

When she sits, she takes in a city turned heavy with dusk, the air scattering with another spring rainstorm.

Opening the envelope, she sees a little page with Mrs. Vanheule's lofty script.

Dearest Evelien,

I have been shamefully slow to sort through Petrus's affairs. But in a pile of his most cherished correspondence, I found this, and with it, my heart aches for all the unseen kindness. Be well.

Anna

Beneath is an older letter with imperfect handwriting that she immediately recognizes. And though she knows it, it makes no sense. She flips the letter over and sees her mother's signature. Then she turns the page back and notes the date: August 13, 1909. The year before Evelien's parents sent her to Bruges.

To Mr. Petrus Vanheule,

My name is Leona Dinneweth, and I am sorry to take your time with this. I realize you have all the help you need and no children yet so have not started thinking of taking on more workers, but if I may plead my case, I have a daughter named Evelien who is young but strong. You'd never have cleaner floors because she'll go over them with a toothbrush if she thinks it's necessary. She is someone you can groom to be the best worker for your house.

You might be wondering why I'm writing to you. Years ago, we were in Paris and went into a gallery where she saw a painting she loved, and she hasn't stopped drawing since. I admit that I did not understand the painting. It was of the Scheldt River in Antwerp by an artist named Georges Braque. When I wrote the gallery, they told me you were the one who bought that painting.

Her father and I are busy with our farm, and we do not have time for art, if I'm being honest. What I am trying to say is that what she'd get in art here is not much, but with you that would not be so. From everyone I have spoken to, you are said to be a good and respected man, and people call you kind. I would not be writing if that were not the report.

I am fortunate to have received a sum of inheritance that I set away and that allows me to make this

*proposition: if you hire her, she will work, and I do not
need compensation. Any money you would pay her, please
keep and give to her when she is grown enough to make
grown decisions. If this is agreeable to you, I ask that you
not tell her or anyone of this arrangement. I have not
always been a wonderful mother, but if her father knew,
he'd expect the payment, when all I want for her is the
chance.*

Please write me when you're able.

Sincerely,
Mrs. Leona Dinneweth

Evelien lowers the page, blinking in the dimming light.
Reeling.

What is it to be a mother, who knows that to save her child, she
must lose her? To have the greatest gift be a future you will never be a
part of? A future without, but because.

Once more, everything Evelien thought she understood has
changed. So many questions, so many varied responses and experiences.
Nothing is absolute, everything nuanced and enigmatic and always
somewhere in between.

Evelien looks at her. Her mother in the painting, across the room.
A woman who understood her more than she'd ever realized, and who
enabled her to have the life she herself might have wanted. There she
is, surrounded by her golden army, back straightened and face tilted to
the sun. Not stooped over and mired with work as Evelien once saw her,
but standing tall and facing the brightness, lit with hope.

Outside, a violet-hued purple night. Already the rain has stopped
and the city before her is drenched in moon-glossed luster, slick with
shine. Buildings from different centuries wake, eyes winking, some half-
shaded and others fully open. The city stirred to life. Music threading,

painters painting, writers taking note. Everyone is hungry, everyone alive.

When she looks down, she sees a man brushing pink cherry blossoms from his shoulders while stamping his feet on the sidewalk, leaving raindrops and flowers behind. And even this—the set of his shoulders, the way he favors one leg and the fact that he must have walked beneath the cherry trees, as she likes to do—has her heart racing. She leans forward, waiting, watching him study a letter in his hand.

And then he looks up at her. And there it is. His face is fuller, but still carved in moonlight.

And she smiles, and thinks once more of how much depends on not just *who* tells the story, but on when the story starts, because life is layered upon life, and nothing is simple. Fluctuations and faults and lies that are a kindness. Green that is not grass and blue that is not sky.

Ends that in fact could be beginnings.

The End (but not really).

Acknowledgments

My great-grandmother, in Belgium during WWI, was in the midst of giving birth to my grandfather when soldiers arrived at their door and told them to leave, that their farm and house were needed. Her response was that everyone would have to wait, because she was having a baby. Another relative was given a pouch she was told to "never open," one that would help with her daughter's medical ailment—a pouch that my mother inherited, and that to this day has remained closed. And one of my great-grandfathers—a man with an edge, you might say—for him it took talking to someone who'd gone through Vietnam to reveal that during the Great War, one of his jobs had been to clear the bodies off the fields.

Often, I've wondered, what did that do to him? Who was he before?

And who was the person who sewed shut a pouch and offered a "cure"?

What was it like to live with war pounding just outside your door?

All of my mother's family is from Belgium, and though I have stories and can trace the dates and locations of their lives, beyond that, there are mysteries. Such is the case with two of my great-grandparents, whose names are listed on a plaque in a small town in Belgium as victims of the war—and yet they were civilians. I may know the dates they died, but the details were lost long ago, and now all I can do is imagine. And imagining, of course, is what writers love to do.

Writing is an excuse to learn. I pick subjects I'm interested in, worlds I'd like to inhabit. As with my last novel, *Take What You Can Carry*, with this book I've chosen to explore my own family's past—only now it's my mother's side. I took some creative liberties, but the truth is the facts of this time and setting were incredible enough on their own.

I must first thank family. My Flemish family, who've shared so much with me, including stories and their time, and who stood patiently by while I stared, entranced, at my ancestors' landscapes. Fernand Vanrobaeys, Moniek Adam, and Lucrèce Liefooghe & Luc Vereecke: my trips to Belgium were remarkable thanks to you. And to Mary Girard Jemming, on this side of the pond, our unofficial family historian, as well as Alixa and Tony Doom and all the Dooms and Verlys and Bulckes and many more who shared their memories and photos and time. And to my brother, Kamaron, and Carmen, my sister-in-law: this last trip to Belgium wouldn't have been nearly as much fun without you there. Thank you both for your support, insight, and cheese plates (Carmen, you deserve an entire page acknowledging your skills in that department, but this will have to do).

And of course the biggest thank-you of all goes to my mother, Addi, who not only read this novel just shy of a million times, but from the start passed along her passion for learning and introduced me to my first love: books. Mom, you fought and worked hard for my education. You fought and worked hard for *me*. I owe you more than I can ever repay, and I love you.

Meg Howrey, Stephanie Stephens, Dianne Schwehr, Becarren Schultz, Rachel Lockwood, Kristin Miller, Tara Hall, Suzanne Unrein, Kathy Doom, and Nika Serras, thank you for invaluable early, middle, and late reads. Nika, down to the wire you were there, and this book is better because of that fact. And Meg, you've been there from the start and are equal parts extraordinary writer and amazing friend, and if not for you, I would've given up long ago. Thank you for talking me off the literary ledge.

None of this would be possible if not for my amazing agent, Lucy Carson, and my incredible editor, Alicia Clancy. Alicia, thank you again for your trust in me and your guidance. I'm honored to be working with you and the entire Lake Union team.

I would also like to thank the Solomon R. Guggenheim Museum, where Georges Braque's *Landscape Near Antwerp* resides, and who generously shared the information they have on "Evelien's" painting. Though Mr. Vanheule is an entirely invented character, and of course not listed in the painting's provenance, I'd like to think that the piece was as loved by its real owners as it was by its fictional ones.

And to my husband, who is my very own Joseph. Joe, I love you. You believe in me, and support me, and so much more—and as repayment, I stole your name for this book. Ha.

And on the subject of names . . . To Maximiliaen, whose name I first saw in a very, very old Bruges census. My amazing little man. Your mind and heart inspire me. I am so lucky to be your mom.

This is the first book I wrote that my father will not be able to read. An amazing artist and human being, his turbulent life in a war-torn country taught him to escape into his mind and into his art. He filled our lives with a love of creativity, and I like to think that wherever he is, he senses these words, and feels just how grateful I am.

Dad, I love you.

Book Club Questions

1. Evelien feels that going to the ruined garden is like coming home. Do you have a place that means that much to you?

2. The role of timing in blame and responsibility is something both Evelien and Coletta struggle with. Have you felt the same about something in your own life?

3. Evelien wants to believe what she's told, that we are not what we do in war. Do you agree or disagree?

4. Coletta encourages Evelien to do something big, and possibly dangerous, by asserting that a little wrong that prevents a lot of wrong is worth it. Do you agree?

5. There is an ongoing question in the novel of whether lies can be not only acceptable but sometimes even good. What are some examples of that in this book? Do you believe in white lies? Have you told lies to help someone that may have backfired? Or do you ever wish you'd told a lie instead of a truth?

6. Evelien is fascinated by life's layers and the starts to stories that are often never known. In your own life, have you learned of any "beginnings" that surprised you or helped to explain a person or situation?

7. Evelien ends up in a relationship of sorts with a man who is not her husband. Did you agree or disagree with that?

8. Coletta believes in fate, and that every loss and every disappointment led her to the child she was supposed to have. Do you have anything you feel that way about?

9. "It's too bad we're not able to be friends with our parents before becoming their children." What have you learned about a parental figure or relative that surprised you?

10. August believes that how someone lives is all that matters, and the Irishman claims that good men don't always do good things. Do you believe one is correct?

11. Do you think Evelien is right to turn off the light the night of the gathering at the vizeadmiral's house? Or should she have left it on?

12. What did you think of Evelien's relationship with the vizeadmiral?

13. Were you surprised to learn of Joseph's tragic connection to Evelien? Or did you see it coming?

14. What did you think of Leona, Evelien's mother, after reading the letter at the end? What are some "unseen kindnesses," or examples of what someone has done without seeking credit, that have surprised you?

15. At the end, after Evelien looks down from her window and sees the man carved in moonlight, what do you think happens next?

About the Author

Gian Sardar was born in Los Angeles, California. Her father was from Kurdistan of Iraq, and her mother is Belgian American and from Minnesota. She studied creative writing at Loyola Marymount University and is the author of the novels *Take What You Can Carry* and *You Were Here* and is coauthor of the memoir *Psychic Junkie*. Her work has appeared in the *New York Times*, Literary Hub, *Confrontation Magazine*, and Salon.com, among other places. She lives in Los Angeles with her husband and son, and enjoys gardening, cooking, and other forms of procrastination. For more information, visit www.giansardar.com.